Those Who
Watch
for the Morning

Those Who Watch

for the

Morning

A Novel

Jonathan C. Page

Published by 1847 Press

Cover design by Matt Roeser
Book design by Lynsey Griswold

Print ISBN: 979-8-9989997-0-3
Digital ISBN: 979-8-9989997-1-0

First edition: July 2025

Those Who Watch for the Morning

I wait for the LORD, my soul waits,

and in his word I hope;

my soul waits for the Lord

more than those who watch for the morning,

more than those who watch for the morning.

Psalm 130:5-6

If the work is burned up, the builder will suffer loss; the builder
will be saved, but only as through fire.

1 Corinthians 3:15

It is often said that the Church is a crutch. Of course it's a crutch.
What makes you think you don't limp?

—Rev. William Sloane Coffin

Chapter 1

Chris Reed shivered in the cold as the heavy door of Widener Library shut behind him. He pulled his wool hat over his ears and zipped his jacket a little more tightly around his neck. There was something about the damp New England cold that seemed to seep between the seams of his coat. Chris pulled his phone from his pocket to check the time: 2:33 pm. Chris was late, but he didn't mind. When he'd arrived for graduate studies at Harvard, he'd discovered everything started late there. They termed it "Harvard time" but it was really just an excuse for overly busy people to try to squeeze more out of each minute. At a place like Harvard, there was never enough time—one of the many things Chris hated about the place.

Walking down the library's wide steps, Chris realized how slippery they were with ice. In the winter, the university installed a wooden cover over the stone steps, but Chris still had to use the railing to steady himself. Once he reached the bottom, he avoided two undergrads who were deep in conversation and oblivious to his presence. When he'd first arrived in Cambridge from Iowa, he invariably said hi to strangers he passed, only to be met with judging glances. Now Chris's own thoughts absorbed him. He had a paper due at the end of the week that he hadn't even started to research. And there was this coffee meeting with Matt, which Chris was late to. What did he want?

Around the backside of the library, Chris left the confines of Harvard Yard and, like every student, jaywalked across the three busy lanes of Massachusetts Avenue. Chris marveled that more students weren't hit by cars every year. After weaving through the winter crowd on the sidewalk, as though he were dodging obstacles rather than people, he entered the coffee shop.

Chris shook the cold out of himself and quickly scanned the room. The ceilings had exposed ductwork, which gave the space a hip, loft-type feeling. Black trim accented lightly colored, varnished wood, and indie dance music played quietly in the background. Most tables were taken by people deep in conversation or by students entranced by the screens in front of them. Across the room, he recognized a familiar face and nodded. Matt raised his cup of coffee in response. The last time Chris had spoken to Matt Jaroslavic, they had both been in Iowa for some family time over the summer. Matt was a year older than Chris. They had been friends and academic competitors in high school and had stayed in touch ever since. Chris missed those days. Life was fun then, and devoid of the constant anxiety that seemed to be a product of twenty-first century adulthood.

"You should've let me know you were coming to town," Chris said after he had sat down. Seeing Matt in person brought a big smile to his face. "I was surprised to get your text."

"I'm in Cambridge recruiting a new analyst for my firm. Last-minute thing. Figured I would see if you were free."

"I'm glad you reached out." Chris thought back to all of the endless debates they used to have. What was going to be the topic today? he wondered. He could use a distraction from the piles of books awaiting him in his carrel.

"I did some thinking on the train ride up. It's time you leave the ivory tower, Chris," Matt replied, as he took another sip of his coffee, his eyes full of mischievous energy. "Come over to the dark side. Put in an application for this job. I'll be sure you get a good look."

Last summer the focus of their conversation had been work. After two years at JP Morgan, Matt had started a job at Sulla Partners, an oil and gas hedge fund out of Greenwich. Chris couldn't help but be jealous, especially after he had heard about Matt's trip to Europe, which he took between leaving one job and starting another. As a history graduate student, Chris couldn't hope to have a vacation like that for at least ten years, if ever.

"Are you serious?" Chris asked. He felt his heart beat faster at what that could mean: no more student debt for him and his wife, Abby. No sharing with another grad student a cramped apartment in Somerville that was too hot in the summer and bled heat in the winter. Enough money that Abby wouldn't have to work and they could finally think about kids. Suddenly, Chris became self-conscious. His old olive-green L.L.Bean parka, which had the style of a sleeping bag, hung over his chair. He was wearing the wool sweater his grandmother had given him eight years ago, and his light brown hair was tousled from his knit hat. Matt, on the other hand, had on a slim-fitting cashmere pullover with a dress shirt underneath. Chris noticed the Canada Goose label on Matt's jacket. His dark hair was flawlessly combed.

"Of course," Matt continued. "If you want to be a grad student for the next six years, that's fine too. I'm sure you'd get one of those tenure-track jobs."

Chris winced when he thought about the prospect of getting a decent job after graduating. Even a place like Harvard had a hard time finding jobs for PhD graduates in history. Maybe half the class would end up in a tenure-track position, and the rest would either teach high school, work as adjuncts for no money, or leave teaching altogether. The lucky remainder found jobs as low-level college administrators.

"Would I have a chance at the job?" Chris wondered aloud.

"You might. You're one of the smartest guys I know. Somehow you beat me at math in high school. I'm still mad at you for that. I'll put in a word for you. Read some Ayn Rand when you have the chance. That will put you in the right frame of mind. The firm's founder, David Sloan, loves Ayn Rand."

Ayn Rand, the great heroine of any aspiring high school capitalist. Chris remembered glancing through some of *Atlas Shrugged* back when Matt couldn't stop talking about her in their junior year of high school. She claimed selfishness as the highest virtue. Any altruism was a sign of weakness, and weakness only bred more weakness. It made Chris's skin crawl at the time, but maybe he should give her another chance. When he was sixteen, the prospect of selfishness and pursuit of money seemed vapid and immoral. Now at twenty-four, with bills to pay and an unpromising career ahead of him, it made more sense.

"Hey, you two!" Both Chris and Matt turned their heads when they heard the familiar voice. Abby Reed made her way across the crowded café and put her arm on her husband's shoulder. Abby was, in many ways, a typical Iowa girl. Kindhearted like her husband, Abby could not have been more out of place in the overly intellectual, highly competitive environment of Cambridge. It felt like everywhere they went, people would reel off their resumes within the first few sentences of meeting.

"I'm trying to convince Chris to apply for a job at my firm," Matt said. "Think you can persuade him?"

Chris could feel Abby squeeze his shoulder a little more tightly. "Abby would prefer us to return to the Midwest," Chris said, knowing that Abby's Midwestern kindness would not allow her to say what was on her mind.

"I don't mean to interrupt," Abby said. "We have this week off for President's Day, and I was running errands in the Square when Chris texted that you were here."

"Nonsense, Abby, you could never interrupt us. Have a seat," Matt insisted.

Abby found a chair, and they all spent the next twenty minutes catching up. Abby filled in Matt as to how her teaching was going: She finally had her own classroom of third graders this year. There was this one problem child, but she was learning to deal with his outbursts. She confessed she spent too much time on her lesson plans. The more experienced teachers assured her things would get easier.

Chris was happy to sit and listen to his wife talk. Abby was impossible not to like with her big brown eyes and her transparent kindness. She became so animated when she mentioned her students. He loved her so much, which made figuring out what to do that much harder.

"What would you think about a move to Connecticut?" Matt asked.

Abby paused. "That's where we'd be if Chris worked for your firm?"

Matt laughed. "It's not all that bad. You'd be able to afford some new clothes."

Chris wasn't sure if that was a dig at Abby's fashion sense or a genuine word of encouragement. "That would be a long way off," Chris said. "Let's not get ahead of ourselves." Chris turned to Abby. "It would mean a different life with a lot more options. And we wouldn't be here for the next five years."

"We'll talk about it later," Abby replied. Chris could tell she didn't love the idea of staying in New England. But what would make her happy? A college job in the Midwest?

They all rose at the same time. Matt had an appointment to make at the university's Office of Career Services. Chris and Abby followed him to Dunster Street in front of the Student Services building. After saying their goodbyes, Chris and Abby crossed the icy street, hand in hand.

"It was great to see Matt," Abby said. "But don't let him pressure you too much. You know I want you to follow your dreams."

"I only wish I knew what those dreams were. This place just isn't for me." Chris replied. "I need to get back to the library. I'll see you later tonight." Chris leaned in to give Abby a kiss and gave her small hand one final squeeze before she walked away. She was still looking back at him as she walked off the curb into the street. Chris loved how beautiful she was, but more than that he loved being around her and how he felt when he was in her presence.

As he turned away, Chris saw Abby fall into the street, her foot slipping on some black ice. From the corner of his eye, he could see a car speeding down the road. Instinctually, he moved to pull her from the car's path, but he was too far away. Everything slowed down. Chris could see the front bumper inching toward Abby as she struggled to get up. The impact was sudden, Abby' small body landing several yards from where she slipped. Chris raced ahead and nearly fell himself before kneeling down next to her.

"Abby? Abby?!" Chris shook her body, but there was no response. "Abby?!" Chris looked around for help, but there was nothing he could do. He glanced down at Abby's bloodied face, and the shock of it began to settle in amidst the sounds of horns blaring.

Chapter 2

April

Somerville, Massachusetts

The sound from the alarm pierced Chris's eardrums. He opened his eyes and read the clock: 10:00 am. He leaned over just far enough to reach the snooze button and smacked it. The blaring stopped. Chris flopped back down and stared at the ceiling. It was time for his meeting at church.

Dragging his legs over the edge of the bed, Chris sat up and winced. His head throbbed with the sudden drop in blood pressure. His mouth was dry and he could taste his sour, dehydrated breath. The ice in the glass on the bed stand had melted but the caramel color from the whiskey remained. "How much did I drink last night?" Chris mumbled as though someone could hear him.

He wobbled to the bathroom and turned on the shower. He had read somewhere that he should finish his shower with ice-cold water, letting the drops beat down on his head. Supposedly it would help the hangover. At this stage, Chris would try anything. The icy water on his head was the kind of numbing self-flagellation he deserved. He knew he would reek of whiskey when he met with Professor Mendes, but that was still an hour away. He just had to make it to the basement of Memorial Church. He could do this, he reassured himself.

Once out of the shower, Chris glanced in the mirror. His light brown hair was a mess from toweling off, and his scrawny body depressed him. Focusing on one task at a time, he shaved, combed his hair—a rarity for him—and put on a collared shirt. Chris hadn't worn anything but t-shirts since the funeral, but somehow it felt important to dress up for a Harvard professor.

It had been nearly two months since Abby's death, but the world still felt vaguely unreal. He was in it. He moved around, and carried on conversations, but he felt like he was viewing himself from outside his body.

Chris shook himself out of his daze and took one last glance at the small room in the two-bedroom apartment he shared with another grad student. Clearly, Abby was the one who had decorated it with some framed posters and laminate furniture from Target. It looked nice. Poor, maybe, but that merely reflected the truth. It had warmth to it, but now it had Chris's clothes and books and general detritus everywhere. Abby would laugh if she saw it.

Chris walked through the streets of Somerville and Cambridge in a daze, not really paying attention to where he was going. Even with three Advil and a stop at Dunkin' for a sausage-and-egg sandwich, Chris felt like crap. The spring air was cool against his skin, and he realized he had not been outside in two days.

Walking down Beacon Street to Kirkland Street, he eventually found himself in the familiar ground of Harvard Yard. The Memorial Church steeple could be seen for miles in every direction. Modeled after the steeple of the Old North Church in Boston, it towered over the other buildings in the Yard. Professor Mendes's executive assistant had said to meet the professor in his office in the basement of the church. It was Chris's second time there. The first time had been when he met with Professor Mendes to plan out Abby's funeral service at the church.

Her sudden death had made the front page of *The Harvard Crimson* and led to talks about safer walking in the streets around campus. The crowd at the funeral had astonished Chris. He didn't know half the people. It felt awkward receiving condolences from strangers. They'd had another service a week later back in Iowa. Chris's parents had tried to encourage him to take time away from school, but the last place he wanted to be was back in Iowa at his parents' home. He knew that would only make his depression worse. Even so, he had barely been able to do any work for the remainder of the semester. The dean had sent an e-mail about starting fresh in the fall. Chris wasn't sure he had it in him to do that.

Professor Mendes's e-mail had surprised Chris. Mendes was a legend on campus. He was the university chaplain and the Plummer Professor of Christian Morals. Chris had heard him preach quite often. He and Abby enjoyed attending Sunday services at Memorial Church. Chris never realized that Mendes even knew who he was. Something about his Lutheran upbringing led him to respond to Professor Mendes's request for a meeting. He felt bad saying no to a minister, let alone the university chaplain.

When he walked into the office, the receptionist told him to take a seat on the couch. He noticed the old-style mechanical clock on the wall. The time there read twelve minutes slow. It clearly needed to be fixed. After a few minutes, the receptionist told Chris he could go in. Chris walked through the door and down a small corridor with the clergy offices on each side. When he got to Professor Mendes's office, the door was slightly ajar. Chris knocked quietly and heard a deep bass voice on the other side. "Come in."

Chris walked across the dark oriental rug to meet Professor Mendes, who came out from behind his desk to shake his hand. Mendes was shorter than Chris, about five foot nine, and was dressed in a tweed sport coat and a bow tie with a colorful silk handkerchief spilling out of his breast pocket. He carried a little extra weight around his frame and had large hands that enveloped Chris's when they shook, putting Chris at ease.

"Sit down, dear boy," Mendes said, using a familiar tone that seemed out of place for how little they knew each other, but eased Chris's anxiety about the meeting. They exchanged a few pleasantries, and then Mendes came right to it.

"You know why I asked you here?"

Chris paused for a moment and then replied, "I imagine because I stopped coming to class, and my dean is worried."

"Your dean certainly is worried about you," Mendes began, "as we all are. My concern, however, is not for your classes. Those will take care of themselves in due time. Although Harvard can seem like a heartless place, you'll discover more support here than you might imagine, at least if you're open to receiving it."

Those words made Chris think about how many e-mails and phone calls he had ignored in the past two months. "I haven't wanted to talk to people," Chris replied.

"Chris, very few who go through a sudden loss feel social. But by cutting yourself off from others you are also preventing yourself from fully grieving."

Chris wanted to burst out, Well, I'm here now, aren't I?! But he held his tongue and sat in silence for what seemed like forever.

Finally, he let it all pour out. He told Mendes about how he met Abby in high school and how he was always the superstar academic. At St. Olaf College, he fell in love with American religious history. His dream was to be a professor. When he got admitted to Harvard's PhD program, everything seemed perfect. Then once he arrived at Harvard, things began to unravel. Abby didn't like Massachusetts and how cold the people were. It took her nearly a year to find a job teaching. Money was impossibly tight. Their roommate was a dirty slob. The classes were a lot more difficult than Chris thought they would be, and over the past year and a half, he'd lost his passion for history. Abby wanted them to move back to Iowa, but it would have felt like such a defeat.

Then there was the accident. What was Chris to do now? He had no interest in going to see his parents or going home and becoming a high school history teacher. And he couldn't get Abby out of his head.

By the time Chris stopped talking, he was in tears.

Mendes pushed a box of tissues across his desk, and Chris reached for one. "It sounds like you need some time away," Mendes said.

"Yeah, but doing what?" Chris asked. Chris looked expectantly at Professor Mendes, who seemed deep in thought.

"Did you grow up in any faith tradition, Chris?"

"I was raised Lutheran. I went through confirmation and all that. I took it seriously back then."

"Does your faith shape your life?"

Chris considered this for a moment. "Honestly, Professor Men-des, after I got to college, I drifted away from God." Chris began to worry that Mendes was judging his lack of introspection. "I mean, I guess I feel about life the way everyone else feels."

Mendes leaned in over his desk. "And how exactly is that? How does everyone feel about life?"

Chris took a deep breath. "You know. The goal is to live a meaningful life that helps others. You get meaning from your family, friendships, work, hobbies."

"And what about death? What happens when you die?"

Chris shuddered at the question. "I was raised a Christian. I believe everyone goes to heaven when they die." Chris slumped back in his chair. He felt exhausted by the conversation. Looking past Professor Mendes, he could see the feet of students walking by outside the window.

"Chris, the sad reality is that we usually don't think deeply about life until something tragic happens. Even students at Harvard usually float from day to day without really internalizing a life philosophy. But pain shapes us. It forces us to see things more clearly, to take a pause. Abby's death two months ago was awful. My heart breaks for you. If you want to get something out of her death, use this time to sort out what you believe and what you want to do. Far too many people never really take the time to do that. Don't let this slip away.

"One of my favorite psalms has always been Psalm 130. It's a cry of anguish in the midst of deep pain. 'Out of the depths I cry to you, O Lord. Lord, hear my voice.' But in the midst of his cry, the psalmist remembers God. Something about his suffering allows him to see God anew. And it's at that moment when the psalmist most realizes his need of God. 'I wait for the Lord, my soul waits, and in his word I hope.' Then he uses this wonderful analogy: 'My soul waits for the Lord more than those who watch for the morning, more than those who watch for the morning.' Sometimes when I'm going through hard times, I think of those who watch for the morning, the night watchmen who wait for the morning so they can be relieved and finally sleep. I find comfort in that because it reminds me that light comes in the morning. It helps me reframe what I'm going through."

Chris let Professor Mendes's words sink in. He hadn't been expecting this type of challenge from the meeting. He assumed it was going to be the normal condolences with a prayer tossed in there for good measure. But perhaps Mendes was right. Could the hellish experience that he was going through lead to something? Could he be like those who watch for the morning?

Chris looked around at all the books that lined the shelves. Many of them were quite old. He thought about all the students who had sat in the very seat he was occupying. Chris decided to trust Mendes, whatever he had in mind.

"What should I do, Professor? Go home to my parents with a reading list from you?"

Mendes smiled. "No, I don't imagine reading in isolation is what you need right now, especially after what you've said about dreading going home."

"Without my stipend from Harvard, I can't afford to stay here in Cambridge. I can barely afford to stay here with it."

"What if you took a trip overseas?" Mendes suggested.

"And where would I get the money for that?" Chris asked.

Mendes told him not to worry about the money. "There is a former student of mine," he said, "who is looking for an assistant. The church has supported his work for many years."

Chris began to wonder where this was going. What was he getting himself into?

"He runs a religious non-profit in Nigeria. Port Harcourt, to be exact. He's a remarkable individual. I think the experience there would change your perspective and give you the time you need to think."

"Nigeria? I've only been out of the United States once."

"Then you're long overdue for a trip. Memorial Church will cover all the costs. Spend the next three months there. If you want to return to the university in the fall, you can. If not, I'll be happy to aid you in your next step."

Chris couldn't believe his ears. Nigeria. Non-profit work. It would certainly get him out of the hole he had been existing in for the past two months. What did he have to lose?

One thing nagged at him though, as he thought about headlines from Nigeria in recent years.

"Is it safe there, Professor?"

"There has been some conflict in the north of the country, but where you'll be going is perfectly safe. I wouldn't worry in the least."

Chapter 3

April

Port Harcourt, Nigeria

Olabisi Bob-Manual pulled her 2000 Toyota Camry into the gravel parking lot. The tires made an audible crunch on the crushed stone as she parked next to an old pickup truck. The clock on the dashboard read 9:55 am. She was early. Glancing in the rearview mirror, she saw one of the long, low buildings of the prison behind her. Olabisi got out and stood by the back of her car. There was no need to get too close to the prison. Ifeanyi would be able to see her. Across the parking lot she saw several guards with semi-automatic rifles lounging on a cement porch. They stared back at her but made no movement, as though the heat prevented them from caring.

The figure that walked toward the Toyota Camry forty minutes later was only vaguely familiar. The naturally muscular body had wasted away during ten years in prison, and the characteristic well-trimmed beard had given way to a straggly one streaked with gray. Then Olabisi saw the eyes—one part of Ifeanyi Okoye that had not changed. Mahogany brown, the eyes had an intensity that caught the casual observer off guard. They were made more dramatic by Ifeanyi's tendency to stare at others, oblivious to the unease it caused. It was the eyes that reassured Olabisi that prison had not broken her hero.

Ifeanyi Okoye had been a leader in the Movement for the Emancipation of the Niger Delta, or MEND. This organization, labeled a terrorist group by the George W. Bush administration, had fought the Nigerian government and the international oil companies from 2004–2010 in a violent culmination of what had originally been a peaceful movement for justice.

As happened in similar situations around the world, international oil companies, in conjunction with the Nigerian National Petroleum Company, had polluted the oil-rich Niger River Delta. Oil spills, gas flaring, pipeline leaks, and lax regulations had left the natural ecology a mess. The tribal fishing villages scattered throughout the delta received little in return for the desecration of their environment. While the elite in Nigeria got rich from oil revenue, the average villager faced many of the same struggles that he did before oil was discovered in 1956 and had to deal with the consequences of pollution.

In the early 1990s, a non-violent movement to redress these wrongs arose and garnered international attention. Many held on to the hope that things might change. There were peaceful marches and demonstrations that called for some of the oil revenue to flow back into the communities from which it came. Then the government cracked down on the protests and nine leaders were executed on trumped-up charges. Even though the Clinton administration publicly protested the Nigerian government's brutality, no move was made to limit the oil that flowed from the delta. Following the Nigerian government's crackdown, new protest movements appeared, which became increasingly violent. If public demonstrations, petitions, and diplomatic pressure did not work, then perhaps bombs would. Repression and a lack of justice had turned non-violence into violence.

By 2004, the largest insurgent groups joined together under the aegis of MEND, and the violence escalated. MEND attacked pipelines and oil installations, kidnapped oil executives and waged a concerted public relations battle against the Nigerian government. The government stepped up its counter-insurgency efforts but eventually came to a compromise with the leaders of MEND. In exchange for funding for the Niger Delta Development Corporation, an organization set up to fund economic development in the region, the Nigerian government granted amnesty to the MEND leaders willing to turn in their arms. The effort was enough to splinter the shaky coalition, and many leaders accepted amnesty. Ifeanyi Okoye was one who did not.

Ifeanyi's arrest and public trial landed him in prison for ten years. His sentence would have been longer were it not for the public outpouring of support for a man who had spoken and written eloquently on behalf of the average citizen of the delta.

Now he was free.

Ifeanyi took his time crossing the gravel parking lot to the waiting Toyota Camry. He wanted the guards to see he was not afraid. He had survived his brutal imprisonment, and their efforts to break his will had failed. When Ifeanyi reached the car, Olabisi embraced him feeling the bony structure under her grasp. She held her breath to protect her senses from the stench of his clothes, drenched and hardened by layers of sweat. It pained her to think how much he had suffered. "Ifeanyi, it's so good to see you free."

Ifeanyi smiled, revealing teeth that looked remarkably well after a stint in a Nigerian prison. "Let's go. I am ready to be rid of this place." When Ifeanyi spoke, the hint of an upper-class British accent created such a stark contrast to his appearance that it made Olabisi sad. Such a

17

man should never be subjected to what he had been. The great insurgent leader would regain his strength, Olabisi assured herself.

Ifeanyi lowered his stiff joints into the worn cloth seats of the Camry and pulled the door shut with a defiant slam. "Where to now?" Olabisi asked as she turned the key in the ignition. "Your apartment?"

"Just drive, Bisi. I want to see the city again. I have dreamed about this day and am in no hurry. I want to see the people of the delta once more."

Olabisi loved when he used her nickname. She nodded and pulled the car out of the lot. Ifeanyi rolled his window down and let his hand drift out into the warm passing air. A song by a new Nigerian artist played on the car radio, the beat energizing and carefree.

Port Harcourt had changed since the last time Ifeanyi had seen it. There were grandiose new houses, showpieces of the local Nigerian elite, with high fences to keep out unwanted people. More banks, built to stash corrupt oil money, lined the major streets. But while he might have been bitter about these changes, in the first flush of freedom, it was the colors that delighted Ifeanyi the most. Everything in prison, including the walls, had been a dismal cement gray, but now everywhere he looked were the vibrant reds, yellows, greens and blues of women's clothing and the street signs. At the many traffic jams, or go-slows, street sellers came to the open car window to hawk their wares: bottled water in a country where no one dared drink the tap water, cheap imitation watches, ties, boiled groundnuts, handkerchiefs, phone chargers. To each of these vendors Ifeanyi smiled and merely waved his hand, indicating he was not interested. It was just as well because he had no money on him. But simply viewing the scene filled him with a deep-seated joy. Even the endless honking of horns was a welcome tune. How he loved Nigeria's pulse.

"Alright, take me home," Ifeanyi finally said after nearly an hour of aimless travel. They drove to Ifeanyi's apartment, a two-room upstairs flat on Trans Amadi Road. He had purchased it years before with a portion of his inheritance, and whenever he was in Port Harcourt, it gave him a place to stay and a refuge from the world. After he opened the familiar door, he scanned the spartan apartment. A well-used wooden desk was pushed against the wall. A table with two plastic chairs sat near a small refrigerator, only recently returned to life with power. Next to it, on the floor, was a hot plate and a few stacked dishes. The available wall space was partially covered with makeshift bookshelves, which were nothing more than concrete blocks with wooden planks. Ifeanyi was pleased to see his books were untouched. By the window was an American-style rocking chair where he would read. A thick layer of dust covered everything, but he noticed that his desk had been cleared off and a laptop computer sat ready to be used.

Ifeanyi turned to his friend. "Thank you, Bisi."

Olabisi felt her heart rate quicken.

"I got a computer for you, just as you had asked. The power is back on, and your friend the tailor downstairs said you could use his Wi-Fi."

"Where did the computer come from?"

"Emeka Nwosu gave it to me. He is now the president of one of the banks in town. You have lots of friends here, Ifeanyi. Lots of people believe in you. Your time in prison made you famous."

"We will see. Support in deeds is the test of true loyalty." He took a deep breath and realized how exhausted he was. "I need some rest."

She couldn't wait to see Ifeanyi's old energy and the command he had over others with his charisma. "I left a few items in your refrigerator and cupboard. You know, there are so many who want to see you."

"Yes," Ifeanyi responded. Olabisi couldn't tell what he meant by that.

"There is a Bible there too," she added. Ifeanyi looked down at the well-worn paperback Bible on the desk near his computer. He went over and flipped open the first few pages before letting the cover fall shut.

Ifeanyi had grown up Catholic, like most Igbos, and had even considered seminary. But he hadn't been to mass in more than a decade. If God hadn't helped his people, why should Ifeanyi care? If God existed, he had proved himself irrelevant to the struggle and therefore to Ifeanyi.

"I'll leave you," Olabisi said. "Some of us want to have you for dinner tonight. Would you feel up for that?"

Ifeanyi nodded, clearly distracted.

"I'll call you later," Olabisi said. He will be back to his old self once he sleeps, she assured herself.

After she left, Ifeanyi went into his bedroom and collapsed on his bed, the cushion of the mattress draining the ache from his bones as he drifted off to sleep. It felt good to be home, to have a brief moment of peace.

When Ifeanyi woke from his nap, he showered and trimmed his beard. In the refrigerator he found some egusi soup with a note attached to it.

Welcome home! Enjoy. —Olabisi

He smiled. She was a good woman. Maybe in a different life there would have been time for something more between them. Ifeanyi heated the soup on his hot plate. He also found instant coffee and plugged in his electric kettle to boil some water. Suitably reenergized, he sat down at his desk and booted up the computer. The laptop was a couple years old, but it had what he needed. While his computer flashed through its starting sequence, he went to the corner of his room near the rocking chair and moved the small table to the side. Then he got down on his knees and lifted one of the floorboards. Thankfully, it hadn't been disturbed in his absence. Underneath was a small space from which he drew a standard-sized notebook. He blew the dust off and cleared the remaining particles with his hand. Flipping it open, he found what he was looking for: a series of e-mail addresses and phone numbers with initials next to them. He returned to his computer and sat down to think.

Ifeanyi's mind drifted to his grandfather, a hero of the Nigerian Civil War who had fought for the losing side. Growing up, he heard story after story about the Biafran War, as it was called. His grandfather never tired of reminding him that it had been the international oil companies that doomed his people. Nigeria had never really been a country, but a loose collection of tribes brought together under British rule. When independence from Britain came in 1960, the three largest tribes—the Hausa in the north, the Yoruba in the west, and the Igbo in the east—divided power amongst themselves in the new government. But the power was never shared equally. Ifeanyi's grandfather remembered when the simmering tensions among the tribes sparked outbreaks of violence, especially against the Igbos, his people, which led the Igbos to declare the eastern part of Nigeria an independent country: Biafra.

The Igbos insisted that Biafra included the oil-rich Niger Delta, which was populated mostly by the smaller tribes. The ruling Hausas and their British allies could not abide the loss of oil revenue. Better equipped and supplied, the armies of the newly independent Nigerian state surrounded Biafra and starved it into submission. Nearly two million Igbos died in the ensuing famine, including several of Ifeanyi's relatives. Their stories were seared into Ifeanyi's psyche. Had the international community recognized Biafra's self-determined right to exist, had the oil companies not sided with the Nigerian government, Ifeanyi's life and the life of his people would have been very different. The fault for all that death lay at the feet of the oil companies and their international masters. If they had supported Biafra, international support would have saved the fledgling Igbo state.

The old wound never healed for some. Ifeanyi Okoye was one of those people. His grandfather had never let him forget what happened or that a different future had been possible.

Ifeanyi's father, like many of his generation, did his best to forget the struggle. He became a successful businessman and, having endured the suffering of the war as a child, devoted his life to building safety and security for his family. Ifeanyi always resented that his father turned his back on the history of his people. Like many wealthy Nigerians, Ifeanyi's father sent his son to a British boarding school. These bastions of English privilege were not always kind to outsiders, and Ifeanyi suffered under harsh student discipline and a constant flow of racist taunts.

While in school and later university in England, his summers in Nigeria became welcome respites, a time to mold his identity. An early interest in religion gave way to a new center of value. He would not devote himself to an absent God, or to money, as his father had done. The struggle became Ifeanyi's life, his cause, his reason for living. The struggle was his faith and religion. From involvement in the youth movement in the late 90s to being a leader in MEND, Ifeanyi focused his whole being on Nigeria's liberation from the vestiges of colonialism. Once Nigerians truly controlled the oil, they could begin to construct a new nation.

Ifeanyi shook himself out of his reverie and opened one of the desk drawers. From inside he pulled a stack of pamphlets and press releases. "The Revolutionary Ideal" by Ifeanyi Okoye. He had written that one shortly after the Ijaw Youth Council was formed in 1998.

He fought back the pull of nostalgia. Emotions were for the weak.

Ifeanyi kept going through the stack of papers until he came to the last pamphlet, one he had written in prison and smuggled out to Olabisi, entitled "The Coming Day of Reckoning." He opened to the first page:

Examine your lives, my friends. You have received your pittance from the oil revenue. How much better is your life now? Were your compromises worth the price, worth giving up the hope for something more? Did you really think the thieves who run this country would stop stealing from you? I am stuck here in prison, and yet I know the corruption still remains. The money continues to flow to buy flashy apartments in London and fancy clothes. Where are YOUR new apartments and Rolex watches?

Corruption. The thought of it brought the anger back. He winced when he thought of his own brother, like so many others, scrambling to get the scraps that fell from the oil companies' table. He kept reading:

Where does it come from, this greed, this corruption? The British taught it to us. The British used Nigeria to extract resources. They taught us how to steal from the land and like good, obedient slaves we have kept doing it. And it has been allowed to happen for so long because of the oil. Two million barrels per day of crude oil come out of our land. That money fuels the evil we see around us. The foreigners taught us to steal and they continue to rob us and pollute our national soul under the friendly guise of the international oil companies. We need a day of wrath, a day of

23

reckoning. Only through violence will we take what is ours by right.

Ifeanyi put the pamphlet down. He wished he'd had more time to edit it. Still, the pamphlet had been widely read and republished online. Its message resonated because it forced people to look at Nigeria's moral decline and the reasons behind it. Once liberation came, there would be time to re-found the nation. It was the nature of the world. Death must precede rebirth.

It helped that Ifeanyi's reputation among the people had never been stronger. In 2009, after the government offered amnesty to the insurgents willing to lay down their arms, Ifeanyi loudly denounced the offer because it did not give the people what they'd always wanted. Going to prison for his uncompromising stand transformed Ifeanyi's reputation and writings in the minds of the people. Discontent was growing. The Boko Haram violence in the north of the country proved it. Ifeanyi had become a symbol of hope for the people of the Niger Delta who had never gotten their due for the damage the oil companies had done to the region.

He got up from his chair and walked over to the window. Outside, people moved up and down Trans Amadi, one of the main streets of Port Harcourt. How much opportunity did most of them have? Little. Billions of dollars of oil money taken out of the ground in the Niger Delta, and what was there to show for it? Ifeanyi took another sip of his coffee. It was the first cup of coffee he had sipped in ten years. He could feel the caffeine buzz work its way through his body. The time had come to start the revolution.

On the computer screen was a blank e-mail, addressed by blind carbon copy to more than fifty e-mail addresses that he had laboriously typed in. They were the names of the old MEND commanders and those interested in the struggle for Biafran independence. They were out there, waiting for a leader. Ifeanyi let his fingers linger over the keyboard as he typed out the words that would ignite a new Nigeria. A spark is a small thing, but with the right fuel, it can lead to a conflagration.

Dear brothers,
     The time has come. Will you join the crusade?
                                        Ifeanyi Okoye

Ifeanyi looked over his e-mail. He pressed send, then watched the moving bar that indicated the e-mail was being delivered across the web. In prison he had carefully worked out his plans. He could foresee how each step would unfold. The next day he would begin texting his contacts. The old machinery would soon come back to life.

Chapter 4

Ifeanyi Okoye relished walking the streets of Port Harcourt. After ten years in prison, the freedom to move about as he wanted helped Ifeanyi relax and think. It was still so new to him that he enjoyed the feeling of treading on uneven pavement and didn't mind the hotspot forming on his left heel. He also got to mingle with people, the average Nigerians for whom he fought. He wandered to the store of a car mechanic he knew and they talked for twenty minutes about the state of the country and the mechanic's sales for the past month.

As the day wore on, however, Ifeanyi could feel the anxiety rising in his body. His mind was full of plans for the days ahead. When he had been in prison, all he saw in his mind was successful attacks on oil installations. Now that he was free and his plans were becoming reality, he kept seeing the faults in his plan, the potential missteps. That morning, he had met with several commanders who would join him in the struggle, but many others had not returned his calls. Had their mobile numbers changed? Had they thrown in their lot with the government? It was impossible for him to know for sure. How long would it be before his movements were reported to the authorities? Time was not on his side.

To distract himself, he approached one of his favorite corn vendors across the road from his apartment. The smell of roasting corn hit his nose, and he smiled at the familiar aroma. Maybe he was worrying too much. Ifeanyi felt his phone vibrate and he reached into his pocket to read the incoming text. The commander he was meeting later was going to be late. He texted a quick response. When he turned his attention back to the corn vendor, he noticed a black Mercedes SUV with government license plates pulling up to the side of the road ten feet away. Part of him had expected the government men to show up, but they had arrived sooner than he thought they would. He considered running but thought better of it.

Ifeanyi looked over the corn arrayed on the grill. One side of the grill had hot coals, the woman slowly rotating each ear. On the other side, the cooked ears were being kept warm over the remnants of fast-dissolving coals. The whole operation was shaded under an old umbrella, which blocked the direct sunlight and made the heat of the grill tolerable for the vendor, who must have been in her mid-fifties, although she looked older than that. A glaze of sweat coated her black arms and face. Ifeanyi pointed to one of the ears on the hot side of the grill. He preferred his corn al dente. It stuck to his teeth less.

"That piece of corn is not cooked enough." The voice was close enough to his neck that Ifeanyi could feel the heat of the man's breath. He knew that voice, though it had been years since he had heard its distinct cadence.

"Hello, Godwin. How nice of you to care for the taste of my food," Ifeanyi said without turning around. His senses were on full alert, his muscles taut under his white cotton button-down shirt. "Why don't you choose one for me?"

Godwin Ogbe leaned over Ifeanyi's shoulder and said something in pidgin to the woman selling the roasted corn. From the warming side of the grill she took the most well-done ear off the heat and handed it to Ifeanyi. Its outer kernels were covered in black char. He took a bite and savored the taste of freshly roasted corn, even if it had more carbon than he liked and he had to tear through the softened kernels with his teeth.

"Aren't you going to pay the woman?" Godwin asked. He was now standing next to Ifeanyi.

"Given your newfound wealth, Godwin, I thought you might be a sport."

"I hate those foolish British schoolboy phrases. Did you use them when you were in prison? I'm sure the scum who were with you must have appreciated that." Godwin took out a bill and handed it to the woman, who was profuse in her thanks for the generous tip. "Let's go for a walk," Godwin added.

The two of them walking side by side—Ifeanyi in his inexpensive button-down shirt and plain khakis, Godwin in a black double-breasted suit lined with brass buttons and a fedora crowning his head—made an unusual pair. Godwin's outfit mirrored that of the former president of Nigeria, who was also from the Niger Delta. He was two inches taller than Ifeanyi but had no beard or facial hair. Under his hat his head was shaved clean. He also outweighed Ifeanyi by nearly forty pounds.

"To what do I owe this pleasure, Godwin?"

Ifeanyi and Godwin had once been friends and fellow revolutionaries during the height of the MEND violence.

"Ifeanyi, I want to save us both unnecessary pain." Neither man looked at the other but kept walking, the crowd on the sidewalk parting before them as if they could sense the fear and tension between the two men.

"I thought you rather enjoyed causing people pain," Ifeanyi replied. Godwin Ogbe had earned a reputation for cruelty when he had worked for MEND before the amnesty. He had once tortured a kidnapped Dutch reporter when his news agency refused to provide the ransom. The mangled body had washed up near Port Harcourt two days later. While Ifeanyi sat in prison, Godwin had accepted the terms of the amnesty offered in 2009 and was rewarded with a well-paying government job. His official title was regional secretary for human affairs in Rivers State, but his actual responsibility was to keep an eye on his fellow former militants and to prevent another insurgency. Once a rebel, now an enforcer. He assumed his new role with as much enthusiasm as he had executed his former one. There were several stories circulating of former militants who had disappeared while in police custody—likely a result of Godwin's interference.

"That e-mail you sent yesterday was foolish. Did you think I would not eventually see it?"

"The e-mail proves nothing. You can't arrest me for that."

While Ifeanyi took another bite of his corn, two young Nigerians came up to him, forcing both the older men to stop. They wore t-shirts with American logos on them—Nike and Gap—practically uniforms for young Nigerians. "Are you Ifeanyi Okoye?" the shorter of the two asked, his words quick with excitement. Ifeanyi guessed the boys were no more than twelve or thirteen years old.

"I am."

"I told you!" The shorter boy said to his friend before turning back to Ifeanyi. "My father says you'll save the country." In turn, the two boys shook Ifeanyi's free hand, pumping it up and down enthusiastically.

Ifeanyi smiled back. "Remember never to be afraid and to stand up for Nigeria," he said. "And say hello to your father."

Afterward, the boys disappeared into the crowd, talking excitedly with one another. To celebrate Ifeanyi's release, one of the major local papers had run a story that morning with his picture on the front page.

Godwin chuckled. "You think your popularity will protect you, but it won't. And those boys won't stand with you when the time comes. You'll see."

"Why are we having this conversation, Godwin? Can't you see I would prefer to eat alone?"

"I am warning you to stop whatever it is you are planning before it's too late. Your schemes won't work. I know too much."

"Perhaps you're assuming too much."

"Ifeanyi, do you really want to return to prison, back to that damp cell, the beatings, the isolation?"

Memories of prison flashed through Ifeanyi's mind, and he shuddered involuntarily. "I'll never go back to prison," he replied.

"I could find you a position in government," Godwin offered. "You could have peace. Find a nice woman to marry. Raise a family."

"And sell out? Leave young boys like those with no opportunity?"

"There are government programs to help them. Your crusade will do them no better."

"Government programs? You and I both know most of the money goes into the pockets of men like you. I saw your house the other day, Godwin. That doesn't come from your official salary." Ifeanyi's voice was loud and distinct. People on the street were staring at them. Two security men who had exited the car with Godwin pulled back their jackets, revealing their holstered sidearms.

"You have always been a foolish ideologue," Godwin said. "You need a cause and you're obsessed with your role as savior. Your ego drives it. What you don't see is that your privileged upbringing gives you the luxury to disdain material things. But if you had grown up in the creeks like me, you would have learned to take what you can get. You never suffered like I suffered."

Ifeanyi stopped and squared up to Godwin, staring him down. "You feel guilty that you gave up the cause. It eats you up inside. I can see that."

"Ifeanyi, you are naïve, and that makes you dangerous." Godwin said in a quiet tone. "The way things are will not change, and you're blind to that. Don't be the cause of unnecessary death. You should be more of a realist, like me. But then it would deny you your much-needed glory and adulation. You'll only end up causing more harm to the people you claim to love."

Ifeanyi turned to face Godwin. "I'll never be like you, happy with the scraps from the tables of the 'Big Men.' I will change things forever." He seethed with hatred for his former comrade.

"That's your ego talking again, Ifeanyi. You need to be one of the 'Big Men.'" Godwin leaned in and pushed his index finger into Ifeanyi's chest for emphasis. "Mark my words. Just because we used to be friends does not mean I won't do my job. I will find evidence against you and when I do, I will embarrass you publicly and send you to prison forever. I won't let you be a martyr like you so desperately wish. If it wasn't for your popularity, I would arrest you here. If only your people had known you twenty years ago as I did, they would see through your act."

"Is that all?"

"For now."

Godwin turned and headed to his waiting Mercedes-Benz across the street. Ifeanyi looked down at his half-eaten ear of corn and tossed it aside. He had lost his appetite.

Chapter 5

Somewhere in the Niger Delta

Pulling into the village, the first thing Ifeanyi Okoye saw was the children. As he parked the old Land Rover he had borrowed from a local supporter, children ran up to it, displaying that fearless curiosity adults lose along the way. Getting out of the SUV, Ifeanyi smiled and questioned them in Ijaw, the local dialect, and they shouted their answer in response. He patted a couple of them on the head and walked down to the center of the village. Some of the women, who were outside smashing cassava root in large wooden bowls, looked at him with suspicion. SUVs did not always mean good things in a village like this one.

Unlike in Port Harcourt, most of the houses in the village were made of wood siding that had been hewn by hand from the many trees that crept right up to the edge of the village. Ifeanyi Okoye had been here before, and he knew the hut he was searching out, though it had been a number of years. No one greeted him as he wandered among the ramshackle dwellings. Even the children had taken the cues from their parents and now gave him his space. Ifeanyi stopped before one of the few concrete houses, this one painted brightly with turquoise and yellow trim, though its tin roof showed signs of rust and age. The acid rain caused by the continuous gas flaring from the oil wells made the roofs wear quickly in this part of the country. Ifeanyi stood and waited outside the house. It was time to rekindle an old friendship.

"There he is!" a voice called from inside the hut. "Back from the dead." Fineface Pepple emerged from his home and embraced Ifeanyi. "It is so good to see you. You are welcome."

Ifeanyi returned the embrace. "It's good to see you too, my friend. I always feel welcome in your village."

Fineface Pepple stood a few inches shorter than Ifeanyi. He had a wiry frame that was lean and muscular, in spite of his age. Unlike Ifeanyi, he was clean-shaven and you could clearly see two scars on each cheek, indicating his tribe, marks that had been given to Pepple when he was only a boy as part of a coming-of-age ritual. He wore an old American t-shirt, brown pants, and sandals—the clothes of a man who gave little thought to his personal appearance.

"Come in." The house itself was modest by any standard. Traditional wood carvings and decorative mats made of shells hung on the walls. The place was clean. In a farther room, Ifeanyi could see Fineface's wife sitting patiently.

"Sit down, my friend." Fineface motioned to a plastic chair near the wooden table. They both took seats. "Esther," he called to the other room, "bring us some palm wine. I need to celebrate seeing my old friend." They sat in silence while Fineface's wife brought them two glasses of the milky liquid that constituted the local alcoholic beverage. Made of freshly fermented sap from the ubiquitous palm trees that surrounded the village, the drink tasted sweet yet tangy as Ifeanyi sipped from his glass. It brought back many memories of his childhood, including the first time he got drunk at age twelve with his friends. For some reason his grandfather had not minded when Ifeanyi had drunk palm wine, perhaps because he thought it linked him more closely with the land. When he had come back from school in England, it was one of the things he craved most.

"I cannot tell you how happy I am to see you," Fineface said, after they had had a few moments to enjoy the refreshment and rest in each other's presence. "So much has changed since you were taken away to prison."

"I can see that. I noticed the new school on the edge of the village."

"Ah, that. Yes, you would think it was made out of gold with how long it took the government to build it. We have only had teachers in two of the past four years." He shook his head. "Some things don't change. The people of the villages never get their due for all the suffering caused by the oil companies."

"How are your men doing?"

"I love them too much. I do. These days most of them want to be in the cities or the larger villages. We don't train like we used to. We come together occasionally to take oil from the pipelines, but I feel more like we are hired hands when we do it. You know how it is." Ifeanyi nodded. He could see the bitterness in Fineface's eyes. It signaled motivation. "But still, it's the main source of income for this village, now that the fishing waters are so polluted."

"Part of me is surprised you stayed in the village. I would've thought that after things calmed down you might find a job like the others."

"Like the others." Fineface tried to push out of his mind the faces of his former MEND colleagues who now worked for the government. Some of them hesitated so little before jumping at the chance for money and security. They wanted to pretend to be "Big Men" in Port Harcourt. But now they skimmed money off the top, money that was supposed to go to the villages and the people. Fineface tried to control his anger by taking another sip of palm wine. A disturbing thought grew in his mind. Was he selling out? In the last few years, Fineface had been stealing oil from the pipelines of the major oil companies, a practice known as oil bunkering. He had been doing it with the active collusion of the Nigerian Navy. These days it was the only way to earn money for his men and his village. Most of the old MEND commanders who hadn't taken amnesty were doing it.

Fineface stared into the last bit of palm wine at the bottom of his glass before raising his eyes to meet Ifeanyi's. Something about Ifeanyi had broken open a festering wound, and as his anger rose he could feel the pus seeping into his soul. "So, Ifeanyi Okoye, the Igbo insurgent, the Unbowed, let us talk about what is to come."

"The time has finally arrived," Ifeanyi said slowly. "We've seen what happens when we try half measures. You and I both know what the real problem is. We have to push them out for good." Ifeanyi did not need to say who "them" referred to. In spite of all the government corruption and collusion, "them" would always be the international oil companies (IOCs) that had taken the best from Nigeria and given as little back as possible.

"You've never been one for small vision, Ifeanyi. The oil companies have weathered a lot in the past. Forcing them out won't be easy." Fineface could feel his nerves tighten as the anger in him built. The passion in Ifeanyi's eyes bordered on obsession.

"Yes, but it is possible. The army is distracted with Boko Haram in the north. The country's stomach for violence is low. And the oil companies are weak. Public opinion has always dominated their thinking in Britain and the US. Shareholders don't like uncertainty. If we could make one big impact, one great act of coordinated violence…it might work."

"We came close in 2006."

"We did. And we can do it again," Ifeanyi assured him. In 2006, MEND's violent attacks had reduced Nigeria's oil output by nearly 30 percent.

Fineface leaned back in his chair and looked at his empty glass of palm wine. "Esther, refill our glasses." Fineface's wife reappeared carrying a plastic jug of the milky palm wine. "Just leave the jug on the table." Esther did as she was asked and left the jug, nodding to her husband and content to remain silent. Fineface refilled both glasses and took another sip.

"So, what exactly is your plan?"

"I'm going to talk with Mama Sandra. We need the women, and not just like in 2002. The women are the key for small attacks, which, taken together, will have a big impact." Ifeanyi and Fineface had been young men in 2002, when the women of the Niger Delta had shut down a major Chevron production facility near Warri, and they both remembered how powerful a statement it was.

"That's wise, Ifeanyi, but now much of the oil is offshore. Not quite so easy to deal with."

"That's why we need to hit more than one offshore platform in addition to attacks all over the delta."

"Ha! You do not lack for ambition. Where are we going to get that level of coordination, let alone materials to carry it out? These days many of the commanders won't be with us. They like their new lives. The amnesty has been good for them."

"True, but with the right leadership, the right inducements, you might be surprised who we could get to help us. I spoke with Ebube in Port Harcourt yesterday."

"That man is a young weasel," Fineface responded.

"Perhaps, but he has men who are ready to fight."

"For a price, I'm sure."

"We all have requirements, Fineface," Ifeanyi said. "I will find the men."

"The reaction would be swift."

"Think, Fineface! Think of all the blood that has been shed already!" Ifeanyi pounded his fist on the red plastic table, making both their glasses shake. "Think of all the destruction, the pollution, the wreckage of our society. Consider all the work we have done. It is possible. We will change Nigeria forever."

"What about the money that'll be needed? The arms?"

"Those I'm working on. There are some weapons that the commanders still have. Buying more arms might be a challenge."

"And the money?"

"Emeka Nwosu claims he has some contacts in Lagos. Men who will support us. Until then we'll need money from oil bunkering."

"Is that a request, Ifeanyi? You want my men to risk their lives to pay off other MEND commanders?" Fineface put his palm wine down and stared at his friend. He was not on good terms with certain commanders, especially those for whom greed was the primary motivation.

"If you're willing, if you think the cause is worth it." Ifeanyi let his words hang in the air, his eyes locked on Fineface's.

"And what about Godwin Ogbe, that traitor? He's a devil. And the others? They know our methods and will find out what is happening. They'll be watching you. I'm sure they already are."

"We shall see." Ifeanyi's face was calm. In his head, he thought about Godwin's warnings to him the day before. Ifeanyi knew they were not idle threats. They would have to work quickly. Which commanders would feed Godwin information? Ifeanyi wished he knew.

"Drink your palm wine, Ifeanyi! Drink up! I will have to be drunk to say yes to this."

Ifeanyi took another sip of his palm wine. He could already feel it making him tipsy.

Fineface rocked back in his chair, twisting the plastic legs. He appreciated Ifeanyi's passion, but part of him distrusted the other man. Fineface's motivation came from seeing the suffering around him, the suffering of his family and tribe. But for Ifeanyi, it came from someplace else. Was it his resentment at growing up with so much privilege? Was it blind ambition? He had often wondered in the past what was behind those eyes. They were of different tribes. Different blood ran in their veins. How far would Ifeanyi be willing to go?

For his part, Fineface had already made up his mind as soon as he read Ifeanyi's e-mail. Ever since he was a child in the village, Fineface had never lacked boldness. He knew this would be his last chance, and at his age, why not take the risk?

Chapter 6

Chris Reed squinted in the bright sun as he stepped out of the Port Harcourt airport terminal. He cursed himself for forgetting to pack sunglasses and held up his arm to block the sunlight. He was surrounded on all sides by Nigerians moving this way and that, all with their bags bumping amongst them. Even though he was finally outside, he felt claustrophobic, almost panicky. He wanted space and someplace where he could feel relaxed. His nerves had been on overdrive ever since he landed in Lagos that morning and had to find his way to his connecting flight to Port Harcourt. A few people came up to Chris to offer him a ride in a taxi. He kept brushing them away, hoping that Paul Wisner would find him. He wished he had some way to call him, but his American cell phone didn't allow him to make outgoing calls. He hated to admit it, but being in a country where he was seemingly the only white person was discomfiting. All his unconscious American racial biases kept bubbling up inside him.

"Chris, my new main man. How's it going, buddy?"

Chris looked around at the sound of the voice and saw Paul walking toward him, just as Chris had imagined he would. About five foot ten, Paul had blond hair, wore a loose-fitting Hawaiian shirt over his tanned body, long shorts and flip flops. He had a broad smile beneath Ray-Ban Wayfarer sunglasses. Chris guessed he was in his late thirties. When

Paul reached Chris, he extended his hand and gave a firm pump of the hand.

"You must be Paul Wisner," Chris said.

"Lucky guess, man. Welcome to Port Harcourt." Paul pushed his sunglasses up on his hair, revealing clear blue eyes that seemed more pronounced against his deep tan. Paul's confidence and radiant joy put Chris immediately at ease.

"I can't tell you how happy I am to see you," Chris blurted out.

"You look worked, bro. But don't worry, we'll get you settled in your new paradise soon enough." Paul reached down and hoisted Chris's bag onto his right shoulder.

"I can take that," Chris insisted.

"No worries, man. Glad you made it safely. Time for you to chill for a bit. God has brought you here, and I'm going to do my best to bring a little of his joy to that face of yours."

"Thank you," Chris managed to say.

"Follow me. Your chariot awaits." Paul strolled leisurely toward the parking lot, seemingly oblivious to the mass of Nigerians around him. Chris could catch him singing as he walked, "Through many dangers, toils, and snares, I have already come." As Paul reached the high note from that verse of "Amazing Grace," he turned to Chris. "'Tis grace that brought me safe thus far, and grace will lead me home." Paul flashed another smile, which involuntarily brought one to Chris's face too.

"Great words to live by," Paul added. "Gotta love John Newton. If God can work miracles through a slave trader, just imagine what he will do with you." Without waiting for a response, Paul turned his face back toward where he was headed and continued whistling the tune of "Amazing Grace" all the way to the car. He popped the trunk and tossed Chris's bag in the back.

"Hop in." Paul motioned to the front seat of a 2009 Honda Civic. Once the car was started, the air conditioning came rushing out of the vents. "That's one thing I like about this car, good AC."

"It feels nice. Pretty hot out there."

"We're in Africa, dude! This isn't Boston. You'll get used to it. I bet you have a heavy coat stuffed in your bag somewhere. Won't need that." As they drove out of the airport, Paul talked, unprompted. "The great city of Port Harcourt, center of the oil industry, teeming with two million people. We have a bit of a drive to the city, so feel free to relax." The car sped along the newly built highway, and Chris stared out the window at the dark green tropical forest, the colors dulled by the glare of late afternoon sun.

"First it was slaves, then it was palm oil, then crude oil and now a shift to natural gas. This land has been stripped bare and had its best extracted from it for years. But the people you'll love. It's why we do what we do. To see God's love reflected in those around us. Doesn't get any better."

Chris was already feeling more like himself. After they had been driving for a few minutes, Chris remarked, "I think the cab driver in Lagos cheated me."

Paul laughed. "It's as common as the heat. When they see a white person—oyibo is the term you'll often hear—the average Nigerian sees a way to make money. Should've warned you about the taxi. My bad." Chris hadn't realized that he would need to take a taxi from the international airport to the domestic airport in Lagos, both of which were confusingly named Murtala Muhammad Airport. "Lemme guess. He charged you five thousand?"

"Ten thousand naira. I think that was over thirty dollars. The taxi driver was a Christian. He talked about faith the whole ride and then he told me the price. There wasn't any meter so I didn't know if I should argue."

"Whew!" Paul whistled loudly. "Yup, you sure got taken. Should have been more like five hundred naira, a thousand if you were feeling generous. That's three bucks. Listen, you've got to understand that the people here don't have much. They don't see it as cheating you. It's more like a business transaction. The person selling a product or service will always try to maximize his profit. It's the same way in the States. The only difference here is that the principle applies to most transactions. Don't worry, you'll get used to it and learn to negotiate."

"I'll have to negotiate for everything?"

"Not everything. Just most things." Paul looked across at his passenger and gave him a friendly slap on the shoulder. "Don't worry about it, dude. It happens to everyone. Look at it this way: you made that cabbie's day. His life probably ain't the easiest. You were a bit of God's grace in his life. You're already doing good work and you didn't even know it." Paul smiled again.

"If you say so," Chris said. Paul's enthusiasm did help. After all, he thought to himself, the money had been a gift from Harvard.

It took about forty minutes for Paul and Chris to reach their destination, a small home just off Rumuola Road, one of the largest and busiest streets in Port Harcourt. Paul leapt out and opened the creaky, half-rusted gate before getting back behind the wheel and driving in. "Here it is! Your new digs."

The house looked old and run-down. Like nearly every building in Port Harcourt, it was made of concrete and was two stories high. Chris noticed a few flicks of light blue paint, as though someone had started painting the house years ago and then given up halfway through. With Chris still staring up at the exterior, Paul had grabbed Chris's bag from the trunk and led the way up the dirt path to the door. The door opened to a small living room that boasted a worn couch, a couple chairs, and several drawings of Jesus as an African. A flight of stairs separated the living room from a kitchen and a small dining area. Before Chris could peek around the corner into the kitchen, Paul was bounding up the stairs with the duffle bag slung over his shoulder.

Trying to stay a few steps behind Paul, Chris was surprised when he heard a voice from above. "You've returned."

"Yup!" Paul called up. He turned to Chris while still walking upstairs. "That's my assistant, Rotimi. Best guy you'll ever meet." At the top of the stairs Paul disappeared into a bedroom and Chris saw Rotimi, whose expressionless face was in distinct contrast to Paul's ebullience. Rotimi was a Nigerian, maybe five foot seven with a slight frame and hair that was buzzed almost down to the scalp. His light blue button-down shirt seemed a size too big and hung off him. He had a little scruff under his chin as though he was trying to seem older than he was.

"Welcome," Rotimi said in a low voice without emotion. "Your bedroom is all set," he added, motioning to the room that Paul had just returned from.

"Uh, thank you," Chris managed in response.

"Rotimi works with me in everything I do here." Then Paul mentioned offhand, "He was living in your bedroom but now we will have to find a new arrangement. Still haven't figured that one out yet."

No wonder Rotimi was a little cold, Chris thought to himself.

"Wonderful to have you here, man!" Paul said as he lightly punched Chris in the upper arm. "Let me take you to the office. Oh, unless you want to shower and change first." He took another look at Chris standing there in his khaki cargo shorts and white t-shirt that he had been wearing since the day before, and said, "Here, we'll be downstairs. Take your time."

"Thanks." Paul left, and Chris looked around at his new quarters.

There was a free-standing wardrobe for his clothes, a twin-sized bed, and nightstand. The window had wooden shutters that could close, but he could see immediately that they would not keep out the light in the morning. He also noticed, above the bed, a net that was pushed off to the side. He inspected it a little more closely and realized it was a mosquito net. Life in Nigeria. Chris sighed. Unzipping his duffle bag, he dumped the contents out on the bed. He looked at the pile of ruffled clothes that constituted his possessions for the months ahead. A few weeks ago he would never have dreamed that he would be here. He really hoped this new adventure wasn't a mistake. But then again, what did he have to lose? As he put his things away, Chris realized that he hadn't thought of Abby all day. Maybe Professor Mendes had been right. Perhaps this was what he needed.

Thirty minutes later, after settling in and taking a shower in the bathroom upstairs, Chris felt rejuvenated, at least as much as he could be after an all-night flight on a cramped 767. Walking down the steps, he heard Rotimi and Paul arguing about something in quiet tones. As soon as they heard him, they stopped speaking.

"Let's go check out the office. We can walk from here, so no need for the car." Without waiting for a response, Paul headed for the door with Chris trailing him and Rotimi a few steps behind. Chris wanted to turn and reassure Rotimi that he was a friendly guy, but thought better of it and instead tried to keep up with Paul.

Winding their way along the main road, they passed the colorful shops and signs of Port Harcourt. The ubiquity of religious posters surprised Chris. They lined the road and were affixed to every telephone pole and streetlight. **Miracles are Forever. You are Next**, one sign read. Apparently, if Chris went to Purpose Living Ministries, he would receive a miracle. The sign had the picture of Pastor Richard Alabere standing with his chest thrust forward in his fine suit. Another poster with similar promises of miracles hung next to it. He tried to push back his skepticism about the brand of Christianity the posters advertised. He was there to learn and expand his thinking.

In the streets, traffic choked the road in both directions. It was late afternoon, and the cars inched along in a mass of metal, horns blaring, a cloud of exhaust fumes lingering over everything. "Is the traffic always like this?" Chris asked.

"Ha!" Paul let out a quick laugh. "Oh, yeah. It's way worse in Lagos though, man. And you'll get used to all the horns. They joke here that the horn is the first thing that needs to be replaced in any car in Nigeria. Totally true. The best is when you get in a traffic jam leaving church. Everyone smiling and praising God, then wild gesticulations, curses and horns five minutes later." He chuckled.

"The funny part is," Paul continued, "that the traffic wouldn't be half as bad if people actually followed some order and some signs, but everyone here is in such an apparent hurry to go nowhere that gridlock is the norm. Traffic signs and lights are for the other drivers. It can take an hour to get through certain intersections when there is no traffic cop on duty. You can see why I like walking."

The sidewalks, if you could call them that, were dirty, and Chris found himself dodging puddles of muddy water that made him regret putting on flip-flops back at the house. It was like walking barefoot through a fraternity after a party. Vendors sold food on the edges of the streets: Nigerian oranges, boiled groundnuts, roasted corn. Music poured out of the shops. Yet it was the piles of trash stacked up or even left by the side of the road that Chris kept noticing. It was as though the people didn't care that the streets and sidewalks were a mess.

A few minutes later they arrived at a storefront next to a hair salon. The sign above had white letters on a red background and read **Emmaus Center**.

The glass front door was propped open, and as they entered, Paul said to the receptionist, "Afternoon to you, Silas."

"Afternoon, sah."

"I want you to meet our newest assistant here: Chris Reed. He'll be visiting from the States for the next couple months. Chris, this is Silas. He runs the office and makes sure everything goes smoothly."

"Nice to meet you, Silas," Chris said as he walked over and shook Silas's hand. Silas leapt up and, deferentially with a slight bow of his head, took Chris's hand and shook it lightly.

"You are welcome, sah. God's blessings to you."

"Follow me. Let me show you the place!" Paul waved his hand toward the hallway in the back. Chris followed Paul across the main reception area, which had Silas's desk on one side and a classroom with twenty chairs and a chalkboard on the other. As they walked down the hallway, Chris noticed a bathroom and a lounge area just beyond it. At the end of the hallway was a set of stairs.

Chris followed Paul upstairs and down the second-floor hallway into the library, which housed an unexpectedly large collection. There must have been a thousand books. Each shelf was carefully labeled, "Biblical Studies," "Theology," "Church History" and the like. Chris saw that one of the labels was for "Healing" and another "Missionary History." Before he could lose himself in the shelves, Paul interrupted him.

"Chris. Great to see you with the books. I know you love those. There will be plenty of time for that. Here, check out your office." Paul led him back down the upper hallway to one of the offices. "You and Rotimi will be in here." Chris leaned his head into his new workspace. There were two metal desks facing each other. One had neatly organized piles of paper and pens lined up in a row. The other was empty. While Chris was taking it all in, Paul turned and walked across the hallway into what was clearly his own office. Paul's office had a faded poster of a surfer on one wall. The opposite wall had a poster of Jesus on a cross, done in a contemporary design. This Jesus was a Black African.

"Take a seat, man." Paul motioned to the blue plastic chair in front of his desk. "Welcome to our palace. What do you think?"

"It's quite a space," Chris said. He hadn't been anywhere like it before. He crossed his legs to prevent himself from fidgeting and showing how nervous he was.

"So, how much did Professor Mendes tell you about what we do here?"

Chris thought back to his conversations in Cambridge. The past month had gone by in whirlwind of activity. Getting a visa, the plane ticket, arranging to take a leave of absence from school, subletting his apartment. It was great to have some direction, but Chris realized how little he actually knew about how he would be spending his time.

"You better tell me everything," Chris admitted.

Paul launched into a spirited description of Emmaus Ministries. Paul had arrived in Port Harcourt fifteen years before, not long after he finished his seminary studies at Fuller Theological Seminary in Pasadena, CA. He was initially drawn to the Niger Delta from all he had read about the injustices of the 1990s and early 2000s. The programs had evolved over the years.

"At first," Paul explained, "I was focused on starting non-profits to help the youth here. So many of them were drawn to violence because there were so few options available. We still have programs that do that. Over time, we made connections with churches all over the region, some in the city and some out in the creeks, as we call the more rural areas near here. Now I try to convince the churches to start their own programs, and we try to facilitate funding and logistical support. There's endless work to be done."

Chris listened intently. The prospect of helping those in need had convinced him to take the leap of faith to come to Nigeria. He did have one nagging reservation though. Finally, he got up the courage to bring it up.

"Paul," Chris began, "that all sounds great, but what if I'm not really much of a Christian? I mean, I was raised a Christian and I went to Memorial Church back in Cambridge from time to time."

"Chris, Christianity is pretty different over here. You'll see. I wouldn't worry about it. There is a lot to learn. And whenever you have questions, just ask. The best thing you can do is to get out there and talk to folks. It's the people, the experiences that open your mind. Reading theology can only get you so far. Professor Mendes said you knew a lot about Christian history." Chris nodded. "That'll come in handy. One of the most important things we do here is teach people about the faith. There is a lot of the Holy Spirit here. You'll see. But not as much deep thinking."

Chris noticed a local newspaper on Paul's desk. He caught a glimpse of a Nigerian on the front page with the headline: Free at Last.

"Who's that?" Chris asked, pointing to the picture that went with the story.

Paul looked down at the paper and paused. There was something about his reaction that worried Chris. For the first time, he saw something other than optimism in Paul's blue eyes.

"Oh, that. Well, things might start to get a little crazy around here. I wouldn't think too much about it."

"Crazy?" Paul's instruction not to think about it made Chris think about it all the more.

"A Nigerian revolutionary was just released from prison. It's got some of the folks here wondering if the violence might start up again."

"That doesn't sound good."

"It's complicated, man. This area has been through a lot. Some folks think that violence is the best path forward." Paul reached for the paper, folded it up in a hurry and put it under his desk.

Paul quickly changed the subject. "It must be a bit overwhelming. All of this. I hear it's a new start for you. Professor Mendes's letter mentioned the accident with your wife. I was sorry to learn that." After a moment of silence, Paul added in a soft tone, "Requiescat in pace."

"Thanks, Paul. It's been a tough past few months." Memories of Abby began rushing back into Chris's mind.

"How long were you two married?"

"We met in high school, then got married a couple years ago before we moved to Cambridge." Chris thought back to that decision to move. If he hadn't been so focused on the glamor of Harvard and the PhD, he would never have entered the program and Abby would still be alive. Chris could hear Abby's voice and see her face in his head. He looked down to avoid eye contact so Paul couldn't see the tears welling up in his eyes. "Sorry," he mumbled.

"Don't be sorry, Chris. Love is hard."

"If you want to know one reason I'm not sure about Christianity, it's Abby's death. There is no way that a good God could have let that happen." Chris dabbed the dampness out from his eyes.

"I wish I had something I could say about that which would put your mind at rest. God is beyond our knowing."

"Then why know him at all?" There was bitterness in Chris' voice. "I loved going to church as a kid. Confirmation, mission trips, helping to lead worship. All of that. Once I got to college, it just seemed less relevant, but I still believed in God. Now I have a hard time repressing my anger at God, if he exists at all."

"Chris, you'd be foolish to think any other way. God can handle your anger. Be angry with him. But don't let go of him. God reveals himself in surprising ways. He'll surprise you here, if you're open to it.

"Let me tell you a story," Paul continued. "My great grandparents lost their only son, my grandmother's older brother, when he was eighteen. He died of a simple infection. Had it happened today, he would still be alive. His death devastated my great grandparents. They were devout Calvinists—God as omnipotent, the ultimate sovereign, and all that. In the midst of their grief, they had a choice. They could either walk away from God, or accept that what had happened was beyond their understanding and return to God. They did the latter. They found a way to keep their faith. I don't know how they did it. Otherwise I'd tell you.

"They were dairy farmers, and during the Great Depression everyone in town knew that they could get food at their place, if they really needed it. Regardless of how little my great grandparents had, they took Jesus's words seriously: 'give to whoever asks.' It meant they ate nothing but cow's tongue and pig's feet, but they fed a lot of people and were rocks in that community. When my father drove around the country in college, he stayed with foster children my great grandparents had taken in and helped raise. They were scattered all over the country, all with families of their own. My great grandparents were the most pious people my father ever knew. They found their faith in tragedy..." Paul's voice trailed off.

"I don't think I'm ready for that."

"Maybe somewhere in this crazy country God will speak to you. I'd recommend getting a little prayer stone, something from around the grounds that strikes you. Have it in your pocket and whenever you touch it, say a short prayer. One advantage of faith in God is that you know you're never alone."

"I wish I could believe that." Chris tried to hide his skepticism. He didn't want to be rude to Paul in their first meeting.

"Alright, dude," Paul nodded to indicate the talk was coming to a close. "I have to go do some work. Know I am here for you. Think, pray if you're so moved, go for walks, and read some of the books in the library, especially the books on Nigeria. You have plenty to learn, buddy. I gotta get some stuff done now though."

As Paul got up from his desk, Chris took it as his sign to leave. He looked forward to some time alone to process everything around him.

"Remember one thing, Chris," Paul said when they were both standing near the door.

"Yes?"

"It's the people. Get to know the people. You'll find it's the most healing thing for you now."

Chapter 7

Port Harcourt, Nigeria

"Rise and shine and give God the glory glory." The singing seeped into Chris Reed's still half-asleep brain. "Rise and shine and give God the glory glory." What is that? Chris thought to himself. "RISE AND SHINE AND"—Chris heard a slap against the wooden bedside table—"GIVE GOD THE GLORY GLORY, children of the Lord."

Chris opened one eye and saw Paul Wisner standing over him. "How early is it?" Chris squeaked.

"Dude, it's totally time to get up." Chris had been slow to adjust to the time change over the past week. Sleeping in every day had not helped. While the clock next to his bed read 7:00 am, his body told him it was more like 4:00 or 5:00 am. There was something about being in a strange place, combined with the extra anxiety of life in Nigeria, that made him tired.

"I don't know, Paul. I'm pretty wiped out. Maybe another hour of sleep."

"Prayer time." Paul got down on one knee and reached out his right hand to grab Chris's unwilling fingers. "Father, you are indeed an awesome God. We praise you for the chance to help others. Inspire your sleeping servant Chris so that he can soar on wings like eagles, run and not grow weary, walk and not be faint. In your holy name we pray. Amen."

Paul looked down on Chris, who, through his half-opened eyes, could see Paul's bright white teeth contrasting with his tan skin.

"It's not fair to use a Bible passage to wake me up. Doesn't God make rules against that or something?" Chris murmured.

"I'm glad to see there is a bit of life in you. Weakness and frailty are good, in small measure. Coffee is downstairs, man, but you gotta move to get it. You'll get used to the time change quickly. If I were you, I would shake out those cobwebs from your brain, and then come down for some eats. You have to be somewhere in a couple hours."

"I do?" Chris's voice croaked. "You didn't mention that yesterday."

"Yeah, well, you can't be reading books and sleeping in every day. There is work to be done. Softly and tenderly Jesus is calling, calling for you and for me." Paul's voice began singing another tune as he rose and went into the hallway, the distinctive sound of flip-flops accompanying his descent down the stairs.

Paul had let Chris ease into his new life in Port Harcourt, and he'd been getting some good reading done and meeting a few people. The place wasn't half bad, after all.

Chris dragged himself from his bed and walked over to his dresser. His clothes were neatly sorted into piles, so it was easy to pick out a t-shirt, gray shorts and the flip-flops he had become used to wearing instead of his running shoes. He looked in the mirror before leaving his room. Des Moines. French for the Moines was blazoned across his t-shirt. He definitely needed new clothes. He would have to ask Paul where to buy them.

Downstairs, Rotimi and Paul were discussing something in the kitchen but broke off when Chris appeared. "Some delicious, imported instant coffee?" Paul offered with a slight smile. "The joys of living in Nigeria. Last time I was stateside I didn't order real coffee for fear that my palette would rebel when I got back here."

"Thanks," Chris managed to say through his exhaustion. He took the cup of coffee and tasted it. He thought about making some re-tort to Paul's wisecracks, but his brain failed him. It was too early. "So where am I off to today?"

"You are about to start your work, man. Today you will be headed to a program handover," Paul announced as if those words explained it all.

"A what?"

"Program handover, bro. One of the local NGO's is handing over their work to the state government where, sadly, most of the work will probably die a slow death. Such is life in Niger Delta. I want you there to represent Emmaus Ministries. We did our best to link the churches in these communities with the program. Tomorrow you and I will be heading out into the creeks. It's time you met some Nigerians outside Port Harcourt."

"That sounds fine to me. Is there anything I am supposed to be doing at this handover?"

"All depends on what you mean by 'doing.' Introduce yourself around. Talk someone into getting lunch with you. Network. Learn. A lot of the work includes tasks that are hard to quantify. Your presence is a sign that God belongs in these programs if they are to succeed long-term."

"How does my presence do that? I'm not sure I'm the best representative for God."

"Don't worry. Be yourself. I think you should be able to handle that. Rotimi here will give you a lift." Chris looked up at Rotimi, who he was convinced bore a grudge against him ever since he took his room and office all in one day. Rotimi now spent most of his nights sleeping on their couch downstairs. True, the couch was big and looked comfortable, but he was out of a room. Chris wondered why he did not get his own place. How expensive were apartments in Port Harcourt anyway?

Thirty minutes later, Chris hopped in the front seat of their Honda Civic and Rotimi settled in behind the wheel. Apparently, Paul was going to do some work from home until Rotimi returned with the car. The car sped off, and Chris sensed the tension between them.

"So where are we headed?" Chris asked.

"To the main Rivers State government complex." Rotimi's voice showed little emotion. Rivers State was one of the thirty-six states that made up Nigeria. Port Harcourt was its capital.

A few minutes went by before Chris tried again. "How long have you been with Emmaus Ministries?"

"Almost seven years now."

Chris looked at Rotimi and tried to guess his age. Chris thought maybe he was a couple years older than him, probably twenty-seven or so.

"Listen, I am sorry I took your room. It wasn't my idea."

"I know."

"I'd like to be friends with you," Chris said.

Rotimi didn't respond.

"So where are you from?" Chris was determined to break the tension.

"I was born outside of Warri." Chris remembered seeing Warri on the map. It was the largest city of Delta State, which bordered Rivers State, and, like Port Harcourt, a center of the oil industry.

"How was growing up there?"

"I don't have many happy memories." Rotimi replied.

"Why is that? I am sorry if I'm being nosey."

Chris could see Rotimi relax slightly. "That's alright. I'm not that talkative. My father got remarried when I was fourteen. He kicked my sister

55

and me out of the house then. His new wife didn't want us around. It wasn't easy for us."

"What happened to your sister?" Chris asked, trying to hide his shock that any parent would do that to their children.

"I don't know where she is now. She's a couple years older than I am. After we were out on the street for a few days, trying to beg for food, she decided it was best if we went our separate ways."

"That sounds awful." Chris started to feel guilty that he hadn't taken the time to get to know Rotimi. "Do you know where your sister went?"

"At the time, I just sat down and cried. It was a few years later when I realized that she must have gone to the bars to find a man. I hope she is married now, but I have no interest in finding out. I understand why she left me."

"But she still left you," Chris said, almost to himself. "How did you survive?"

"It was hard. I remember being so hungry that I went through the trash heaps on the side of the road and chewed on chicken bones. God saved me. A woman from a church in Warri took me in. She said she could not bear to watch me starve. Later they found out I could sing and that got me into church work. After a few years of working with the church in Warri, the pastor took me to Ghana, where we went to start a new church. After a couple years there, I told him I wanted to go back to Nigeria. He was disappointed but still helped me get to Port Harcourt. I have been here ever since. I would be dead if it wasn't for the church."

"I hope to hear you sing sometime," Chris said as he looked at Rotimi. He had expressive brown eyes and almost boyish features.

"I am sure you will, my brotha," Rotimi responded. It was the first time Chris had seen joy in Rotimi's face.

Suddenly, a car cut in front of their Civic, and Rotimi slammed on the brakes. "Ah! What does he think he is doing?!" Rotimi shouted. Chris was taken aback by Rotimi's outburst. Before he could say anything, the car behind them rammed into their trunk. The seatbelt caught Chris as his body was thrown forward. Rotimi turned his head to stare down the car that hit them, a newer-model Infiniti SUV.

"What now?" Chris asked, his heart racing.

Without answering, Rotimi honked his horn several times and rolled down his window. The Infiniti had pulled out from behind them and was next to Rotimi's window. "Man, what are you doing?" Rotimi shouted at the Infiniti, gesticulating with his left hand.

Chris could see the man in the Infiniti shouting back but his windows were rolled up, and he couldn't make out the words. Chris looked behind him. He could see the trunk flapping up and down as they inched forward. He heard the muffler dragging along the pavement beneath them. The car in front, an early 90s Ford hatchback, inched along in the traffic as though it had not caused the accident and nothing was out of the ordinary.

Rotimi shook his head and stopped the car on the side of the road. Even though they tried to pull off to the side, their car still blocked a lane of traffic. Rotimi put on his hazard lights and got out to survey the damage. Chris followed. He could feel the hot, late morning sun on his back and arms. People in the cars around them were shouting and honking their horns. Expletives filled the air. As Rotimi bent down to look underneath the car, he was already on his cell phone.

"Isn't the Infiniti going to stop?" Chris asked. Rotimi shook his head and waved off Chris before talking rapidly into his phone. He guessed it was Paul on the other line. Chris turned to the sidewalk. People were watching them, more honking filling the air around them. Chris felt the stares of some of the younger men on the side of the road. Were he and

Rotimi stranded? Did they have tow trucks in Port Harcourt?

"Chris, you should walk to the government building," Rotimi said, pointing to a large tower maybe a mile away. "The meeting is in the tall one, on the second floor."

"What will you do?"

"Paul is coming to pick me up with some rope. We will fix the car and drive it to a garage. These things happen. You can call on your mobile if something comes up."

Chris swallowed nervously. "Right." Chris pulled his new phone out of his pocket, a cheap Nokia that cost him only five thousand naira, or about thirty dollars. He quickly double-checked to make sure he could find Rotimi's number in his contact list.

Chris peered down the street and started walking in the direction Rotimi had indicated. He heard a few people call out to him, but he kept his gaze fixed forward and tried to ignore everything but the big building in front of him. After a few minutes, he began to relax. Why was he so paranoid walking the street of a major city in the daylight? He scolded himself for being such a stereotypical American white guy. "It's just a normal city, Chris," he kept saying to himself.

Chapter 8

The Rivers State government buildings mostly dated from the
1970s, when the oil shocks, the rise in oil prices due to supply cutbacks
by the newly formed OPEC, brought huge amounts of wealth to Port Harcourt. The buildings all shared a similar modernist design—lots of gray
concrete, large, imposing, unfriendly. They looked as though they would
have been impressive in decades past. Now, most of them showed signs
of disrepair: discoloration on the concrete and the occasional broken window with chipping paint around the trim. As Chris Reed approached the
tallest building, people around him paid him no attention. They were all
government professionals, mostly dressed in suits or smart-looking
skirts, going about their business.

The main foyer of the building had a low ceiling, and no lights were
on. The light from outside was sufficient to illuminate the room, but the
darkness made the entrance unwelcoming. Chris guessed they were trying save on electricity in a city where the power supply was unpredictable
and the cost of generators scandalously high. The click-clack of dress
shoes on the laminated cement floor melded with the muffled voices of
bureaucrats moving about. Chris walked across the room to the small
staircase in back and wound his way up to the second floor. At the landing, he saw a crudely made sign on paper that pointed to the conference
room. Chris wandered in that direction and found the room. A young man
with a New York Yankees baseball cap sat at a table in front of the entrance to the room. He looked up when Chris arrived.

"What's your name?" the boy in the Yankees hat asked.

"Chris Reed. I'm here with Emmaus Ministries."

The boy smiled. "Ah, Emmaus Ministries. Where is Pastor Paul?" With these words, the boy looked down the hallway, expecting Paul to appear.

"He sent me as his representative."

"Oh." Chris could see the obvious disappointment on the boy's face. "Fill out a name tag, if you would, sir."

Chris leaned over the table and started writing out his name. He decided to stick to just his first name and then, in larger block letters, he wrote *Emmaus* underneath. While still leaning over the table, he heard, "So who are you?" It was a woman's voice with an evident American accent. Chris stood up and turned around, carefully placing his name tag over his right breast. He found himself face-to-face with a white woman a couple years older than him. She had mid-length black hair and black-rimmed glasses, and she stood a few inches shorter than Chris. She wore pressed gray wool slacks and a button-down shirt.

"I'm Chris Reed. I work for Emmaus Ministries."

"Ah, another zealous missionary type. Where's Paul?"

"I'm not a zealous missionary type, if you must know," Chris corrected her. "And I'm not sure where Paul is. He asked me to come in his place."

"I'm not surprised," the woman responded. "He hates these events. You missed it, by the way."

"Missed what?"

"The program handover." The woman nodded to the room behind her. Chris could see about twenty people milling around.

"I had some car troubles."

"Welcome to Nigeria." The woman suppressed a smile. "So, are you Paul's new assistant or something?"

"Something like that. Just moved here from Massachusetts."

"That's obvious. You dress like an American and look totally out of place. You sure you're not from Iowa? Good choice for a t-shirt."

Chris blushed. He wished Paul had given him some hint of what to wear. "Um, it's nice to meet you too," he said. "What's your name?"

"I'm Julia O'Keefe. I work for the New Africa Initiative." The name New Africa Initiative vaguely rang a bell in Chris's head, but he couldn't recall any details about the organization. Julia's confidence threw Chris off. He stood staring at her.

"What kind of work do you do?" Chris asked, wondering if Julia could sense his nervousness.

"You just missed a whole presentation on it."

"Yeah, I'm sorry."

"What are you doing for lunch?" Julia asked. Chris detected the first hint of sympathy in her voice. Perhaps she did have compassion for an out-of-place American.

"Nothing, actually."

"Right. Come join me. I can tell you a bit about my work, and you can have something to report to Paul. Do you have a car?"

"No. Car troubles, remember?"

"Ah, yes. Ride with me." Julia led the way down the hallway, not bothering to see if Chris was following.

"I'm in the mood for some fast food," Julia said matter-of-factly, in between two horn bursts. The brightness of the sun and glare off the other cars was a stark contrast to the Rivers State government building. Chris wished he had brought along his new sunglasses.

"That works for me," Chris replied. "I didn't know that Nigeria had fast food."

"Of course they do. This isn't some primitive society." Julia's condescending tone annoyed Chris. But he had to admit she was a good driver, unfazed by the starts and stops and cars cutting her off. Chris's blood pressure rose just riding in the car with her, especially after the accident with Rotimi. They weaved in and out of traffic for a few minutes before Julia finally pulled into a parking lot in desperate need of re-paving. Their car rocked back and forth over the uneven ground until they found a parking spot. The sign over the restaurant read **Chicken Republic**. In contrast to the deteriorated parking lot, the building looked new, with glass gleaming across the front facade.

"This is my favorite fast food place here. The chicken is pretty good." Walking up to the glass door, Chris thanked the security guard who held the door for them. Julia ignored the guard as she walked by him. "Here they expect a tip for most things," Julia added, "but I'm pretty stingy."

The interior was sun filled and white, clean even by American standards. Behind the counter were several piles of fried chicken under heat lamps in a large Plexiglas container. Chris noticed miniature plastic containers filled with side dishes stacked next to the piles of chicken. Behind the counter stood three servers, their black skin contrasting sharply with the white shirts and hats emblazoned with the Chicken Republic logo. Without even looking at the menu, Julia ordered. "A double chickwich with fries and a Coke."

Chris examined the menu above the clerk and ordered two pieces of their chicken with fries and a Fanta.

They sat down opposite each other at a clean white plastic table with chrome chairs, which fit the overall decor of an 1950s American diner with a chic modern appeal.

"So where are you from?" Chris asked in his attempt to start an actual conversation.

"I grew up in New York City."

"Wow! This must have been a bit of a change."

"It was. I got tired of New York. It's a great city. It's still home. But I wanted to make a difference in the world. Most people in New York are obsessed with money or status or being in the center of the action. I'll go back at some point, but not now." Julia stared at Chris from behind her glasses. Chris could sense she was sizing him up, almost like a prize-fighter searching for weaknesses in the opening rounds. The two of them sparred back and forth while they filled each other in on their respective backgrounds. Chris talked about growing up in Iowa and heading to Harvard for his PhD. He left out any mention of Abby though when he related what brought him to Nigeria.

"So, you got burned-out from your studies? Wanted to go find yourself in a strange land?" Julia asked.

"Something like that."

"So why hitch your wagon to the crazy Christians? You could've volunteered with any NGO here. I like Paul. I just wish he would ditch the Christian nonsense."

"Christian nonsense?" Chris asked. Julia's acerbic tone caught him off guard. In Iowa, even if someone wasn't a Christian, they generally had some respect for it. But he had run into Julia's type at Harvard: the secular crusader, a know-it-all who liked to hide behind her confidence while she substituted "doing good" for any faith in the supernatural. "I would hardly consider a religion that has two billion adherents 'crazy.'"

"I'm an atheist. Let's go pick up our food." Without waiting for a rejoinder, Julia stood up and went over to the counter, grabbing both trays and bringing them back. Meanwhile, Chris sat preparing a response. These types of conversations energized him. He missed his high school debating days.

"And before you start on your Christian apology," Julia continued, "I was raised Catholic."

"How old were you when you decided that the Catholic Church was wrong?" Chris asked, genuinely interested in what gave someone such strident certainty.

"I stopped going to church at eleven and then refused to be confirmed," Julia responded with a hint of defiance in her voice.

Chris leaned forward. He was going to enjoy this. "Let me get this straight. At the grand age of eleven you decided that two thousand years of Christian doctrine did not make sense?" Chris tried to repress his sarcasm. "What part exactly?"

"The God bit. I couldn't find any evidence for God."

"I see. And you assumed you were the first person to come to that conclusion? That no Catholic or other believer on the planet had thought through the evidence before? At age eleven, no less!" Chris started laughing. "Congratulations. You were a born philosopher of religion. And I'm assuming you have read a lot on the subject since then?"

"I read Richard Dawkins a couple years ago," Julia said. Chris could see she was getting defensive, a position, he guessed, she was unaccustomed to.

Chris pressed his advantage. "So the opinion of one evolutionary biologist writing on a subject that is not evolutionary biology must be the final word on God?" Chris changed his tone and lifted his eyes to the ceiling. "God, billions of people thought you existed, but then Saint Richard pointed out our collective delusion. Now you no longer exist. K. Thanks. Bye."

"You know, for a Midwesterner, you're awfully sassy."

"I had to come to the Northeast to learn that. I found that privileged Northeastern, liberal, secular humanists don't understand any other language."

"I can see we are going to get along," Julia replied, deadpan. "Try the chicken."

Chris took a bite and then washed it down with a sip of Fanta. "Pretty good."

"Welcome to the finer things of Port Harcourt."

"Why, thank you," Chris said. "Getting back to this whole God question."

"Yes?"

"So you don't believe there is anything supernatural? No higher power? No spiritual anything?"

"No. Why would I believe that?"

"We're only a collection of atoms, and everything is governed by their physical interaction?"

"You say that as though it's a problem."

"Well, it just means that we are no more special than this chicken, whose head was mercilessly chopped off and whose body was fried for my pleasure and sustenance." Chris took an aggressive bite of his chicken for effect. He smiled slightly as he chewed to see if he could get a reaction.

"Correct. Humans are no different from other animals. And I'm happy that your chicken provides you with such pleasure." Julia smiled.

"But that means we are the same as a rock too. Do you really believe that? Nothing is sacred or inherently better than anything else. We are all just atoms. Why treat one set of atoms, like a rock, any differently than humans?"

"Well, that's true, but my morals are not determined by the fact that nothing has inherent worth. I care for my fellow humans because I choose to value humanity. That is why I do what I do for work," Julia said.

"How very noble of you! But you see the problem though, right? I happen to agree with your compassionate approach, but, as you said, it is something you chose. It's arbitrary. Can't I choose to be cruel and selfish and make that my moral system? You happen to value other humans, but what if I didn't? What if I chose to make a ton of money, even if it meant trampling on the little guy? How can you say that's wrong?"

"It's wrong because humans deserve to be treated well."

"So they now have inherent worth?"

"Are we really having this debate at Chicken Republic in Port Harcourt, Nigeria?" Julia asked.

"Are you afraid of a little debate?"

"Chris, I have to say that you are the first person I've met in Nigeria who tries to make friends by arguing."

"Sorry." Chris looked around to see if anyone else had been listening.

"I guess I just got carried away."

"No, it's refreshing. And fun. But I thought you said you weren't a Christian like Paul."

"I appreciate Christianity and I've studied it a bit. I guess I just haven't made up my mind yet." Chris thought back to Abby and her accident. How could God have let that happen? He could feel himself getting agitated.

"Let's change the subject," Chris said. "What kind of work do you do?" Chris took a final bite of his food and tried to focus on that. He liked the chicken's spice and crunch. The fries, though, were a little soggy.

"In Nigeria I work mostly on health issues, especially malaria prevention and treatment."

"Sounds like admirable work."

"I like to think so. Although events like today's program handover can be tough. It's unclear how committed the government will be to carry on the work. The funding could dry up tomorrow."

"I guess that's the risk of any government program," Chris said.

"It is in places where the government doesn't prioritize human health and welfare."

"I felt like you were about to say, 'Like in the US.'" Chris guessed Julia was a Democrat. She certainly fit the mold.

"The thought did cross my mind," Julia admitted, "but I didn't want to bring up both religion and politics on our first meeting."

"Yeah, what else would we have to talk about next time?"

Julia shook her head and smiled. Chris smiled back, happy that his charms were working. He had to admit that it felt great to talk to another American.

"Where are you staying?" Julia asked. "I can drop you off there."

"You can take me to the Emmaus Ministries office. Know where it is?"

"I do," said Julia, finishing the last bite of her sandwich. "You are an intriguing person, Christopher Reed. You're wrong about all the God stuff, but at least you're not boring."

Chris smiled. "You're just full of compliments today, aren't you?"

"Something like that." Julia stared at Chris's eyes, and Chris looked away, suddenly self-conscious. "By the way," she added, "if you ever want to see some of the work that the New Africa Initiative does, let me know. I'd be happy to show you. I'm sure Paul would approve."

"I'd like that. I really would."

Chapter 9

New York, New York

David Sloan disliked charity events. There were too many black-tie fundraisers in New York anyway. His wife, on the other hand, lived for them, and, as part of their separation agreement, David had agreed to go. After all, they were still technically married and, as far as their New York social circle was concerned, still a couple even though they had not lived together for the past four years. David had a condominium in Greenwich, Connecticut, and Sally lived in their apartment on the Upper West Side. Their two daughters were off at boarding school most of the year, and the arrangement worked.

David Sloan could not remember what the event was that night, but he was happy to have the chance to drive his new sports car into the city. He was not into wine or golf or the adventure tourism that some of his hedge fund colleagues treated like the ultimate test of manhood, as though climbing a mountain or swimming the Dardanelles somehow proved something. But he did like fast cars. There was nothing like the feeling of being in control of that much power. His favorite at the moment was his Bentley coupe. He had recently read the early James Bond novels in which Bond drives a Bentley. It had inspired him. He had told Sally he would pick her up at seven o'clock, the time cocktails were due to begin. He hated chitchat and was happy to avoid as much of it as he could.

Going against the grain of traffic, he made good time. He had the best radar detector on the market and loved pushing the car as much as other cars and the roads would allow. The curves of the tree-lined New York–area parkways made for great driving when the traffic was light. He called Sally the moment he hit the Henry Hudson Bridge. David Sloan hated waiting for anyone, especially Sally, who seemed to take pride in making him readjust his schedule to suit hers. Even with the advance warning, she was not downstairs when he pulled up to the building, which was just off Central Park West. He redialed her number from his car.

"Dearest, I am waiting."

"I'm on my way. You're on time, for a change. You can't blame me for assuming your customary tardiness." David hung up the phone without answering. She was uniquely skilled at making him lose his temper, and he was not going to give her that satisfaction.

Five minutes later, Sally appeared under the awning of her building. At forty-two, David still found her stunning. Their money allowed her to keep up her well-toned dyed hair, flawless skin, and clothes chosen by talented personal shoppers. There was something about her that David could never resist. They'd always had great chemistry between them, both in and out of the bedroom. Too bad she was a total bitch, David thought. Note to self: marry for comfort, not for mutual entertainment. The doorman hurried in front of her and opened the car door.

"I hate when you drive this thing. You should be more considerate of ladies in high heels and cocktail dresses."

David smiled in response to Sally's opening salvo.

"Get in. You'd complain if I showed up in a stretch limo." It did give David a certain pleasure to see Sally awkwardly collapse into the front seat as she tried to maintain her balance in a tight-fitting black dress.

"When have you ever showed up in a stretch limo?" she said, glaring at him.

"Nice to see you too, darling," David said. "No kiss?"

"Go," Sally said as she gestured toward Central Park. "I want to make it in time for some of the canapés. Absorbs the champagne."

"Ah, yes, the New York socialite dinner."

"Would you prefer me to be fat?"

"I don't think it's my opinion you care about. What's his name these days? Enrico? From what I recall, you have a taste for young Latin lovers."

"I'm surprised you even care. And don't get me started. Those in glass houses shouldn't throw stones." Sally was right. David had no interest in talking about his girlfriends. He pressed the accelerator but never went above second gear all the way to the New York Public Library. He enjoyed the acceleration and handling at higher RPMs.

The event that night was a fundraiser for the charity du jour among the New York social elite. David had long since lost track of them. He knew as well as anyone that the event was more about socializing than charity. Besides, David didn't believe in charity, which did nothing but assuage the consciences of the wealthy, and his conscience was not bothered by poverty. David cared for himself and himself alone. Everyone did, according to David. Some people were just more honest about it than others. He embraced selfishness. There wasn't any inherent meaning in the world. It would be stupid not take what you could get, and the world had offered him plenty.

The valet in front of the library smiled as he hopped into the Bentley after David handed him the keys and two twenty-dollar bills. Walking up the steps of the grand entrance, he and Sally made quite the pair. David, also forty-two, was dressed in black-tie. He had brown hair, sprinkled with gray, which he kept clean cut and short. He was six foot three with an athletic build and kept in good shape despite the hours he put in at the office. The most noticeable aspect of David Sloan was his confidence.

Ever since he was a boy, his mother had told him how great he was, and he believed it. He had experienced enough success in life that doubt seldom crept into his mind. It was something Sally always liked about David, regardless of how their relationship had deteriorated. Wherever they went, people looked. They made a great pair for a night out.

"Oh, Sally, how are you? You look wonderful." They heard a voice come at them from the top of the steps.

"Thank you, Ruth." Sally reached out her right hand and squeezed Ruth's. "Great to see you, as always." David tried not to smirk. He knew Sally couldn't stand Ruth and thought her fashion choices were as bland as her personality.

The typical gauntlet of polite greetings met them in the foyer. A uniformed waiter came over and offered them champagne, which they gladly accepted. David did a quick scan of the room as he took his first sip. Unlike his wife, David had no interest in who was there from the social register. He was on the lookout for his competitors. The world of commodities hedge funds in New York was not large, at least at the top. Six years ago, David had started his own shop—Sulla Partners—which specialized in oil and gas futures but also made a variety of related investments. He had a good track record, but his fund did not have the capital of the heavy hitters. They had just topped two billion dollars. Impressive by most standards, but David was intensely competitive. He did not like playing second fiddle to anyone.

A few of the usual managers were in attendance. Then he spotted Josh Cohn walking toward him.

"David, Sally, how are you both doing?" Josh's eyes already glowed from champagne and perhaps a cocktail or two beforehand.

"I've never been better, Josh," Sally responded. "Thank you for asking." Sally was always the first to speak. She leaned in and kissed Josh on the cheek.

71

"You're looking well, Josh," David managed to say.

"Thank you, David. I need to be."

"Didn't I tell you, honey? Josh is the recipient of the leading philan-thropist award at the dinner tonight. Is your speech ready?" Sally was a master of flattery and, more to the point, she knew how much it rankled David to see one of his rivals honored in any way. It was even more gall-ing because David and Josh had known each other at Yale and had, for a time, worked at the same firm. Josh's own fund had more than six billion under management and was currently the darling of the commodities hedge fund world.

"Congratulations, Josh," David heard himself say. "I am sure the cause loves to have your money."

"Jealousy suits you so well, David. Don't ever grow up." Josh turned back to Sally. "I hope you have a good seat at the dinner." He nodded graciously before walking away.

"He just wanted to gloat," David muttered.

"And with a reaction like the one you gave him, who could blame him?" Sally looked him in the eyes. "David, you really are juvenile some-times."

Their table was not a good one. They had only given the minimum amount, and Sally was not involved in the charity, which meant they were squeezed near the wall. Yet from his seat, David had a perfect view of the back of Josh Cohn's head. He could see him laughing and relishing being the center of attention at the head table.

Interrupting his thoughts, Sally leaned over and said, "You know, I might have to take another date next time. You're worse than usual."

David glanced around at the table. "Sorry, darling." They were the youngest people at the table, and David had not met any of the others before. David discovered one was an architect and another was in real estate, two things David had no interest in. He didn't catch the professions of the people across the table when they introduced themselves, but feigned as though he had heard them. What was the point of asking them to repeat it when he did not intend to engage them in conversation?

The food was disappointing, which was typical of these events. A mediocre shrimp cocktail atop assorted greens, followed by nondescript beef with a brown sauce, potato, and julienne vegetables. Even the flower arrangements on the tables weren't good. Apparently, this charity did not have any decent society gays involved.

The most galling part of the evening was Josh Cohn's speech. Long, boring, sprinkled with bad jokes. David merely shook his head. "And he thinks people are loving it," he whispered to Sally.

"It's the booze," she replied, a little too loudly. "Josh has always been a lightweight. I hate when people don't write out their remarks. Where did he go to prep school? Did he learn nothing?"

"Enough to write a big check." David leaned back in his chair and looked at his half-eaten chocolate torte. The more he heard Josh Cohn drone on, the angrier he became. He hated being jealous, almost as much as he hated playing second fiddle to anyone. "I will embarrass you someday at your own game, Joshua Cohn," David whispered to himself. "Whatever it takes." David's ego fueled his anger, and he loved it.

Chapter 10

Every Monday morning at 7:00 am, Sulla Partners had its weekly strategy meeting. The whole firm, all sixteen of them, met at their office in Greenwich, Connecticut, in a large conference room that David Sloan had never liked. One side of the room faced the tree-lined parking lot and the other, which faced the hallway, had frosted glass with the name of the firm etched in a contemporary font. He would have preferred a nice wood-paneled conference room with a skylight, but he wasn't willing to pay to have the whole office space redone to suit his whims. It also mildly annoyed him that his wife had chosen the paintings that hung on the walls. They were done by some artist he had never heard of and cost far more than David thought they were worth. Sitting there at 6:50 am, looking at the yellow legal pad of notes in front of him, he decided he would have the paintings removed in the new year. No more pseudo-modernist crap done by wannabe Communists from Brooklyn. He wrote it down at the top of his pad.

David looked up. A few minutes before seven, and two people were still missing. He detested waiting for other people. He adjusted himself in his seat. A pack of Nicorette gum rested on the table in front of him, and he instinctively grabbed another piece and popped it in his mouth. David didn't love the taste but he was hopelessly addicted to nicotine, and the gum was a lot better than the dip he did when he was just out of Yale.

He looked at his watch again. Time to start. "Catherine," he said, turning to his left, "begin." Catherine Dunlop was the firm's head of research. Each Monday morning meeting, she began by giving a rundown of all the news over the past week that related to the global energy sector, the impact it might have on supply and demand, and any changes in their price expectations for the quarter. David insisted on the whole firm's involvement in their price analysis. He wanted to make sure nothing was missed.

"Political tensions with Russia continue to abate," Catherine started to read from the sheet in front of her. "Crude production was slightly hurt in the past year, but most analysts think that their export volume should remain at current levels..."

Catherine's report continued in the same vein, with David Sloan asking the occasional follow-up question. The rest of the room, out of fear of earning a tongue-lashing from Sloan, usually kept silent.

"So, any changes in our price predictions for the upcoming six months?" David had come to the heart of the matter. The price predictions determined the firm's trades for the week.

"Given the weak global economy, prices should stay the same or trend downward." Catherine was about to say something else, but held back.

"What is it?" David asked. "What were you about to say?"

"I had Matt look into an assessment of global supply last week. It surprised me."

David turned to Matt Jaroslavic, who sat three chairs down from Catherine. He had only been at the firm for eight months and was their most junior researcher. His recruiting trip to Cambridge in February hadn't yielded any good candidates, so his workload forced him to practically live at the office.

"Well, Matt?" David said, seemingly annoyed that Matt had not already come out with it.

"Um…it's just that supply is tighter than I would expect, given the price today."

"What do you mean?"

"There really isn't any excess capacity. Oil-dependent countries are pumping as much as they can to make up for the drop in prices. Russia, Iraq, pretty much everyone is at full production, even though they probably shouldn't be. I mean, the Saudis used to have excess capacity, but those days are gone. Because of low prices, new fracking in the US has essentially stopped. There are some big offshore fields that should come online in Africa and Brazil, but those are still years off. And the North Sea continues to disappoint."

"So?"

Matt swallowed hard. "Even though demand is weak, any sudden change could send the spot market through the roof." The spot oil market was the market for immediate delivery of oil. It accounted for only a small proportion of global oil sales, but the price of the spot market helped determine the price of futures contracts.

"Interesting," David said. So the market was more fragile than most people thought, and prices could jump at any time if the supply was suddenly restricted. He liked it when his analysts looked for what his competitors might not see. David then turned his attention to James Li, the head trader at Sulla Partners. "What can you tell me about the markets,

James?"

"Crude prices across the major markets continue to trend downward this week, in line with the weak demand Catherine outlined," James said. "West Texas Intermediate dropped a surprising two dollars per barrel last week. Brent saw a drop of a dollar ninety. Over-the-counter trades followed a similar trend. There was moderate volume across the board. I talked with one of my friends at Credit Suisse to find out why prices had dropped more than expected. He said that Fraser Asset Management was reformulating their pension positions, but that would only account for a small part of the rapid drop."

"Anything else?" demanded David. "Unexplained drops in prices make me nervous."

"There was some unusual movement toward the end of the day on Friday. When the mercantile exchange opens today, I bet we will see a significant drop in West Texas Intermediate." West Texas Intermediate crude was sold on the New York Mercantile Exchange and was the most heavily traded oil type and most liquid oil market in the world. Its price was often used as a benchmark for other crude oil types.

"Say more."

"I don't know who it is, but someone seems to be building a large short position. They are betting the price will continue to drop. At the end of the day Friday, I got a call and was asked if I could move four hundred million dollars of futures this week. He was looking to sell. Wouldn't say who the client was. But it has to be one of the big funds. Looks like a purely speculative play."

David was staring at the conference table in front of him and pushing down the button on his pen, which made a distinct click each time.

The rest of the room was silent.

Unexpected downward pressure on prices. Someone trying to sell large blocks of futures. One of his competitors must be up to something. But who?

"Okay," he spoke up. "Let's say that is a piece of a larger short sell by one of the big players. Why and who? James, any idea of how big the trade is?"

"Hard to tell right now. We'll know more when we see how much the market shifts this morning. If they were trying to move four hundred million through us, I'm guessing it's a multibillion-dollar play."

"It could be a short-term gamble on the Ford announcement," Matt offered. Ford was expected to come out with plans for a new electric car that week.

"It's not the Ford announcement," David said, a little exasperated. He hated being on the wrong side of a move he was left guessing about. "Alright, I want to focus on this today. James, find out the person building the short position. Call around. I want a name, and I want it this morning. Catherine, get your people to ferret out what we are not seeing. Perhaps one of the majors is opening up a new field that might push the prices down in the near term. Get your people to rescan press releases from last week. And make some calls. If we should be moving our positions, we need to know now. I do not want to be caught with our pants down on this one."

David stood, an obvious indication that the meeting was over. He wanted to think this through in his office. As he walked down the hall, his secretary walked a step behind him. "Martha, you want to get me another cup of coffee? I could use it. And no disturbances."

"Of course," Martha replied. Martha was in her early fifties and was a highly qualified executive assistant. David thought she might have been his best hire when the firm opened.

David's office was in the corner suite and looked out over the small garden in front of the office building. Not too inspiring, but it was the best space available, and he enjoyed thinking while gazing out his window. Without him noticing, Martha walked in with a cup of black coffee and set it on his desk. A knock on the door broke up David's train of thought.

"Yes?" David asked. "Anything new?

James Li walked across the carpet.

"Turns out finding the truth was easier than I thought. I called up my former roommate, who works with Josh Cohn." At the mention of Cohn's name, David's face darkened. "He laughed when I asked about their positions. Said their big fund was taking a short position on crude futures across the board. A long-term play. Obviously, the firm is not shy about the information. They are convinced the global slowdown will worsen this summer. He said they have been selling for the past four weeks off the winter high. That means their positions already have a nice cushion, which is why they are being so open."

"And now that others know about their position, they are betting that more will follow the momentum and drag prices down," David said.

"Do you want us to start selling? Would be a great way to make some easy money once more people know what's going on." James was clearly eager to use this newfound information.

"Let me think about it."

James Li knew it meant the end of the conversation and quietly departed, leaving David Sloan with his thoughts. David swiveled his chair around to look outside again. "If I sell and follow Cohn, I could make money. James is right," he said aloud. "Might not be much, but it would be easy. But then I would be putting money in Cohn's pocket. And what if it's not a long-term play? What if he has something else up his sleeve? That bastard."

Just then his secretary buzzed on the intercom.

"Yes?" David's voice was curt.

"There is a phone call for you. A long-distance call."

"I'm not expecting a call this morning, am I?"

"No, Mr. Sloan."

"Where is the call from?"

"Nigeria. He is on line one."

David picked up the phone. "Hello."

"Hello, Mr. Sloan?" David could discern an American accent, but he had a hard time placing it. In college he had made a drinking game of picking out regional accents. This one was a mystery.

"Yes. Who is this?" David asked.

"This is Eli Schrimpf. We met in Nigeria a couple years ago. You said to call if I had anything that might be of interest to you." A smile crept across David's face. For a while he made contacts when he traveled to oil-producing regions. With a nominal payment, he kept people on the payroll if he thought they might be able to give him some useful tips. Overall, it was a small investment. He got a few bits and pieces of information now and again that made it worthwhile. He vaguely remembered Schrimpf. In his late forties or early fifties with a typical American paunch, Schrimpf did environmental cleanups in Nigeria for Octagon Petroleum, one of the supermajor oil companies. When they met, David detected the personality of a man whose ethics were, well, flexible.

"Go on, Mr. Schrimpf. It's good to hear from you."

"It's not a social call, Mr. Sloan."

"Of course not. As you would expect, I reward people who reward me. Why the call?"

"Looks like the violence in the Niger Delta will return."

David was intrigued. "Really? How do you know?"

"I was a little cautious when I first heard the rumors, but I have looked into it and there seems to be something to this one. A former insurgent leader got out of prison not long ago. The word is that he has been recruiting other insurgents, aggressively."

"What are the chances that this will have an effect on supply?"

"Hard to say. This insurgent means business. He's a sworn enemy of the oil industry, and he decided to serve a prison sentence rather than take the amnesty deal ten years back. Prison in Nigeria ain't pleasant. It could be a minor thing, but the people I spoke to don't think so. He's fixin' to do something big. The police and military are already searching him out for questioning. They're worried, and these guys don't get worried over spilled milk."

"Thank you, Mr. Schrimpf. It might be time for a trip to Nigeria."

"Let me know if you are coming, Mr. Sloan. I could have you meet with some of my contacts."

"Good. We'll be in touch." The phone went dead. David Sloan stood up and grabbed another piece of Nicorette gum. A smile crept across his face. It was time for a gamble. Major violence in Nigeria would lead to a sudden drop in supply, which would push prices up, wrecking Josh Cohn's numbers for the year. Leaning over his desk, David picked up the phone again and dialed a three-number extension.

"James, it's David. I want you to buy that four hundred million of futures this morning."

"Buy? Are you sure? Cohn might know something. That puts us on the wrong side of his position. It's not smart to go against him."

"I don't care what Cohn knows. What's our leverage now?"

"A pretty safe ten to one."

"See how much more we can get. And free up as much capital as you can this week without taking any losses."

"Can you tell me what this is about, David?"

"Just do it, James." David leaned over and ended the call. Then he dialed another extension. "Martha, get me a plane to Nigeria. I want to be there before the week is out."

"Yes, Mr. Sloan. Anything else?"

"If anyone asks where I am going, don't tell them."

Chapter 11

Fineface Pepple was an expert at oil bunkering, and the location he chose was ideal. The pipeline went close to a bend in the creek, which allowed the oil storage barge to moor close to the shore. Dense green trees spread out on both sides of the clearing, giving Fineface and his crew ample protection from any potential intruders. Pepple had fifteen of his men with him. They called themselves the Lord Rules Brigade. In the last twelve months, they had punctured eleven pipelines in the area, but this particular one was the largest by far. He estimated they could get between three and five thousand barrels of crude out of it, which would fund their own preparations as a part of Ifeanyi's planned assault. As Pepple watched his men at work, he thought back to his conversation with Ifeanyi the week before. This might be the time when things would change for good, he had told his soldiers. Pepple could see the new light in their eyes, the first glimmer of hope for something new in years.

Pepple had three soldiers who specialized as "engineers," all of whom used to work for oil companies. Their job was to cut a hole in the pipe and attach a metal collar with an expandable rubber gasket, which was capable of taking the pressurized oil without problems. A hose from the collar would convey the oil to the storage tanker, which sat a little over a hundred feet away and was also manned by people who knew their jobs well. Pepple stood back, carefully surveying the scene as they went to work.

"Spread out to discourage any villagers from wandering this way," Fineface ordered his other men. Without replying, the men took up positions around the pipeline. They wore a range of dark t-shirts, some of which had the labels of American designers, indicating they were donated castoffs that ended up in Nigeria. Most of them carried AK-47s, which were relatively easy to acquire, reliable, and, since the Nigerian soldiers used them as well, easy to replace and find ammunition for. His "soldiers" were a ragtag group from the creeks and villages in the area. While some were former oil workers with college degrees, most of them were unemployed youth, victims of an economy that offered them few options. Pepple had found the one standing closest to him on the streets, a half-starved teenager. His growth had been stunted, as it had been for many people in the area. The money he earned in the Lord Rules Brigade helped support his sister, who had moved to Nembe, not far away. If the government actually used its billions of dollars' worth of oil revenue every year to help young Nigerians, Fineface would be out of business. Pepple shook his head at the irony of it.

"Almost there!" Fineface heard one of his engineers yell.

BANG! Metal broke free from the pipe and hit the top of the circular pipe cutter, making a loud noise. Fineface Pepple didn't even flinch. He was unconcerned about the authorities. They would get their cut, as would the others involved in every step of the operation. Fineface looked around at his men. There was an energy and focus that had been missing in the recent past. Everyone knew that this effort was a part of something greater, part of the cause.

Ifeanyi had done that. His writings, his courage.

Letting his eyes rest on one man after another, Fineface wondered what would become of them in the weeks ahead. Who will live? Who will die?

The crude oil began to trickle around Fineface's feet, and he knelt down to rub some between his fingers. He felt it was good luck, like he was touching a part of the Niger Delta's very heart, part of its soul brought up from the depths of the earth. He also loved the color of the sweet Nigerian crude, some of the highest-quality crude oil in the world. He smiled as he felt it and then brought his fingers up to his nose. It had a distinctive odor, but none of the rotten-egg smell from the hydrogen sulfide that is found in many other crude types.

"Hurry it up!" Fineface yelled at his people as he watched more valuable crude spill onto the ground. His engineers on the pipe dripped with oil, which made their task more difficult. They finally managed to get the collar attached. Pepple looked at his phone. It would take about five hours to fill up the barge. He turned to the woods around him and slapped a mosquito that landed on his arm. He wished he could grab a cigarette, but with so much crude around, the one cardinal rule of these operations was no flames. There were plenty of stories of idiots who died doing something stupid like lighting a cigarette at the wrong time. He looked down at the now taut hose. Black gold. Far better than selling useless trinkets on the streets of Port Harcourt like he had as a teenager.

"Get your commander on the phone!" Eli Schrimpf shouted at the soldier nearby. Eli Schrimpf was the head of environmental cleanup for Octagon Petroleum in Nigeria. That morning he had been on a routine tour of one of the major flow stations for Octagon.

A flow station was a central collecting point for oil from nearby wells.

From the flow station, the oil was separated from its associated water and natural gas before being pumped through pipelines to the coast. While doing a normal check, Eli had noticed a rapid drop in the pressure of the main pipeline, which indicated a major leak. Eli guessed there were thieves trying to steal the oil.

It was rare for Eli to be in the creeks when oil bunkering was going on. He now had a chance, and the responsibility, to stop the thieves. One thought flashed through his head: he might have to confront armed insurgents. Eli had no experience with firearms and even less desire to be shot at.

Eli's sudden outburst surprised the soldier. At the height of the violence over a decade ago, the Nigerian government had established an elite task force to deal with the insurgents. This group was known as the Joint Task Force, or JTF. The JTF was still in operation, and its men were often hired by the international oil companies to protect their property. Theoretically, they were more skilled and less susceptible to corruption than the regular army, two things that Eli doubted. The soldier looked at Eli, unsure of what to do.

"What are you waiting for? Who pays you?" Eli demanded. "We do. Now get your commander on the phone."

"I can try, sir," the solider answered uneasily.

"Don't try. Make it happen." Eli impressed himself with how firm and confident he was. This would make a good story to tell the other oil guys back at the compound.

Schrimpf turned his back to the soldier and took out his cell phone. He began making calls to his cleanup team. Every minute of delay was one more minute of lost oil. Octagon, like most oil companies, relied on the natural pressure of the oil well to send the oil to the coast. Since they had no storage tanks at the flow station, he had no way to turn off the flow of oil down the pipeline. He had to find the exact location of the leak so he could direct his team to it. Fortunately, they were well trained and had had far more practice at cleanup and pipeline repair due to oil bunkering than the Octagon executives would like.

After making his calls, Eli stood next to the soldier and watched over him while he fiddled with his radio. The soldier seemed to be stalling. With each moment that passed, Eli could feel his anger rising inside him. Before the soldier could say more than a few words into his radio, Eli snatched it away from him. Although he had no experience in military matters, Eli was not intimidated by a JTF uniform.

"Hello?" Eli said into the walkie-talkie. He thought he could hear breathing on the other end. "Hello!" he demanded again.

"Yes. Who is this?" The voice on the other end was calm and self-assured.

"This is Eli Schrimpf from Octagon Petroleum. Who's this?"

"I've never heard of you."

"I'm a chief engineer and in charge of repairs and cleanups. We have a problem with the pipeline from Flow Station Eight. I'd like it checked out immediately."

There was a pause on the other end of the walkie-talkie before the voice said, "I wish I could help you, Mr. Schrimpf. I am afraid my units are all tied up at the moment."

"All tied up? With what?"

"With other operations," the voice replied with a touch of anger. He was clearly annoyed that he had to take orders from a civilian, and an American at that.

"Aren't there some men or a boat close by that could, at least, survey the pipeline?"

"That would be difficult. I'll see what I can do. The last thing we want is oil leaking out of your pipelines." Eli shook his head in disgust. He didn't believe for a moment the commander was unhappy. Eli wondered what his cut was.

"What's your name, commander?"

"Commander Musa."

"Good. I look forward to reporting that to my superiors."

"Please do. That way, when we send Octagon Petroleum the bill for moving men down the pipeline, they'll know we didn't make it up." Eli could almost see his smirk on the other end of the radio.

"Right. Be as quick as you can," Eli snapped.

"Oh, we will, Mr. Schrimpf. Oil lost from your pipelines is less money for the Nigerian citizens. We don't want that." The commander was referring to the fact that Octagon was in a joint venture with the Nigerian National Petroleum Company (NNPC). Fifty-five percent of all revenues from the oil went directly to the NNPC and into the government's coffers.

"Thank you for your help, Commander," Eli replied, his voice laced with sarcasm. He handed the radio back to the soldier, who had a hard time repressing a faint smile.

Thirty minutes later, Eli Schrimpf set out in a JTF Defender patrol boat accompanied by eight heavily armed soldiers. Eli was shocked at the speed of the response. He had expected more delays and equivocating. Something must have happened between his radio call with Commander Musa and the arrival of the patrol boat. Eli could sense the difference in the soldiers around him. "Tense" was the only way he could describe it. Normally, the security forces, especially the Nigerian navy, had a cushy relationship with those engaged in oil bunkering. The thieves would steal the oil and then pay off whomever they needed to.

This time, something was clearly different. The soldiers meant business.

Riding along the silent river, Eli noticed how the entire shore looked the same. Mangrove trees grew everywhere with their roots eerily exposed like the legs of an insect. Dense vegetation choked the shore beyond the mangroves. The boat's wake pushed the mass of discarded plastic bottles and other trash to the water's edge. Eli could also make out a sheen on the water from former oil spills. Roughly one hundred times the amount of oil spilled in the Exxon Valdez accident had spilled into the Niger Delta over the past fifty years. Remarkable. Cruising along the waters of the delta, that figure was easy to believe.

After gazing out at the water, Eli surveyed the soldiers around him. Three were up in the bow near a small, mounted machine gun. In the small cabin with him were Commander Musa, who remained silent for most of the trip, and the driver. Three more soldiers were in the stern, each sitting on the gray polyethylene foam that encircled the boat and protected it from objects close to shore. The soldiers seemed experienced enough. None looked like teenagers, and they held their guns as though they were accustomed to using them, which Eli took to be a good, if ominous, sign. Sitting on a hard aluminum seat, Eli shifted back and forth to prevent circulation from being cut off from his legs. The extra weight he carried in his gut made him even more uncomfortable. As eager as he was to get the operation started, he couldn't wait until it was all over. Even though the side windows were open, the cabin air still felt stifling.

Soon the boat slowed down. The soldiers up front began talking, but Eli could not hear them in the cabin or see what they were talking about. He looked off to the side and noticed an area where fresh crude oil was spreading out into the water.

He could feel his stomach seizing up.

A few hundred yards away, up on shore, Fineface Pepple knew the game was up. The sound of the patrol boat's engine was unmistakable. He had been afraid it might happen. Earlier in the day, Pepple had called his contact in the Nigerian navy. They had exchanged their usual banter, and Pepple mentioned that they might "need help" that day. The contact said he would get back to him. They had been working together for years and never had any issues. But Pepple had not received a return call. Alarmed, he had considered cancelling the mission before remembering Ifeanyi. They needed this.

At the sound of the engine, Pepple ordered his men to take cover. As they had trained countless times before, the men scattered in the dense forest and got their guns ready. The JTF meant business. Pepple guessed there would be ten or more soldiers, and they would have a large-caliber gun on board the boat, which could keep them pinned down. He hoped their motorboat could outrun the Nigerian navy, but he doubted it. The fresh crude oil on the water and the ground made the situation combustible, literally. Now Pepple had to figure out how he was going to get them out of this alive.

"Over there," the commander spoke up, his voice carrying through-out the boat. The patrol boat edged its way over in the direction of the oil slick. As they cleared the nearest bend in the river, Eli saw an eighty-foot-long oil barge moored around the corner, maybe two hundred yards away. He heard several of the soldiers cock their guns. Eli noticed the driver in front of him was sweating down his neck.

Toward shore, there was scurrying in the woods near the barge.

The insurgents had seen them. Eli's breathing slowed. Then the large diesel engines in the oil barge came to life. The soldiers, crouching beneath the gunwales for protection, readied their guns. The quietness surprised Eli. The barge began to move away from the shore.

"What now?" Eli asked, almost afraid to speak too loudly.

Just then, a bullet hit the water not more than five feet from their boat. Shocked, Eli threw his heavy body onto the aluminum deck. The JTF soldiers fired back in the direction of the woods, brass shells littering the stern of the boat. Eli could hear scattered gunshots coming from the woods a few hundred yards away. Then the shooting stopped. Eli got to his feet in the cramped cabin, keeping his head low. He scanned the shore but couldn't see anyone in the woods.

"What's going on, Commander?"

"The insurgents are using the barge as cover," Commander Musa said with a hint of frustration.

"Can we move in on them?" Eli asked.

"The barge is full of oil. Firing at it might run the risk of an explosion. It's probably only half-full, so the inside of the tank has lots of evaporated gas. That insurgent, whoever he is, knows what he is doing. He's also got big balls, gambling that we won't try to blow up the barge." At the mention of the exploding barge, Eli's eyes widened. "Don't worry," Musa added. "I'm not going to risk my men, or you."

A few more gunshots rang out from shore, gradually becoming steadier and more consistent. The patrol boat started to reverse direction. One bullet hit the side of the boat with an audible thud in the polyethylene foam. Then another. The patrol boat gained speed as it moved backward to safety.

"There has to be something we can do," Eli said.

"Stay low," Commander Musa cautioned. "We found the source of your leak."

"Are they getting away?" Eli asked, his body hunkered awkwardly beneath the JTF commander.

Looking at the thigh of Commander Musa, Eli realized he was embarrassing himself and stood. The patrol boat was safely out of the line of fire from the shore. Eli's shirt clung to his chest from water and sweat.

"They won't get far," the commander replied. "The barge doesn't move quickly. I radioed the navy, and they'll intercept it. You'll get to keep some of your precious oil."

"So the militants will escape?" Eli asked. His heartbeat refused to calm down, even though they were in relative safety. In all his years in the oil industry, he had never been fired on before.

"That's up to you," Musa replied, bringing his binoculars up to his eyes to scan the water in the distance. "Would you like to follow the militants or inspect your precious leaking pipe?"

"My job is the pipeline," Eli said. "Your job is the militants."

"You have to choose. They're getting away."

Part of Eli wanted to chase down the militants and prove to the commander he was not a coward, especially after throwing his body to the deck. But he knew there was only one response he would give. "The pipeline," Eli said. "Take us to the pipeline."

"Very well," the commander replied. "You are letting the militants get away." Eli remained silent, inwardly despising the commander. He guessed the feeling was mutual.

Their boat slowly crept back around the promontory, and they could see the barge floating downriver. There was no sign of the militants' boat. Eli tried to hide his relief. Where the barge had been moored, the underbrush had been cut away. Oil was pouring directly into the water from a hose. Eli shook his head. The target had indeed been well chosen. It was rare for such a large pipeline to be so close to the water.

As the bow slid into the small landing area, two soldiers jumped out into the oil slick and began scanning the area. Another soldier hopped down afterward with the bowline in his hand. With some effort, he dragged the boat right up to the shore and tied off the line onto a nearby tree.

Eli was already on his phone, calling his cleanup crew to coordinate their next move. He estimated they could be at the site in forty minutes or less. After putting his phone away, Eli jumped over the side of the boat into the shallow water, his feet splashing into crude oil and sinking into the mud below. He hurried up to the pipe. With each step, a distinctive sucking sound trailed him as the mud clung to his soles. The job was cleanly done, and no oil was leaking from the hole on top of the pipe where the hose was attached.

"It will be a long night," Eli said aloud. He still couldn't figure out why the JTF risked a confrontation with the insurgents. It was so unlike them. And for the oil thieves to strike such a major pipeline was also rare. It meant Eli had been right. Things were heating up in the Niger Delta, and they were going to get a lot worse. At least he'd have something to report to David Sloan when he got to Nigeria.

Chapter 12

Lagos, Nigeria

David Sloan stepped off the private jet and walked sprightly down the steps onto the tarmac. The bright sun reflected off the faded pavement, and he reached into the breast pocket of his suit jacket for his sunglasses. Looking around, he could see an official walking toward the plane. Rather than wait, he walked over to meet him. His assistants would have to catch up.

The uniformed Nigerian greeted David, "You are welcome, sir!"

"Thank you," David replied without any emotion. He kept walking toward the low-lying building attached to Murtala Muhammad Airport that served as the small terminal for private jets.

The uniformed man had to turn quickly to keep up with David. "Sir, do you have a visa?"

Without slowing his pace, David replied, "My executive assistant was on the phone to your embassy in Washington. They said I could take care of my visa when I arrived."

"Well, yes, sir, for businessmen like you that is no problem, but there will still be the fees and the necessary paperwork."

David Sloan stopped and squared up to the man, looking him in the eyes from behind his dark Ray-Bans. Sloan wore a pink dress shirt under his navy suit, its top two buttons undone. "My executive assistant arranged for someone to take care of those details. She should be meeting us at the terminal." He looked toward the terminal and pointed. "I'm going there." He started walking again.

"Sir, this is something we must take care of." David ignored the man. When they reached the terminal, a nicely dressed woman walked toward them.

"You must be Mr. David Sloan." She was beautiful with a well-tailored navy suit, and she spoke unaccented American English.

"Why, yes, I am. And you are?"

"Carol Opara," she offered her hand. "Welcome to Nigeria, Mr. Sloan. Your assistant, Martha Childs, was very thorough on the phone."

When the uniformed immigration officer saw Carol, his demeanor changed. He nodded to her. "Excuse me for a moment," Carol said before she walked over to speak with the immigration official. She returned a moment later. "Mr. Sloan, if you will come with me, we can take care of the immigration and customs details now."

David Sloan followed her. By this point, two other people from Sulla Partners had caught up with him. Catherine Dunlop, the head of research for oil and gas, had joined him on his right, and behind her was Matt Jaroslavic, the young associate. They soon found themselves in a small office adjacent to the main room that processed overseas immigration. An open window provided the only light, and there were green filing cabinets and stacks of paper everywhere. When they entered the cramped room, Carol turned to them. "If you can hand me your passports, we can take care of the immigration visas now. I assume you have nothing to declare for customs?"

"Nothing to declare," David answered for the three Americans. They stood there silently while the officer, the head of immigration services, looked over their materials. David could feel himself sweating in the stuffy room.

"Here for business?" he inquired.

"Yes," David replied. "We're making investments in the oil and gas industry." The immigration official offered no response. After a minute more of turning pages, which David assumed was just for show, the officer took a stamp off his desk and brought it down sharply onto a blank page of each passport before dating their three visas in pen. He handed the passports to Carol.

"Enjoy your stay in Nigeria," the official said without emotion. With that they left the office, Carol leading the way.

"How much did that cost me?" David asked.

"Do you really want to know?" Carol answered. "The immigration line is across the other terminal, if you would prefer." David took one look down the connecting hallway at the long, snaking line and turned back to Carol.

"A good investment."

"Don't worry. You haven't been cheated. There are cars outside to take us to your hotel." Exiting the airport, they found two black SUVs waiting for them. A minute later they were on their way. Wealth had its privileges.

"Why exactly are we in Lagos?" Catherine Dunlop finally asked. They were lounging in David Sloan's suite at the Wheatbaker Hotel in Ikoyi, Lagos. David was standing by the small bar and fixing himself a drink while Catherine was laying out papers on the desk. It was 11:30 am.

"Would you like something?" David asked, holding up his glass.

"Should I, or do I have a long day ahead?"

"Your work here will be straightforward. Nothing too intense."

"A whisky for me would do fine then. I don't like plane travel any more than you do. Even if it is on a nice rent-a-jet."

"Neat okay?" David said, pouring one of the fifty milliliter bottles of Johnnie Walker into an old-fashioned glass.

"Yes. Although I'm sure the ice in a hotel like this is fine."

Catherine walked over and David handed her a glass, raising his own. "Cheers. To taking a gamble."

Catherine's and David's glasses clinked. "Would be nice to know what this gamble is," she said, savoring the slight burn in her throat from the whisky.

"I got a call from one of my people here in Nigeria earlier this week. He said he has reliable information that the Niger Delta is about to explode again with violence." David fixed his gaze on Catherine to gauge her response.

"And we are here to investigate and determine the extent to which we want to take advantage of that information?"

"Precisely."

"So the meetings we have this afternoon with the major oil companies are window dressing."

"Not exactly," David said. "Assuming the information is correct, we have to see what the oil companies might know. If the impending violence is common knowledge, we can assume it will affect the price sooner rather than later. We could also assume that the authorities are aware of the risk, which might change our gamble."

David sat down in one of the leather chairs and finished the remainder of his whisky before continuing.

"We also need to assess what exactly we should buy to take full advantage of any information we receive."

"Which is where I come in," Catherine replied, looking down at him.

David smiled. "This could be big," he said.

"You do realize we are betting on an insurgency. People will die in this."

"Catherine, they will die whether we make money off of it or not. And yes, the bigger and bloodier the better." David leaned back in the chair and closed his eyes. "Let's make sure we're ready to work our press contacts when the time comes."

"You could always tell the authorities," Catherine offered, "and be the one to stop all of this."

David sat up. "You mean tell the corrupt plutocrats who run this country? Do we really need to help them?"

"It's not them we would be helping. It's the average Nigerian. People like them always suffer during violence."

David shrugged. "Perhaps. Honestly, that's not my problem. I'm looking out for myself, and if that means promoting and profiting off an insurgency, so be it. You know those things don't bother my conscience. It shows weakness."

"You are one of a kind, David." Catherine shook her head as she took another sip of her drink. "You're one of the few unapologetic nihilists I know. But as far as the insurgency is concerned, I'll reserve my judgment until I see it. One of us has to watch after the firm's capital."

"That's why I like you, Catherine. You're the perfect counterbalance to me."

"By the way, don't get too tipsy before our meetings today. We need to be polite with Octagon Petroleum."

David dismissed the remark with a wave of his hand. "Don't you know how much business gets done over a three-martini lunch?"

Chapter 13

Olufemi Adebayo was annoyed that his schedule had to be hastily rearranged. All the same, he could not turn away Sulla Partners. It was one of the larger oil and gas hedge funds and could have a direct impact of Octagon Petroleum's bottom line in Nigeria. These hedge fund managers had notoriously large egos and were known to harbor grudges against people or firms when they felt slighted. Olufemi assumed David Sloan was no different. It was a good thing that Olufemi had his own agenda as well.

As president of Octagon Petroleum in Nigeria, Olufemi Adebayo had the best office in their Lagos headquarters, complete with a view of the lagoon next to Lagos Island that gave the city its name. As always, Olufemi was impeccably dressed, this time in a Savile Row navy suit, a light blue shirt with a spread collar, and a Windsor-knotted pink silk tie, complete with a matching Hermes pocket square. Looking across his oversized desk at David, he could not help but think there was something more going on, though he could not figure out what. Why make the trip to Nigeria at such an early stage of investment research? It was also clear that he had been drinking. Whisky, from the faint odor. Who had he met with over lunch?

Adebayo refocused on the conversation. While the Sulla Partners chief research analyst talked, some junior suit was busy taking notes—a child, Olufemi thought, who looked no more than twenty-one or twenty-two years old.

"As you can see from our income statement, Octagon's operations in Nigeria are highly profitable." Olufemi's posh English accent was so pronounced that even the Anglophile David thought him pompous.

"Yes, Mr. Adebayo," Catherine Dunlop said. She was feeling the effect of one drink, which, combined with little sleep on the plane and the heat of Lagos, made her more aggressive than normal. "We have looked over your public income balance sheets, but we are trying to get a better sense of what's behind the numbers. Oil theft is starting to make a serious impact."

"That is true," Olufemi admitted. "The government has been unable to find and prosecute the thieves. These bandits might force us to sell some, or all, of our onshore operations."

"If Octagon and other producers did sell their onshore assets, what would be the effect?"

"We have already been selling off some of our lesser-producing wells to local oil companies, who can extract the remaining oil at lower costs. Further sales would open up opportunities for enterprising traders like yourselves."

"Enterprising traders?" Catherine was intrigued.

"Yes. New producers would mean new contracts with great potential for profit. This is where having inside connections could help a firm like yours." Olufemi smiled.

Inside David Sloan was laughing, but he kept his eyes fixed on Adebayo. Was he implying what David thought he was implying?

When he got no obvious response, Olufemi continued, "In a place like Nigeria, those connections would come with a cost, but I think you would find those costs worthwhile." Olufemi paused for effect so that the full import of his last statement could be felt. The implication that some money under the table could help Sulla Partners did have its attractions. Sloan was sure there were hefty profits to be made buying oil from lower-producing wells at a discount. However, David had already decided he could not trust Olufemi Adebayo, and he wanted to avoid any potential corruption charges in the United States. If Adebayo was willing to deal with Sulla Partners, he was certainly making the same pitch to others.

"I wonder if I could change the direction of the conversation slightly," David interrupted. He had remained largely silent so far.

"Of course, Mr. Sloan. You are the one who requested the meeting." David could sense Olufemi Adebayo's frustration.

"What about the security situation?" David asked.

"The security situation?"

"Yes, Mr. Adebayo. There has been violence in the Niger Delta in the past. And I'm not talking about stolen oil. This violence at one point shut down over 30 percent of total production, not to mention the additional costs in security measures as well as ransoms for those who were kidnapped. I'm sure you can see how that would make any investor uneasy."

"You bring up a sore subject, Mr. Sloan. Several of my colleagues were victims of kidnapping during that period. It took a great deal of our energies to deal with the violence. We have no interest in returning to that situation."

"But, with a new president in office, surely there is some risk of the conflict reigniting."

"Mr. Sloan, you'll have to forgive me. I am quite tired, so I am perhaps more blunt than I might be otherwise. The amnesty that ended the violence over ten years ago was effective. Nearly all of the insurgency's commanders surrendered to the authorities and are quite content with the current situation, as I understand it. Most of the insurgents' weapons were seized. Yes, there are still militants in the mangrove swamps of the delta, but they are not a current threat. It is the oil theft with the possible collusion of government forces that concerns us now."

David thought for a moment. "Let's say, hypothetically speaking, that the insurgency were to return. Would you know in advance?"

"Most likely. To be frank, I would not withhold your investment in Nigeria on that threat. Nigeria is fast becoming a different place. It's an ideal time to invest, especially in the expanding natural gas sector. If I were you, I would seek out allies in the government and also with us at Octagon Petroleum." Olufemi grinned and wondered how much money David Sloan was personally worth.

"Thank you for putting my concerns to rest. I am sure we will be in touch going forward."

"Indeed. I look forward to it," Olufemi said. "I'll have our people communicate with you about opportunities for partnering with Octagon."

David rose from his seat and extended his hand across Olufemi's desk. Given the width of the desk, David had to reach, putting himself in an awkward position, but he thought a sign of humility might be helpful. "Thank you for taking so much time on such short notice."

Olufemi shook his hand rather weakly. David, who had always thought weak handshakes said a lot about a person, did his best to hide his smirk. Catherine and Matt were already on their feet and followed their boss into the hallway, where an Octagon employee there waiting to show them out.

"What now?" Matt asked his bosses.

"We head back to the Wheatbaker Hotel. Review your notes and create a summary sheet for me to look at. Once that is done, enjoy what Lagos has to offer. Catherine, we'll speak later tonight. I hope you got a taste of how things work in Nigeria."

•••

David Sloan looked down at his empty glass. He probably shouldn't have another whisky, but why not? He glanced at his watch, an absurd luxury item in a world of ubiquitous cell phones. It was 9:07 pm. It was five hours earlier back in New York, and the booze would help him sleep. He got up and walked over to the small bar in his room. David's mind had been racing all day. Everything depended on knowing the certainty of this insurgency. Without the violence and with Josh Cohn putting downward pressure on oil prices through his short selling and rumors spreading, David's positions were already taking a hit. If he were to dramatically increase his bet and the violence were to never happen, he would lose a lot. One bad year in this industry could make investors flee, like rats from a demolition site in lower Manhattan. But damn, he loved the risk-taking, the thrill of it. Catherine was right. He needed her more sober guidance.

In the midst of pouring yet another Johnnie Walker fifty milliliter bottle into his glass, his phone rang. David looked down at the number and smiled.

"Hello, Mr. Schrimpf. I've been expecting your call." His words had a slight slur to them. He hoped Schrimpf didn't notice. He didn't want Schrimpf to think he was weak under pressure, which he most certainly was not.

"Glad you made it safely to Nigeria. Up for a drink and a chat tonight?"

"Sure," David responded. "I'm always up for a drink if the conversation matches."

"Great. Can you meet me at the bar of the Intercontinental at ten?"

David took one more look at his watch. "No problem. I'll be there."

"Looking forward to it," Eli Schrimpf said.

David hung up the phone. "Oh, I am too, Eli. I am too."

Chapter 14

At just past 10:00 pm, David Sloan walked into the Ariya Terrace
Bar on the fifth floor of the Hotel Intercontinental on the north shore of
Victoria Island, one of the nicest sections of Lagos. Originally an island,
landfill in the mid-twentieth century connected Victoria Island, or VI, to
the Lekki peninsula to the east. Its north shore faced the lagoon, and
beyond that Lagos Island and Ikoyi, where Sloan had just come from.
VI's tony north shore had a string of fancy hotels and the consulates of
the major European countries and the US. The Ariya Terrace Bar, like
the rest of the Intercontinental, was relatively new and had a large outdoor terrace overlooking Victoria Island. Through the glass doors, David
could see the lights of the nearest hotels in the steadily darkening night.
David had forgotten what Eli Schrimpf's face looked like, so he kept scanning the room for a middle-aged white guy. There were several groups
gathered around tables, a mix of Nigerians and foreigners.

"Dave!" Sloan turned to see a guy in his late forties walking toward
him. He had on an untucked white button-down and khaki pants that
looked like linen from afar. Even with his loose-fitting shirt, Sloan could
see that Eli carried a few extra pounds. His hair was gray and long and
had been slicked back with a handful of gel. He also wore a close-
cropped beard. David was glad he had changed out of his suit and into
slacks and a casual button-down. The contrast between the two men
would be less conspicuous.

"You must be Eli."

"You got it, pal." Eli Schrimpf smiled broadly and shook David Sloan's hand. Schrimpf's informality was in stark contrast to his earlier demeanor on the phone.

Sloan was eager to keep attention away from them, so he made small talk. "So where in the States are you from?"

"Born in Cincinnati, grew up east of Houston, but have lived all over. A wandering soul, you might call me. Here, let's get a drink. I'm thirsty." Eli grabbed David by the elbow and led him to the bar. Even in his slightly inebriated state, David could tell that Eli was a number of drinks ahead of him.

"This is the lovely Doris," Eli said, motioning to the female bartender, who gazed back without emotion. David imagined she was used to dealing with drunk foreign businessmen. "A real black beauty, wouldn't you say?" Eli's familiarity both with him and the bartender made David uncomfortable.

"Let's have some cognac." Eli slapped David on the back. "The Nigerians love cognac. Biggest consumers of cognac outside of France. Can you believe it? These people do like fine things." He turned to Doris and added, "Two Hennessys on the rocks."

"Thanks," David said. He would have preferred to stay with whisky but decided not to argue. They both sat down with their backs to the bar so they could survey the other diners.

"You know, Dave," Eli said, turning toward him. "Do you mind if I call you Dave?"

"It's David."

"Right. David, Lagos is a great place, a fine city. I've been all over the world, and this place is alright. Poor, which is easy to see, and rich, very rich, side by side. The traffic is horrible. The roads frightful. The whole damn city floods with just a little rain because the drainage system is so bad. There is filth on the sidewalks and the buildings look dingy, but there is life here!" Eli slapped his hands together enthusiastically. "And good people. You'll like it."

"Well, we're off to Port Harcourt tomorrow. I guess I'll need to make a return trip," David responded.

"Eek. PH is not like Lagos. Not as nice. But it's functional, and, let's be honest, we are all in Nigeria for something, and it ain't tourism. There ain't a tourist in this whole damn country. But there is money to be made." David was grateful when Eli turned his attention back toward his newly filled Hennessy, which he had swooped up off the bar, the momentum alone propelling half of tumbler's contents down Eli's throat. David sipped carefully. He wanted to maintain focus for when the talk turned to business.

"So Port Harcourt is worse than here," David remarked, playing along. "When we drove in from the airport today, I couldn't help but notice the slums by the water. It looked like the houses were floating in fog."

"Makoko," Eli replied. "That's the name of the slum. The largest in Lagos. And the houses, if you can call them that, are built on the water. It wasn't fog you saw. It was smoke. They char the wood they use for their houses so it rots more slowly, or so I was told. Quite the sight to greet you, eh?"

"That explains the smell. It looked like something out of a horror film."

"Lots of people live there. They must make it somehow. But you want to talk horror films. Whew!" David realized that drunk Eli would dominate the conversation, which was just as well. Sloan assumed it came from nervousness about their meeting. "My first time in Lagos," Eli continued without missing a beat, "over twenty years ago, I was coming in from the airport along that same long bridge you were on, and we passed a guy mangled on the road. Still alive though. Cars were whizzing by him like it was nothing. Crazy. Never seen anything like it. The poor man was dying. I tapped my driver on the shoulder and told him to pull over to help the wounded guy. The driver waved me off and kept going. So I yelled at him. I mean, this was my driver, after all. Then he turns to me and says, 'Sorry, sir. We cannot stop. If we stop, the police will think we hit the man and we will have to pay for the funeral and cleanup.' We kept driving like everyone else. Used to happen all the time until they changed the laws and banned those damn motorcycles from Lagos." Eli shook his head at the memory.

"Tragic."

"Yeah, that was the past though. Down your glass, buddy." Eli stood up and put his empty glass on the bar. "We'll go grab some eats in Ikoyi. There's a fun place over there that has real African flavor. You'll like it. The food is not bad, as far as Nigerian food goes. You like spicy, right?"

"I tolerate it," David said. Looking around at the clientele, David agreed it would be better to talk business elsewhere. "It would be good to taste some Nigerian food while I'm here."

"A man after my own heart. Try the local flavors. All of them, if you know what I mean." Eli winked at David, and David tried not to show his exasperation at Eli's routine. "Why don't you give Doris here your card and we can move along."

"It would be my pleasure." David slid his card to Doris, who seemed grateful they would be moving on. Glancing at the bill, he realized Eli had had four doubles on his tab before he arrived. David included a nice tip when he signed. He was sure Doris could use it after dealing with Eli.

Downstairs at the hotel, Eli had a car waiting. He waved his hand and the car pulled up. "Hop in, buddy. This is my driver in Lagos. Quiet and knows how to drive, which I like." Before David had closed the rear door of the Camry, Eli turned to his driver. "Adamu, Bogobiri House. Pronto."

With that the car sped off into the night. The drive was only a few minutes over the Falomo Bridge from the hotel. Driving over the bridge, David gazed up and down the lagoon that gave Lagos its name. There were some ships moored along the shore but not much movement on the water. Over the bridge, they dodged in and out of traffic. Horns filled the night air. While David briefly considered putting on his seat belt, they abruptly pulled onto a side street that was under construction. It looked like a dirt road in the darkness, and they drove slowly to avoid the potholes.

"As I was saying, the roads here are crap. Don't worry. You get used to it." Eli bent his head and peered out the window. "We're here."

David looked up to see a gate with a homemade sign of cowrie shells that read **Bogobiri House**. As they got out of the car, the sound of live music poured out into the dark street.

"Food's inside," Eli said as he led the way through the small courtyard filled with African art and a handful of smokers—some black and some white—seated around a small table and absorbed in a heated conversation. David thought he caught something about them reporting news in a different part of the country. Once inside the cramped restaurant, they maneuvered to a table and sat down. The tables and chairs were of dark wood that had a vague African rustic feel. The live music David had heard on the street came from the dance floor in the next building over. On the restaurant side, the music was muffled, but combined with the steady murmur of voices, it gave them cover to talk about whatever they wanted without fear of eavesdroppers. A waiter came over and dropped off two menus. "Star beer," Eli told him, holding up two fingers. "You drink beer, right?"

"Yes," David answered. "So what's good here?"

"Try the jollof rice with shrimp or chicken. Will be the best for a newcomer. Think spicy rice with stewed chicken bits. You'll have to watch out for the bones though."

"What are you going to have?"

"Their goat meat soup. Spicy as hell. Not for the fainthearted. Just what I need to clear the sinuses." The two of them settled back into their seats and took in the scene. David was glad to have a break in the conversation. The works of local artists decorated the walls, paintings and prints with a Rastafarian feel. He recognized Bob Marley in one of them. A singer and two accompanists were setting up their instruments in the corner. Background music, David guessed. Those who wanted to dance would go across the courtyard. A mixed crowd of Nigerians and expatriates chatted at their respective tables. David took a sip of his Star beer. Not bad. An American-style lager, a little watery but refreshing.

"Nigeria, my friend. It's a messed-up country," Eli remarked, almost as though he were speaking to himself.

David leaned in. This is what he had come for. "Say more. Let's get down to business."

"Two days ago, I was in the creeks, down near PH. We caught some buggers stealing oil from one of our main pipes, one of the big ones, you see."

"And? I thought that kind of thing happened all the time."

"Not this way. Usually they go for one of the smaller pipelines. They're scattered all over the delta. Not that hard to do, really. This group was different. They were heavily armed and knew what they were doing. They wanted a big score."

"Okay, and this is why I'm here?"

"No. No, you're not listening, Dave." Eli was becoming agitated as he remembered the scene. "The security forces weren't in on this one. Or if they were, they double-crossed the thieves. It was a professional job. Shit is gettin' real."

"You think it's a sign of things to come?"

"Listen, this one insurgent, Ifeanyi Okoye, is a serious motherfucker. As soon as he got released, my local contacts started chatting. Apparently, he's planning something big. Everyone knows it. At least all the locals sense it. The security forces know it too. The only reason I can think of for hitting that pipeline is that they need money to buy arms. That wasn't a small local thing."

"So it's really happening then."

"Unless the security forces can stop it."

David leaned back in his wooden chair and thought for a moment. "What are the chances of that happening?"

"I don't know. No one knows. I'll get you in touch with some of the locals when we're in PH. You make the call."

"A lot is riding on this, Eli." David considered how much of a risk he was taking.

"Speaking of which, what's my cut?"

"Your cut?"

"Yeah, I'm putting my neck out for you. What's in it for me?"

"If this works out, I'll get you three hundred thousand."

"And if it doesn't?"

"If it doesn't, I'm out a lot more than that."

"Fuck, I need another drink." Eli chugged the remainder of his Star beer and motioned to the waiter to come over. "Another round?"

"Sure," David replied, looking at his half-filled beer. Time to do some drinking. It would help him sleep, he rationalized.

Eli passed the message to the waiter. "So you met with my man

Femi today." David's mind went back to the brief conversation with the Octagon Petroleum country manager.

"He's more British than the Brits."

Eli chuckled. "All the upper-class Nigerians send their kids to British boarding schools. A legacy of colonialism and crappy schools here. Femi's like most high-up Nigerians: corrupt as can be, but careful."

"How much does he know about the insurgency?"

"Most people like Femi don't take these rumors too seriously. They're stuck in their offices in Lagos. Nigerians are good at seeing the upside of things. They're not so good at hedging their bets."

"Right." A waiter appeared carrying two plates, which interrupted David's train of thought. "Ah, the food," Eli said. "Time for some serious spice. Let's eat."

David's dish was a generous portion of rice with a red sauce poured generously over the top. Just as Eli had warned, the chicken was chopped up into large chunks but still attached to the bone. David looked across at Eli's bowl of brownish soup. Not the most appetizing color. David took a big bite of his own dish.

"Whoa! This has got a kick to it," David exclaimed, putting his fork down.

"Your taste buds need some practice. Nothing compared to this soup, my friend." Eli took a spoonful and smiled as his face flushed. "Love it though," he croaked.

"I'd rather save the S&M for something other than my taste buds."

"Alright," Eli said after taking a few more bites, "let's focus on other issues: getting another round and having some fun."

"Why not?" David replied.

An hour later, David and Eli's car pulled up to Pat's Bar on Victoria Island. The bar did not look particularly fancy from the outside. At least

Eli's taste in late-night bars was close to David's own: the seedier the better. The slight swaying of their walk up the short path spoke to the Hennessys and Star beers already in their systems. Eli nodded to the man at the door as they walked through. The bar was crowded. Immediately to their left, a band played, far too loudly for a bar its size. After glancing around the room, David leaned over to Eli and said, "There are a lot more girls here than guys. I like it."

Eli smiled. "Yup, my friend. This place is great. Been a popular expat bar for years!"

On their way to the bar, one Nigerian woman—David guessed she was in her early twenties—came up to David and rubbed against him. David smiled. She looked up and smiled back. At the bar, Eli ordered two more Star beers. The expat next to David said something, but he didn't catch it with the loud noise of the band. David nodded. "Yeah," he said back before turning to Eli.

"Now, there are a few things you have to know about these ladies, my friend," Eli cautioned, putting his face right up to David's ear.

"What's that?" David shouted back.

"If you take one of them back to your hotel room, remember they are expecting a little cash at the end."

"Not a shock," David said under his breath.

"Consider it a tip. But fair warning: if I were you, I would be sure to pay the tip. Some young guy last year came here and took home one of the girls. The next morning she insisted on money, and this guy got all indignant and tried to get her out of the hotel room. In his carelessness near the door, she surprised him and pushed him out, locking the door behind him. This American guy was banging on the door in his skivvies while he could hear the girl breaking things in his room. An ugly scene. Let's just say it's worth it to pay them."

"Noted," David said. The same woman who had rubbed against him earlier was back. She strolled over to him at the bar. "Hello there," she said in a thick Nigerian accent. "You rubbed against my bum."

David couldn't quite make out what she was saying and pointed to his ear to indicate he had not heard. "What was that?"

"Ya rubbed against my bum." She smiled and got close to him. Eli laughed out loud. David looked up and could see a few other women eyeing him.

"I can see why you expats like Nigeria."

"What happens in Lagos stays in Lagos," Eli said.

David looked at the woman next to him and turned back to Eli. "Honestly, I'm fine for now." David had no interest in picking up an STD, and he didn't know enough about these women to trust them.

"Suit yourself," Eli said. "I don't feel like spending the night alone." David turned back to the bartender and let Eli work his magic. It was too loud for small talk. He felt the gazes of the women. The handful of white guys in the bar were all at least fifteen years older than David; some were in their mid-sixties. He wondered if some of the oil service companies gave out Viagra as part of their overseas package. David couldn't help but reflect on the imperialist nature of it all. Western countries come here to make money and act like they owned the place. One more example of money ruling all, David thought.

Two drinks later, after Eli had done a little dancing in front of the horrible band, he stumbled back over to David. "Let's go, buddy." There was a Nigerian woman holding tightly on to Eli's upper arm, almost as though she was afraid to let him go.

"Sure." David put the remainder of his beer on the bar while Eli signaled to the bartender and settled the tab. Walking outside, David pulled out his cell phone. He still had Carol Opara's number from earlier in the day. He could still see her figure at the airport. She was more his taste.

Fuck it, why not? he thought before sending her a text inviting her for a drink at the Wheatbaker.

A minute later he got a text back: I can meet you there in thirty minutes.

David smiled. Nigeria was his type of place. Eli wasn't going to be the only one having fun that night.

Chapter 15

Port Harcourt

Chris Reed decided to take Julia up on her offer to see some of the work that the New Africa Initiative did around Port Harcourt. They spent a day in the city itself and finished it off with a casual dinner at one of Julia's favorite spots. Their dinner conversation had been significantly less confrontational than their first lunch at Chicken Republic. It turned out they had more in common than Chris had originally thought. Julia had grown up with more privilege than Chris, but they both wanted to change the world for the better. Julia said her par-ents were constantly bugging her to return to New York, but she liked Nigeria. Here, she was making a difference.

They shared stories of their friends who were off making money and posting endless Snapchat and Instagram stories of late-night partying. "When is that going to get old?" Julia wondered aloud. She was the only other American Chris had met who was around his age, and it was a comfort to spend time with her that night after all the work he had been doing for Emmaus Ministries, which amounted to whatever Paul wanted on that particular day. Chris felt relaxed around her. All through the din-ner, he kept staring at her lips before catching himself. He knew he shouldn't be attracted to her. After all, it had only been a few months since Abby's accident. When Julia dropped him off, she invited him out to see some of the initiative's work outside the city. Without thinking, Chris said yes. At least he could tell Paul he was networking in the city, although he would feel more justified saying that if Julia were sixty-seven and ugly.

Their destination the next day, a so-called "village," was more of a city than a village and was about an hour's drive north. Julia O'Keefe estimated the population to be somewhere around fifty thousand people. The scenery looked much like the rest of this part of the country, palm trees and greenery lining the road once they got outside the boundaries of Port Harcourt.

"Sounds like you've been enjoying your time here." Julia's voice broke a long silence.

"Definitely been the change I needed," Chris responded.

"Tired of the cold in Massachusetts?" Julia joked, keeping her eyes on the road.

"No." Chris hesitated. He hadn't brought up Abby with anyone other than Paul. Then he said, "More like grief therapy."

"Grief therapy?"

"My wife. She died back in February. A car hit her while crossing a busy street. The police said she died instantly. I watched the whole thing."

"I'm really sorry to hear that, Chris. I didn't know you were married. You're so young."

"She was my high school sweetheart. We married right out of college. It's not that uncommon in Iowa."

"I'm sorry." Julia got flustered. "That came out all wrong. I didn't mean to imply something wrong. I—oh, forget about it." Julia looked back ahead at the road.

"Forget about what?"

"Just a different world, that's all. I couldn't imagine being married already," Julia said. "Thank you for sharing. It must be hard to talk about."

"It is, but somehow it doesn't feel awkward around you. I think you two would have gotten along. She'd be happy to know I had someone to talk to."

Neither of them said anything more until they reached the village, which seemed to Chris Reed like a smaller version of Port Harcourt, only less densely packed with buildings. The sidewalks were not as crowded with people, but there were the same women selling oranges and roasted corn and boiled groundnuts. The pace here was definitely slower. Chris noticed a number of people casually chatting on the side of the road as though there was nothing else to do. There were also fewer posters and church advertisements.

The New Africa Initiative truck slowed and pulled through a worn-out metal gate that had a broken top hinge, which left the gate stuck in the ground. The rusted lettering read **Health Center**. The building itself was not in much better shape than the gate. It badly needed a paint job and some basic landscaping. When they arrived, there were probably a half dozen other cars parked over the patchy lawn. Chris guessed there were twenty or so people milling around outside, presumably waiting for them.

"What are we here for again?" Chris asked.

"Malaria treatment work." Hopping down from the driver's seat, Julia called, "Give me a hand with these boxes."

Chris grabbed several out of the back of the pickup, accidently brushing against Julia in the process—a brief touch that made his heart beat a little faster. Following her to the side of the health center, they walked up a few steps and into a large room with a table at the front. Maybe a dozen more people were in this room, several noticeably sweating, even though it was one of the cooler days Chris had experienced in Nigeria. Julia put down her boxes and Chris stacked his on top.

"Would you mind grabbing the other boxes?" Julia asked Chris.

"Sure. No problem. What's in them?"

"Medication. There are labels on the side. You should stack them up here by label." Julia motioned behind her. "They have different doses for different ages."

Chris nodded, and as he walked out to the truck, he looked back to catch another glimpse of Julia. Their eyes met briefly, and neither one of them turned away. When he returned with another armful of boxes, Julia had set up her station at the front table and was already talking with the first patient, a mother whose eight-year-old daughter was sick outside the village. She had walked two hours into town to buy the malaria medication she needed.

"What symptoms does your daughter have?" Chris overheard Julia ask.

"Fevers, and her body has been aching."

"How long has this been going on for?"

"Four days now," the woman said.

"Has she gotten any worse?"

"Yes. That's why I walked here today. Thank you for bringing the medicine." The woman smiled. Chris could see the joy in the woman's eyes at the relief her daughter would get. Julia and the woman talked for another minute and then the woman paid Julia, who reached into the nearest brown box for a smaller box with the medications and instructions. Julia then made a mark on a large yellow ledger book that she had brought with her. Julia seemed to be in her element. Nothing about the run-down health center outwardly bothered her. Being able to help made everything normal, which Chris admired.

Chris scanned the faces of those waiting in line. Some seemed quite ill. One older man, his face ashen, his body weak, sat in a chair next to the line. Chris had been taking his own malaria medication and was vigilant about sleeping under his mosquito net at night. He had no interest in showing up at a similar clinic in Port Harcourt. Pushing that thought out of his mind, he wandered outside to look around the health center. He was shocked by its dirtiness. In one hallway, he found a pile of open bags with used needles. He shuddered when he thought of the viruses and bacteria that could be on those needles, especially with the rates of HIV/AIDS in the region. Disposal couldn't be that hard.

Strolling around front, he entered through the main door and walked down the hallway before stopping in front of one of the examination rooms. There was a little boy, no more than six years old, lying on the bed and sweating profusely. The boy suddenly shook, and his mother reached over to hold him down during what appeared to be a seizure. After thirty seconds, the boy stopped moving. The boy's eyes, which darted in different directions, frightened him.

"I'm afraid the malaria has attacked the brain. Perhaps if he had been able to get treatment earlier, it might be different," Chris heard the physician say. "There is not much we can do for him." The mother began to sob, and Chris felt ashamed observing someone else's pain. All because of a damn mosquito.

When he walked back to the other room, Julia was nearing the end of the patient line. By the entrance, Chris saw a boy holding a jar with pineapple slices in it. The pineapples looked as though they had been in the jar for a while. He could see several of them darkening, indicating that they were beginning to turn. As Chris approached, he made no attempt to sell them to Chris. The boy seemed content sitting on the ground and watching the people around him.

"Hungry?"

Chris turned around to see Julia holding a bag lunch for him.

"Yes, actually. Thank you." Chris smiled. He looked inside the bag and found a plastic container with rice and some nondescript beef dish in red sauce. They both walked out onto the grass, where they sat down for a little picnic.

"How'd it go today?" Chris asked.

"Well. Sold a lot of boxes. There were one or two cases that seemed distressing."

"Sold the boxes? Why don't you just give them away?"

"When we give away the meds, people value them less and tend not to follow the instructions and recommended dosages."

"That's human nature for you, I guess. That's one thing I have always thought Christianity had right."

"Is that so?" Julia replied. "You buy all of that sin stuff in Christianity?"

"You have to admit that human beings sin."

"Honestly, I hate that word. I'll give you the fact that human beings mess up, which is why education matters so much."

"Education?" Chris asked, raising on eyebrow. "Aren't the instructions on the side of the meds education enough?"

"Whatever," she said. "The good news is that we've made progress. Malaria deaths in our area are way down over the past several years. Now we need more mosquito nets and, ideally, spraying of wet areas with insecticide."

"They don't do that?"

"Not enough money. Someday we'll get the funding. Little by little the Niger Delta is becoming a new place. If we keep at it, things will improve."

"I think you overestimate our capacity to bring about a utopia. Plenty of oil money around here. Strange that it requires a New Yorker to make things better." Julia gave him a mocking stare, made more pronounced by her dark-rimmed glasses. After taking a bite of his food, he added, "What would your friends back in the US think of all of this?"

"Who knows? Their version of helping is giving fifty dollars to an MS150 bike ride. They drop more than that on a weekday dinner."

"Didn't Jesus say, 'For where your treasure is, there your heart will be also'?" Chris offered.

Julia gave him another look and rolled her eyes. "For a non-Christian, you're full of Christianity."

Chris shrugged his shoulders. "I was raised in Iowa. Christianity is in the water there."

"I believe they call it 'brainwashing,'" Julia retorted.

Chris changed the subject. "Shouldn't that kid over there be in school and not selling pineapple?"

"Definitely. I wish they would enforce truancy laws in this country."

"Or that people would tell the kid to get to school," Chris added.

"I'm sure his parents need the extra money he brings in. Your white privilege is showing."

"I guess I didn't consider that." Chris felt guilty for his American instinct to judge Nigeria.

"Don't worry," Julia said, reaching out to touch his shoulder. "Just try to be more generous in your views until you spend a little more time here. Ready to head off?"

"Ready when you are," Chris said. "These malaria cases depress me. I'm glad I don't live in the tropics."

"You do now."

They made good time on the road back to Port Harcourt, Julia driving like a New Yorker, the speedometer constantly edging past one hundred and ten kph.

"The palm trees are pretty," Chris remarked.

"Good for palm wine too."

"Palm wine?"

"It's the local booze. They make it by fermenting the sap from the palm trees. Maybe we should pick some up. It might even cheer you up." Julia turned her head to Chris and gave him a wink.

Chris shook his head and smiled. "Sure. Why not?"

"No time like the present."

Julia eyed some shacks up ahead on the side of the road and pulled the pickup into a clearing in front of them. Next to the shacks was a lean-to with a long wooden table set up next to a large pot of boiling water over a portable gas stove. Behind the table stood a man, stripped to the waist, chopping up a large snake. Others casually looked on.

"Is that a python?" Chris asked, astounded.

"You are so observant, Chris." They got out of the truck, and Chris walked over to the man to watch him do his work. The snake must have been six feet long. He slid his machete back and forth over its body to descale it. Satisfied that he had gotten everything, he lifted the snake off the table with one hand and brushed the scales onto the ground with the other. He then placed the snake back on the wood and began slicing it with his machete. Each swift blow cut right through the thick skin and spine. After chopping it into foot-long pieces, he dropped each one into a nearby pot of boiling water.

"All set?" Julia walked over to Chris while carrying two one-gallon containers filled with a milky liquid.

"Yeah, yeah. Does python taste any good?"

"Couldn't say. Never tried it."

"Wait, did you just buy those jugs here?" Chris asked, looking down at the old plastic containers with dirt coatings the outside.

"Of course I did. Places like this are the best for palm wine."

"But this place looks unsanitary."

"If it is good enough for the residents here, it's good enough for me.

"Hop in the truck, tough guy."

Chris watched Julia walking toward the truck. Her dark blue capri pants reached down to her shins, and she wore a lighter blue top. Chris caught himself staring and hurried to catch up to her.

"So when do we get to try this palm wine?" Chris called after her.

From inside the car, Julia responded, "When you come over to my apartment for a drink."

"Is that an invitation?" Chris tried to hide his excitement at the prospect.

"Get in. I want to miss the after-work traffic."

Driving back down the road toward Port Harcourt, Chris couldn't stop thinking about Julia. She was unlike any woman he had ever met, so confident with such a good heart—at least once you cracked the New York exterior. He had his normal Midwestern biases against East Coast elitists: that they had no moral compass and were obsessed with money and class. But here was Julia, devoting her life to saving others, eschewing materialism. She was doing so much more than most Christians he had ever met back home. Perhaps Christianity was no better than Humanism, at least a well-considered Humanism like Julia's. And Nigeria was nothing like he had expected. Everyone seemed so welcoming. In a place like this, he wondered, what could possibly go wrong?

Chapter 16

Chris Reed was in the best mood he had been in since arriving in Nigeria. His friendship with Julia was getting better by the day, and work was more fun than ever. Professor Mendes had been right. This really was what he had needed.

That morning, he was teaching a class on early Christian history, something he loved, in the classroom on the first floor of the Emmaus Center. It was a chance to use some of that fancy education he had. Chris looked at the clock on the wall opposite him in the classroom of the Emmaus Center. Two minutes past noon. The past two hours had flown by. "Alright, class," he said. "That's enough for today."

"Thank you, Chris," one of the men in the front row said.

"I look forward to seeing you all here next week at the same time. You will see on the handout instructions for your assignment. You can find the reading online, or I can print out copies for you. It is a passage from William Lloyd Garrison's The Liberator. Read through it several times. It is the best introduction to the American abolition movement." The eight students got up from their chairs. "Have an awesome week," Chris added.

"You too," one of the students said.

Finally, Chris felt useful. He wasn't just meeting people and attending events around the city. He was doing something. The course he was teaching focused on the development of American Christianity and its lessons for Nigeria. It was Paul's idea. He knew Chris had studied American religious history, and he'd helped recruit the first students. Chris had been given full freedom in designing the course. That day he had been talking about the start of the Second Great Awakening. Everyone had listened intently as Chris described the debates over what it meant to be regenerated or "born again" in early nineteenth-century America. They then had written personal accounts of what being born again meant to them and discussed how much the concept had changed over time. The students were riveted.

Chris decided to go home from the Emmaus Ministries offices to grab lunch. Paul was working from home, and Chris wanted to surprise him and tell him all about the class. Leaving the office, he waved to Silas at the front desk and strolled up the road. Port Harcourt no longer seemed strange to him. He had become accustomed to the heat and the layer of sweat that covered his body for most of the day. Miracle of miracles, he was even developing a tan. He felt comfortable walking into local shops and was beginning to get used to bartering for every item he purchased. The incessant noise of cars honking no longer bothered him, and neither did the piles of trash lying on the sidewalk. He even liked the Nigerian pop music that played from the car parts shop he passed on the way home.

Approaching their house, Chris was glad to see the familiar Honda in the driveway. Paul was home. Without knocking, he opened the door and walked in. Paul was nowhere in the living room, where Chris assumed he would have been working. He poked his head around the wall, expecting to see him in the kitchen, but, again, no Paul. Chris bounded up the stairs and threw open the door to Paul's room.

"Paul! You will never guess—" Chris froze. On the bed were Paul and Rotimi, naked and on top of each other. Stunned, Chris stood there not knowing what to do. It was something Chris had never seen before: two men having sex.

Paul looked over at him. "Chris…"

Chris backed out of the room without a noise, turned toward the stairs and went outside. He could hear Paul yelling behind him, "Chris, wait!" But Chris was already out the front door, walking briskly. He turned down the main road, ignoring the people around him.

Chris was shaken, as though he had violated Paul's privacy. Paul and Rotimi? They were…they were gay. Chris scolded himself for being such a Puritan about it. Being gay was totally natural. He had known plenty of gay people in college and grad school. But he hadn't suspected Paul and Rotimi. Part of it was the Christianity. He was sure the church folks at Emmaus Ministries wouldn't approve. And Nigeria? Chris had heard stories about how homophobic Nigeria was. They put people in jail for being gay. What would happen to them if the secret got out? The more Chris thought about it, the more other things made sense. That's why Rotimi had been living there. That's why Chris's arrival had caused such tension in the house.

After an hour, Chris found himself back at the Emmaus Center. He entered and Silas said, "Hey, Chris. You're back. Welcome. Paul is in his office and wants to see you upstairs." Silas went back to reading something at his desk. Behind him on the wall was a map of the area around Port Harcourt, with little red pins marking the churches they worked with. Does he know? Chris asked himself. He hoped not, for Paul and Rotimi's sake.

"Thanks, Silas," Chris finally said out loud as he walked toward the stairs. Out of the corner of his eye, he caught his notes on the whiteboard from that morning. It seemed like ages ago. When he got to the top of the stairs, he noticed Paul's door was closed. Chris knocked. "Always knock before entering," Chris said under his breath. "A new mantra."

"Come in," he heard Paul call from within. Chris opened the door and walked in. Paul was standing behind his desk in his trademark loose-fitting button down and faded shorts.

"Heya, Chris. Mind closing the door?" Paul said, his voice significantly weaker than normal. Chris turned and pushed the door closed, waiting for the click of the latch. "Man, I'm sorry you had to see that earlier." Paul tried to feign a little lightheartedness. "Surprise!"

"I'm sorry, Paul. I really am," Chris said. "I should never have barged in on you like that. I—"

"You're good, man. I guess we should have told you. We just didn't know how you would react..." Paul's voice trailed off. Chris could see the concern on his face.

"Paul, this the twenty-first century. I don't have any problem with you being gay," Chris assured him. "It might require us to have some better boundaries about privacy, but I want you to be happy."

Paul exhaled. "Thank you for understanding, Chris. I—I really can't thank you enough for that." Emotionally drained, Paul sat down.

Chris could see the pain in Paul's eyes, and it moved him. Chris sat down in the chair opposite the desk. Paul looked so shaken, Chris wanted to reach out and touch him. They both remained there silently for a few minutes.

"How many people know?" Chris asked.

"No one," Paul replied. "It would ruin everything." Paul put his hands to his face as he thought about what might happen. "I love him so much," Paul added, his voice soft. "Rotimi has saved me. He really has."

"I'm sure he feels the same way, Paul. Your secret is safe with me."

Chris and Paul talked for a while about how he and Rotimi had met, how they had been together for the past three years. Paul said it was the best three years of his life.

"Have you thought about going home?" Chris asked. "I worry about what it could mean for you two here, especially given the climate of Nigeria toward these things."

"We've talked about it. But we both love the work, and we love it here. If we left, what would happen?"

Chris thought about the class that morning and about the other work that Emmaus was doing in the community. Everywhere he went, people knew Paul and admired him.

"I want you to feel free to be yourselves around me, Paul. Displaying affection is nice. You deserve to have you own safe space." Chris thought it might be a perfect time to spend an evening with Julia. He was sure Paul and Rotimi would have a lot to discuss. "Can you answer me something though?"

Paul nodded.

"How do you square this with Christianity? Historically, Christians have not been the most supportive of gay people."

Paul smiled. "That's putting it mildly. Truth is, I didn't do anything sexual for a long time. I suppressed my feelings, ignored them. I hated myself for having them. Honestly, dude, that's one of the reasons I came to Nigeria. If I could get away, if I could do something big for God, then he would reward me by taking away my urges. He didn't. I prayed endlessly. I kept myself as busy as I could to distract myself. For years, Chris. Years."

"That sounds so lonely," Chris said, realizing how much easier he had it being straight.

"Chris, I can't even tell you how much I hated myself for my sexual desires. Dude, I grew up in Northern California. AIDS was everywhere when I was a kid. If there was one thing I knew, it was that being gay was hella bad. About ten years ago, I was reading through the Bible and came across one of the laments of Jeremiah. I wrote it down and posted it above my bed. I read it every morning. It became a part of my routine."

Paul reached into his desk drawer and pulled out a white sheet of paper with writing on it. The paper was creased and had several holes in the top where Paul had stuck a pushpin through it. He slid it across the desk for Chris, who picked it up and read the words aloud:

> *Cursed be the day*
> *on which I was born!*
>
> *The day when my mother bore me,*
> *let it not be blessed!*
>
> *Cursed be the man*
> *who brought the news to my father, saying,*
>
> *"A child is born to you, a son,"*
> *making him very glad.*
>
> *Let that man be like the cities*
> *that the LORD overthrew without pity;*
>
> *let him hear a cry in the morning*
> *and an alarm at noon,*
>
> *because he did not kill me in the womb;*
> *so my mother would have been my grave,*
> *and her womb forever great.*
>
> *Why did I come forth from the womb*
> *to see toil and sorrow,*
> *and spend my days in shame?*
>
> *—Jeremiah 20:14-18*

"You had this above your bed?" Chris asked. "Jesus, I guess I never knew how hard it could be for gay Christians."

"You're also a lot younger than me. A lot's changed in the past twenty years. Anyway, one day, I strung a piece of rope around my neck, hung it from a hook I had screwed into the ceiling and kicked out the chair I was standing on."

Chris was shocked at what Paul was saying but remained silent.

"Miraculously," Paul continued, "I woke up. The circulation to my brain was cut off, but at some point the hook I had screwed into the ceiling came loose, and I fell to the ground. I had a nasty bruise on my head but was fine otherwise. I can't tell you what it is like to die and then be reborn. I mean, really reborn. I remember walking down the street shortly afterward when a little girl came up to me and said, 'Thank you.' At that point we were running a food pantry out of the office. These days, several of the churches do that, but then we were the only place that served a regular meal along with the food we gave away. I had raised the money and set up the food pantry so people like that little girl had something to eat. Suddenly, it hit me: I was doing God's work, and yet I had just tried to take my own life because of something that God put within me.

"I know my New Testament, Chris. I am a sinner. Like everyone, I don't do enough for the poor and marginalized. I get angry and lose my temper. I'm not perfect. But I believe God has redeemed me, all of me. I live by grace, Chris. We all do. We can do it no other way. Without grace, there is nothing. But of all the things I do wrong, I can't believe God judges me for loving Rotimi. Other things maybe, but not for loving someone else, even if that someone is a man. Once I finally learned that lesson, I began to see being gay in a different light. I learned I'm a child of God."

"And Rotimi?" Chris asked. "What about him?"

"I had never known real love with another person until I met Rotimi. He's amazing and caring and lets me do my thing and just smiles. Dear Lord, I love him. I thank God every day for him. I do. I thank God for bringing me to Nigeria so I could meet him. I wish you knew him like I do. He is such a good soul and is twice the Christian I am. I have never felt more connected with God than when I am with him."

"I love to hear that, Paul," Chris said, smiling. He realized he needed to spend more time with Rotimi. "What about the Bible stuff? That's one thing I heard at home. 'The Bible says being gay is wrong.'"

"The Bible? People who say that don't know much about the Bible. How many times does the word 'homosexual' appear in the Bible?"

Chris shrugged. "I don't know. Like three or four times?"

"Nope. Zero. It doesn't appear in the Bible at all because it's a nineteenth-century concept. In biblical times there was no sense that someone was gay by nature. People like the Apostle Paul assumed men had sex with men because of an excess of lust, not because they were hard-wired to be gay. Nearly all the references to same-sex attraction in the Bible have to do with prostitution and rape, not loving relationships."

"I wish more people knew that," Chris said.

"Me too. But it's more than that. The Bible talks about slavery as a normal thing, and yet no one today claims the Bible supports slavery. Sabbath keeping is one of the Ten Commandments, and yet how many conservative Christians keep the Sabbath, or even think about it? Jesus prohibits divorces, and yet Christians get divorced all the time. When someone was ill in the New Testament, it was believed an evil spirit caused it. Now we go to the hospital to get better and not to an exorcist. If there is one thing that drives me nuts about Christians and the Bible, it is how often the Bible has been used to hurt others and cause harm. People have even interpreted the Bible to defend killing others. It's nuts.

"A while back, I read something from St. Augustine on biblical interpretation. I wish I could remember the exact phrase. Basically, he said that our interpretation of a text should either lead to a greater love of God or to a greater love of our neighbor. If it doesn't, then we're clearly not interpreting the Bible correctly. Go back and read it again. That's always stuck with me. Even the Apostle Paul, who is quoted to justify homophobia all the time, wrote, 'Owe no one anything, except to love one another; for the one who loves another has fulfilled the law.' It really is that simple."

They both sat silently for a while. Finally, Chris said, "I should give you some space. Thanks for being so honest."

"No, Chris," Paul replied. "Thank you for being so understanding. You can't imagine how much that means to me, man. I feel like a huge weight has been lifted."

Chris stood up to go. There were some things he wanted to get done, and he needed his own time to think.

"Chris, one more thing," Paul said.

"Yeah?"

"Give me a little warning before you come home next time."

Chris managed a smile himself. "You can be sure of that, Paul."

Chris left Paul's office and walked into his own. He found Julia's number in his phone and pressed send.

"Hey," Julia said. Chris loved the sound of her voice.

"I was wondering if I could come over to your place to talk later. Maybe we can try some of that palm wine."

"Is everything okay?" she asked. "Your voice sounds a little off."

Chris thought for a moment, then said, "I'm actually good, really good. But I'd love to see you."

"I'll be home in a couple hours. I can text you the address."

Chris smiled at the thought of hanging out with Julia. All that talk of love got him thinking.

Chapter 17

Port Harcourt

"Thanks for letting me come," Chris said to Julia, almost before she opened the door. Chris' body kept moving to dispel some of his nervous energy. He couldn't believe he was about to hang out with Julia at her place.

"No problem. I wanted to make you dinner sometime anyway. Why not tonight?" Julia shrugged her shoulders and broke into a smile. "We have been doing enough professional stuff together," she added. "Honestly, I don't have many friends in Port Harcourt."

"Me neither. I appreciate it." Chris walked inside but couldn't keep his eyes off Julia, who was wearing a loose-fitting white button-down shirt, the outline of her bra visible underneath. This was the first time that he had allowed himself to see her in a sexual light, and he was transfixed. Catching himself, Chris did his best to look at the paintings and wood carvings on the light pink walls. "You have a nice apartment."

"The art was all made by local artists I know." Julia walked over to the kitchen area, which adjoined the living room. "Can I get you a drink?" she called out. "Perhaps some of that palm wine we bought the other day?"

"Sure. I'd love some. It's alcoholic, right?"

"You'll like it. It's a cultural experience." Julia already had two glasses on the counter and was fishing out some ice from her freezer.

She lifted one of the gallon jugs she had bought the other day on the side of the road and began pouring two generous glasses. Chris's eyes drifted down to Julia's loose-fitting sky-blue lounge pants, but he averted his gaze when she turned around. Walking back to the living room, she handed a glass to Chris. "Enjoy."

"Thanks. And thanks for having me over." Chris raised his glass and took a sip. The palm wine was better than he was expecting, both sweet and tangy. Julia smiled when she saw he was drinking it. She walked to the kitchen and brought back a small dish with peanuts in it.

"It goes well with groundnuts," she said, offering the dish to Chris. Chris grabbed a handful and took another sip of his drink. "Want to sit down?" Julia motioned to a beige two-person loveseat near them.

The couch was small enough that their legs brushed up against each other's. Chris took several large sips of his palm wine.

"So, what's going on? I was a little surprised to get your call."

"It's nothing. I'm just happy that Paul and I are getting to know one another better. He's full of surprises."

"I can imagine. As much as I don't love his beliefs, he does great work. I bet you're learning a lot." Julia's eyes met Chris's, and neither of them looked away.

"I also came over because I wanted to see you." Chris quickly added, "I wanted some space." He looked down at his glass and began tapping its side with his fingers. Julia reached her hand over and touched Chris's hand to calm it down. With the touch of her hand, Chris closed his eyes. His heart was racing.

"What do you want to talk about? The weather?" Julia smiled.

Chris sat awkwardly for a minute. When he opened his eyes and turned his head, Julia was right there. He gazed into her light brown eyes, framed by her glasses. She leaned in and touched her lips to his. They both stayed there for a moment before Chris pulled back.

"That was nice," he said, his breathing shallow and rapid.

"Come here, missionary boy." Julia grabbed Chris's head and brought it close to hers. Their lips touched again, and this time Julia slid her tongue in Chris's mouth. The pent-up sexual tension between them finally had some release. Chris moved his hands to her body and felt her rounded breasts under his fingers. Julia leaned backward until her head rested on the arm of the couch, and she pulled Chris's slender body down with her. Chris's erection pressed against his shorts as he slowly ground his pelvis into hers. Suddenly, he stopped.

"What is it?" Julia whispered into Chris's ear.

Chris sat up. "We shouldn't."

"Is it your wife?"

"Something like that. It's just too much right now. I...we..."

"Don't worry about it, Chris. We don't have to do anything."

Julia sat up and let her right hand rest on Chris's thigh. She then patted his thigh twice and stood, grabbing her empty glass before walking to the kitchen. "Sorry, I got a little carried away," she said. She dropped a few more ice cubes in her glass and filled it up with palm wine again. "Let's make some dinner and pretend like that never happened."

"I'm the one who should be sorry, Julia. I was in an odd headspace when I came here," Chris called from the couch. Julia said nothing. "Paul Wisner is gay." Chris bit his lip, angry at himself for saying anything.

Julia put the jug down on the counter. "What?" She turned around to look at Chris across the room.

"Damn it. I know I shouldn't tell you. I caught him and Rotimi having sex together earlier today..."

Julia just stood in the kitchen. "So you came over here because you couldn't deal with them being gay?"

"No, I'm actually fine with it," Chris said, defending himself. "It surprised me and—"

"It surprises me too. I wasn't expecting Paul to be a hypocrite."

Chris walked toward Julia. "Julia, that's not fair."

"No, it is fair. Why do you think this country is so homophobic? It's because of Christians like Paul."

"Julia, Paul is not like that at all." Chris raised his voice. "He's not a judgmental person. Why can't Paul find love too?"

Julia stared back at Chris. After a few moments, she said, "I'm sorry. You're right. I'm sure it's not easy on Paul. But the homophobia stuff is one of the things I hate about Christianity. I have so many gay friends back in New York."

"Christianity doesn't have to be like that," Chris said.

"Tell that to the Christians you see here."

"I wish I could."

"Can't you?" She sighed. "Let's make some dinner. I can see why you wanted to give Paul his space. You can stay on the couch tonight if you want."

Chris wanted to pour out his heart to Julia. He wanted to say that Paul's love for Rotimi got him thinking about her and how he wished to be with her. But the sexual tension had dissipated, and it felt wrong to say.

"Thank you, Julia," Chris said, still wishing he could say more.

"You see, even atheists can be vehicles of grace, except we prefer to call it kindness and understanding." A smirk appeared on Julia's face. "Come on, Chris. I'm glad you came over. Let's not talk about Paul. Now you can earn your keep and chop some vegetables for me."

Chris felt the awkwardness ease in the room and walked over to Julia at the kitchen counter. "Here I am. Ready for service. I'm not much of a cook."

"One of these days I should attend one of your history classes so I can see what you are good at," Julia replied lightheartedly.

They chuckled, and Julia leaned her body into Chris before pulling down a cutting board from the shelf.

"How'd you sleep?"

Chris opened his eyes at the sound of Julia's voice, sat up and tried to stretch the kink out of his neck, unsuccessfully. The love seat was too small for him to stretch out on, so he'd slept uncomfortably on his side. His light brown hair was a tangled mop, and he could smell his own body odor mixed with the smell of palm wine. He desperately needed a shower.

"Well, you slept for a while."

"I guess all that palm wine helped."

"For a man who claimed he didn't drink much, you weren't shy. You reminded me of a freshman in high school." Julia laughed.

"I didn't say anything stupid, did I?"

"Let me think." Julia put her hands to her chin in mock reflection. "Other than professing your love for me? Not really."

"That's all?" Chris rubbed his eyes. "I need some water."

"You know where it is, mister. We don't do the whole women-serving-men thing in this apartment."

"There should be an 'off' button for you." Chris stood slowly and wandered over to the small kitchen. Palm wine sure gave him an intense hangover. He fumbled through the cabinets to find a glass and grabbed some filtered water out of the fridge. "Do you have any Advil?" Chris called out.

"I'll get you some, trooper."

Five minutes later they were both back on the couch. Chris began rubbing his temples to ease the pain while Julia looked at him. He could sense she wanted to say something. Finally, she asked, "How are you doing this morning?"

"What?" Chris shook himself out of his brain fog.

"Well, there is the gay thing, which you shouldn't have told me. Then there is Abby, who you kept bringing up last night the more you drank." Chris didn't respond, but Julia noticed a change in his expression. She decided to press a little more. "I was sorry about making out with you last night. I can only imagine how hard things must be after Abby's death."

Chris was silent for a moment, and he tried to think clearly. "You're right. I should never have told you about Paul. Please don't say anything."

"I won't. And you're really okay with him being gay?"

"I've never lived with a gay couple before, but I like them. I want them to be happy. Also, Paul said some things about gays and Christianity that made a lot of sense."

"Maybe I should ask him about it." Chris's face lost all its color. "Just kidding," Julia quickly added.

"I loved Abby and I miss her. But I can't dwell on what happened. At some point I have to move on," Chris said. "What about you? Have you ever loved someone?"

"Years ago," Julia replied. "That was back in New York."

"And you haven't been lonely here?"

"I made out with you last night. Doesn't that say anything?"

"I kinda hoped it meant you were attracted to me." Chris laughed.

Julia smiled. "Maybe I am." She stood up and declared, "I think it's time for breakfast. I'm starving."

"Breakfast sounds great." Chris took a big sip of water and followed Julia to the kitchen. He'd enjoyed cooking with her the night before. "Thanks for having me over, Julia."

"It was my pleasure." She leaned over and gave him a peck on the cheek. "Now you can get the eggs out of the fridge. Any more thoughts on Paul, by the way?"

"God is working through Paul and Emmaus Ministries. I feel that now more than ever. I also appreciate the honesty between him and me."

"You're a good man, Chris. It's all about helping people. So much has improved since the end of the violence. The Niger Delta will keep getting better and better."

Chapter 18

Lagos

Ifeanyi Okoye ran through his plans in his head once more. He had heard back from over a dozen of the former MEND commanders who had pledged to join the insurgency. Mama Sandra, the only female MEND leader, had not yet said whether she would commit her women, but Ifeanyi was not concerned about her. She hated the oil companies and the corruption of Nigeria even more than he did. The one lingering issue was financing. How would they get the money for arms and payments to the commanders? Nearly everyone said they would not attack without money up front. After Fineface's attempt at oil bunkering was foiled, the situation had become even more desperate. So, against his better judgment, Ifeanyi flew to Lagos to meet with a businessman who went by Henry, whom his good friend, Emeka Nwosu, said might help. Apparently, he led a group of moneymen who wanted a new Nigeria. Ifeanyi ground his teeth together in frustration. He hated having to beg for money, but he was out of options.

He also had never liked Lagos, which held the title of the largest city in Africa. For him, Lagos epitomized everything that was wrong with Nigeria. The city teemed with people who left behind their villages for a Western-style metropolis, as though fleeing their roots would solve their problems. The city served as the center of British influence for nearly a century and embodied Nigeria's colonial past. The old British clubs and colonial houses still existed as living monuments of that fact. But most of all, Ifeanyi hated the bleak contrast between wealth and poverty. Rents in Ikoyi and Victoria Island, the two nicest neighborhoods in Lagos, were as high as New York or London, while just a couple miles away, Nigerians dwelt in some of the worst slums in Africa. On every main thoroughfare, luxurious imported cars vied with the small yellow tricycle taxis and broken-down vans stuffed with people. Despite its tremendous wealth, its infrastructure was woefully inadequate.

Ifeanyi took out his phone. 12:43 pm. A few minutes until his meeting. He had left Port Harcourt early that morning and had arrived in Lagos an hour ago. Eschewing a comfortable taxi ride from the airport, Ifeanyi had opted for the overcrowded vans that most average Nigerians relied on. Sweat seeped through his new dress shirt while his suit jacket lay on his knees, but he didn't care. He hated all things "posh," as they used to say in school. The two men squeezed next to him argued the whole way about the failings of the Nigerian national soccer team. Soccer provided a convenient distraction for many people. Distractions were fine, provided they didn't take away from the main focus. It bothered Ifeanyi that soccer was like a religion for some. For the fanatics, it provided meaning in their lives. How could he get people like that to see the reality of things? Violence. Violence was the key. Only violence would shake them out of their false religion and see the importance of the cause.

In the city center, Ifeanyi hailed a cab for the remainder of his trip to Ikoyi. Emeka Nwosu, his friend who had set up the meeting, had insisted Ifeanyi buy a suit and tie before the trip. After the ride in the crowded van, the air conditioning in the taxi helped him dry off and gave him a chance to think about how to handle the conversation with this fellow Henry. What was his game? Ifeanyi would have to do his best to hide his contempt for moneymen, people like his brother, who lived in Lagos and to whom Ifeanyi had not spoken in a dozen years.

He got out of his cab on Glover Road and scanned both directions before entering a nondescript metal gate with the street number painted in white. Dressed the part and with his British public-school training and his upper-class British accent, Ifeanyi would not raise any suspicions. But he had to do his best to hide his contempt for the people inside.

Across the street, another taxi pulled up and sat idle while Ifeanyi walked through the gate. The Nigerian in the back seat paid his driver and pretended not to notice which building Ifeanyi had entered. Rather than follow Ifeanyi inside, he walked a short way up the street and began bargaining with a vendor selling clay pots along the side of the road. The man was dressed smartly like a Nigerian businessman. His navy suit was close-fitting, showing off his muscular body. He kept the jacket unbuttoned so the bulge from the pistol under his jacket was barely noticeable.

The man carried on bargaining with the vendor. His disinterest only made the vendor try that much harder to make a sale. The spot gave the man a clear view of the gate but kept him out of the line of sight for anyone exiting. Ifeanyi had not seen him on the flight from Port Harcourt. Godwin Ogbe's instructions had been quite clear: scope out the criminal activity Ifeanyi was up to and then arrest him for questioning. Godwin wanted the arrest to happen in Lagos, far from Ifeanyi's base of power. By the time his friends in Port Harcourt discovered something was wrong, Godwin's men would have extracted all the information they needed.

The man kept a close eye on who was coming and going, trying to spot the person Ifeanyi was meeting. He didn't want to make the arrest in such a posh neighborhood. The question running through the man's mind was where Ifeanyi would go next. Wherever it was, Godwin's man would not be far behind.

143

•••

Inside the gate, Ifeanyi strolled across a clean gravel car park filled with a half-dozen expensive foreign cars. Without paying them any attention, he walked through the entrance of a small restaurant. Unlike in many parts of the world, restaurants in Lagos that catered to a wealthy clientele often liked to keep a low profile. The resulting exclusivity and good food made this particular place a popular lunch spot with the Ikoyi business crowd. Ifeanyi waited near the hostess. He had been told his lunch companion would recognize him. Not wanting to appear nervous, he asked for a menu and glanced over the items, quickly choosing what he wanted before surveying the room. Every table seemed engrossed in its own conversation, and no one had taken notice of him. One couple was clearly enjoying their wine, which provided a convenient distraction for him while he waited. No one would pay him any notice.

"Mr. Okoye." Ifeanyi turned his head to see a man a little shorter than himself, well-dressed in an expensive suit with a protruding belly and flecks of gray hair. His accent revealed he also had gone to a British boarding school.

"You can call me Henry. I'm pleased to make your acquaintance," the man said, offering his somewhat limp hand. Ifeanyi closed the menu and shook Henry's hand while trying to read the eyes of the other man, who seemed unintimidated by Ifeanyi's intense gaze and offered a thin smile. What was Henry getting out of supporting him? Ifeanyi guessed he had to involved in the oil industry in some way. Pushing out the international oil companies, or even rattling them, could profit Henry immensely, Ifeanyi surmised.

"Let's find a seat," Ifeanyi said. He turned to the hostess. "Two for lunch." The hostess grabbed one menu for Henry and led the way.

Approaching a table in the center of the small dining area, Henry gently touched the hostess's arm. "If we could have that table in the corner, I would be much obliged."

"Of course, sir," the hostess replied, a little taken aback by Henry's excessive politeness.

Once they had seated, Henry said, "I would like some mineral water, please." Ifeanyi had not taken his eyes off Henry the whole time.

"And for you, sir?" the hostess asked Ifeanyi.

Without looking at her, he replied, "The same."

The two men sat silently for a moment while Henry took out a pack of Benson & Hedges. "Do you smoke?" He offered the pack to Ifeanyi, who merely shook his head. Henry exhaled the smoke carefully to the side so that it did not get in Ifeanyi's face.

"So, Henry, what public school did you attend?" Ifeanyi asked, referring to the fancy boarding schools in England, which had longstanding rivalries. It was a convenient way to size up the man across the table.

"Rugby."

"I'm a Harrovian," Ifeanyi replied, trying to hide a subtle smile. Harrow's reputation was far better than that of Rugby.

Henry ignored the comparison. "It is a pleasure finally to meet you," he said. "We share a similar vision for Nigeria."

"Do we?" Ifeanyi instinctively distrusted wealthy men in Nigeria. So few of them earned their money without the taint of corruption.

"Yes." Henry took another drag on his cigarette and let the smoke settle into his lungs before exhaling again. "I'd like to see legitimate development in this country, but in order to do that, Nigerians must control the oil. The vested interests are too well entrenched. Violence is the only way to change things. As your friend Emeka has no doubt mentioned to you, I represent a collection of businessmen here in Lagos who, for various reasons, support your efforts. We understand you need financial help to pursue your plans."

"We do." Ifeanyi wondered if they knew how desperately they needed the help.

"Before we commit funds, I wanted to get a better sense of your strategy. You can understand, I'm sure, that our financial support exposes us to certain risks."

"I can assure you, Henry, that your risks are no greater than those my men and I are taking." Ifeanyi could hear the harsh edge in his voice, his irritation tensing the muscles of his face. "We will unleash a sudden shock to the international oil companies and rattle their corporate masters overseas. As you know, some IOCs already want to scale back their efforts. A series of coordinated attacks would drive them out for good."

"Potentially." Henry took a long final drag from his cigarette before delicately crushing it in an ashtray. "And then what? What happens to the oil then?" Ifeanyi smiled. They were finally getting down to business.

Before Ifeanyi spoke, their waiter appeared. They both ordered their respective dishes, Henry without even looking at the menu. Once the waiter left, Ifeanyi continued, "The oil is a secondary concern to me."

"Yes, but the oil has to be managed by someone. Your influence could make the difference in terms of who has ultimate control. We wouldn't want our precious national resources to end up with people who don't support your development goals."

So that's how this will work, Ifeanyi thought to himself. They give a paltry sum of money in return for access to billions of dollars' worth of oil reserves.

"What specific support would you want from me?" he said aloud. "What would it include?"

"That will depend. I want us to be friends, Ifeanyi. My colleagues want to be friends. Friends help other friends out. It's not the 'how' that matters in Nigeria. It's the 'for whom'. Surely a man of your experience can understand that. But when the time comes, we'll need your public support."

"Yes," Ifeanyi responded coldly. "If you know anything about me— and I'm certain you've done your research—you know that I'm loyal to my friends."

"Very well. I'll take that as an agreement. Let me talk to my colleagues. We will communicate directly with your friend Emeka to arrange the details. My friends will want more concrete assurances."

"I'm sure they will. I'm also certain you have an idea of what that will look like." Ifeanyi could see the greed in Henry's eyes and wondered what his plan was. After Ifeanyi had the money, anything could happen. He had to keep his anger in check until then.

"Excellent. Much depends on how successful you are. We are committed to that. And be sure to keep a low profile," Henry cautioned. "Any investment in you is worthless if you get arrested. Some of these government men are wiser than you think." The sudden change in tone from politeness to condescension amused Ifeanyi. Anyone arrogant enough to advise Ifeanyi on his own safety must think he could control events. This was a man who thought he was in charge. That illusion of control meant "Henry," or whatever his real name was, and his colleagues were willing to take a big risk. It remained to be seen how substantial the investment would be.

Both men ate their meals in relative silence, punctured by a few comments on the weather and the governor of Lagos's new program for infrastructure improvements. When the meal was done, no bill arrived, which was just as well with Ifeanyi. It avoided the awkward discussion over the bill and Ifeanyi's eventual capitulation out of deference. Playing the role of suppliant was something he preferred to avoid.

Still, Ifeanyi's lunch companion intrigued him. He was someone who

147

thought he could have it all, blind to the trade-offs that came with his materialism. What if he lost his precious money? Would he still value the cause? Ifeanyi doubted it. That was always how you could tell what someone truly valued. Take away their comforts. Put them in a desperate situation and you'd see what mattered most, what their center of value was, what they put their true faith in.

Once outside the restaurant, Ifeanyi waved down the first taxi he saw. He got in quickly and never bothered to look if anyone was following him. His mind was preoccupied making preparations. How much would this Henry and his cronies give them, and would it be enough? Ifeanyi checked the time on his phone. He had a few hours before his plane left.

Ifeanyi made the impulse decision to get out at Balogun Street on Lagos Island, which had the largest outdoor market in the city. He wanted to buy something colorful and fun for Olabisi as thanks for all she had done since his release from prison. Wandering through the stalls, Ifeanyi thought about the peace of a domestic life, a life he knew he would never experience. Maybe it would happen after all the violence was over. Olabisi would make a great wife. Ifeanyi looked over the different fabrics and tried to think what she might like. A blue scarf caught his eye, and he walked over to take a closer look.

Ten steps behind Ifeanyi, Godwin Ogbe's security man dodged someone pushing a cart of bread. The distance between him and Ifeanyi began to narrow. Ifeanyi turned around to check out the stalls on the other side of the crowded street. Godwin's man was weaving between people too quickly for it to be a coincidence. Ifeanyi caught the man's expression and realized he had been followed.

Adrenaline pulsed through his body. Pretending like he did not see his pursuer, Ifeanyi walked diagonally across the street, rapidly closing the distance to the man, who couldn't change direction without making his intentions obvious.

Godwin's man reached for the gun underneath his suit jacket. Ifeanyi caught the rapid motion out of the corner of his eye. They were nearly on top of each other. Instinctively, Ifeanyi brought his right arm down on the man's forearm. The action took Godwin's man by surprise and the force of the blow knocked the gun to the pavement. As the man reached down to pick up his weapon, Ifeanyi put his left hand on the back of the man's head and brought it down onto Ifeanyi's right knee, which he lifted rapidly for maximum impact. The force of the blow broke the man's nose and left him stunned.

Using his powerful upper body, Ifeanyi thrust the man onto the pavement and snatched up the handgun by its barrel. Without thinking, Ifeanyi brought the butt of the gun down on the man's forehead. Blood spattered the pavement. Two more rapid blows in the same spot, and Ifeanyi knew his skull was cracked. Just as the crowd began to realize what had happened, Ifeanyi was on his feet moving swiftly away. The whole incident lasted no more than ten seconds.

Ifeanyi was already halfway down the block when the first person screamed. Glancing down at his right sleeve, he noticed it was covered with the man's blood. Commotion was building behind him. He ducked into the first alley he saw and took off his suit jacket. No one followed him. Working quickly, he pulled out his wallet and phone and put them into the pockets of his trousers. Then he used his suit jacket to wipe any handprints off the gun before dabbing the few spots of blood he noticed on his right leg. The jacket had been custom made for him the week before in Port Harcourt and had no identifying tags. Wrapping the gun in his jacket, he walked back out onto the main street. Twenty feet down the road he stuffed his jacket into a trash can and pulled a piece of trash over it. Without waiting to see if he was noticed, he crossed the street and began walking to the Carter Bridge in the distance.

As Ifeanyi passed one of the street sellers, he noticed a cheap khaki jacket for sale, the type that fits tightly around the waist and zips up the front. He wasn't sure if there were any bloodstains on his shirt and wanted something to cover himself up for the plane trip to Port Harcourt.

"How much?" Ifeanyi barked at the man standing next to his wares.

Ifeanyi noticed the fear in the man's eyes and took a breath before saying more calmly, "How much money for that jacket?"

"Four thousand naira," the man replied, his eyes darting down the street at the commotion in the distance. Ifeanyi knew he could bargain him down, but he didn't want to waste time. He handed over the money and snatched the jacket out of the seller's hand. As he put the jacket on, he looked for the nearest taxi.

Approaching an open taxi window, he ordered, "Murtala Muhammad. The domestic airport." He climbed into the back seat and then asked, "How much?"

"Three thousand naira," the driver said. Ifeanyi merely waved him onward, indicating he agreed with the price. Then he allowed him-self to sink into the seat. The man he'd assaulted must have followed him from Port Harcourt. He knew Godwin Ogbe. Godwin would not have entrusted his arrest to someone in Lagos. He wanted that pleasure for himself so he could control any interrogation that followed. In that case, the Lagos police might not be able to identify the dead man right away. He had to rely on that fact. The last thing Ifeanyi wanted was Godwin Ogbe waiting for him at the Port Harcourt airport.

Chapter 19

Port Harcourt

When Ifeanyi Okoye stepped off the plane in Port Harcourt, he glanced around the tarmac in front of him, trying to be as discreet as possible among the passengers jostling to get down the metal stairs. No security men were waiting for him, but he knew it was just a matter of time before Godwin Ogbe would be looking for him. Fortunately, he reasoned to himself, the authorities could not prove anything. Lagos was a violent place. He doubted any eyewitness could identify him. Many in Lagos might know him by reputation, but few outside Port Harcourt knew what he looked like. That that would not prevent Godwin and his henchmen from bringing him in for questioning, and the questioning would not be the soft kind. He had to get his papers and laptop out of his apartment, and fast.

Ifeanyi took the precaution of getting dropped off a half mile from where he lived. As usual, there were street vendors selling a range of goods, and Ifeanyi bought new pants, a new shirt, and a baseball cap. He wanted to blend into the crowd as much as possible. After changing in a restaurant bathroom, he approached his apartment from the opposite side of the street, which gave him a better view of anyone who might be lingering by his door. Trans Amadi Road was busy with pedestrians, and Ifeanyi walked with the flow of the crowd on the sidewalk. Only his beard might give him away to someone on the lookout for him. Ifeanyi avoided eye contact with the people he recognized along the side of the road. He didn't want to draw any unnecessary attention to himself. About a hundred feet from his door, he paused and pretended to examine the oranges that one woman had for sale. He turned toward his apartment and scanned the road for anything out of the ordinary. Everything seemed normal, at first. But then he spotted them.

Ten feet from the door, a car was parked with its engine running. Two men sat in the front seat, not talking to each other. Ifeanyi, staying on the opposite side of the street, moved closer. He glanced over again. The car had not moved. He began running through scenarios in his head. How could he get to the apartment without anyone seeing? What if they found his laptop? Would they be able to crack his passcode? Maybe he could convince someone to enter the apartment for him. If they were here, surely—

"Welcome back to town." The voice from behind him interrupted Ifeanyi's thoughts. He considered making a run for it but didn't know if the man had a gun. There was little he could do.

"I suppose I should walk over and see your friends," Ifeanyi replied loudly without turning around. He wasn't sure how the people around him might react.

"That's right. You have some explaining to do. Start walking."

Ifeanyi turned toward the government car and casually began to cross the street. The traffic was light for that time of day. He had to pause to let several cars go by. How far behind him was that man? He jogged across during a break in the traffic and knew the man would have to rush to keep up. Without warning, Ifeanyi turned. The man was right behind him, and Ifeanyi grabbed him by his right shoulder. Using his strength and the man's momentum from running, Ifeanyi flung him into oncoming traffic and sprinted back to the opposite side of the street. He heard cars honking and tires scarring the pavement. He didn't look back for fear it would slow him down.

A gunshot went off somewhere behind him, and Ifeanyi ran down the small road that connected Trans Amadi with the street behind it. He had been a champion sprinter at boarding school in England and relied on that speed now. Reaching the smaller parallel street, Ifeanyi moved to his left behind the nearest building to protect himself from any bullets that might come his way. Frantically, he looked around. Ten feet ahead, a young man straddled an okada, or motorcycle, while chatting with a young woman. Okadas were technically illegal within the city limits of Port Harcourt, but the law was rarely enforced as long as they stayed off the main roads. Rushing to the okada, Ifeanyi glanced back over his shoulder at the entrance to the alley but saw no one yet.

"Man, take me away from here!" Ifeanyi insisted. Bewildered, the young man looked back at Ifeanyi. "Five thousand naira to take me away. Now!" Ifeanyi said.

The young man nodded to Ifeanyi, who hopped onto the back of the small motorcycle. The driver waved to his girlfriend and started the engine. Okadas were unstable and often death traps in the chaotic Nigerian traffic. People who could afford other options avoided them. But good okada drivers were fearless around any obstacle, which was just what Ifeanyi needed.

The okada sped down the street with Ifeanyi holding on to the young man's torso. He looked back. A man stood near the alley and was aiming a gun in their direction. "Faster!" Ifeanyi whispered. The driver aggressively rotated the bike handle downward, and the engine kicked into high gear. The sudden burst of speed helped them dodge the bullet. The loud crack was unmistakable. The driver now had the bike at top speed.

"We need to lose them! Quickly!" Ifeanyi said. The driver nodded.

He knew his own life was now on the line. He didn't dare turn his head while going full speed, dodging the loose collection of cars and people scattered in their way. The okada wound through several back streets and reached the expressway, where the driver had to slow down. Ifeanyi hopped off the back and quickly pulled out five thousand naira, handing it to the driver, who didn't wait before he sped off in another direction.

Darting in and out of the late afternoon expressway traffic jam, Ifeanyi made it to the other side of the road. He saw no one behind him, but took no risks and alternated between walking and jogging for another ten minutes to Obasanjo Way. Walking up the street, he entered the parking lot of Victory Bank, one of four banks on that stretch of road. Sweat poured down his face, and he could feel the dampness in his armpits. He hoped the guards would not prevent him from entering the bank. He took off his hat and rolled up his sleeves to make himself seem more confident, more in control.

Like he would at many Nigerian bank branches, to enter Victory Bank, Ifeanyi had to walk into a circular sealed-off antechamber. On the other side of the bulletproof Plexiglas, the guard eyed him suspiciously but let him enter the bank without problems. Walking into the main room, Ifeanyi moved to the line to wait for a teller. He could see Olabisi helping a customer. When he got to the front of the line, a teller opened up, but he indicated he was waiting for Olabisi. The man behind him in line smirked and then went to the open window staffed by a man.

"Well, sir, how can I help you today?" Olabisi asked, trying to hide a smile. This was the first time Ifeanyi had seen Olabisi in her new job.

"I'm here to inquire about a deposit. I wondered if I could speak with your manager about it. It's a large deposit."

"Hold on one second." Olabisi stepped back and picked up her phone. After speaking a few words, she said, "Follow me, sir," and indicated a set of stairs at the end of the line of tellers. At the top of the stairs, she knocked on frosted glass door that had the word **President** painted on it in black letters.

"Come in," a voice called from within.

Once the door was closed, Emeka Nwosu got up from his chair to greet his friend. "Ifeanyi, you look like you just ran a race." Emeka's expensively tailored suit and brightly patterned tie contrasted sharply with Ifeanyi's cheap, sweat-soaked clothes.

"I will tell you about that in a moment. Any word on the money from Lagos?"

"Take a seat. Olabisi, you stay too." Emeka went back to his desk and sat down. "This morning we received a transfer of five million naira."

"A good start," Ifeanyi remarked, "but far less than we hoped for."

"My contacts said they wanted to pay in installments in case any difficulties arose. They were especially concerned that if something happened to you, the whole effort would collapse. They don't want to lose their investment, so to speak."

"Right," Ifeanyi replied and began tapping his finger on the plastic armrest. "Did you tell them we have payments pending to several MEND commanders? We need the money up front for anything to happen. Five million isn't enough."

"I mentioned that to them. They want to be in control of the situation."

"So, they want the attacks to happen but not to be too drastic. What game are they playing?" Ifeanyi put his hands together and tried to think, but he was too distracted.

"What should we do?" Olabisi asked.

"We might have to push our time frame out a bit," Emeka replied. "Delay things by a few weeks. That might reassure them and give us more time to make sure everything is in place."

"No!" Ifeanyi's voice was stern. "We'll have to seek other options."

"Other options? What other options do we have? Money like that doesn't just appear." Emeka took a deep breath to calm himself down and said, "We can afford to wait."

"We can't. Not anymore."

"What do you mean, Ifeanyi?" Olabisi asked. The tone of her voice revealed her concern.

"Godwin Ogbe has men trailing me."

"How do you know?" Emeka asked, leaning forward with his forearms on his large executive desk, his eyes narrowing in on Ifeanyi.

"In Lagos, one of his men got a little too close. I reacted."

"And?" In the silence that followed, they all could hear the ticking of the fancy clock on Emeka's desk. Ifeanyi remained still, and Emeka and Olabisi could see in his eyes what had happened.

"Bloody hell!" Emeka blurted out, slamming his hand down on his leather-topped desk.

"And when I arrived home, they were waiting for me at my apartment. They must know that I killed their man."

"They'll hunt you down," Olabisi said quietly. "You need to be safe. Where will you hide?"

"You should go to the countryside and wait there," Emeka declared. "This is moving too fast. Now we have to postpone things. And if the people in Lagos find out about this, there'll be no more funds."

"We can't stop our preparations now, Emeka," Ifeanyi said, blotting the sweat from his brow with his sleeve. "Things will work out. We have to think clearly and act with speed. Can I stay with you, Bisi, in the meantime?"

"Of course. My place is not very big, but I have a couch. Do you think they might come looking for you there?"

"That's not likely. Your couch sounds perfect to me. I'll have to travel around a lot anyhow," Ifeanyi replied. "And they've now got my computer.

Let's hope they don't know what to do with it."

Emeka remained silent.

"How are the preparations going? Any more word from Mama San-dra?" Olabisi asked.

"No," Ifeanyi replied. "She had indicated she was interested. I'm confident she'll come through."

"But where will she get her weapons from?" Emeka asked. "Her ex-plosives?"

The tension in the room was palpable.

"I'm not sure," Ifeanyi replied. "To be honest, hers is the only part of this whole operation I'm not concerned about." Ifeanyi looked at Emeka. "Don't worry, my friend. Anything worth doing has uncertainty. Believe me. We will succeed."

"Don't get caught, Ifeanyi," Emeka said. "I would lose everything."

"Emeka, if I get caught, you will be the least of my worries."

Chapter 20

Port Harcourt

"I'm surprised you decided to come, Julia."

Chris Reed was walking just ahead of her as they crossed the parking lot of God's Redeeming Grace Church in Port Harcourt. It was a large parking lot, and Chris guessed there were already over two hundred cars in it. Other worshippers, dressed in shirts, slacks, and colorful dresses, moved around them toward a large building that looked almost like a warehouse.

"This is a sociological trip for me, Chris. Nothing more."

"I'm still glad you are coming," Chris replied. "This is an inside look at another part of Nigeria. You can't understand the country without experiencing its churches. At least that's what Paul says."

"Paul would say that."

"I can't believe you haven't been to a church since you were twelve."

"Eleven," Julia corrected him. "I was eleven when I stopped going to church."

Chris smiled. "You know what I mean. I'm always surprised by how many secular people critique Christianity without ever having gone to a church as an adult."

"Well, you people don't exactly get the best press in the US."

"But you'd think that smart, liberal-minded people would actually check it out before making judgments."

"I'm here, aren't I?" Julia said with a mock defensive tone.

"You're a rarity. Last year I was at a cocktail party and some guy started berating Christians. When I asked him if had been to church, he said no. When I asked him if he had ever read the Bible, the most influential book in history, he said no. But he had no qualms having fully formed, and quite emotional things to say about Christianity."

"You have to admit there is some pretty bad stuff in the Bible."

"Like any ancient text, it requires interpretation. There is some weird stuff in Buddhist texts too. Or the Bhagavad Gita? That takes place in the middle of a battle. My point is that in the US, secular people judge Christianity differently. They tend not to be rational about it."

"That's because it does a lot of harm," Julia said.

"It does even more good, if you bother to take a closer look."

"Whatever. By the way, do you smile this much every time you go to church? I thought you told me you disagreed with a lot of what this church preached."

"That's true. You'll see." Chris hopped around to face her and began walking backwards. "But maybe I'm smiling because I get to spend time with you." After the night in Julia's apartment, Chris had been looking forward to seeing her again. Church was a good excuse to invite her along.

"I have to admit, your enthusiasm makes this a less painful experience."

"I'll be sure to be extra enthusiastic for you." Chris turned back to the church and reached down for Julia's hand.

"You sure that's not too much of a public display of affection? This is a church, after all."

"No one here knows us. And, as far as they know, this is how friends behave in the US." Julia let out a small chuckle. She wasn't complaining. And Chris was right, none of Julia's colleagues went to church here.

Fifty feet behind Chris and Julia, Olabisi Bob-Manual clutched her Bible tightly with her right hand. The past several days had been stressful with Ifeanyi moving into her small apartment and the constant concern that something might happen to him. If there was any time that she needed God's guidance and protection, it was now. God's Redeeming Grace Church had been Olabisi's spiritual home for several years. Coming here always made her feel more at peace and connected to God. She hoped the pastor would have a good message for them that morning. Even though she knew some of the people in the crowd around her, she preferred to focus her thoughts on God as she entered the sanctuary, ready to receive the Holy Spirit.

Julia and Chris made their way through the crowd gathering in front of the church and entered through one of the main doors. The space was set up like an indoor amphitheater with a circular lower area and upper deck. They walked to the front and sat in the first row. Chris wanted them to have the full experience. An elevated stage, reminiscent of a boxing arena, rose up in front of them, surrounded on all sides by seats. To their left were several musical instruments, and directly next to them stood the choir. Closer to the stage, air conditioners blew cold air on the congregation, though none were directed at them. Large television screens were mounted on the upper deck in each corner. Chris glanced around at the steadily growing group of people. Chris and Julia were the only two white people in the congregation of nearly fifteen hundred.

"Why this particular church?" she asked.

"Someone I met in Port Harcourt goes here, and I wanted to check it out. He is a good guy."

"They are probably all good guys to you," Julia remarked. She noticed that they were the only two people without their Bibles on their laps. "You forgot your Bible," she said.

"I guess we both did. I'm sure they'll show the relevant verses on

160

the screens. You ready?"

Julia shrugged. "As ready as I'll ever be."

When the band started, Julia was startled by the volume. She was tempted to put her hands to her ears but didn't want to be rude. "Are they always this loud?" Julia shouted over the music.

"It helps you get fully immersed."

After maybe ten minutes of music, a new song began as a woman climbed onstage. She started to sing, and the people in the congregation rose to their feet.

"Let's stand," Chris said, reaching out to grab Julia's arm. Everyone around them started to clap along to the music, which Julia refused to do. Chris began clapping, and Julia smiled when she noticed how off the beat he was. She tried to listen to the lyrics, but the sound system was poor and the singer had a thick Nigerian accent. Julia could hear references to Jesus and his awesomeness. One man in front of the choir was dancing in circles and swinging his arms around.

"Is that guy okay?" Julia yelled into Chris's ear.

Chris looked over and shrugged his shoulders. "Don't be so judgmental. Try to see things from a different perspective. It's called being open-minded," he yelled back.

After about ten minutes of singing, a man in a suit got onstage and the music wound down. The singer left the stage, and the man approached the clear plastic lectern.

"Praise the Lord!" he yelled into the handheld microphone. "Praise the Lord! Praise the Lord!"

The congregation shouted back, "Praise the Lord!"

"Praise the Lord for our salvation in Jesus Christ!" The leader started speaking faster. "Praise the Lord for our salvation in Jesus Christ!"

The congregation responded repeatedly with "Amen!"

The speaker's pace quickened even more. "Praise Jesus Christ, who saved us from sin! Praise Jesus, who brings us what we need! God is good! God is great! We love the Lord, who saves us!" The phrases rose to a crescendo. Chris responded to each phrase with his "Amen" in line with the congregation. Julia observed, subtly shaking her head.

After a couple of minutes, the speaker stopped. He then said, "Let us now pray." From his pocket he drew a folded sheet of white paper, which he laid on the lectern. The words of the prayer were posted on the screens overhead.

"Lord Jesus," the speaker began, "as we lift up our praise to you in this month of May, let us look back on the month and see when you were granting us your blessing." The prayer continued in the same vein for another couple minutes, each phrase highlighting something in the past month for which the people should be thankful.

In the next section of seats over from Julia and Chris, Olabisi Bob-Manual raised her hands into the air. She closed her eyes and let the Holy Spirit wash over her. Without thinking she began to pray, the words pouring out of her, all of the emotion and fear over Ifeanyi's dangerous situation. Her soul overflowed with thanks that he was able to escape arrest and that so many in the delta had welcomed him. He was truly a beloved servant of God and the people. Into her mind came all the blessings of her work as a bank teller. A job that paid and allowed her to care for her elderly mother. It was so much bounty. Thank you, God. God is great. God is merciful. Thank you. Thank you. Olabisi felt the Spirit subside in her and heard the pastor at the lectern say, "Amen." She opened her eyes. Sitting down, she felt at peace.

The man on stage slowly walked off and was replaced by another man at the lectern. He too took out a sheet of white paper from his pocket and said, "Let us pray." Once more, the words appeared on the screens above.

Julia leaned over to Chris. "Are we really going to go through this again?"

"Try to put yourself in the minds of the people here, Julia." Chris looked her in the eyes in an attempt to shame her into taking this seriously, and she turned her attention to the screens.

The new pastor began, "Father, we pray to you that you might grant us your salvation in the month ahead. And not just salvation for us, but for our family and friends. Give us life, health and prosperity..." The pastor listed out the many things that people might want in their lives in the coming month. "Amen" echoed around the amphitheater throughout the prayer.

Olabisi rose again and felt the Holy Spirit return to her. She became weak in the knees and cried out, "Jesus!" The prospect of the month ahead was too much. She let it all pour out to the Lord. May Ifeanyi live! May the violence finally free Nigeria of foreign interference! May the people here have some relief of their suffering! Lord, you know these people love you. Show them your mercy and blessing. Let them have abundance and an end to their ills. In Jesus's name! May his name be praised! Olabisi again felt the Spirit in the room begin to subside and heard the pastor add, "Amen." Everyone took their seats.

A well-dressed man in his thirties climbed onto the stage. Instead of a white sheet of paper, he had with him an e-tablet, which he placed on the lectern. The sermon was about to begin. "Our message for today," he said, looking around at the congregation, "is the mystery of salvation." The preacher was considerably louder than the people who had led the prayers and was nearly shouting into the microphone he held.

"The first message the Bible has about the mystery of salvation is that the past is gone. We live in a new creation. Do you hear that? If something bad happened to you yesterday, don't worry! You are a new creation. Paul writes in 2 Corinthians 5:17..."

Olabisi raised her hands up. Yes, thank you, Lord. The past does not determine me. Thank you for allowing me to be a new person in you. You give me the courage to fight for freedom in the delta with Ifeanyi. You strengthen me. I am not a scared little girl anymore. Olabisi felt the Lord was speaking to her through the preacher.

"...now that you know that the past is gone, you can focus on salvation. Salvation comes to us through the cross of Jesus. And what is this salvation of the cross? It is riches, long life, healing, and righteousness. Revelation 5:12 says, 'Worthy is the Lamb that was slaughtered to receive power and wealth and wisdom and might and honor and glory and blessing!' That is salvation."

In the front row Julia let out a noticeable sigh. Turning to Chris, she shouted into his ear, "If you believe in Jesus, you get a long life and riches? That's salvation? Why do people believe this stuff?"

Chris looked and her shook his head, then pointed to the stage. "Listen," he said.

The pastor continued. "But some of you here might be wondering, 'Why have I not received my own riches? Why am I or a family member sick?' The answer is clear in the Bible. Knowledge is the key to salvation. Proverbs says..."

Julia turned back to Chris. She couldn't help herself. "So, I need knowledge to get long life and riches. Does a good college education count?"

Chris ignored this latest commentary of Julia's.

"...You don't take the word of God seriously enough. God says in Revelation 3:16, 'So, because you are lukewarm, and neither cold nor hot, I am about to spit you out of my mouth.' You must love the Lord with all of your heart! Don't be lukewarm..."

Olabisi chided herself for the ignorance she'd shown for so long. She was far too lukewarm in her belief. It had gotten her nowhere. Ever since she joined this church and committed fully to the Lord, her life had changed. What blessings she had received from God's hand. Her job. A clear purpose in life. Tears began to form in her eyes, and she wiped them away.

After the preacher finished, an older man walked onto the stage and the whole congregation quieted down.

"Brothers and sisters, it has been a great day to worship the Lord! The Lord is good to us when we are good to the Lord." Loud "amens" came from the congregation in response. "Now we ask you to be generous with your offering. We are told to give without counting the cost. Isn't that what you want God to do for you? To give to you, not according to what you deserve, but abundantly and without hesitation? It is time for you to show how much you want the Lord's favor."

When the offering basket came by Chris, he deposited a five-hundred-naira note. Disgusted, Julia passed it along and added nothing. Shortly thereafter, there was a final benediction, and they got up to leave.

"What did you think?" Chris asked Julia once they got outside.

"It was an experience."

"New experiences are a good thing. Let's go have lunch with Paul and Rotimi."

"Where were they during this spectacle? I'm surprised they missed it."

"They went to a different church," Chris said. "Paul usually visits different churches so he can keep up relationships with the pastors in town."

"I guess he's seen it all."

"So, I hear you went to church this morning, Julia." Paul was at the kitchen counter cutting vegetables for brunch. Rotimi was next to him and broke into a slight smile.

"I did, Mr. Missionary. It was something else."

Paul turned around to face Julia, who was sitting at the kitchen table with Chris. "Tell us what you learned."

"I can't say that I learned anything new about Christianity, considering that the service only reinforced all of my previously held beliefs."

"Ah, I see," Paul responded. "Still a little skeptical,"

"How could I not be? The service was all about money, how you could become rich and live a long time! Heck, we all want that!" Julia threw her hands up in exasperation.

"It wasn't only about money, Julia," Chris added. "Let's be fair."

"Okay. It was about giving yourself over to Jesus and then getting money. And if you don't have money, then you clearly need to recommit yourself to Jesus. How is that not being fair?"

"Dude, which church did you guys go to?" Paul asked Chris.

"God's Redeeming Grace."

Paul chuckled. "Pastor David is a prosperity gospel preacher, for sure. That's pretty common in Port Harcourt."

"You say that like it's some kind of harmless diagnosis, as though it's not an issue," Julia said. Her frustration with the Christianity was starting to show. "If greed is the main problem of Nigeria with all its oil, then how is preaching about getting more money going to change that?"

"She's got a point, eh, Rotimi? Maybe we should give it all up." Paul looked to his shorter companion by his side, and Rotimi said nothing back. "I'm actually kinda curious what young Chris has to say about Pastor David. Time to see if all that fancy education can give us any insights." Paul had been carelessly waving the knife around in his hand as he spoke. "So, Chris, any thoughts?"

"Yeah, I'm also a little curious to hear this," Julia chimed in, adjusting herself in her seat to face Chris. "What about all the money talk?"

Chris took a deep breath. "Well," he started, feeling very put on the spot, "there is a lot about salvation being linked to long life and riches in the Old Testament, but from my reading it's more complicated than that. In the New Testament, Jesus and others are clear that money, while not bad in and of itself, has some major pitfalls. And, yes, the part where the preacher today claimed the cross is about long life and riches is just nonsense. The cross is an instrument of torture and death. Jesus died at thirty-three, voluntarily penniless."

"This is some of the stuff that Emmaus Ministries works on, Julia," Paul added. "We try to bring a closer fidelity to the text." Paul stopped himself, "Oh, I like that, a closer fidelity to the text. Rotimi, we should write that down." Paul nudged Rotimi, who broke into a broad smile. Chris loved seeing these little signs of affection between them.

"Why don't you just admit it is all a bunch of nonsense and ditch it?" Julia asked.

"Is it a bunch of nonsense?" Paul asked. "The average Nigerian has very little in terms of material wealth. It's hardly surprising that having more for one's family is a common prayer here. This is not the Upper West Side. And the churches here provide more community and support for those in need than the government does. Do you really think Nigeria would be better without the spiritual and material support of churches? Would you rather Nigerians get rid of Christianity and determine morality for themselves without the insights of Jesus or other holy men?"

"Frankly, yes!" Julia responded without hesitation. "I believe that we all have a natural moral compass within ourselves. Without the delusion of religion, we can focus on that."

"Now who is being naive?" Paul said. "Christianity gives us a chance to change people's souls, to invite them to a better life. It provides the type of community and social capital that people need to be happy. It also gives us a language that we can use to talk about morality. At least with Christianity I can point out greedy people and show them how they are not living a Christian life. Without religion, how do you determine what the morals of society should be? If some innate moral sense governs us, why don't we see it more often?"

"Most people can agree on what is moral. Be kind to your neighbor. Don't be too greedy or selfish."

"But how do we hold ourselves accountable even to those low standards?" Paul asked. "How do we not fall into justifications for our own selfishness?"

"Religion has the same issue as Secular Humanism, and it brings its own problems," Julia said.

"Of course it does, but Christianity has a text and a tradition that can guide us. I can talk to the pastors here in Port Harcourt and show them the problems with the prosperity gospel. How could I do that without the shared language and tradition of the faith? Yes, religion has its problems, but so do foreign NGOs like the New Africa Initiative."

"And how is that?" Julia raised her voice. "How do NGOs have problems?" Chris reached over and put his hand on Julia's lap to calm her down.

"Because by trying to take care of Nigeria's problems, you let the Nigerian government off the hook. Nigeria has the money to fight malaria, but why should they if you and the Gates Foundation take care of it?"

"We are helping people. Period," Julia asserted. "Anyway, it's not NGOs you should be attacking. What about the oil companies or the blood-sucking financiers?" Julia was now nearly yelling.

"Struck a nerve there, eh?" Paul retorted. "The New York girl doesn't like bankers?"

"I know too many of them."

"Including someone in your own family?"

"What's for brunch?" Chris asked, interrupting the conversation.

"Eggs with sautéed fresh vegetables and toast," Rotimi said, equally happy to ease the tension. "We have some good chili sauce that I made on the side, if you want it."

"Actually sounds pretty good right now," Julia admitted. "A lot more appetizing than talking about American capitalists."

Chapter 21

Port Harcourt

David Sloan's second stop in Port Harcourt, after dropping off his luggage at his hotel, was to tour the Octagon Petroleum facilities and to meet with one of their chief engineers. Ever since arriving in Port Harcourt, his senses had been on full alert, taking everything in. His career depended on this move, and he was trying not to second-guess himself. Catherine Dunlop kept planting little seeds of doubt in his mind, but Sloan felt in his gut that this was the time for boldness. He didn't want Catherine or Matt to distract him while he scoped out the Octagon compound, so he had them wait at the Novotel.

The Octagon Petroleum compound in Port Harcourt was surrounded by an eight-foot-high metal fence with barbed wire on top. When his driver reached the main entrance, he had to go through two security checks, complete with an armed guard checking beneath the car for explosives. Once inside, they followed a gently curving paved road that led to a large parking lot that was mostly full of cars. On each side of the road were well-manicured lawns that bordered a collection of buildings painted bright yellow, all with flat roofs, and all looking dated. Sloan guessed they had been built during the oil boom in the 1970s.

Some lower-level Octagon employee, who was Nigerian, met David at his car and escorted him to the main building. Most of the employees he saw were Nigerian, or at least David supposed they were Nigerian from the color of their skin.

Inside the main building, a security man talked with his escort before letting them through. Sloan followed his escort up a flight of concrete steps and down the corridor to their left. The walls were painted a boring off-white with various cheaply framed posters along the wall. Clearly, no one had spent much time or money on interior design. They stopped in front of a wooden door that had a nameplate under a small glass window that read Timothy McAuliffe. His escort knocked twice and then opened the door once he heard a voice on the other side.

"Welcome to Port Harcourt, Mr. Sloan," said Tim McAuliffe, coming around his plain metal desk to greet Sloan. McAuliffe wore a bright red Octagon Petroleum polo shirt and khakis. From his accent, Sloan guessed he was a Midwesterner.

"Impressive facilities, Mr. McAuliffe," Sloan lied as he reached out to shake Tim's hand. Tim had dark brown hair and a slender build. He looked bookish like most engineers he had met.

"Thank you, Mr. Sloan. I can't really claim much credit for it, but Octagon Petroleum does everything very professionally."

"Feel free to call me David. Mind if I call you Tim?"

"Tim's fine. Please, sit down." Tim McAuliffe's office had a couple worn wooden chairs and white walls with yet more framed posters depicting Octagon Petroleum's operations. On one wall was a detailed map of the delta region. David noticed different-colored pins and markings, which presumably highlighted all of Octagon's wells, pipelines, drilling rigs and flow stations. He was tempted to take a closer look at the map, but he didn't want to seem overly curious. The light in the room came from bright florescent lights on the ceiling and a window with cheap horizontal blinds. Not the most inspiring work environment.

David could tell that Tim McAuliffe was sizing him up as they sat across from each other. He guessed it was the first time Tim had met with a potential investor. He could see Tim shift anxiously in his seat, and small beads of sweat appeared on his temples. Olufemi Adebayo had told him Tim would answer any specific questions he might have about their Niger Delta operations. David considered toying with him by asking him increasingly aggressive technical questions until Tim had to say, "I don't know." It would be fun to watch Tim sweat even more, but David decided not to be cruel. He had a specific agenda.

"So, what do you miss most about home?" David asked. "I heard you arrived not long ago."

"Yeah, it's only been a few weeks. Honestly, I hate having guards everywhere and feeling like a prisoner. It sounds odd, but what I will most relish when I get back to Houston is walking down the street by myself."

"With your wife and kids?"

"Yes, with my wife and daughter."

"Family is what it's all about." David marveled at people who could be so simple and still somehow be happy. He steered Tim McAuliffe to the topic he wanted most to discuss. "They must be worried about your safety here."

"We don't talk about it."

"Is Nigeria as dangerous as I've heard?" Sloan asked.

"Hard to say. I spend most of my time behind the walls of this compound. Believe it or not, back during the worst of the violence, the insurgents attacked our compound in Warri. They say there is still a risk of kidnapping, but it hasn't happened in a while. They make sure we have insurance for that kind of thing."

"Sounds like that insurance is a wise investment. Any concern around here about a renewal of the insurgency?"

"The insurgency? Like violence? Oh God, I certainly hope not. People steal oil from the pipelines all the time. It's a major problem and one of the reasons I'm here. We have to decide which, if any, of our assets we want to sell. Olufemi's been pushing me hard on that. He says we need to focus on the most profitable wells and sell what we can while prices are strong."

"Sounds smart to me. I bet Olufemi has nothing but the company's best interests at heart," David assured him. "Seems like an honest chap to me."

"It's the NNPC that's the real problem," Tim offered. "That and the military."

"Say more," David encouraged him. "You have my full attention."

"As you probably know, the Nigerian National Petroleum Company—or NNPC—has a controlling interest in Octagon Petroleum in Nigeria. They own 55% of the business but invest zero capital. They are supposed to, but rarely do. Instead they just skim money off the top. Lord knows where it all goes. And the military is hopelessly corrupt. We have complained about the theft of oil for years. These days, they don't seem to care, although this past week they did foil a major attempt. We're hoping that means things will get safer."

"I'm sure things are getting safer by the day," David agreed. "What could possibly go wrong?"

"I don't know. This is my first time in Nigeria."

"What's your impression so far?"

"Whew!" Tim let out a big sigh. "It's not like any place I've been. There's money to be made, for sure. But I'm more of a numbers guy. The other day—" Tim stopped himself.

"Yes?" David asked, his voice calm and reassuring. "The other day what?"

"Well, the other day I went car shopping with one of my Nigerian colleagues. Paid for the car in cash. He had a duffle bag full of it. After he paid—and you'll never believe this—he took a gun from the trunk of his car and fired off a round into the back window of his brand-new Toyota Land Cruiser. I nearly jumped out of my skin. He wanted to be sure the windows were bulletproof."

Sloan could see from Tim's flushed face that he was in way over his head in Nigeria. Then again, if Tim were working for Sloan in Houston, he was just the kind of naively honest guy he'd want looking into the oil bunkering.

"That's Port Harcourt, I guess. By the way," David asked, "is there any way I could see some of the delta? I came all this way to make big decisions about investing with you. I think Nigerian oil and Octagon, in particular, are greatly undervalued. It would be a shame if I couldn't see a little more of how things operate on the ground. Just to put my mind at ease, you know."

"That's understandable. In fact, in a couple days, I'm heading to one of the villages in the delta. We are opening a new school. You can see the good work that Octagon is doing in Nigeria."

"I'd love that," David said. "I'm staying at the Novotel here in Port Harcourt. Just let me know where to be and when."

"You can ride out with me. That will save you the trouble of arranging security."

"How nice of you."

Tim reached out to shake David's hand. "Too bad you're not staying a little longer in Port Harcourt. It's nice to have another American to talk to. Life gets boring here."

"I'm sure the boredom is only temporary," David said.

•••

Peering through the tinted window from the back of his SUV, David Sloan made out the faded sign that read **Jack's Bar**. He guessed this qualified as a discreet place to meet even though it was dead smack in the middle of the Port Harcourt bustle. Crowded places could provide good cover, but he stuck out like a wine stain on a white dress. David got out of his car and walked between two people on the sidewalk who were looking at his SUV. He pushed open a swinging door with metal mosquito netting on it that made a loud noise as it swung back into place. The area in front looked more like a convenience store with stacks of candies, tobacco, and other nonperishable goods for sale. The Nigerian woman at the counter merely pointed down the hallway toward the back. David took the hint and walked in that direction. He wondered what she was thinking. A tall white guy in a three-thousand-dollar suit was probably not an everyday occurrence.

The long dark hallway opened up into a surprisingly bright and clean back bar with well-used green plastic chairs and tables. The walls were all open and covered in mosquito netting, which let a gentle breeze drift through. Port Harcourt was not as hot as Sloan had expected, which suited him just fine. At a table sat Eli Schrimpf, whom he hoped was more sober this time. Eli wore a blue polo with the Octagon Petroleum logo over the left breast. Must be the expat uniform, David mused to himself. But he wondered if it was wise for Eli to broadcast his employer in a place like this. Next to him sat a Nigerian. They were the only two in the bar.

"Dave," Eli's voice called out, a little too loud for David's liking. "Come meet my friend." David strode over and held out his hand. The

Nigerian stood up. David could tell this man liked his food. He was even more overweight than Eli and wore black tracksuit bottoms and a yellow t-shirt on top with the matching tracksuit warm-up jacket zipped up part-way. His handshake was disappointingly weak with not much feeling in it.

"David Sloan, meet Fela. Fela, this is the man I wanted you to meet, the American banker."

"How do you do?" Fela said, deep bass to his voice.

"I'm doing well. Thank you. May I sit?"

Eli nodded and pointed to the open seat. "Fela's mother was a big fan of the singer," Eli said by way of explanation.

"I'm not sure I follow you," David replied.

"Fela Kuti, the famous Nigerian singer. You've never heard of him?"

"Should I have?"

"I suppose that depends on how thorough your research of Nigeria has been," Eli said.

David ignored the unnecessary jab and wrote it off as a product of Eli's nervousness. "My visit to Nigeria has one purpose. I don't waste time on extraneous details."

"Right," Eli responded, sensing he might have gone too far, then added, "Fela is a commander in MEND. You've heard of the Movement for the Emancipation of the Niger Delta?"

The grandstanding of insignificant people like Eli Schrimpf rarely concerned David. He focused his gaze on Fela. So, this man is a killer, David reflected as he looked at the heavyset Nigerian. "What can you tell me about your plans?"

"You are very direct," Fela responded. He took a bite of the food in front of him and wiped his mouth with his paper napkin. "What do you want to know?" Fela's accent was heavy, and David had trouble making out his words.

"I want to know the extent of the plans, whether they will actually happen, and how much damage might be caused." David tried to gauge Fela's reaction. "I want to help," he added.

Fela stared at David before turning to Eli Schrimpf and asking, "Why should I trust this man?"

"That's a good question, Fela," Eli answered. "The answer is simple. He will make money if you attack the oil industry. Lots of money."

Fela smiled widely. "I feel like I know this man then very well. There are many people like him in Nigeria."

"He is a 'Big Man' in the United States," Eli added.

Fela nodded. "I am a MEND commander. Giving you this information could get me killed. If I come to harm because of you, I will kill you. You understand?"

David replied, "Yes. You are being quite clear." David resisted the urge to make any nervous movements.

"Good. For security, MEND commanders do not know what other commanders are doing. There is broad communication but few details. You understand?"

"It makes perfect sense to me, Fela."

"Good. One of the leaders of MEND, a true revolutionary, Ifeanyi Okoye, was released from prison not long ago. He contacted the old commanders. He contacted me to see if I would attack the refinery in Port Harcourt along with the supplies in the harbor at Onne. Onne provides all of the repair equipment for the offshore rigs."

"Do you intend to follow through and attack those targets?" David asked.

"Yes, we will destroy them. The security, especially in the harbor, is very light. This leader indicated that other big attacks would be going on at the same time."

"When will the attacks be carried out?"

"I do not know that for sure. He said to be ready by next week. We will be ready."

David sat back in his plastic chair, which was buckling under his weight. "What about the actual oil wells? Will production of oil be slowed?"

"Yes. I heard that Mama Sandra is involved. Mama will do her part."

"Who is Mama?" David asked Eli.

"Mama is the name given to a woman who organizes the local women in Bayelsa State and most of Rivers State," Eli Schrimpf explained. "I've never met her, only heard talk of her. Supposedly, she was organizing protests and actions against the oil companies back in the 1970s, long before anything started on a larger scale."

"Haha!" Fela laughed at the description of Mama. "You don't know the half of Mama, my friend. She organized the women of many communities for support against lazy and violent men and those who didn't take responsibility for their families. You do not trouble these women. Long ago, a man violently beat his wife, which happens." Fela shrugged his shoulders. "This woman was in Mama's group. Two days later, the man woke up without a penis. Some women had gotten him drunk and drugged him. They tied him, cut it off, and nailed it to his front door. Men are scared of Mama." Fela laughed again. "Nigerian men are tough, but they also love to have sex. Mama was very smart."

"American men also love to have sex," David said. He thought about the hot twenty-six-year-old he was banging back home. He made a mental note to text her on the return flight. "How did the women get away with it?"

"It was not women from that village but from other villages. The men of that village could do very little."

"If Mama is on board with the violence, we should be good. Remind me not to be in Nigeria then," David said. "I'd like to keep my manhood intact. One final question for you, Fela. You've been very helpful so far." Fela nodded. "Where do you get your money?"

"It always comes back to money. Different commanders get money in different ways. Some steal and sell oil, others kidnap and get ransom money. Some get money for not attacking. Some get money from the government. There is also money that comes from other sources. It depends. Ifeanyi has not paid me yet. He will have to pay me before I attack."

"And he didn't say when he would pay you?"

"'Soon' was all he said."

"Thank you," said David. "You've been most helpful. I wish you luck in your endeavor."

"And you, Mr. Sloan. I wish you luck in your moneymaking. Nigeria is a good place for you."

David stood up and turned to Eli Schrimpf. "Eli, good to see you. We'll be in touch soon."

"Wait." Eli stood and pulled David over to the corner of the bar, out of earshot of Fela, who returned to his food. "So, Dave, what about that payment you promised?"

"David. It's David. And I need to see how this insurgency plays out."

"Whoa, whoa, David. I've done my part. You owe me," Eli pleaded. "Don't make me blow the whistle on this one."

David Sloan thought for a moment. "Ok, I'll have my people wire you a hundred fifty now and a hundred fifty after the violence starts." David hated the uncertainty of the operation, given how much he was risking.

A smile appeared on Eli Schrimpf's face. "Good. That's good."

"Now let's just hope these insurgents are ready. The last thing we need is amateur hour."

Chapter 22

Bight of Bonny

"Silence!"

Fineface Pepple looked down the length of the motorboat. Some-one had been talking. The perpetrator would have to answer to him when they returned. In the darkness, the only light came from the faint half-moon above, and he could barely make out the shapes of the men with him. Pepple turned back toward the bow. The twenty-six-foot-long boat had an open deck where eight men of the Lord Rules Brigade, including him, sat with their AK-47s pointed toward the black water. For the past several days, Fineface's two motorboats had been on the water in the middle of the night. His men had rigged up muffler boxes over the en-gines, simple wooden contraptions that dampened the sound of the mo-tors. The boxes limited the oxygen flow to the engines, but the tradeoff in noise reduction made them worth it on the open water.

Fineface glanced over to his left and saw the outline of the other boat close by. It was six feet shorter than his boat, and he had limited it to five men. Both boats could carry more men, but the priority was on speed and fuel conservation over a long distance. The extra fuel took up enough weight. They wouldn't need the fuel that night, but he wanted the drivers to know how the boats handled when fully loaded. There were also several bags on the floors of the boats, loaded with rocks. The men knew enough not to ask what the bags were supposed to simulate. These were not sightseeing journeys. They were practicing for the most danger-ous mission they had ever attempted: the destruction of an offshore oil platform. Ifeanyi had said it was the most important element in the entire plan. The IOCs had to know the insurgents could destroy their most val-uable assets if they were going to be chased out of Nigeria for good. But Fineface and his men had never ventured out to the open sea. Everything was different out there, from the currents to the navigation to the risks they faced from the Nigerian navy.

Fineface peered through the darkness, trying to make out ships on the horizon. They had passed the last island and were moving into open water. Here, there were no places to hide. The run-in with the JTF at the oil bunkering site had made him extra cautious.

"There."

The soldier next to Fineface pointed to a small speck of artificial light in the distance. Fineface lifted his binoculars and examined the spot. He could make out a vessel with red and green bow lights and a white light in the stern. It was difficult to determine whether it was the Nigerian navy or not. He continued to pan across the horizon. He could clearly see two large oil tankers and a midsize cargo ship, possibly one of the ships that delivered parts to the oil rigs just offshore. Those ships didn't concern him. They would rarely raise any alarm over a small vessel unless that vessel seemed hostile. Unfortunately, with eight armed men in an open boat, it was difficult to hide their intentions, but there was only a slight chance of distant merchant ships taking notice. The Nigerian navy was a different story. Their patrols were actively looking for boats like theirs.

Pepple looked down at his cell phone. 2:12 am. Maybe they should turn around now. He had planned to head farther out to sea before doing some exercises close to land that would mimic approaching a rig and placing a bomb on its legs. To make the exercise worthwhile, it had to be done in the dark and with a minimal sound. Even though an oil rig's radar would pick them up on their approach, there was a good chance that in the middle of the night someone might not be monitoring the radar. The darkness and low profile of their boats would also make it difficult to identify them. Their only hope of survival was to surprise the rig and detonate a bomb before the alarm was raised. Then they had to hope their speed carried them back to safety.

Pepple made the decision to keep going farther into open water. He could not panic at the sight of every ship. It would send the wrong message to his men.

In the silent darkness, Pepple kept planning. Of the seven other men on board his boat now, he would choose four for the mission. All four of them would have to know how to navigate, drive and set the bombs in case someone got wounded or killed. The specific rig they would target was still not determined. He would meet with Ifeanyi in a few days to settle that question. He was also waiting for the explosives, which Ifeanyi claimed were on their way.

Something made Fineface shudder. Was it the cold? Despite growing up on the water, Fineface did not like the open ocean. Too much uncertainty. Too much risk. Out here, his mouth was dry from anxiety, even though he told himself they would be fine. He could sense the water spirits who lived in the ocean. They were different from those in the creeks. Fineface was a Christian, but that didn't mean he ignored the water spirits. Looking down at his gun, he muttered a silent prayer.

"Sir!"

Fineface glanced back at a soldier crouched down on the starboard side of the boat. Once he saw he had Fineface's attention, the soldier pointed behind them.

He lifted his binoculars. "Shit," Fineface said. A navy patrol boat was about a mile off their stern, between them and the safety of the creeks. It looked to be closing in on them. The chances of outrunning the boat were slim. Nigerian patrol boats had bigger and better engines and were designed for speed. More importantly, they were armed with 20mm cannons on their foredecks, which packed far more firepower than anything he had on board. Pepple knew they should have turned back sooner.

"Dump the rocks! Do it discreetly!" he said in a loud whisper so his voice would not carry too far. If the boat pursued them, they would need every bit of speed they could manage. Meanwhile, he made his way to the stern of the boat, keeping a low profile in the hope that the patrol boat would not spot the movement. Glancing at their companion boat, he could see they were taking a cue from him and also dumping their rocks.

While crouching at the stern and eyeing the approaching patrol boat, Pepple took out his phone and dialed. It rang twice before a voice came on. "George," he said to the driver of the other boat. "Turn left and return home. If the patrol boat follows us, take the muffler off the engine and go full throttle. Once we get closer to the creeks, we split up."

"Yes, Commander."

Fineface looked to port and saw the other boat begin to turn. His own boat dutifully followed. Everyone was silent and tried to keep low. The patrol boat had certainly seen them. Would it turn to pursue? He hoped the opposing commander was feeling lazy that night. Perhaps he would let them go. Fineface brought the binoculars up to his eyes. In the darkness he had a hard time making out the figures on the patrol boat, but it was indeed staying on their tail.

Pepple turned to the soldier next to him. "Help me." The two of them lifted the makeshift muffler off the large outboard engine. Gas fumes filled the air around them, and the noise of the engine echoed across the night sky. Without the cover, the engine could get more oxygen and would cool more easily, allowing them to increase the throttle to full power.

"Open it up!" Fineface said with his head facing the driver. "Maximum throttle back to the creeks!" The boat surged ahead, and the bow rose dramatically out of the water before settling down and skimming the surface. He looked back at the patrol boat. A floodlight appeared and shone in their direction. They had increased their speed and were gaining on them.

Fineface did a quick calculation in his head. They were a little over a thousand yards off his stern. He guessed they could do between five and ten miles per hour faster than his boat. That gave him a matter of minutes. Looking to the bow, he could see the mouth of the river and the relative safety of the islands. But the islands were no guarantee that they would be free, even if they could make it that far.

"Everyone, stay low! Keep your guns out of sight," he ordered. At some point the patrol boat might open fire from its 20mm cannon to slow them down. If they caught up, they would certainly board and probably arrest all of them—although, if it was a commander Pepple had worked with on stealing oil, he might let them go for a hefty fee. All of Pepple's men's guns were technically illegal. Yet, even if they dumped the guns in the ocean, they might face arrest or worse.

The patrol boat was getting closer, but it still had not opened fire.

Fineface looked again at the coast in front of them. He needed to buy some time. They might start firing soon. "You," he said to the soldier near him. "On three, we are going to throw this gas tank in the water. First, get it up on the gunwales. One...two...three!" They heaved the green plastic twenty-five-gallon tank onto the edge of the boat. The boat began to list. Instinctively, two of the men leaned over the other side for balance. Fineface looked around the floor of the boat and found one of the rocks that had fallen out of the bag as it went overboard.

"Give me your bandanna," he said to the soldier behind him. He wrapped the stone with the bandanna. Then he grabbed his knife and began jabbing at the tank. His blade barely punctured the heavy plastic, but gas began to spill out. He kept slicing it. The gas soaked the bandanna-covered rock.

"Slow down," he yelled to the driver, who eased back on throttle. Then, Fineface pushed the tank over the side of the boat. It bobbed in the water and floated behind them. Fineface took out his lighter and lit the bandanna. Without hesitating, he hurled the rock at the tank in the water. The gasoline on the surface caught fire. "Go!" Fineface yelled back as the flame began to spread. The sudden throttle knocked him off-balance, but he had enough sense to plunge his hand into the water over the side of the boat, dousing the flame that had begun to creep up his arm. He turned to watch the growing blaze behind him. A loud sound punctured the night sky as the floating gas tank exploded in front of the Nigerian patrol boat. Fineface grinned when the patrol boat was forced to slow down and then came to a complete stop. Its driver wasn't sure whether he should back up or go through the spreading flames.

Fineface turned forward and pulled out his phone. He hit the send button and redialed George. "Dump your extra gas. Light it. Head in a direction different from ours."

"Yes, sir."

Fineface hung up the phone and moved up to the console in the center of the boat. "Turn toward that island!" he told the driver. The boat lurched in the direction of Pepple's outstretched arm. Pepple looked back at his wake. The patrol boat had backed out of the flames and was continuing to follow them, but it had lost ground in the process. His ploy might have bought them enough time. He wanted to see which of the boats it would pursue.

Shots rang out across the water, but, in the dark, Fineface could not see who fired them or where they were aiming. More shots followed, and he realized that it was George's boat attempting to shoot the floating gas tanks to get them to ignite. The gunfire had the effect of drawing the Nigerian patrol boat in that direction. Pepple's boat was putting more and more distance between them and the Nigerian navy. Fineface heard the distinctive sound of the 20mm cannon spraying fire at the other boat. The echo of the cannon across the water was frightening, but he couldn't see what was happening. He closed his eyes to say a prayer for his men while his boat sped away to safety.

Twenty minutes later, Pepple's boat pulled into a secluded place near the shore and waited. They heard nothing. He tried calling George on his cell phone, but it just rang and rang. There was no one on the other end to answer.

Chapter 23

Port Harcourt

Julia O'Keefe arrived early to the Elkan Terrace hotel in Port Har-court. Everything had to be perfect for the big dinner with people from the Wellingstone Foundation. Three months ago, she'd gotten a call from her boss in Washington that their previous grant had run out and would not be renewed. The foundation that had previously supported the New Africa Initiative had a new executive director and new priorities. Malaria prevention in Nigeria was not flashy enough, didn't make a "long-term impact," or so they were told. Her boss had assured Julia that everything would be fine and that finding money for malaria work would be easy. But, so far, the only interest in funding had come from the Wellingstone Foundation in Philadelphia. Two of its employees were in Port Harcourt to observe NAI and one other NGO in the region.

To underscore the importance of the dinner that night, Julia's boss had called her that afternoon to check in. She had never done that in the three plus years Julia had worked at the New Africa Initiative.

Walking into the Elkan Terrace's lobby, Julia headed to the front desk. She was dressed in a blue blouse, a light khaki skirt, with a pink patterned silk scarf around her neck for a little variation. She'd picked out a pair of blue-rimmed Warby Parker glasses to complete the outfit. She wanted to project an air of relaxed professionalism.

"Can I help you?" asked the well-dressed Nigerian at the front desk.

"Yes, I would like to see Helge." Helge was the manager of the hotel, a German who had been in Nigeria for ten years.

"Yes, of course. Just wait here one minute." The man behind the desk nodded and whispered something to his assistant, who disappeared into the back offices. Julia looked at her cell phone. She still had thirty minutes before the guests were to arrive for dinner. Slightly impatient, she drummed her fingers on the green Formica countertop. Hanging above the receptionist were the familiar portraits of the Rivers State governor and the new president.

"Julia, I'm glad to see you here. What can I help you with?" Helge's voice had a noticeable German accent. Julia liked him because he was one of the best hotel managers in town and took an interest in every detail of the hotel's operation.

"I wanted to double-check that everything was all set for dinner tonight."

"Follow me and I'll show you the table we have reserved. Also, let me know if you have any special instructions for the waitstaff." Helge led the way across the lobby to the dining area. There were a few scattered diners and a large buffet set up against the far wall. The Elkan Terrace wasn't the nicest or most expensive place in town, but the food was good and they had a great bar area upstairs. Julia thought it was unwise to seem too extravagant while she was begging for money. Helge went through the menu for the night and introduced Julia to their waiter. Julia made it clear she wanted drinks served as soon as they sat down, no waiting around.

"Sorry if I seem a bit neurotic," Julia said to Helge as they both walked back to the lobby. "It's an important dinner for us tonight."

"I'm glad you chose to have it here." Helge smiled. "Let me know if there is anything else you need. I'll be sure to check in personally with your table during dinner."

"Thank you," Julia responded. She let out a small sigh and went over to the black leather couches near the front entrance. She sank into their soft cushions, the plan for dinner playing in her head. A few minutes later, a couple SUVs pulled up and Julia rose to her feet, but then she saw several Nigerian businessmen, all smartly dressed, getting out of the cars. No doubt they were ready to begin a big night. Julia sat back down and began going through her e-mails on her phone.

"Julia! There you are!" She looked up to see her colleague Ken Tuepolu walking toward her with two white people in tow.

"Ken, good to see you." Julia went over to the other two guests. "Cynthia, Ian, welcome to the Elkan Terrace." Julia smiled broadly and shook both of their hands. "I hope you are both settling in well."

"Yes, the Novotel is nice. Thank you for the recommendation," Cynthia said. Cynthia Powers was in charge of all grants to public health organizations for the Wellingstone Foundation. She prided herself on knowing Africa well and made a yearly trip to the continent to meet potential recipients. Elizabeth Wellingstone, the elderly matron whose late husband set up the foundation, loved Cynthia. Over the past five years, the foundation had dramatically increased its gifts to American NGOs that worked in Africa.

"Let's go to our table," Julia said. "Cynthia, this is your first time in Nigeria, right?"

"Yes, it is. We've supported an organization in Ghana for the past several years. I thought it was time to see Nigeria. Most of our other work has been in East Africa." No surprise there, Julia thought to herself. Not only was East Africa prettier, but the British had colonized the area far more thoroughly. Even after independence, there was a significant white population that helped draw a large number of American NGOs to the area.

"I'm sure you'll enjoy your visit. There's a lot of great work being

189

done in this country. The Niger Delta is not the war-torn place it was a few years ago. NGOs like the New Africa Initiative are helping transform the region," Julia replied.

They sat down at a table in the corner, away from any noise from other diners, and the waitress came over with their menus. Like most hotels in Port Harcourt, the Elkan Terrace offered both Nigerian and American food options.

"I would be happy to recommend something, if you'd like to try some local food," Julia offered. "But first, would anyone like a drink?"

"I'd love one," replied Ian Montrose. Ian was a lawyer with the Wellingstone Foundation. Trained in trusts and estate law, he had only recently joined the foundation so he could "do well while doing good," as he liked to tell his friends. Julia had to suppress a smile when she saw he was wearing ExOfficio travel clothes as though he were on a safari.

"How about a gin and tonic?" Ian said. "That way I'll keep with the colonial feel of the place." Julia winced at Ian's comment. He clearly had not spent much time in postcolonial Africa. The wounds were a little too deep for offhand slights. She looked over at her colleague, Ken, who had not missed the comment either.

"Sparkling water is fine for me," Cynthia said. Julia gave her own order to the waitress—also a gin and tonic—and Ken got a Heineken.

The table ordered their respective dinners, and then Cynthia said, "You're from New York, Julia, right?"

"Yes, I grew up in Manhattan, but I have been here in Nigeria with the New Africa Initiative for the past three years."

"And you, Ken? Where are you from?" Cynthia asked, putting her menu aside.

"I grew up not far from here. I was in Lagos for two years, but I prefer being closer to home." Ken took a sip of his beer. He was the only one at the table in a suit.

"The involvement of locals is crucial to the success of these ventures. Can't make it all the white man's burden, as Kipling would say," Ian added, happy to be able to include his British colonial literary reference.

"Yes, that's very true," Ken replied. "The white man has carried such a burden." As Ken took a sip of his beer Julia could sense him trying to control his anger. She resisted the temptation to list the effects of European colonization for Ian.

They carried on with basic introductions until the food arrived, each of them nursing their drink. Slow drinking was not a good sign, Julia remarked to herself. Cynthia seemed most curious about the political situation since the recent election. During the last spate of violence in the Delta, Goodluck Jonathan, who is from the Niger Delta, was elected Vice President, in part, to placate the people of the region. Since he left office, the region's population has been left without significant representation in the national government, which controlled the oil revenue. The most recent election only continued that trend.

"The election has certainly caused more tension in these parts," Julia said. "I don't think it is anything to be concerned about, however. Nigeria is a country with an estimated three hundred different tribes. They are used to disagreements. It won't lead to renewed violence."

"I hope not," Cynthia responded. "That would certainly affect our investment."

"There must be close to three hundred different ethnic groups in the US, with all the immigrants arriving every day, but we manage to get along," Ian said. "They should try the melting pot mentality here. Everyone sure looks the same to me."

"Yes, immigrants joining an established culture and a foreign power colonizing three hundred different tribes is basically the same thing," Ken replied. "And I'm glad we all look alike. I guess you could say the same thing about the Greeks and the Irish."

"Well," Ian said, "at least you all speak the same language."

"We don't, actually. English came from somewhere else."

"I think you will be impressed with our operations," Julia said quickly, wanting to segue into a different topic of conversation. She stared down Ken in an attempt to keep him quiet.

"Yes, I look forward to seeing them in the next few days," Cynthia replied. "Our big requirement is that you have clear metrics for success. We don't want to throw money down a rabbit hole, so to speak. Far too many NGOs carry on projects without really knowing if they're succeeding."

"We keep accurate records on all of our work. The last thing we want is misspent money."

"I was impressed by how many people you reach with your anti-malarial work," Ian added.

"Well, the anti-malarial work does give an indication of the difficulty of dwelling solely on numbers," Julia said, trying to refocus. "Our goal is to have the number of cases decrease. If we do our job well, there will be no more cases to report. But we would still need money to keep that going. Regular spraying of wet areas and the distribution of mosquito nets are the two things that would be most effective. Unfortunately, those efforts would take far more resources. For now, we are glad to be able to treat the new infections that arise."

"I can see how that makes sense," Cynthia admitted. "But it might be hard to convince Elizabeth Wellingstone of that." She paused, looking down at her food. "This dish is interesting. I have never had snails done this way." Cynthia took another bite and then continued chewing the small, rubbery mollusks.

"I'd like to take a close look at your books in the next couple days," Ian said. "I often find that summary reports in Washington for organizations like the New Africa Initiative do not give the full picture of expenses. I am sure there are areas for more efficiency. At least, there usually are."

"I can appreciate that," Julia said. "But I can tell you that we do spend a lot of money on salaries. We believe in paying our people well. We think it makes for effective programs."

"I can see you would want to be paid well," Ian replied. "But I am sure that salaries are lower for local help. This is Nigeria, after all."

"Yes, the local labor does come cheaply," Ken said, no longer able to repress the anger in his voice.

"What I think my colleague meant to say," Cynthia interjected, "is that we like to see a high proportion of dollars spent on programs rather than administrative salaries. You can understand that, I'm sure."

"I think you'll be pleased with our accounting, Cynthia. And don't worry, Ian, they keep my salary low." Julia forced a laugh. Shouting from the group of Nigerian businessmen interrupted their conversation. There is one table that is having more fun than we are, Julia thought. "Would anyone like some more drinks? There is a great bar upstairs, as well. It would be fun to get you excited about some of our work."

"Another drink would be great," Ian said without hesitation. "Do they have any whisky here?"

"For sure," Julia replied. "Nigerians drink a lot of scotch. Let me get the attention of our waitress." Julia turned to flag down their waitress but couldn't see her anywhere.

"These people seem like good people. I'm glad we can help them. They sure need it," Ian said.

"Yes," Ken replied. "We Nigerians need all the help we can get. White people have been so helpful through the years."

"You know, this money from the Wellingstone Foundation could make a real difference," Ian said. "I am prouder of my work with Welling-stone than anything else I've done. Now, where is that scotch?"

"There will be plenty of time for pictures tomorrow, right, Julia?" Cynthia asked.

"Yes, of course."

"Good. We will need plenty of good photos when we present things to Elizabeth Wellingstone. She likes the visual. It also will be good for our website."

"Nothing like smiling black children for a good website," Ken added.

"I think I'll have another drink too," Julia said. "It's been a long day for all of us at the office."

"I've never been to this bar before," Chris Reed said, looking out at the view from the Elkan Terrace hotel bar. He could see several other hotels lit up in the black night. With so few tall buildings around, the scattered trees made the city seem greener, wilder from two floors up.

"Yeah, it's a good place, especially on a night like tonight. The terrace is peaceful, and we're high enough off the ground to avoid the mosquitoes." Standing next to Chris, Julia took another sip of her gin and tonic. She forgot what number this drink was. "Thanks for coming down."

"Well, it sounded like you could use a designated driver. I don't want anything to happen to you." Chris was delighted when she had invited him out. He wanted to hear how the big meeting had gone. He was even wearing the new pants and shirt that Julia had bought him when they went shopping together to update his wardrobe.

The waitress, wearing a maroon polo shirt and carrying a tray with two extra-large Heinekens, came over and interrupted them. "Excuse me, sir, do you want a drink?"

"Do you have an orange Fanta?" he asked. The waitress nodded and walked away without another word.

"No drink?"

"I figure one of us could be sober."

"So I've had too many already, Dad?" Julia had a glazed look in her eye.

"Let's sit down." Chris led the way to a couple of chairs next to a low-lying table. The chairs were comfortable, made of black woven webbing. The soft night air felt nice and relaxing. "So, what happened? I haven't seen you like this before."

"The meeting didn't go well."

"Sorry to hear it," Chris said. The waitress came over and dropped off his Fanta. As he took a sip, he noticed a sadness in Julia's eyes that he had never seen before.

"Apparently, Americans with money can solve all the problems that have eluded humanity for thousands of years. Wave the Stars and Stripes covered wand, and whoop, it's done."

"That's just the drinks in you talking, Julia. I know you care about your work."

"I do. I don't know how much good we're doing though. We help people, but look around. What's changed? Then you have to deal with people like the Wellingstone Foundation, who like to come here and tell us how to do our work. We have to kowtow to them to get their money."

"And it didn't work?"

"I don't think so. It didn't help that my assistant kept dropping snarky comments. He was justified, but we need their money. We'll see how things go tomorrow." Julia took another sip of her drink and leaned her head back.

"Is this a big deal?"

Julia looked back at Chris. "It just means I have to go back to the oil companies and beg for money. I've done it before. I'll do it again."

"I can imagine how much you hate doing that."

Julia shrugged. "Giving money away helps their image. So we polish up their image and then ignore all the gas flaring and oil leaks and mis-appropriation of resources and bad politics they foster. It's a little game we play. They pretend to help. We pretend the problems are being solved." Julia smiled drunkenly.

"You don't have to do it, you know."

"Do what?"

"Work with the oil companies."

"I will after tonight. It's the way the world works, Chris. You can't be too stuck on your morals. It's for the greater good."

"Is it? Or is it just for the good of your organization?"

"Churches do the same thing."

"Some do. I'm not up for an argument now. Let me take you home." Chris stood up and left the remainder of his drink on the table.

"Now that's something I can get behind. Come on, handsome. You are adorable, you know. And that's not just the booze talking." Julia got up, slung her arm around Chris, and gently kissed his neck. Chris closed his eyes. He loved the feel of her lips on his skin.

"Not going to stop me?" Julia chided him.

"A little kiss won't hurt. But we should go."

"Maybe I can convince you to stay at my place for a nightcap."

Chris hesitated. "I...I don't know. Let's get out of here though."

"Lead the way!"

Chris took Julia's hand and began walking to the exit. He knew one of these days the timing would be right. If he was being honest, he was looking forward to it.

Chapter 24

Port Harcourt

In the week after Ifeanyi Okoye had killed his man in Lagos, Godwin Ogbe had been obsessed with finding him. Part of it was personal. It infuriated Ogbe that a man under his command had been killed. That it had been at the hands of Ifeanyi Okoye made it worse. But an equal part of Godwin's obsession was professional. Ensuring there was no new insurgency was his responsibility, and Ifeanyi was the key. Arrest Ifeanyi, and things would be under control. Let him go free, and Godwin had no idea what might happen. He had already heard rumors that former MEND commanders were preparing for attacks, and he guessed that Ifeanyi was the only one who knew the extent of those plans. If Ifeanyi succeeded, it would jeopardize Godwin's whole career.

After several days of searching, Godwin Ogbe had a breakthrough. Poring over visitor records for Ifeanyi while he was in prison, Godwin discovered one name that came up more often than any other: Olabisi Bob-Manual. She was a teller at a local bank. Why would a young bank teller be so interested in Ifeanyi Okoye? What was their connection? Godwin was convinced she would know where to find Ifeanyi. She might even know his plans.

Given that he was now leading a murder investigation, any and all means were at his disposal. But, since Olabisi had a registered car, finding her apartment wasn't too difficult.

Olabisi Bob-Manual kept a low profile. She avoided attention, rarely went to bars, and never spoke about her relationship with Ifeanyi Okoye. Her small apartment was near the river, across the street from some of Port Harcourt's most notorious slums. Olabisi knew that area well because that was where she'd spent most of her childhood. She moved into her current apartment because it allowed her to be close to her aging mother, a Yoruba woman who had moved to Port Harcourt to marry Olabisi's long-deceased father. Her mother still insisted on staying in her own hut, even though during the rainy season the area would flood when the banks of the river became swollen.

After Ifeanyi moved in, Olabisi's small apartment was even more cramped than before. She never complained, but Ifeanyi tried to be out of the apartment whenever he could.

On that particular morning, he was lucky. Olabisi was not.

Leaving her apartment, Olabisi noticed dark clouds overhead. It was sure to rain sooner in the day than normal. While she walked toward her car, she was trying to remember if she had an umbrella at work and didn't notice the military truck parked a block away. Dashing across the busy street, Olabisi nearly ran into two military men in camouflage fatigues standing near her Camry. She hesitated.

"Hey you, fancy woman with the car! Don't turn away. We want to talk with you. Is your name Olabisi Bob-Manual?"

Olabisi backed up slowly, trying to decide what she should do. Cars whizzed behind her. No one paid the soldiers any attention. Maybe they just wanted some dash, Olabisi reasoned—a bribe from someone who looked like she had some money to take. If she sprinted by them to the shanties on the river's edge, her knowledge of the slum's makeshift streets might give her a chance to get away. While she paused, two other soldiers came up behind her.

"You can walk up the street now, woman. No need to run anywhere. We have real bullets in these guns." Olabisi turned around to see two barrels pointed at her chest. To demonstrate that they meant business, one of the soldiers fired a shot into the muddy ground a dozen feet away, the sound giving Olabisi a start.

"Okay, okay. I'll come with you." Olabisi walked up the mud-soaked path along the street, frantically turning over her options. Run. Stay. Would they really shoot her? If she ran, where could she even go? Certainly not to her mother's.

The soldier who had fired into the mud kept his gun at Olabisi's back while she climbed up onto a black pickup truck, which was parked near her Camry and had seats in the flatbed. Two other soldiers climbed up after her. Once they were settled and Olabisi had handcuffs put tightly on her wrists, the last soldier hopped up and banged the side of the truck to signal they were set to go. As they drove off, she could see one of the boys she knew in the slum. He waved at her, a confused look in his eyes.

Thirty minutes later, Olabisi nervously glanced around at her sur-roundings. She had been taken to a military installation, not to police headquarters. The room was around twelve feet by twelve feet, the walls bare concrete painted a dull green and without windows. There were two metal chairs. Olabisi sat on one of them with her still-handcuffed hands behind her back. Despite the chill in the room, her hands were sweating. The few questions she had asked in the truck had been met with silence. She did not know what she was doing there, but she was sure it had to do with Ifeanyi.

Finally, the door opened. Three men walked in. They wore olive military uniforms, but Olabisi noticed no ranks, name patches, or identifying information on them. The oldest of the three spoke first. "How are you doing?" he asked. He brought the second chair close to Olabisi and sat down.

Olabisi looked around, confused, and said nothing back. The soldier slapped her face and asked again, "I said, how are you doing? When I ask a question, you answer. Is that clear?"

Shocked from the blow, Olabisi nodded.

"I am thirsty."

"Ah, she is thirsty." The interrogator looked at the other two soldiers, who were standing on either side of Olabisi's chair. "You will get plenty to drink later. First, I want you to tell me about your friend Ifeanyi. You see, we know he is planning something. We know most of what will happen. We just need you to fill in a few details."

Olabisi stared back at her interrogator and said nothing. Fear crept into her eyes.

"This can either be an easy process or a hard one. I don't like causing pain. I really don't, especially to a woman. But my friends here? They are bad men. They are sick men and have no sense of chivalry. Do you know what I mean, Olabisi? Uche here was beaten by his father nearly every night when he was a boy. When he hits people, he likes to think it is his father's face he is hitting, even if it's a woman's. Are you beginning to get the picture?" Olabisi remained silent. Her mouth was dry. She tried to see if she could loosen her hands, but the metal from the handcuffs only dug into her dark skin.

"Let's start with a few questions." The interrogator rested his elbows on his knees. "Some of the questions I will ask you I already know the answers to. Others I do not. I mix them in to make sure you are telling me the truth. I don't like when people lie. Uche really does not like when people lie. So, Olabisi, tell us. Where is Ifeanyi Okoye?"

"He...I don't know." Her voice was weak.

"I see this is going to take a little longer than I hoped. Let's try again. Where is Ifeanyi Okoye? I know you have the answer. I can see it in your eyes. If you don't tell me, we will have to try a different method."

"I told you, I don't know," she said more forcefully.

"You see, now you are lying. I said I don't like liars. Uche, do you like liars?"

Before Olabisi could turn her head to look up at Uche, a strong blow landed on the side of her face. She felt an exploding pain in her jaw. Olabisi tried, and failed, to free herself from her chair, shaking it violently.

"You see what I mean, Olabisi? Cooperation is important. I will ask you again. Tell me where Ifeanyi is and who his accomplices are."

"I don't know what you're talking about," Olabisi muttered.

The interrogator sat up in the chair and nodded again to Uche over Olabisi's shoulder.

Wham! Olabisi's face absorbed another hard blow on the left side. She could feel her jaw slightly dislodge. The skin on her face felt hot, and then the pain came.

"Enough. If we break her jaw, she won't be able to speak." The interrogator turned back to Olabisi. "Are you ready to cooperate?"

She remained silent.

"Part of me was hoping for that. Strip her," he said with a loud voice.

The soldiers stood Olabisi up and unlocked her handcuffs while the interrogator left the room. The one called Uche said, "Take your clothes off." Olabisi hesitated for a moment and then gave in to the inevitable. She wondered which one would go first.

Once she was naked, the soldiers kicked her clothes to the side.

The soldiers stared at her young black body. Her breasts were still firm, and she could feel them gazing at the tuft of wiry hair between her legs. Finally, the door opened, and the interrogator returned with two more soldiers carrying a long wooden board, which had leather straps to tie someone down. The two soldiers laid the board on the ground and left.

Once they were gone, Uche said, "Down," and pointed at the board. A shaking Olabisi got down on her knees and pressed her back against the board. One of the soldiers tightened the leather straps around her wrists and ankles. Naked and spread out, her arms and legs bound, she was completely exposed.

"I like that view," the interrogator said and laughed. "You are a beautiful young woman. Too bad it's all wasted."

The door opened again, and someone entered the room carrying a black box with wires coming out of it. The wires had clips on the ends of them.

"Do you know what this is?" the interrogator asked Olabisi, pointing to the device. She shook her head. "It is a device that delivers electric shocks. Simple, but very effective." The interrogator nodded to the soldier carrying the device. He leaned over Olabisi and attached one clip to her upper arm and a second clip to the big toe on her right foot.

The interrogator pulled up his chair so it was next to Olabisi's head. He then leaned down so he was close to her ear. "Now, we are going to try these questions again. I want to know what Ifeanyi Okoye is planning. I want details and names. You can begin by telling me where Ifeanyi is hiding out."

Olabisi merely shook her head. She saw Ifeanyi in her mind, and tears came to her eyes. She tried to focus on that image. "Give me strength, God," she prayed, her lips moving as she repeated the prayer over and over.

The interrogator turned to the man with the black box and nodded. The soldier turned the dial on the machine. Pain shot through Olabisi's body, and her muscles tensed, lifting her up off the wooden board. After a few seconds the searing pain stopped, and Olabisi opened her eyes. The soldier with the machine had a big smile on his face.

"How does that feel? Good, eh? That was at pain level four. The dial goes all the way to ten. Each time you give me an unsatisfactory answer, we will increase the power. Do you understand?"

Olabisi said nothing in response. She closed her eyes and began to pray again, but this time more weakly. She didn't hear the next question. A moment passed and the pain began again, more intense than before. It shook her whole body. She screamed out. Mercifully, it stopped.

"Just let me know when you are ready to start talking. We have all day and all night. How many hours of pain do you want? You will talk with us eventually. Everyone does. Make it easy on yourself."

When Olabisi said nothing, the interrogator nodded again to the soldier. The screaming could be heard down the hallway.

Two hours later, Godwin Ogbe stood in the damp, concrete hallway outside the interrogation room. "Do you have anything from her yet?"

"No," the chief interrogator responded. "I'm surprised by her resilience."

"Maybe you're not trying hard enough." Godwin's voice showed his frustration.

"For some reason, women tend to be harder to break than men."

Godwin squared up to the interrogator, his large frame overshadowing the smaller man. "Lives are at stake here. Your efforts will save lives."

"I'll see what I can do, but I can't make any promises. At this stage, the results are often uncertain. She's quite beautiful. When we are done, Uche wanted to have a go with her."

"No." Godwin plunged his forefinger into the interrogator's chest. "We are not animals."

"Of course, sir."

"Call me as soon as you know something. When you are done with the girl, put her back where you found her." Godwin turned and walked down the hallway, wondering where Ifeanyi was now.

Chapter 25

Port Harcourt

"Emeka, have you heard from Olabisi?" Ifeanyi's concern was evident over the phone.

"No. Why?"

"When I dropped by the apartment earlier, her car was still there, but she was nowhere. Your manager at the bank says that she never reported for work this morning, and she is not answering her mobile."

"You think she might have taken a day off and gone off by herself? This has been a stressful time. Maybe she lost her phone."

"No. I even checked her mother's place, and she wasn't there. That's not like her. Something's happened."

"Don't be paranoid, Ifeanyi. You really—"

"Listen to me, Emeka. I have a bad feeling about this. Leave the bank now. Don't tell your secretary where you are going. Don't take your car. Meet me where we used to go swimming as kids." Emeka Nwosu was silent. The Boat Club in the old port. Both of their fathers had been members. The building had not been in use for some time. Emeka thought a bit more, and the seriousness of what Ifeanyi was saying began to sink in. If the police had taken Olabisi, it was only a matter of time before they showed up at the bank looking for him.

"I'll meet you there." Emeka tried to hide the panic that was rising in his body.

"I'm going to head back to her apartment once more. If something has happened to her, we need to make plans."

Ifeanyi hung up his phone and tried not to let his thoughts get too far ahead. He had to think clearly. What did Olabisi know? What might be in jeopardy? She knew the general scope of the attacks, but she'd had no connection with the MEND commanders involved. She knew something of the finances, but again, no names. The biggest threat was to Ifeanyi and Emeka. They had to leave Port Harcourt that afternoon, with or without Olabisi.

Approaching Olabisi's apartment, Ifeanyi drove slowly in the old Land Rover he had been using. His senses were on full alert. The early afternoon rain gave his car some cover, and he was thankful that the authorities didn't know what car he drove. It was not registered to him, but to a friend of Emeka's. Did Olabisi share that information? He scanned the road for any sign of the JTF or other police presence. Olabisi's old Camry came into view. He pulled up behind it and took one more look around before shutting off the engine.

The ground was muddy. The rain had come late this year, but it had been consistently wet every afternoon for the past several days. The land near the river was partially flooded. He didn't know how the people who lived here coped with the water. He got out and felt the drops soak through his shirt. As a matter of habit, Ifeanyi wore no raincoat. Nigerian rain was warm, and he hated the steamy feeling that raincoats gave him. Looking both ways for traffic, he was about to cross the street to the apartment when he spotted something. Up the road, in a place that the Camry had blocked from his view, a body lay on the ground. He rushed toward it, taking a few furtive glances as he did so.

"Oh, no," he said under his breath. Olabisi was lying flat on the wet ground, her face to the side. Her chest rose and fell with each labored breath. He knelt next to the body and put his hand on Olabisi's back.

"Bisi." He shook her. "My dear friend, can you hear me?"

"Ifeanyi," Olabisi muttered weakly.

"God forgive me," Ifeanyi said, raising his eyes skyward. With effort, he picked up her body. Despite her small frame, she was heavy and limp. "Bisi, put your feet down. Try to stand." Shakily, Olabisi rose, using Ifeanyi's muscular frame for support. Ifeanyi put his arm under Olabisi's shoulder and half dragged her to the Land Rover. With his free hand, he opened the back door and lifted Olabisi up onto the seat. Her nice work clothes were covered in mud and soaking wet, which made getting a good grip on her difficult. With Olabisi uneasily resting in the back seat, Ifeanyi hurried to the driver's side. He turned the key and, as soon as the engine turned over, he put the car into drive. Barely looking over his left shoulder, he accelerated into the light traffic. A horn blared at him, but he ignored it.

"Bisi, can you hear me? Are you alright?" He heard a moan from the back seat and adjusted the rearview mirror so he could look at her. Damn. He took out his phone and hit the call button, dialing the most recent number.

"Emeka?"

"Yes? I am in a taxi headed to the old town."

"It's worse than I thought."

"What's the matter?"

"I have Bisi with me. She's in a bad state. It looks like the police roughed her up." Ifeanyi could feel the rage building within him. He was afraid he might run down a police officer if he saw one.

There was a silence on the other end of the line. "Does she need a doctor?"

"Yes. See if you can convince one to meet us at the Boat Club. It's the most secure place I know of right now."

"I wish there was some other place we could have gone," Emeka Nwosu said as he closed the creaky door behind him. The main dining area of the old Boat Club was bare of furniture and littered with trash. The greenish-blue paint was peeling off the walls, and black mold was noticeable in several spots. The building had long since been abandoned after the Boat Club built its new facility two miles upstream. The Club had been unable to sell it because no one wanted property in the old, dilapidated port area. The lock on the large wooden front door had been broken by looters long ago. "What if someone shows up?" he asked.

"Then we make something up. I didn't know where else to come on such short notice," Ifeanyi replied, his voice louder than normal, reverberating through the empty, dark space. The only light came from the wall of windows that faced the river.

Emeka looked over at Olabisi, who was resting on a jacket that Ifeanyi had put down on the floor. "How is she?"

"She will live. Hard to say beyond that. Where's the doctor?" Ifeanyi asked.

"He's on his way."

"What did you tell him?"

"I told him the truth: that I needed a doctor to care for a friend," Emeka said.

"Can you trust this doctor?" Ifeanyi asked.

"Yes, he's my brother-in-law. He knows of my involvement with MEND and has always been supportive." Emeka looked at Olabisi more closely. The left side of her face was swollen, perhaps from a broken jaw. "Do you know what happened to her, Ifeanyi?"

"She hasn't spoken much. From the condition of her body, I would guess they used electricity. They might also have done waterboarding. I hear that can be even more effective. The French were masters of it in Algeria and passed their knowledge along to the Americans. Now, it's apparently in vogue." Ifeanyi shook his head when he thought of the pain that Olabisi had suffered.

"What does this mean for the operation?" Emeka asked.

"I can't say. We still don't know what she told them."

"We have a problem, by the way. I was going to tell you today."

"A problem?"

"Yes, our main source of income has dried up."

"Completely?" Ifeanyi asked.

"It looks that way for now. After the initial two payments, we have received nothing. I called up my contact in Lagos, and he said they had found out that you killed an officer. They said it's too dangerous to have any connection with us. Attacking the international oil companies is one thing. Attacking the police and military is another."

"Bloody hell. Let me think." Ifeanyi scratched his beard. His dark brown eyes moved furtively around the room. "I can't stall the commanders for much longer. We still have at least a half dozen that expect some payment up front or no attacks."

A knock on the outer door interrupted their discussion, and they both looked in that direction. Ifeanyi quickly ran through his head what he would do if it was an overly curious local or drifter. He would have to be silenced. Before he could move, a middle-aged man dressed in a brown suit appeared.

Emeka went up to him, and they embraced. "My brother, you are welcome." He turned to Ifeanyi. "This is Doctor Okonkwo." Turning back to the doctor, he said, "Ike, this is a matter of extreme delicacy and secrecy. Can you examine this woman?"

Ike Okonkwo walked over to Olabisi and knelt down. He carefully removed her clothing and examined her body. She was too exhausted to resist. "This woman has been tortured," he declared.

"We know," Ifeanyi replied. "How is her health?"

The doctor took out a stethoscope and listened to Olabisi's heart and breathing. "Your friend has suffered much." He looked up at Ifeanyi, who was standing near Olabisi's head. "She will have permanent scars from the electricity burns. Her bruises will obviously heal. Her heart is weakened. I would guess that her jaw is not broken, but I would need an x-ray to confirm. Most of all, she needs rest. The biggest impact, judging from the extent of her suffering, will be psychological."

The doctor stood up and walked over to Emeka. "I can get you pre-scriptions for some painkillers and some anti-anxiety medication. Be careful, my brother. There should not have been a woman involved in this." Emeka could tell from Ike's tone that Olabisi's condition angered him.

"Thank you, Ike. She's a special woman."

Ike Okonkwo embraced his brother-in-law and then showed himself out the door.

After they heard the door close, Ifeanyi spoke. "We need to find out what the authorities know. If they know the names of the commanders involved, my guess is that Godwin Ogbe will try to buy them off. I'm sure he has access to funds. Even if he doesn't know who has agreed to help, he will begin contacting his old friends. Time is short either way. And you must leave the city. Soon!"

"What are we going to do about the money shortage? In addition to the payments to the commanders, we still need funds for the ex-plosives and other weapons," Emeka added. Ifeanyi could tell he was worried.

"We might have to resort to the old methods," Ifeanyi said. "We knew this would not be easy. I've already been in touch with Fineface, and we talked money. He is a good man. He knows how to handle the situation. I'll give him the green light to go ahead." Ifeanyi knelt next to Olabisi. He put his hand on her forehead. "I am sorry, Bisi." He clasped her hand and squeezed it. "Know that I am sorry."

"Ifeanyi," she said, turning her head to him, her voice low and weak. "I did just what you told me."

"What was that?" Ifeanyi's eyes were now wet as he struggled not to weep for his friend.

"After it started, I screamed and screamed. Every time it came on, I screamed." Olabisi paused to rest. "When they asked questions, I just kept saying 'no.' Finally the pain was too great, and I lost consciousness. I don't remember what I told them." There were tears in her eyes. "I'm so sorry."

"Oh, my friend, you have more courage than any of us." Ifeanyi squeezed her hand more tightly. Then he leaned over and placed a kiss on her forehead. "Please rest." Ifeanyi stood up and faced Emeka. "We have to move her out of here and head to the creeks. I know places we can go."

"I need to go to my house to pick up some things."

"No." Ifeanyi's voice was stern. "This could be you next."

Emeka took another look at Olabisi and shuddered.

Chapter 26

Julia O'Keefe wore her best suit, a light gray wool-and-linen blend that her father had bought for her at Neiman Marcus. The sky-blue blouse matched perfectly, and with her hair done up, she felt as though she could stroll comfortably into any boardroom. But it wasn't a boardroom she was walking into. Today she was the public face of the New Africa Initiative with Octagon Petroleum in Nigeria. During the past week, she had been in touch with Olivia Wike, who was in charge of Octagon Petroleum's charitable efforts, and Julia was pretty certain they could get a grant for the upcoming year. Julia told Olivia she was happy to be at the opening of the new school in Ichewa and to give whatever laudatory quotes Olivia wanted for the newspapers.

Despite how drunk she had been, Julia had not forgotten her conversation with Chris on the deck of the Elkan Terrace Hotel about her qualms with being close to Octagon Petroleum. In the mid-1990s, Octagon had colluded with Sani Abacha, the brutal dictator at the time, to suppress peaceful protests in the Niger Delta. The show trials and subsequent execution of the leaders of that movement had brought unwanted international attention to human rights abuses in Nigeria. Octagon Petroleum had its hands dirty, for sure. But the company was different now, or so Julia told herself. The fact that they had a designated person to work with local communities and NGOs proved it. Besides, she needed this money or NAI's operation in Nigeria might have to stop. Every good deed came with tradeoffs. Is there any truly morally pure work? she asked herself.

When Julia arrived at the Emmaus Center, Chris was waiting for her out front. "You're looking great," he said, once he was settled in the front seat. "I wish I had something nicer to wear." Chris had on a white button-down with khaki cargo shorts and flip-flops.

"We're going to play with the bigwig corporate and government people today. I have to look professional." Julia put the New Africa Initiative truck into drive and pulled into traffic.

"So, when it comes to the oil companies, you dress up. What do I have to do to earn that privilege?"

"I'm not opposed to playing dress-up," she replied, winking at Chris. Chris's heart began to beat more rapidly. He wished he could lean over and kiss her.

"So what's this event again? A school opening?"

"Yes, Octagon Petroleum gives money every year for projects in the area. This is their most recent project: a new school for one of the larger villages, along with a government commitment of funds for teachers and supplies." Julia honked twice at a car that pulled in front of them on the main road.

"It sounds like a great project, Julia. You shouldn't feel bad about doing it," Chris said, remembering their conversation from the other night.

"I'm over it. They get pictures with me and get to use the NAI name, and we might get some money to save lives."

"Sounds worthwhile. Thanks for letting me tag along." Chris paused for a moment, then added, "I was kinda hoping we could make dinner at your place afterward." He glanced at her, trying to gauge her reaction.

The car stopped in the inevitable morning "go-slow," and Julia was focused on the road. Chris worried he had pushed a little too far.

"Dinner would be great," Julia replied. "Perhaps this time we can make it off the couch." Julia smiled, and Chris felt a tingling warmth throughout his whole body. This was going to be a fantastic day.

Outside the main office building of the Octagon Petroleum com-
pound, a small group gathered on the well-manicured lawn. At the center
was Tim McAuliffe, the American executive David Sloan had met the
other day. He was confirming details for their trip to the opening of a
school in the Niger Delta. Two Toyota Land Cruisers with tinted windows
were parked nearby. The drivers, dressed in military fatigues, were leaning against the hood of the front vehicle, chatting casually.

David Sloan stood not far off, chewing a piece of nicotine gum. That
morning, he had sent Catherine Dunlop and the young analyst Matt back
to New York. They'd had had an intense strategy session the night before
at the Novotel, where they laid out a plan for oil and gas purchases. Catherine was going to put together a proposal with specific trades and timing,
including margin financing, as soon as she got back to Connecticut.
Standing on the grounds, waiting to venture into the Niger Delta, David
could feel the rush of a gambler's life. At that moment, it seemed as
though his entire future was at stake. If this play worked out, it would
make his career and potentially crush Josh Cohn. If it failed, he could
lose most of his investors.

David would join Catherine and the rest of the team in Connecticut
in few days. But before going all in, he wanted to see what it was like in
the heart of the delta. He trusted his intuition, but he wanted a better feel
for the situation. This ribbon-cutting event for the new school would give
him the chance to talk with locals. Afterward, they would see a major flow
station. It was his last chance for second-guessing.

They climbed in their respective SUVs, and the caravan got under
way. David noted they were only forty minutes behind schedule. Good
for Nigeria. He rode in one car, and the Octagon people were in the car

ahead. A pickup truck with armed soldiers led the way.

David wondered about the quality of these soldiers. Would they fight when the attacks came? Was he wrong to bet so heavily on the insurgents? He popped another stick of nicotine gum and distracted himself by watching the okadas, the classic Nigerian motorcycles, maneuver past them. David noticed that none of the okada drivers wore helmets, despite the law that required them. At least it confirmed that Nigeria was a place for risk-takers. David did his best to relax as the cars sped onward.

As they approached the village of Ichewa two hours later, the new school came into view. The bright glare of the late morning sun made the building stand out against the trees behind it. It was two stories tall, with yellow-painted stucco and a flat roof. There was a broad open space in front of the school with a large green sports field off to the side. Facing the school was a collection of houses, which looked new. David surmised that the center of the village was farther down the road. In front of the main entrance to the school was a large red-and-blue ribbon. A couple dozen Nigerians, some in brightly colored traditional garb and others in European-style clothing, stood around and talked casually, in what would certainly make a good photo op.

Their caravan pulled off the road next to the sports field, and everyone got out. The heat had worsened. David put on his sunglasses and hoped there was some air-conditioned space nearby. Otherwise he might sweat through his shirt, and he hated looking unkempt, especially in a bespoke suit.

David had little interest in making small talk with Tim McAuliffe and looked around for someone more intriguing. He spied a pretty young American in a light gray suit and designer glasses off to the side chatting with someone. She was the first attractive American he had seen in Nigeria, so naturally he strolled over.

"Hello there," David said to Julia O'Keefe, interrupting her conversation. He stood right next to her, ignoring her Nigerian interlocutor.

"Hello," Julia said, a little annoyed, and then, not waiting for a response, she returned to her conversation.

"What do you do for Octagon?" David asked.

Julia turned back to him. "I'm actually in the middle of something, in case you failed to notice."

"It's alright, Julia. I'll talk to you later." The man Julia had been chatting with walked off. She turned to David.

"Well, that was rude of you. No, I don't work for Octagon Petroleum. Do you?"

"No. Just here visiting."

Julia looked at him more closely. "A white guy in a suit with an Hermès tie? Typical tourist, I would say."

"It's an Alexander Olch tie, and I'm here on a business trip."

"And what kind of business do you do?" she asked, feigning interest.

"I invest in oil and gas."

"Am I supposed to be impressed?"

"Yes, you are. I'm good at it."

"I should hope so. You're certainly not very good at hitting on women." Julia turned and walked off to find Chris Reed. She hoped he had not wandered toward the village. David looked at her walking away and admired the lines of her legs. He sighed. It was time to locate Tim McAuliffe.

The nervous expression on Tim's face amused David when he caught up to him. From the look of it, he had never done this sort of thing before and was worried he might screw up. Clearly, he didn't know how these things worked. Tim represented money, so he could do whatever he wanted. It was the other guys who should be nervous.

"Mr. McAuliffe?" Tim looked over when he heard his name. It came from a well-dressed woman in her early forties, who was walking over from the crowd near the school's entrance. "Olivia Wike. I am in charge of public relations for Octagon Petroleum in Nigeria. Welcome to Ichewa."

"Thank you," Tim said. "Olivia, I want you to meet David Sloan." Tim placed his hand on David's shoulder. "He's an investor from the US. Here to see the good work Octagon does in the community."

"I love seeing money going to good causes," David added. He smiled and wondered if Olivia caught his facetious tone.

"I hope you'll be impressed," Olivia replied. "Gentlemen, follow me. We will begin with a tour of the facility. As usual, we have our photographer here as well as some people from the press. We're hoping to get coverage not only here in the Port Harcourt area, but also in some of the Lagos papers. After our tour, we'll do a ribbon cutting in front of the school, and then we have a lunch set up on the football pitch. That will give us a chance to have a meal with local leaders. A few of the children will have a presentation for Octagon at that point."

"Sounds good to me," Tim said. "Show us the way. I'm looking forward to seeing a Nigerian school. Should be interesting to compare it to schools back home." Tim's naïve enthusiasm was beginning to annoy David.

"Oh yes, should be good fun," David said, his eyes scanning the environment for anything that seemed out of place, any hint that something was wrong. Everything appeared normal, too normal for David's liking.

As Olivia led the way to the school, David watched the people setting up for lunch and noticed there was no tent to block the sun. Damn, he thought to himself. He had neglected to bring sunscreen. When they reached the entrance, Julia O'Keefe joined them, trying to avoid eye contact with David. Inside, the hallway was painted a dark blue, and the cool shade of the building was a welcome change.

"We have classrooms here for up to four hundred children," Olivia began. "Thanks to Octagon's generosity, there is a new computer lab as well as a small library." They strolled down the hallway, which had new tile over a cement floor. A photographer trailed them, snapping photos in rapid succession. They poked their heads into several classrooms, all of which had school desks set up in neat rows.

"This looks like it could be a school in the US," Tim said, obviously impressed. "How large is the average classroom size?"

"Each class should have about thirty students. The pedagogy here is still focused primarily on lectures, although there are one or two rooms that are set up seminar style for a class discussion. The facility itself is cutting-edge for public education in Nigeria, let me assure you. We're hoping that this will become a model for the schools in Rivers State. There are a couple similar schools in Port Harcourt, but this is part of a larger effort to improve educational standards throughout the region."

"Impressed?" Julia asked David as they climbed the stairs to the second floor. She had decided he was the most interesting person there and gave up ignoring him.

"Me? Oh, I think I'll reserve my judgment for ten years."

"Why's that? This school will give the villagers a chance at a decent education. This is the future of Nigeria."

"I've seen enough top-down government solutions to intractable problems. I'll wait to see how this one works out," David replied.

"That's awfully cynical of you," Julia said. "I would've expected you to be a fan of education. I'm guessing you got your fair share of it. Schools are where long-term development begins."

"Are they?"

"You don't think so?"

"Look around you, Julia. Who do you see? Any locals here on this grand tour? Ultimately, who is responsible for education? The parents of children. This whole thing has been planned out by Octagon and the government. It might work, but I'm not holding my breath."

"I'm happy with it," Tim said, interjecting.

"I hope so," David said. "You guys are paying for it."

The tour continued through the library, whose shelves were mostly bare, and ended with the computer lab. When they arrived at the main door for the ribbon cutting, Olivia introduced Tim to the various government officials. David had little interest in glad-handing and walked down the steps from the front entrance to find some shade. He took his jacket off to cool down before lunch.

Ten minutes later, the visiting dignitaries stood with the local community leaders in front of the new school building for their photo op. David, off to the side, admired the awkwardness of the photo. No wonder Olufemi Adebayo, the Octagon country head, didn't want to make the trip. Nigerians next to white Americans made for better press. The cold fish, Julia, seemed more at ease in the photo than most, David noticed. She probably had a lot more experience at this kind of thing. He had found out she was a do-gooder NGO type. Right then, the white guy Julia had been talking with after the tour wandered over to him.

"David Sloan." He put out his hand.

"Chris Reed. Nice to meet you."

"What brings you out here?" David asked, impressed with Chris's firm handshake.

"I could ask you the same thing."

David smiled. He liked being challenged. Perhaps Chris was more than his bad taste in clothing indicated. "I'm a finance guy from New York, scoping out some investments."

The name David Sloan rang a bell in Chris's mind. "You don't happen to know Matt Jaroslavic, do you?"

"Matt? Of course. He works for me. You just missed him. He flew out of Port Harcourt this morning."

"Really?" Chris asked excitedly. "He was one of my best friends in high school. I just saw him a few months ago in Cambridge." The memory of that day flashed through Chris's head.

"Harvard guy?" David asked. Chris didn't reply. He stared straight ahead, lost in his thoughts. "Chris?"

"Sorry," Chris said, trying to regain his composure. "I got distracted. Yeah, I'm a Harvard grad student. Just here taking some time off to help others and do some thinking."

"Another do-gooder." David attempted to hide his contempt. "So, are you and Julia joining us for the trip to the flow station?"

"The flow station?" Chris asked.

"Yes, where the wells pump the crude oil. There it's separated and sent in pressurized pipes down the coast. You ever been to one?"

"No. It would be cool to see, though." Chris was eager to put his mind on something other than that day in Cambridge.

"Well, if you and your friend Julia want to join, I'm sure we can arrange that. It's not like these places are a big secret." David smiled. It would give him more time to talk with Julia O'Keefe. She was pretty, but more than that, she had an attitude. David loved women like that. "I'll mention it to Tim."

"Tim?"

David pointed to where the photo group was breaking up. "He's the white guy in the center of the photo who looks like he has heatstroke."

The lunch that followed was typical Nigerian fare, which meant

David Sloan hated it. Too spicy. Unusual flavors. Why couldn't the French have colonized Nigeria? David thought to himself as he lazily poked the green mush, which was next to a white ball of something starchy. The heat from the sun made the meal even more unbearable. The Coca-Cola, made with real sugar, was about the lunch's only redeeming factor. He said a few pleasantries to the low-level government official sitting next to him but was more interested in people-watching.

Supposedly, an insurgency was about to begin at any time, yet he saw no sign of it. Either that was a good sign, and the attacks would come as a complete surprise, or a bad sign that they were not going to amount to anything. He wished he could pull aside one of the younger locals and grill him or her with questions. He had tried approaching one person before the food was served, but the man had quickly walked away.

As soon as the lunch finished, David moved over to Julia. "You again," she said.

David smiled. "Yup. Little ole me. By the way, your friend Chris said he wanted to join us on our trip to the local flow station."

Julia gave David an inquisitive stare. "Really?"

"We were chatting, and I mentioned where I was going. He seemed excited. New experiences and all. More time spent with me."

Julia stared at him and let out a noticeable sigh. What is with these banker types? They think they can get everything they want. "Sure, I guess we can go. I didn't make any plans for this afternoon. Always hard to know how long these events will last."

"Wonderful." David stepped away, but after a few steps turned back to Julia and said, "You know, there is room in my car if you want to save your driver the trip."

"I drove myself. But thank you." Julia went to find Chris. He would get words for this.

221

•••

The route to the local flow station from Ichewa was a poorly main-tained dirt road. Octagon Petroleum vehicles did not usually arrive at the flow station via the village, which meant neither Octagon nor the government, had much incentive to invest in the road. They drove slowly to avoid the potholes, which appeared to grow out of the ground and were eager to swallow up the nearest tire. Four-wheel-drive cars were a necessity. The soldiers led the caravan in their black pickup truck. Tim's car was next, followed by David's, and in the rear was the New Africa Initiative's white pickup with Julia at the wheel.

David kept looking over his shoulder to catch a glimpse of Julia. Each time she seemed to be staring back at him. Good sign? Without a doubt.

While he was looking back over his shoulder, his SUV suddenly stopped, and David had to catch himself against the front seat. "What is it?" David asked his driver.

"Not sure, sir. The car in front stopped."

"Damn it," David said under his breath. He took out his cell phone and dialed Tim McAuliffe, who had given him his number that morning. "Tim, what's going on?"

David couldn't see Tim in his SUV, which, unlike David's, had tinted windows. Thick jungle surrounded the road on both sides. "There's a tree across the road," Tim said. "It must have fallen recently. We might have to turn back."

"You've got to be kidding me! How are we supposed to turn around on this road? It's barely wide enough for one car."

"Hey." Tim sounded defensive on the phone. "Don't get mad at me. This is not one of our roads." David looked back at Julia again and shrugged his shoulders in an exaggerated manner as if to say, I don't know.

"Well, do you think you can move the tree?" David asked Tim. "There should be enough soldiers to make it happen."

"Maybe. Let me—"

Suddenly, a large explosive detonated behind the caravan. The noise was deafening, and the blast rocked Julia and Chris's truck forward. Dirt and branches rained down on the vehicles. Gunshots rang out, while shouting was heard up ahead.

"What the fuck was that?" David said to Tim over the phone. David could see Julia and Chris frantically looking around them. Behind their car, as the dust began to settle, he could make out figures moving.

"They're ambushing us!" Tim's voice yelled through the phone's receiver.

"Who?" David screamed, his heart pounding in his chest.

"Insurgents!"

David looked up ahead. Some of the insurgents were surrounding the lead truck, the one with their armed escort in it. Men with bandanas wrapped around their noses and mouths, carrying semi-automatic rifles, walked toward his car. He heard more shots, but he couldn't tell who was firing. When the insurgents got to David's SUV, one of them tapped on the glass with his gun barrel and yelled, "Get out! Get out of the car!" David sat there, unsure of what to do. "Get out!" the same man yelled again, motioning more forcefully with his gun. The man pointed his gun right at David through the window.

"Okay, okay," David said. He reached for the door, unlocked it, and got out. Up the line of cars, other militants were escorting Tim. Julia and Chris were in a similar situation behind him. All four of them found themselves walking past Julia's white truck and around the ten-foot-wide crater in the ground created by the blast. Fifty yards up the road, the insurgents nudged them along a path that led to several well-camouflaged trucks that they had missed when driving past. Following instructions, they climbed up into the same truck. David leaned over to Tim and asked, "What happened to our security? And our drivers?"

"They are out of their cars and tied up near the fallen tree. Apparently, these militants have no need for them," Tim responded.

"Does anyone know where they're taking us?"

"Probably to their camp," Julia replied.

Tim whispered to Julia, "Should we make a run for it?"

"Run where?" Julia asked in a normal tone of voice. "They have guns, and we're miles from the nearest village."

"Be quiet!" One of the soldiers yelled. "No talking." Once the prisoners were on one of the trucks, two soldiers climbed up onto the bed with them. The trucks started their engines and drove off. While one soldier kept his gun on the prisoners, the other began blindfolding the captives. The blindfolds were knotted with such force that David winced as his was tightened.

As the soldier moved toward them, Julia could see that Chris was wide-eyed with terror. "Don't worry," Julia said to calm him down. "We're ransom money to them. We won't be harmed."

"Yeah, but what if you don't have anyone who can pay the ransom?"

Chapter 27

Somewhere in the Niger Delta

Chris Reed estimated that the trip to the camp lasted about an hour and a half. It was hard to tell since they were blindfolded and disoriented. Once the trucks had started moving, the guard in the truck with them had demanded silence. No one had been in the mood to argue. They had taken their cell phones away, so even if Chris had not been blindfolded, he still could not have accurately gauged the time. The trip was bumpy and hot. Chris had done his best to push any bad thoughts from his mind like whether he would make it out of there alive or, if so, in what condition.

When the trucks stopped, the guard took off their blindfolds. Chris blinked and looked around at the place. They were in the jungle. There were about a half-dozen concrete buildings scattered a ways off from the small clearing, presumably so no helicopter could see the encampment. Chris noticed that the zinc roofs of the buildings were painted dark green. One soldier came up and opened the door to the truck bed, and they each jumped to the ground. At gunpoint, they were led to an area outside the largest building and told to sit down. After a few minutes, a slender man of medium height walked over them. He was wearing green-colored fatigues like most of the other men and had his shirt open, revealing an olive undershirt. He had a red bandanna wrapped around his head as a sweatband. He carried a sidearm but no other weapon.

"So, these are my new prisoners," the man in fatigues said to no one in particular. He looked at them one by one. "A well-dressed group. Let me tell you what will happen. Each of you will be able to make a phone call with this phone." The leader held up a basic Nokia phone for them to see. "You will tell your friends and associates you are my prisoner, and that they should pay the ransom we demand. Then you will hand the phone to me, and we will do the negotiating. We do not want to harm you, but we will if you cause any problems. I hope your capture proved to you that we mean business and that we are professionals. There is no place to escape from here. You are miles from the nearest settlement and will likely face many more problems if you try to run. There will be a guard with you at all times. Let the guard know if you need to use the toilet. You will sleep here. Any questions?"

The five prisoners kept silent. There was not much they could say.

"Good," the man in fatigues said and then walked away with three of the soldiers following him. Two armed guards took a seat nearby on small stools that they brought with them from the closest hut. They laid their guns across their laps, their eyes resting on the prisoners.

"This is pretty shitty," David said.

"Damn it. How could this happen?" Tim tried to hide the fear and frustration in his voice.

"Someone obviously tipped them off," David said. "Ours was not the usual route to the flow station. The ambush was set for us."

"But who?" Tim asked. "Do you think it was someone at Octagon Petroleum?"

"Possibly," David said, almost to himself. He looked over at Chris, who had his head bent down in prayer. "Praying for God to save us?"

Chris didn't respond.

"It'll be alright, Chris," Julia assured him. "Don't worry."

"I'm scared, Julia."

"So am I," Julia said. "We just got caught in the wrong place at the wrong time. Maybe we can talk our way into getting released."

"Not likely with people like this," David responded.

"So what now?" Tim asked.

"We wait," David said. "We wait and rely on the fact that we have good insurance." He chuckled.

"This isn't funny," Julia said to David. "Thanks, by the way, for convincing us to come."

"My pleasure," David said, making a gesture as though he were tipping his hat to the lady, even though he had no hat. "Anyone know any good jokes?"

"I don't know how you can be so coldhearted in a situation like this," Tim said to him.

"What's the proper response to have? Getting worked up won't do any good. We'll be fine. We're money to our captor. He's not going to do anything to harm us."

"The mosquitoes might though."

"What was that?" Tim asked.

"The mosquitoes," Julia said. "We're out in the open. Once it gets dark, we'll be feasted upon. At least you'll be able to tell your wife in Houston you know what malaria is like." Tim blotted his sweat on his sleeve. "It's not going to kill you," Julia assured him.

David started whistling to himself. He then took his jacket off. He was sweating profusely. "Hey, you!" he called out to one of the guards. "Yes, you. I'd like some water."

"Be quiet," the guard said back.

"I'm sweating and losing a lot of water. I'd like something to drink."

"You'll get something when it's time for dinner."

"He's not very friendly," David said.

Julia also took off her jacket. Her suit was covered in dust and mud from driving through the woods and sitting on the ground. She turned to David and asked, "So, hotshot, what is it that you do?"

"Small talk is good," David said. "I like your thinking. We need to pass the time somehow. I manage a hedge fund that deals in oil and gas."

"So, you bet on the price of oil and gas?" Julia asked.

"Basically, but I prefer to see it as investing. We also provide liquidity to the market. We make it easier for oil and gas companies to move their products to the optimal buyers. And we allow companies to hedge against fluctuations in price."

"Sounds almost altruistic when you put it that way, although I'm not really sure what all of that means," Julia responded.

"I read about you guys once in Rolling Stone, I think," Chris offered. "You were responsible for the run-up in oil prices in 2008. You guys made gas go to four dollars a gallon."

David laughed. "I wish I were responsible for that. I'd be worth a lot more than I am now. But I was working for a big firm then, and we did our part. Made some good money."

"That rise in gas prices cost a lot of people," Julia chimed in. "Average people with long commutes, people trying to grow food in the developing world. Even if it wasn't you alone, people like you did a lot of harm, all to make a buck."

"Ah, a couple of crusaders, how nice. And now you are stuck in the jungle with a money-hungry bastard like me," David said. "It must drive you nuts."

"Unlike you, we're trying to make the world a better place," Julia said with anger building in her voice.

"What if I told you I don't buy into your go-help-the-world nonsense, Julia? Why? What do I owe the world? I'm going to take what I can out of this world because I can. I like buying things, but more importantly, I like the power that comes with money. Because I have money, people look at me differently. They treat me with deference and respect. I get to order other people around and make sure that every whim is satisfied. I don't need to be nice or polite or kind if I don't want to. People will always suck up to me no matter what."

"You're heartless and you're selfish. That's what you are," Chris said to him.

"I am selfish, but so are you and so is your friend Matt, who works for me. You seek what's best for you. I seek what's best for me. Just because I'm not constrained by some illusion of God or morality should not be held against me. I saw you praying earlier, Chris. What are you, a Christian? Jesus suffered on a cross. He was tortured to death. That's your example of a God? You know what I think? Pathetic. I'll never worship a God who loses." Chris shook his head. "What?" David continued, "God wins out in the end with resurrection? We'll see when I die. But I'll tell you what, Chris, wherever I end up, I'll have a lot of company."

"If there is any truth to Christianity," Chris replied, "you'll be judged for your actions."

"Then I will await my judgment. And in the meantime, I will enjoy making money and the privileges it brings. Julia knows what I mean. I write one check to her charity, and she will be at my beck and call."

"You're an even more disgusting human being than I thought," Julia said.

"Why? Because I'm honest?" David replied. "Honest about my own self-interest? Honest about my goals and how the world functions? You act as though there are some eternal moral laws in the universe that I'm violating. No. What gets under your skin is that you know I'm right."

"David, there's an inherent goodness to the world and to humans," Julia said. "That moral fabric is there, regardless of whether you believe in God or not. Some of us, apparently, were so wounded as kids that we do our best to suppress it."

"You must be joking, Julia. A moral fabric to the universe? War has existed as long as humanity has existed. War, greed—these things are also a part of what it means to be human. There is nothing eternal about your values. Why be compassionate? Because it's right, or because it feels good and it makes you happier? As soon as you admit that any set of rules is arbitrary, the only measure of morality is how happy or fulfilled something makes us. I'm happy and fulfilled making money and having power over other people. You are happy pretending you're saving lives and changing the world. We both do what we do because it makes us happy. There's no moral difference between our lives. That's just nonsense you were taught as a child, and you stupidly still believe it."

"You know what? I hope you're getting your reward, because I can tell you that I am happier and more fulfilled than you are," Julia retorted.

"Are you still going to believe that when I am walking out of here first because I have money? Enjoy getting eaten by mosquitoes, Julia. I'm sure you'll find it fulfilling."

Tim had been silent during this whole discussion. He didn't have the energy for an argument, but he was content listening. At least it had distracted him from the reality of his capture.

Some time later, a militant came up to the group and pointed at David. "You. Come with me."

David looked up at him. "Me?"

"Yes, you. Follow me."

David got up and grabbed his jacket from off the ground. He dusted off the sleeves and put it on. A little dirty but better than nothing. They walked across the clearing to a smaller hut that had a covered porch. With his gun slung over his shoulder, the guard grabbed David's elbow to lead him along. He pushed David up the two stairs of the hut and onto the porch, and David cautiously entered through the door.

The room was sparsely decorated with a desk and several maps on the wall. Standing with his back to David was the same man who had addressed them earlier. David saw for the first time that he had some gray in his hair.

Hearing him enter, the leader turned around.

"How are you faring?"

"I've been better," David answered. "Do you have any water?"

"Get him some water," the leader said to the soldier who had brought David in. The soldier nodded and left. "Take a seat." David sat on a nearby wooden stool and folded his hands on his lap. The leader came over to him and handed him the cell phone he had held up earlier. "Make a call to your people."

"I will need the contacts from my other phone."

"Of course." The leader opened a drawer in his desk and pulled out a bunch of cell phones, laying them on the desk. "Which one is yours?"

David peered at the phones and pointed to one on the end. The leader walked it over to him. "I'll watch you. If you turn on any sort of location finder, I'll beat you. Understood?"

"Now, why would I do a thing like that?" David noticed they had turned off his phone. He powered it up, let his thumbprint unlock it and found Catherine Dunlop's number. He dialed it on the Nokia. It rang several times before someone picked up.

"Hello?"

"Catherine?"

"David? Why are you calling me from this number?"

"I've been kidnapped."

There was silence on the other end of the line. Then, "Oh my God, you're serious."

"I am. I need you to contact the insurance company."

"Of course, of course. I'm sure I can track that down. Are you alright? Should they call this number back?" David looked up at his kidnapper, who nodded.

"Yes, they should. And I'll be fine as long as the insurance company pays up. The quicker the better, Catherine."

"We'll be back in touch with you soon," Catherine promised. "I can't believe this is happening. Don't do anything rash. We'll get through this."

"We will. Thank you, Catherine." David hung up the phone and handed it back to its owner. "What now?"

"We wait to hear back from your people."

"Fair enough." David realized that kidnapping insurance was probably his best-ever return on an investment. "So, how much of the ransom money will Eli Schrimpf get?"

His kidnapper smiled. "Eli Schrimpf?"

"Yes, Eli. The overweight guy who works for Octagon. The man I gave our itinerary to."

"So you're the one. I suspected that."

"A simple way for my insurance company to help the cause. I couldn't exactly write you a check, now could I?"

The guard came into the room and gave David a cup of water. He sipped it calmly while looking at his chief captor. "I hope you use the money wisely. By the way, do you have a cigarette?"

Chapter 28

Chris woke up with mosquito bites all over. It felt as though his whole body was swollen, and he ached more than he itched. The insects had bitten through his button-down shirt, and he regretted wearing flip-flops. His feet seemed to be prime targets.

Maybe he had slept a couple of hours. When he awoke, Julia was looking at him.

"Morning."

"I noticed you didn't say 'good morning.'"

"That would be a lie." Julia smiled at him. There was something different about her expression. Maybe it was her glasses, which were smudged with dirt and sweat that she couldn't seem to clean with her blouse.

"Sexy look for me, eh?" Chris joked.

"I might have to throw this suit out," she replied. Julia looked horrible, Chris thought. Tired, filthy, hungry and covered in red bites. Still, he kept looking at her. He couldn't imagine how he looked. Good thing there were no mirrors.

"I have a headache too," Chris said.

"Not enough water."

Chris thought back to the events of the day before. They had taken each person one by one to see the leader and make calls. His call, he assumed, had been the shortest.

"Paul! Paul, it's Chris." He was sure the desperation showed in his voice.

"What's up, man?" Paul responded casually.

"I...I have been kidnapped. I'm in the creeks somewhere," he said, the words pouring out of his mouth.

There was an odd silence on the other end of the phone. "Hand the phone back to the men there. I'll see what I can do."

That was it. That was the sum total of his conversation with Paul. Obviously, he did not have the money for a ransom. He was convinced he would die in these woods. Abby died on a street in Cambridge, Massachusetts, and he would die in a jungle in the Niger Delta.

"Do you think the New Africa Initiative people will be able to get us out?" Chris asked Julia, returning from his thoughts.

"They were a little panicked when I called yesterday," Julia admitted. "I hope they will call back today." Julia reached out and grabbed Chris's hand. Involuntarily, Chris could feel himself getting aroused. Was this what happened when you were about to die? You sought comfort in the hope of sex?

Tim McAuliffe was staring at them. "At least you two have each other."

Chris turned to Tim. "I'm sure the Octagon Petroleum people will have you out soon. They have protocols for things like this, right?" he asked.

Tim shrugged. "They do. It figures that Octagon would have a procedure even for kidnapping. Engineers run the company. A plan for everything."

Only David Sloan seemed relaxed. He was bitten like the rest of them but seemed oddly at peace with it all.

"Get any sleep there, David?" Tim asked him.

"Probably about the same as you. I wish I had brought bug repellent. DEET, DEET, my kingdom for DEET!" he yelled in a mock Shakespearean tone. "I have never liked the outdoors. I could never understand the attraction of camping. When I was a kid, my parents sent me to overnight camp in New Hampshire. I enjoyed it about as much as this. Dirty. Tired. Buggy."

"You poor, suffering soul," Julia said to him.

"Not suffering. Just stating facts."

Their breakfast that morning consisted of bread, water, and fruit. Chris drank his water so quickly it spilled down the front of his shirt. He didn't even notice.

"What we need is a game to play," David said finally. "I feel like I am in the car with my brothers driving to see family in upstate New York." No one responded to his proposal. "Think of the stories you'll be able to tell. 'I once got kidnapped in the jungle of Nigeria. No, seriously.' I'm sure it will be worth at least one drink at a bar for you in Greenwich Village or Williamsburg, Julia."

She gave him a nasty look.

"I hope you write a check to the New Africa Initiative for the money they will spend getting me out of here."

"Always coming back to money, Julia. Tsk, tsk. Whatever happened to altruism?"

Julia turned to Chris. "Talk to me, Chris. I think I might strangle the financier."

"Are we in high school here? Let's be civil," Tim interjected.

"The Houstonian speaks," David said. "How does this compare with the woods of Houston? Are there any woods in Houston, Tim?"

Tim stayed quiet.

Time passed in a daze. They were tired enough that most of them dozed off or tried to. Making small talk took effort.

Mid-morning, Chris could see some commotion in camp. An SUV

had driven up, and he could not see who was in it, but it was obviously someone important. Militants gathered around the car and talked excitedly. The prisoners were suddenly interested.

"What's going on?" Chris asked.

"No idea," Julia said. "I guess we'll find out."

Chris's heart nearly stopped. It couldn't be, but it was: Paul Wisner strolled around from behind the leader's hut. Walking next to him was an athletic-looking Nigerian with a beard in a blue button-down and khakis. He looked vaguely familiar.

The soldiers crowded around the Nigerian visitor excitedly. The leader of the camp was with them too, and they were heading over to where the prisoners were sitting.

"Ifeanyi Okoye," Chris said at last.

"Who?" Tim asked.

"It's the former MEND commander who was recently released from prison," Chris remarked, remembering the newspaper article he had read about Ifeanyi. "The one commander who would rather endure prison than compromise with the government. He has written a lot about the Niger Delta struggle."

"No wonder he's so popular," Tim responded. "I hope this means he has come to set us free."

"Not likely to happen without paying him money," David added.

As the crowd neared the prisoners, they all stood up. "So where is this friend of yours, Paul?" Ifeanyi said, his rich baritone voice carrying through the camp. "Let me guess. That one." He pointed directly at Chris. Everyone turned to look at Chris, who felt suddenly uncomfortable.

"Great guess, Ifeanyi." Paul laughed. "The one dude who doesn't belong in a group like this." Chris looked down at his soiled shirt and cargo shorts.

"He doesn't look like the type to get us any money. Hopefully, he can offer some prayers though." Ifeanyi slapped Paul on the back and turned away from the prisoners. He headed over to the leader's hut without waiting for a response. Paul stood looking at Chris for a moment.

"You ready to go?" he asked.

"Paul, how did you find me?"

"Let's just say that if you live around this area long enough, you know a lot of people. Ifeanyi is an old friend." Paul nodded in the direction of the hut. "Let's jet. Ifeanyi is going to stay in camp for the day and get a ride back to PH with someone else. You probably want a shower and some food."

Chris began to move, then stopped. "Could Julia come with us?"

Paul looked at Julia. "Very professional in that suit, Julia. I almost didn't recognize you. Need a ride as well? I don't imagine our friends will be crushed to be losing your company. I doubt the New Africa Initiative can pay much."

"I'd love to go." A relieved Julia looked Chris in the eyes. "Thank you."

"Why are you thanking him?" Paul said and chuckled. Without waiting for them, he began to walk toward the car. Chris was dumbfounded. Paul seemed to think this was just another day in Nigeria.

"What about us?" Tim asked, a hint of desperation in his voice.

Paul turned back. "Ah, the money boys. I think you'll be fine chillin' here. Look at all the nice local scenery you get to enjoy." He waved his hands around. "This, my friend, is Nigeria. You can even get a nice view of the water from over there." Paul pointed to his left and then walked off without another word. Chris grabbed Julia by the hand and hurried after him.

"Hang out in the car. I'll be back in a moment," Paul said before walking away toward a group of soldiers. Julia watched him wander away and shook her head.

"I don't get it. How does Paul know these people?" Julia asked.

"As he said, he has spent years in the villages around Port Harcourt. I guess he has made lots of friends."

"Yeah, but these people? These people are violent. They have guns. They kidnap people! He is all buddy-buddy with them."

"Let's just get in the car." Chris put his arm around Julia and gently pushed her toward the door. "You sit in front."

"I suppose it has begun."

"Something has begun, Ifeanyi. You said yourself there was no other way."

"Of course," Ifeanyi replied as he sat down on the stool opposite Fineface Pepple's desk in his hut. Fineface sat on the edge of his desk and looked down at his old comrade.

"We should get nearly four million dollars for them. The hedge fund manager alone will bring in two and a half million."

Ifeanyi smiled at this news. "Wonderful. Well done, Fineface. I wish we could have waited, but several of the commanders said they would do nothing without their payments."

"It's hard to blame them. We still don't know how the government will respond to our attacks. This insurgency might cost the commanders everything."

"And it might win us everything, too," Ifeanyi replied, his eyes aglow as he thought about how close they were to achieving his dream. "When do you think you'll have the money?"

"I would guess in two days, no more," Fineface replied.

"Good. I'll be back then to pick it up."

"Minus the commission for my men."

"Yes, Fineface, minus an appropriate commission. You have taken a big risk."

Fineface nodded, pleased with how well things had gone. One advantage of oil bunkering was that it put militants like Fineface in contact with certain people in the oil industry, like Eli Schrimpf. His tip-off could not have come at a better time, with Ifeanyi having just given the go-ahead for targeted kidnappings.

"We still have an arms problem," Fineface added, as he reached into his pocket for a cigarette. "I got you what I could from my sources, but we need more weapons, especially explosives. Time is short."

"Time is very short. We need to launch the attacks next week, before the government moves too many more troops into the area. There is one place we could go for arms once I have the money."

"It has to work, Ifeanyi. We have come too far. The gods have favored us."

"Yes, something like that," Ifeanyi said as he watched Fineface take a long draw from the cigarette. "Those things will kill you."

"If I have to wait for these things to kill me, Ifeanyi, I will have lived a full life." Fineface smiled. "If only we knew how the next week would go."

"If only."

Paul, Chris, and Julia did not say much to one another on the first part of the trip back to Port Harcourt. Paul knew the roads well even though there were no signs. He hummed hymns to himself as he drove.

Chris remained quiet in back, sensing the tension between the two in the front seat.

"So what was that all about, Paul?"

"What do you mean, Julia?"

"You know what I mean. MEND insurgents? You're friends with them?"

Paul stopped his humming. "I am. I know them from my work."

There was a long silence.

"You're going to have to explain this. Maybe it's because I am being ignorant, but how can that be Christian, Paul? Those people are killers. They held us at gunpoint. They detonated a bomb right near us. They could have killed your protégé back there." Julia took a deep breath to let out some of her anger.

"Julia, I'm sorry you had to go through that. I really am. I know that was tough, but you weren't in any serious danger," Paul said. "I'm glad you're safe now. You and I take very different approaches to the problems in the delta."

"Yeah, no shit." Julia could tell her stress and exhaustion were getting the better of her, but she didn't care. "Enlighten me on your reasoning."

"Your approach, Julia, is based on a materialist view of the world. You see people suffering, so you give them medicine. You see young people involved in an insurgency, so you dream up employment programs for youths. You assume that the best way to justice is to reduce suffering as much as you can. You raise money and create new initiatives. And I applaud your work. You help a lot of people."

"And you, Mr. Missionary? How is your approach any different?"

"Well, I don't see either the problems or the solutions as being fundamentally material in nature. Relieving suffering with medicine and starting job programs are great. We do charitable work and support NGOs like yours. But I see that work as secondary to the spiritual problems in society, and that's where we differ."

"So you focus on saving souls for eternity, right? Well, what if eternity doesn't exist, huh? You waste your time preaching a bunch of nonsense while I'm saving lives."

"Come on, Julia. Look around you. What is the problem in the Niger Delta? It's the corruption of the government officials and army officers. It's the greed of the oil companies. It's the self-righteousness of people like you who come here to solve the world's problems, and yet you usually end up perpetuating an unjust system. You were in Ichewa to support Octagon Petroleum. Many of the foundations you rely on for your funding earned their money through exploiting others. You collude with those in power, and, in doing so, you uphold the system and prevent real change from happening. How is the Niger Delta going to change with a few less cases of malaria or a dozen youth having jobs? Those are important efforts, but they miss the key problem. We need to transform society."

"We are making progress. I do the best I can to help people! And talk about collusion with those in power. You work with insurgents!" Julia was shouting now.

"Julia, I can understand your emotions, but you're missing something important. You think people are fundamentally good. If they are given the right materials for their well-being, then they will act in a good, moral fashion. It's all about materialism. That is where you and I differ. I see human beings as sinners by nature. The root of sin is separation from God. When we are separated from God, we seek our own self-interest, even if we have all the material goods we could ever want.

"The way to help the Niger Delta is to attack the cause of the suffering. If people acknowledge God in their lives, if they can see Jesus as a path to God and let him into their hearts, then they can find a connection with God and pray for the grace to be better. People have to see love as the ultimate good to put aside their self-interest, and they can only do that through a transformation of their souls. God has to be involved, otherwise you are missing the fundamental problem."

"This is all a bunch of religious nonsense."

"Is it, Julia? Ask yourself why you are here. Be brutally honest. What brought you to Nigeria? Yes, you want to help people and alleviate suffering. But isn't it also so you can find deeper meaning in your life? Isn't it so you can feel connected to God, the ground of being and the source of love?"

Julia had to think for a moment. "Yes, I do find meaning in helping others. I do want to feel connected to the love in the world. But that has nothing to do with a belief in God."

"Julia, perhaps we're not as far apart as you assume. Let's say you do believe in a deeper spiritual reality to the world that is rooted in love. That deeper spiritual reality is God. When you are connected to it and motivated by it, you are being guided by God, whether you call it that or not. That same God called me here, or at least, I'd like to think so. Since I acknowledge God, I think the solution lies in getting others to feel that same connection, the same connection you also feel through love. That is the goal above any material end. I work with churches so they can see and feel the love of God in their lives and then do transformative work in the delta. I want Nigerians, not Americans, to start soup kitchens and job programs. I want them to lobby the government for real change and write articles exposing corruption. The kingdom of God, Jesus's great guiding vision, can only take hold here if everyone works for it and is inspired by the Holy Spirit that calls them to love and compassion.

"I work with government officials to make them see that they can be disciples of Christ in their workplaces through compassionate living. And yes, I also work with the insurgents because I want them, as much as anyone else, to be more loving, compassionate, and focused on God. Maybe they will try methods other than violence. Maybe they will use their share of the oil money for their communities and not for a new house in Port Harcourt. It is the spiritual change that's needed, Julia. That's how things will become better. When it becomes solely about materialism, it leads to selfishness and self-aggrandizement."

"If the problems are all spiritual, why hasn't God done more to bring about change?"

"Maybe God is bringing about change right now. Because of your capture, I got the chance to ride out here with Ifeanyi Okoye. What do you think we talked about? We talked about the injustices of the delta. We talked about the struggle. I tried to talk him into a more loving and less violent approach. His writing makes a difference. His moral stance against corruption makes a difference. Because I have a relationship with him, he was willing to listen to me.

"Sadly, I don't think I got through to him. He is so wounded from his past that all he sees is his obsession with expelling the oil companies. The cause—his revolution—has become his idol, his god, not love. But even if he succeeds, I'm not convinced it'll bring the change he imagines. All of us need to continually seek connection with God because only by making God our ultimate concern will things change. And when things change, you can feel the love in the air. It's the Holy Spirit at work."

"So is it the Holy Spirit that helped you with being gay?" Julia blurted out.

Paul was stunned. That was one thing he hadn't expected.

No one said anything. The only sounds Chris heard were the blowers for the AC and the faint hum of the engine.

Finally, Paul spoke. "In that, as with everything, I try to seek love. I happen to have found love by being true to who God made me. In spite of what some other Christians believe, I think I am following God."

"I'm sorry, Paul. I shouldn't have said that."

"No, it's fine. You've had a rough couple of days. And you're right that I should be more out. I should take a bolder stance on being gay. I guess I'm just afraid that it would jeopardize the other work I do."

"For what it's worth, I don't care that you're gay. And I do respect the work you do. I have to admit, I have never thought about God the way you phrase it. You're making me think."

"Thinking is good. It's probably good for all of us right now."

Chris kept silent in the back seat but felt pangs of guilt for telling Julia about Paul. At least everything was out in the open now.

Julia found the button that adjusted her seat backwards. She tried closing her eyes, then gave up on rest and stared at the palm trees passing by her window.

Chapter 29

After Julia and Chris left the militants' camp, conversation between David and Tim became less frequent. Tim wasn't much fun for David to talk to and usually ignored his verbal potshots. David tried to entertain himself by focusing on his plans and how he could maximize the money he would make off this uncomfortable little sojourn into the jungle. His firm, Sulla Partners, was already planning its trades in anticipation of the violence and a subsequent rise in oil prices. Since the rise would likely be ten dollars per barrel, more if they were lucky, they could only make big money through heavily leveraging all their assets. Two things would help him out: a general panic in the market and ensuring the violence in the Niger Delta was as damaging as possible.

The first part was tricky. Once they were building their position in the market, David had to spread rumors to build a panic. Rumors put him in dicey legal territory, but he was willing to take the risk. His whole firm was at stake. He knew who he would talk to as soon as he was headed back to Connecticut.

The second part he still hadn't figured out. How could he prevent the government's crackdown from succeeding? The insurgents who'd kidnapped them were clearly professionals. How many others like them were there? As an aside, he thought he might take up Olufemi Adebayo on his offer to invest in some wells that would be sold. If the violence took off, he was sure companies like Octagon would begin to divest from

Nigeria. The potential upside was huge. He would just have to find a way to do business like the Nigerians. If it all worked, he'd have the hottest commodities fund around. David began dreaming about additional investors and the money they would bring in. A little time in the jungle was a small price to pay. Still, he couldn't wait until it was over.

After a rather bland lunch, the leader of the militants, whose name David had discovered was Fineface, came over to the two of them and said, "You are going back today."

Tim McAuliffe let out a sigh. "Hallelujah."

"You better hope your friends have the money all ready."

"Oh, I am praying for that. Don't worry," Tim replied.

"Good," Fineface responded. He motioned to the guards near them. "Get on your feet, both of you." The two prisoners stood up. David felt the soreness in his knees from so much sitting. Then the guards came over and wrapped blindfolds around their heads. A guard grabbed David's arm and began escorting him away from the spot that had been their home for the past three days.

Once out of the camp, David realized they were descending along a path. He stumbled a couple times on rocks he could not see, but the guard holding his arm caught him. He felt like asking the guard to be more careful, but thought better of it.

When they stopped, David heard gently lapping waves near them. They were at the water's edge. He envisioned the waters of Long Island Sound, which helped calm him. Water is good, he thought. Should be a quicker trip.

"Get in the boats," Fineface ordered.

"With pleasure," David responded.

"Boats?" Tim asked.

"Yes, we are traveling by water. Unless you'd like to take the longer route through the creeks," Fineface replied.

"No, no. The water works for me."

Fineface snickered at Tim's eagerness to get the ordeal over with.

Getting in the boats was a bit tricky with blindfolds on, but David figured it was a necessary precaution. The militants did not want to risk giving away the location of their camp. There was no telling what David or Tim might be able to recognize later.

David went first and had little trouble getting into the boat. After rowing for so many years, finding his balance on the water was second nature. When his butt settled on the metal floor of the boat, the water that had collected there soaked through his pants and briefs. Given how filthy he was already, David didn't care. He heard some commotion in the next boat over. It sounded like Tim McAuliffe had fallen over while trying to get over the boat's gunwales.

When they got under way, David caught a few words that the militants exchanged with one another, but he tried not to pay attention. The less he knew, the better. At this point, he couldn't wait to be back in Port Harcourt and on his way back to the US. Thankfully, the water was calm and the sea breeze felt good on his face. He focused on the days ahead.

When the boat slowed down some thirty minutes later, the engine and wind noise quieted, as well, which put David's senses on high alert. He could feel tension in the air. One of the militants loosened David's blindfold, and his eyes blinked instinctively to adjust to the glare off the water. Up ahead was a dock, and behind the dock were buildings that David guessed were part of a larger village. He had no idea where they were in the delta. It all looked the same to him.

Tied up at the dock was a larger vessel, painted in a dull navy gray with its bow pointed toward them. It had a large-caliber machine gun mounted on the deck and a half dozen uniformed men standing around the ship, each with his own semi-automatic rifle.

For the first time, fear welled up inside David. What if something went wrong? On the dock, he saw several Nigerians in suits and one white person along with more armed, uniformed personnel. David sat up and stiffened when he felt the barrel of a gun at his back. These militants were not taking any chances. He was their protection until they got their money. Sweat formed on his brow and dripped from his armpits. He watched the distance slowly close between the bow of the boat and the dock.

The lead boat, the one David was in, glided into the dock first. As the bow neared the first pylon, one of the militants on their boat grabbed the dock while another began to tie the bowline. A JTF soldier on the dock reached for the line, but the nearest militant slapped his hand away. The militant and the soldier stared at each other before the soldier on the dock backed off.

"Fineface, I didn't know you were back in this dirty game!" The loud voice came from a larger, well-dressed Nigerian man on the dock, his clean-shaven head glistening in the sunlight.

"Well, Godwin, some of us don't like bowing down to people in suits," Fineface yelled back. The two men glared at each other. David could sense there was no love lost between these men. "Kindly pass over the money, and we will make this exchange as quickly as possible. I don't want to look at you any longer than I have to," Fineface added.

Godwin Ogbe nodded to one of the men in uniform, who passed the large black duffle bag from the dock to the boat. David noticed the white person look nervously at the bag. An Octagon Petroleum lawyer? The bag was handed to the boat, and Fineface unzipped it and looked inside. David caught a glance and saw US dollars, lots of them. Fineface turned to David and said, "Off the boat."

David got to his feet and quickly moved up the boat. One of the JTF soldiers on the dock reached out, and David used it to help him onto the dock. He had never been so grateful to be on solid land. He straightened out his soiled suit jacket and stood next to the white lawyer.

Once David was out of the boat, the insurgent in the bow unwrapped the line from the pier and pushed off. The boat carefully backed out, avoiding the larger naval vessel. When Fineface's boat was safely out of its path, the other boat made its way to the dock. The driver of that boat was not quite so skilled, and David felt the dock shake under his feet as the bow hit one of the pylons. Rather than tie the boat to the dock, the insurgent in the bow merely held on with his hand for a more rapid departure. Tim McAuliffe awkwardly shuffled forward until he too was on the dock, and the second boat backed away rapidly.

Once Tim was standing next to David, two soldiers put their bodies between them and the water and started corralling the former prisoners off the dock.

"Easy there, boys," David said, feeling a particularly strong shove toward the shore.

David could sense something was wrong. Then shots rang out. He looked over his shoulder and could see the naval vessel opening fire on the two smaller boats with its machine gun. David turned from the gunfire and ran as fast as he could toward the cover of the village. Tim and the Nigerians were not far behind him.

"What the fuck was that about?" David said once they made it behind the nearest building. "Those assholes," he added between heavy breaths.

"Assholes? They were shooting at the bad guys," Tim said.

"Yeah, but they lured them in under false pretense. I wonder how many of them got hit." David peered out from behind the concrete building and could make out both of the MEND boats moving at high speed into the distance. At least the boats made it out okay.

"Don't you want those guys to get what they deserve?" Tim asked.

"I thought you were a good American. Don't you care about honesty and integrity? A little suffering and your virtuous ideals go out the window." David caught himself and took a deep breath. He added, "These government guys are no saints. They are a bunch of corrupt criminals."

"But these government guys didn't just kidnap me either. Al-though, I admit, I'm shocked they started firing."

David looked toward the water again. The boats were off in the distance, and the shooting had stopped. He came out of hiding to see the government people walking briskly up the shore from the dock. When Godwin got close, David said, "Get any of those bastards?"

"We shot several," he replied.

"But you didn't want to chase them with the navy?" David asked him.

"No, let them run. If we chased them, we would probably lose some men too. Safer to dust their boats with some bullets before they can respond." David noticed that Godwin seemed happy with himself.

"Are you going to track them down?" Tim asked.

Godwin stopped and stared at him with his dark brown eyes. "Yes, we will. All in good time," he said.

A few hundred yards away, Fineface's two boats were finally in the clear. "That traitor Godwin! I should have known not to trust him," Fineface said when they were sure they were out of sight of the dock. He walked to the bow, where two of his men lay. One was wounded in the shoulder, but the other one had taken a bullet through his skull. Fineface shook his head. "At least that idiot with the machine gun doesn't know how to shoot. Otherwise, we might all be dead."

Fineface waved the other boat over. Miraculously, only one of their men was wounded.

"What are we going to do now, Commander?"

"We are going to head back and get the money where it needs to be. We will get our revenge when Ifeanyi's plan comes through. Look at these men, my friends," Fineface said, pointing to his dead and wounded soldiers. "This is why we fight!"

Chapter 30

Port Harcourt

Standing outside the door to Julia's apartment, Chris took a deep breath before knocking. He had called Julia beforehand to be sure she was home. The kidnapping incident had gotten him thinking about their relationship. Living in Nigeria was risky. He didn't know what might happen to either one of them. Maybe now was the time to take things to the next level. Their time in captivity had made him realize how much he cared for her.

"Hello, Chris," Julia said, after opening the door, her voice void of enthusiasm.

"Julia! How are you?" Chris could feel his heart beating faster. Something about her just-out-of-bed look made her seem even more attractive.

"Doing okay, I guess," Julia replied. "Come on in." He walked over to the couch, the same beige love seat where they had shared their first kiss, and sat down.

"Would you join me here?" Chris said, patting the cushion next to him. "I'd like to talk."

"Sure." Julia flopped down next to Chris.

Chris reached over and took her right hand in his. "You know, Julia, I have been doing a lot of thinking about us, especially after the past few days, and—"

"Before you start, I want to say something. I've been doing a lot of thinking the past day."

"Me too, which is why I wanted—"

Julia let go of Chris' hand and held hers up to stop him.

"Let me go first. I've been thinking a lot about what Paul had to say. For so much of my life, I've had the most negative view possible about Christians. It all seemed so stupid to me. I mean, who could believe in an old white man in the sky who controlled everything? All the miracles. Then there are the conservative Christians in the US who hate gays and obsess over abortion. Jerry Falwell. Pat Robertson. That's always been my impression of Christians."

"They're not all like that, Julia."

"I know, I know. If I had thought more about it, I would have realized that, but, frankly, I've never really considered it at all. I keep coming back to what Paul said. He said that God was the source of love in the world. I guess I see what he means, that love is a power in the world, that it seems to come from outside us, or at least transcend us. But I'm not sure how to reconcile that with the impression I have of God. It seems more like a parlor trick or a play on words. That's not the God of the Bible, at least from what I remember of it."

"The Bible does say 'God is love, and those who abide in love abide in God, and God abides in them.'" Chris was happy that he was able to remember that quotation from confirmation.

"The Bible says that? Well, it also has God walking in the Garden of Eden and smiting his enemies."

"I mean, Julia, the Bible has a lot of bad things in it, but there are also a lot of great things. Read it all the way through, and you'll see how the themes of love and compassion rise to the top. Anyone can quote a few verses that are offensive, but it's about the whole message."

"Really?" Julia said. "Which of us is being fair about the Bible?"

Chris reached out to hold her hand again. "Julia, I don't want to get into an argument about the Bible. I want to talk about us."

"This is about us, Chris." Julia's tone made Chris realize the conversation was not going to go the way he wanted. "I can't deal with the Christian stuff, especially after seeing Paul fraternizing with our kidnappers. I don't know about you, but that experience was a living hell. I want nothing to do with Paul now."

"Julia, I think you're overreacting."

"No," Julia replied firmly, staring dead ahead at Chris. "I'm not overreacting. We can't have whatever relationship you want if you side with Paul. It's me or him."

"I can't stop working for him, Julia."

"I'm not asking you to. What I am asking is for you to reject his Christian nonsense. He's in league with militants who could have killed us. That is not ok. You can work for him, and you can also make it clear that you reject his whole worldview."

Chris leaned back on the couch and stared at the ceiling. Julia had a point, and he knew it. If Paul's Christianity led him to hang out with militants, maybe Chris needed to distance himself from Paul. Chris looked back at Julia and felt his heart ache. He so desperately wanted to be with her.

"I understand what you're saying, Julia," Chris replied. "And I agree with you. But what about all the stuff Paul said about the need for spiritual renewal? That made a lot of sense."

"I guess he's right in a certain manner of speaking. Yes, people need to be less selfish and need to overcome corruption. I get that. And I see how it seems that the work I do can seem more like Band-Aids than cures. But I still don't fully agree with him."

Chris looked at Julia's face. He wanted to lean over and give her a hug. He tried to push his feelings out of his head and focus. "What was it that you didn't fully agree with?" he asked.

"I just think his model seems overly idealistic. You know what I mean?"

"I'm not sure I do. Sorry."

"The material stuff matters more than Paul thinks. Good schools like in Ichewa. Healthcare. Access to new opportunities. These things do make a difference."

"I don't think that was what Paul meant. Of course, those things matter. But maybe the spiritual change in people, the focusing on goodness and love and not on self-interest, needs to come first, or at least alongside those other things."

"Yeah, maybe." Julia let out a sigh. "Then again, perhaps it's just about the rule of law. If the laws about corruption were actually enforced, we would be in a different situation. If government programs were put in place according to the law, there wouldn't be so much skimming off the top and useless programs. I'd love to give the law a chance. Despite what Paul says, people are good. If everyone follows the rules, if the bad people are punished, then all the material stuff would work. We wouldn't need a bunch of stupid preaching if the laws were enforced."

Chris looked across at Julia. He so admired her passion and commitment to helping others. "Laws. Enforcing the laws. That'll do it?" he asked with a hint of skepticism in his voice.

"Without a doubt, Chris. They just need to give that a chance in Nigeria."

"What about the chance of letting me kiss you?"

Julia shook her head. "Chris, I'm not in the mood. Let's save the kissing for another time."

"Fair enough," Chris replied. He didn't want to leave Julia on that note, and he knew that if he left then, he would obsess over her ultimatum to distance himself from Paul. "How about a board game then? Would you be in the mood for that?"

"You're on," Julia said. "Just be prepared to lose."

Chris started to look around the apartment for the games.

"Over there, stud," Julia said, pointing to the bottom of one of her bookshelves. "And if you do manage to beat me, then we can talk about that kiss."

Later in the afternoon, after leaving Julia's place, Chris raced back to the Emmaus Center. Once inside, he darted past Silas and bounded up the stairs before knocking on Paul's office door.

"Come on in!" Chris heard from the other side of the light green wooden door.

Letting himself in, Chris apologized, "Sorry to keep you waiting, Paul. I know we had a meeting at two." Chris guessed it was close to 2:30 but resisted the temptation to check his phone. "I was spending time with Julia and lost track of time."

"No worries, man. I've got plenty to do here. You're the one who wanted to chat."

Chris sat down opposite Paul and launched into what he wanted to say. "I wanted to apologize again for telling Julia about you being gay. I—"

"Chris, it's okay," Paul interrupted him. "I was a little mad when it first came out, but I prayed about it and I get that you had to tell sbmeone. I should've expected that. We're good, dude. No worries."

Chris was immensely relieved. "Thanks, Paul. I still don't know what to say."

"It's a good thing in its own way. I need to be more comfortable with people knowing. Julia is about as a safe a person as you could have told."

"She's one of the things I wanted to talk about."

"I'm all ears, man," Paul said, leaning back in his chair and putting his arms behind his head.

"Well, I really like her. I do feel guilty having feelings for someone only a few months after Abby died. And, I...I'm so confused right now." Chris started to involuntarily chew on his fingernails, something he hadn't done in years.

"You're human, dude. To be honest, I'm probably not the best person to give relationship advice." Paul chuckled and rocked his chair forward and put his forearms on his desk. "But seriously, go with your heart, Chris. God moves in mysterious ways."

"He sure does." Chris took a deep breath before continuing, "But there is another issue. Julia was pretty shaken up from the kidnapping. She still can't believe you know Ifeanyi Okoye. She says your relationship with him shows that your Christianity is a fraud." Chris held back from mentioning her ultimatum over Chris's feelings toward Paul. He felt torn and needed to hear what Paul had to say.

"Chris, my relationship with Ifeanyi comes down to two things. The first is what I mentioned in the car. I'd rather have a relationship with him and try to sway him to seek non-violence than to cut him off altogether."

"I get that," Chris replied. "But you said yourself it didn't work and is not likely to work."

"True, it's a long shot. But there is another reason for my relationship with him. It has to do with Liberation Theology. Are you familiar with Liberation Theology?"

"No. I've never heard of it. It didn't come up in my church back home."

"I wouldn't expect it to. Liberation Theology arose in the 1960s in response to suffering. Christians saw the suffering of those around them and the indifference of many Christians to that suffering. Poor people were told to believe in Jesus and focus on the next life, which only justified continued oppression. These theologians looked at Jesus and saw someone whose entire mission in life was to bring good news to those who were poor, blind, in debt or oppressed in any way. It was Jesus's radical message of liberation that challenged the status quo so much that it got him killed. Liberation Theology claims that Christians must interpret the Bible and theology from the lived experience of those on the margins. We need a preferential option for the poor. From my own reading of the Bible, I think Liberation Theologians were dead-on right. That's one of the things that brought me to Nigeria in the first place."

Chris was nodding as Paul kept talking. Everything he was saying made perfect sense to Chris. What had always inspired Chris about Christianity was Jesus and his message.

"One key element of Liberation Theology," Paul continued, "is the way it characterizes sin. Sin is the structures of power that keep people oppressed. Poverty is sin. Racism is sin. The abuses of capitalism are sin. Just as Jesus worked to liberate people from sin, we must do the same thing. That is what I admire so much about Ifeanyi Okoye. He is working to dismantle the sinful structures in Nigeria that keep people oppressed and in poverty. I might disagree vehemently with his methods, but I agree with his ends. People like Julia don't see it. They don't see how their actions only perpetuate harmful structures. Ifeanyi's writings call out that hypocrisy. He is a symbol of hope for many poor Nigerians in the delta. He is on the side of the marginalized and oppressed. I wish Julia could see that."

After Paul finished speaking, the two of them sat for a while in silence. Chris kept turning Paul's words over in his head. He did see what

Paul was talking about, and he understood why Paul would rather keep company with those working to end oppression than with those in power.

"Isn't Liberation Theology unrealistic though?" Chris asked. "While it might sound good to overturn systems of oppression, wouldn't it be better to work with the powers that be to alleviate suffering rather than risk the violence that someone like Ifeanyi might bring?"

"That's why Christianity matters, Chris. Ifeanyi needs to see the end goal as liberation in line with Jesus's model. Jesus could have led a violent insurrection himself. Many of his supporters wanted that. Instead, he voluntarily went to the cross. But the cross is not the end of the story. Resurrection happens. Resurrection happens when we follow God. We have to believe that and continue to work for it."

"What about the rule of law?" Chris asked, echoing what Julia had told him. "Don't we need that to make sure people aren't oppressed?"

"The law is not always on the side of good. It's often used by those in power to maintain their power."

"But we have to start somewhere. We need the rule of law."

"Perhaps, Chris. But we also need Jesus and his message to influence the law."

But why can't we start with the law here in Nigeria? Chris thought to himself. Chris appreciated what Paul had to say, but in his heart, he wanted Julia. He wanted to be with Julia, and he knew what he needed to do.

Chapter 31

The dingy reception area where Chris was waiting had the smell of antiseptic solution, which reminded him of the cleaning products they used on the wrestling mats in high school. He thought it was an unpleasant odor then, and now, seven years later, he hadn't changed his mind.

That morning he had been to the police department in Port Harcourt to report his kidnapping. He wanted to tell the authorities what he knew about the insurgents. The police had listened to Chris and then made him wait while they made several phone calls. After another wait, he found himself going to one of the government administrative buildings in downtown Port Harcourt to meet with a man named Godwin Ogbe.

"What does this guy do?" Chris asked the young Nigerian behind the reception desk outside Ogbe's office.

"He is regional secretary for human affairs here in Rivers State. He is a very powerful man."

"I see. Does he have anything to do with fighting insurgents?" Chris didn't want to get shuffled around to another meeting and another office.

"Mr. Ogbe has lots of jobs and responsibilities. You might have to wait awhile. Mr. Ogbe is a busy man." The young Nigerian seemed in awe of his boss.

Chris hoped he was doing the right thing. This was his first time dealing with Nigerian bureaucracy, and he was not impressed. His appointment was for 3:00 pm. Chris glanced at his phone, which read 4:08. People had been coming and going from Godwin Ogbe's office ever since he arrived, while Chris sat on the couch outside. Unlike in American waiting rooms, there were no magazines or newspapers to distract Chris. He wished he had brought a book with him.

"I hope the wait is not too much longer," Chris said. The receptionist merely shrugged. "I should have been at the office today."

Chris's head felt like it had been spinning for the past several days. First there was the kidnapping, then the appearance of Paul in the camp, and finally Paul and Julia's argument. He respected Julia's work so much, and he knew how good a person she was. Chris hoped that his talking with the authorities would show Julia that he was listening to her. The rule of law mattered.

He really did want to make something more of their relationship. His thoughts drifted to intimacy with her. He pictured her dorky glasses and loose-fitting clothes and then imagined what she looked like naked. He hadn't thought about sex in so long, but now it seemed like it was the only thing he could think about. It was as though he was sixteen in gym class again.

"You can go into Mr. Ogbe's office now." The words from the man behind the desk shook him out of his daydreaming. The receptionist pointed to the door, which Chris had been looking at for the past hour and a half.

"Time to get his over with," Chris said aloud, knowing that the receptionist was not paying attention. "Maybe all this waiting will do some good."

When he entered the room, the man behind the metal desk barely noticed him. On the wall to his right hung framed photographs of the same man, who Chris assumed was Godwin Ogbe, with various political leaders throughout the delta and the country. He noticed one photograph of him with the former president. Impressive. Chris stood there, not knowing whether he should say something.

"So, what brings you into my office?" the man finally said. His intensity caught Chris off guard. It was as though Godwin was looking through him with his large eyes, which were more pronounced with his cleanly shaven head.

"Um, I would like to make a report about MEND," Chris said haltingly. "Along with several others, I was kidnapped and taken to a camp." Then he added without waiting for Godwin's response, "I know who did it."

"You were kidnapped?" Godwin's voice became calmer, almost eerily soothing. "And how did you get free? These insurgents can be nasty people."

Chris hesitated. Should he mention Paul's role? He hadn't really thought about what he would say, and now he felt like an idiot.

"When were you kidnapped? Let's start there." Godwin looked at the young American and tried not to let his impatience show.

"We were kidnapped four days ago," Chris said.

"Where did this happen?"

"We were in a convoy from Ichewa to an Octagon Petroleum facility. A tree blocked the road. The insurgents then surprised us and set off a bomb behind us." Chris added details so Godwin knew he was not making it up.

"How many others were kidnapped?"

"Three others. One with the New Africa Initiative, and the others were with Octagon Petroleum," Chris explained. "Well, one was a hedge fund manager."

Godwin leaned back in his chair and put his fingers together. "I see. And you escaped?"

"I was released," Chris said and then added quickly, "They found out I wasn't worth any ransom. I work for an NGO here in Port Harcourt."

262

Godwin remained silent.

"I'm convinced that people in Ichewa were involved the kidnapping. I don't know any other way they could have known we were taking that route to the Octagon facility."

"Say more. What do you mean?"

"As I was told, the trip from Ichewa to the flow station had not been advertised or planned far in advance. It was a road that was seldom, if ever, used. At the last minute, I joined the convoy in Ichewa so that I could see an oil facility." Chris was surprised how rapidly words were coming out of his mouth.

"So there are insurgents in Ichewa. That's good to know," Godwin replied.

"I wanted to make sure you knew that. Something should be done. This type of behavior can't be allowed. People have to respect the law," Chris said, trying to seem authoritative.

"Indeed they do. These insurgents are a big problem. They undermine society," Godwin said. "Thank you for your information."

"I'm going to write a letter to the US Consulate in Lagos. I think they should know too. I am worried about the safety of American citizens in Nigeria," Chris said. He wanted to get this over with, but also to be thorough.

"So am I. Americans are our friends, although I'm not sure that letter will be necessary. We will take care of the insurgency. Don't worry. The interests of Nigeria and the United States are closely aligned on this matter."

Godwin spoke with such steadiness that it unnerved Chris. He didn't trust him. "The people there seemed kind and peace loving," Chris said. "But I know there are bad people everywhere."

"You have done the right thing. Trust me. Anything else you would like to add? I have much to do today."

"No, not that I can think of. Thank you for your time," Chris replied. He hoped he wasn't forgetting anything.

"Good. Have a nice day." With that, Godwin picked up some papers on his desk and began looking over them. Chris, who had never been offered a seat, had been standing the whole time. He turned and left.

After Chris left Godwin's office, the phone on his desk buzzed. "Yes?" Godwin said, annoyed at the interruption.

"It's a phone call for you, Mr. Ogbe."

"Who is it?" Godwin was eager to leave for the day and hated things that came up late in the afternoon.

"Sorry, Mr. Ogbe. It's someone from Octagon Petroleum named Timothy McAuliffe."

The name was familiar to Godwin. This Tim McAuliffe was one of the people he had rescued from Fineface Pepple and his insurgents. He was tempted to have his secretary take a message, but then he thought better of it. Perhaps Mr. McAuliffe could be of use.

Godwin punched the button for line one and picked up the receiver.

"Mr. McAuliffe, it is good to see you looking so well." Godwin Ogbe shook Tim's hand as he came around his desk to welcome Godwin to his office at the Octagon Petroleum compound.

It always disappointed Godwin that Octagon didn't put more money into their offices. Wealth, like power, was meant to be displayed. Tim's office seemed particularly bland.

"Thank you. I feel not so great, but at least I am safe. Thanks to you."

Ogbe was dressed in a suit that accentuated his muscular frame. He liked to use his size to intimidate others. After Ogbe released Tim's hand, Tim said, "Please have a seat. I'm happy you were able to make time on such short notice."

"For a top executive of Octagon Petroleum in Nigeria, I can always make time." Godwin grinned.

"That is good to know. We appreciate it."

"In Nigeria, we know how to look after good businesses."

"Yes, well, that's the reason I wanted to speak with you. As you can imagine, my superiors in the United States are now deeply concerned about the security of the Niger Delta."

"That is understandable. Your kidnapping must have been quite an ordeal."

"Yes, it was. But my superiors are more worried about the possibility of the insurgency reigniting. I will reassure them that this was a one-time event, but I wanted to check with you first."

Godwin's face was expressionless. Tim had a hard time figuring out what was going on behind his eyes. His pause made Tim shift uncomfortably in his seat.

"There might be a problem, Mr. McAuliffe. My department is looking into it."

"There might be a problem? What kind of problem?" Tim's voice rose with alarm.

"Mr. McAuliffe, I do not want Octagon Petroleum to be overly concerned, but it seems that one of the insurgents is trying to cause trouble." Godwin emphasized the word "one."

Tim began fidgeting with his mouse, moving it back and forth across the mouse pad on his desk. "What kind of trouble?"

"It looks as though this insurgent wants to cut production for the oil industry."

"Oh, hell!" Tim slapped his hand on the table. "This is just what we need." Ogbe observed Tim trying to control his emotions. The stress from the kidnapping clearly rattled Tim.

"We're always looking for allies in the oil industry, Mr. McAuliffe."

"What do you need? Is there anything we can do? More security? Are there places we should put on alert?"

"Now that you mention it, there might be some things you can do. I would recommend heavier security around your facilities in both Rivers State and Bayelsa State."

"Okay, more security." Tim picked up his pen and began writing on a yellow pad.

"As we have before, I am sure the Nigerian Joint Task Force would be able to help with security. The fees might be higher than normal. This could turn into a crisis. But if Octagon commits enough resources now, it could prevent a lot of damage."

"That's a good idea. I'll talk to the people in Houston and see what we can do. I will try to get as much money as possible for security for the next several months."

"That's wise, Mr. McAuliffe. You can work through my office directly, and we can make sure the funds go to the right places and the best units."

"That makes sense to me. Anything else you might recommend?"

"Helicopters. We do not have many helicopters. In a time like this, they can be quite helpful for monitoring the militants using the waterways and for transporting our soldiers."

"You will have access to whatever helicopters I can provide. I'll put in a call to Rostow Helicopters today." Rostow Helicopters was one of two firms that specialized in providing helicopters to oil and gas companies throughout the world. They had a large presence in Port Harcourt and Warri.

Godwin paused. He wanted to seem as calm and in control as he could. It was in striking contrast to Tim McAuliffe's obvious anxiety and would reinforce Tim's faith in him. Godwin spent the moment thinking about how much extra money the new security would mean for his own pocket. He guessed his services would be worth 25 percent of the total contract. Maybe he would take a shopping trip to Dubai with his girlfriend.

"All of that sounds good to me," Godwin finally said. "Please do not hesitate to call my office directly with anything you might need or find useful."

"Thank you for all your help. I really do wish you good luck in your work."

"You are so kind," Godwin responded. Tim got up from his seat, and Godwin rose as well, though intentionally more slowly. "There is one more thing you could do, Mr. McAuliffe."

"Yes, of course, what is it?"

"It might help if you called the Rivers State governor personally. It would help my efforts if he knew that we had the backing of a company like Octagon Petroleum."

"It would be my pleasure, Mr. Ogbe. You've been a great help to me. I will be sure to let him know. He's lucky to have you in his government."

Godwin nodded. "I am so glad you are feeling better. Good day to you."

Chapter 32

Harrison, New York

When David Sloan's flight from Lagos landed, he could feel the anxiety in his body ease. He prided himself on self-control, but that trip had tested his limits. He took a final glance at Catherine Dunlop's plan for oil and gas purchases. She had e-mailed it to him while he was in flight on the NetJets plane that Martha had booked. David made some final notes and then involuntarily scratched his arms. The mosquito bites on his ankles were even worse. Why couldn't they have locked them up inside a building? As the plane taxied to a stop, he gathered his yellow legal pad and other papers in front of him, putting them into his briefcase with his laptop. He guessed the violence would start in a week. One week to get things ready.

Slinging his briefcase over his shoulder, he grabbed the folded garment bag off the seat next to him and walked toward the exit. The pilots opened the cockpit door to wish him well. David merely waved with his hand, not looking up. He had his phone contacts open and was scrolling through them. He found the number and dialed it.

"Hello, Greenwich Medical Associates," a young female voice said over the phone.

"Hello, I need to speak to Dr. Podolsky's nurse."

"May I ask what this is in regard to?"

"I need to be treated for malaria."

"Malaria? Hold on one second."

David walked down the few steps of the plane and then across the tarmac to the small terminal at the Westchester airport. Martha, his executive assistant, had a car waiting to pick him up.

"Hello, this is Stephanie."

"Stephanie, it's David Sloan. I have just returned from Nigeria, and I'm pretty sure that I have malaria."

"David Sloan. Hold on one second while I get your record. How are you feeling now?"

"A little tired."

"What makes you think you have malaria?"

"I slept outside somewhere in the Niger Delta without any bug repellent and was bitten by, conservatively, about six dozen mosquitoes."

"Okay, you should definitely come in for tests, David. If you actually have malaria, that can be life-threatening, depending on the type."

"I have to go to my office. Can't you send someone there?"

"I'm afraid that's not possible. If you are feeling ill, you need to come in to see us."

"I'm at the airport now. I can be there in an hour." David hung up the phone. Damn it. Why didn't he have a doctor who could make office calls? He walked up to immigration and customs at the small airport. After a short exchange with the officer, he strolled toward the airport exit and dialed again.

"Catherine."

"David? David, how are you doing?"

"I'm fine. Listen, I have to run to the doctor's office now, but I'll head to the office from there." In front of the small terminal, David found his driver and nodded to him. The black SUV came over, and David handed the driver his garment bag before getting in the back seat.

"David, are you sure? You should probably get some rest at home."

He could sense Catherine Dunlop's concern.

"Catherine, it's not like you to seem worried," David said. He let the dark leather seats of the Lincoln Navigator slowly conform to his body. One thing he liked about American cars was the overstuffed seats.

"David, as hard as this might seem for you to believe, I care about your health."

"How nice of you. Is James at the office?"

"Of course."

"Good, I should be there in a couple hours. I want to meet with you and James as soon as I arrive."

"David, you should really take time to recover. We can handle things at the office."

"Catherine, I did not fly to Nigeria so I could rest. I'll see you in two hours."

He hung up the phone. The last thing he wanted was pity or concern. He would need to stop at a pharmacy for some Tylenol though. He felt awful. Maybe he could rest a bit in the car, but he had no qualms pushing his body. That's what got him to where he was now.

Greenwich, Connecticut

True to his word, a little over two hours later David Sloan walked into the Sulla Partners offices. He had insisted on starting malaria treatment and had also taken three Tylenol and a caffeine pill. His body still ached and itched. But when he entered the reception area, his excitement overtook him. He waved to the receptionist and walked straight to his office.

"Martha, are Catherine and James in?" David asked, passing her desk.

"Of course, Mr. Sloan."

"Send them to my office."

"How are you feeling, Mr. Sloan?" Before he could answer, he had already closed his office door. He went over to his desk and pressed the on button to his computer. His four different screens sprang to life and began to feed him the numbers he had missed while in Nigeria. It was good to be home. A few moments later, there was a knock on his door.

"Come in," he said. Catherine Dunlop and James Li entered his office. Without waiting for them even to sit down, David asked, "How's the buying going?"

"For the past four or five days we've been building up a position in West Texas Intermediate," James began. "We have focused on contracts that are due in the next four months. So far everything has been done under the radar. I have made the purchases through several different traders I know. None of the individual orders were large enough to raise any suspicion, at least not that I can tell."

If the price spiked in the next four months, they would be sure to sell their contracts at a nice profit. They had to sell them before the contract expired, otherwise they would have an actual quantity of oil on their hands.

David said nothing. His right knee was slowly tapping the center drawer of his desk, a nervous movement. Even though he knew he shouldn't, he reached for a stick of nicotine gum. "How about the other markets?" he asked. The other major exchange, the Intercontinental Exchange, based in London, sold futures contracts for Brent Crude from the fields in the North Sea.

"You had said you wanted to keep things quiet," James replied.

"Not anymore," David said. "I want you to buy oil from everywhere you can." David paused. "Except Nigeria. Focus on contracts due in the next three months."

"That is a lot of oil, David," Catherine said. "How much money do you intend to spend?"

"How much do we have?"

Catherine and James looked at each other.

"Get the maximum margin financing for our capital," David ordered. Oil traders traded in multiples of the amount of capital, or cash, they had on hand. The rest of the investment was borrowed. Firms often leveraged their capital ten to one, or more. "Once you secure financing, I want half of our available funds invested now and half to be reserved for when the violence begins. Get out of our more liquid investments to free up more cash for this play."

"The violence?" James asked. "What do you mean, David?"

"The violence in the Niger Delta. Nigeria is about to explode again, and I intend to make as much money off of it as I can."

James hesitated and then asked, "How certain are you that violence will occur?"

"Pretty certain that something will happen. The scale of it, I don't know yet."

"Do you know when it might happen?"

"From what I could gather from listening to my kidnappers, I'd guess sometime in the next two weeks, probably sooner."

Catherine spoke up. "The situation there did not seem about to explode, David. Are you sure you want to bet so much? I don't think we should make any rash decisions."

"Are you implying that my health or my kidnapping might be affecting my judgment?"

Both Catherine and James were silent.

"If I want to risk my firm on this, that's my decision." David's voice had a harsh edge to it. "Here's what I want you to do. Start buying, and this time, I want people to know you're buying." David leaned forward in his chair and began pointing with his finger. "Specifically, I want Josh Cohn's people to know you're buying. If I know Josh, he'll sell even more just to squeeze us. The more people who know something is up, the better. Others will be looking to jump over Josh or us when something changes. That way, even if the violence in the Niger Delta does not amount to much, it might be enough to rattle the other players in the market. I want to be sure we have enough in reserve to start capitalizing on the news when it hits. If we can push Josh Cohn into more exposure, even a small rise in the market might really hurt him. And if we're lucky, the violence will be big. In that case, we'll all be rich and Cohn's fund will have its worst year yet."

James, who had never seen his boss so worked up, hesitated before saying, "If you say so, David. I trust you."

"Good." David went back to looking at his screens. James turned to leave, but Catherine waited behind.

After James left, Catherine said, "So, what did you find out in the creeks?"

"Everything that my contact told me was confirmed. The militant who captured me had not been actively involved in the insurgency for several years, other than the occasional oil bunkering. A few weeks ago, the leader, this Ifeanyi character, started recruiting his old comrades. That tells me that there must be several people mobilizing for some kind of attack. Catherine, all we need is a few pieces of news."

"Of course. I guess I'm just nervous about going head-to-head with Josh Cohn. I don't want your personal rivalry with him to interfere with business."

"It's time to knock him down a few pegs. And I'm right on this one. Don't worry." David heard his office phone ringing. He picked it up.

"Mr. Sloan." David recognized Martha Child's voice. "Your wife is on the phone."

"Excuse me for a moment, Catherine. It's time for me to get a tongue-lashing."

"You haven't called your wife?" Catherine exclaimed. David shrugged his shoulders and then pressed the button on his phone that patched Sally through.

"You got kidnapped and never told me!" The voice was a high-pitched screeching into David's ear.

"I'm fine. Thank you for asking."

"David, don't give me that crap. You must be fine or you wouldn't be in the office. Well, knowing you, you might feel like shit and still show up to work."

"Listen, Sally, you were my next call. Trust me."

"David, I wouldn't mind as much if it wasn't for your daughters. The insurance company people called to tell us about it."

"You told the girls?"

"Of course I told the girls. Their father was being held captive by Nigerian militants! What did you want me to say? I was a mess."

"I guess I should give them a call."

"You can try. I'm not sure they want to talk with you. I believe Mary said 'Good' when I told her. This should make the St. Luke's graduation even more interesting. You have that on your calendar, don't you?"

"Yes, I do. Sally, it would be nice if you could support me for once." David could feel his exhaustion getting the better of him. "Not because I need it, but it would make you seem like less of a bitch."

"David." Sally's voice became calm. "I'm mad because I care about you. We all do. What is consistently amazing is that you never seem to care much about us."

"Thank you for the call, Sally. Goodbye."

"David, take care of yourself."

David ended the call and then pressed the button for his secretary.

"Martha, can you get the St. Luke's school main number? I should really call up the girls."

"I already left it on your desk, Mr. Sloan. Just in case."

Chapter 33

When they reached the line of trucks, they knew they were getting close. For several miles, trucks, some loaded with cement and other goods and some empty, were parked along the side of the road, waiting outside Onne, the major port for Port Harcourt. Ifeanyi and Olabisi passed one truck after another as they made their way down the newly paved main road. The road was not too crowded at that time of day, mostly okadas weaving and bobbing around them. It was early evening, and the sun was rapidly disappearing behind them. Olabisi turned on the headlights, and Ifeanyi glanced at the fake papers in his hands, a manifest of parts for the maintenance of oil wells. He hoped it would do the trick. They were not picking up spare parts for oil wells but rather doing something decidedly more dangerous.

"How are you doing?" he asked Olabisi. It was her first job since her arrest and torture.

"I'm good," she responded. Ifeanyi could sense her anxiety, but he needed her on this trip. There were few people he could trust.

"It will be alright."

They both wore uniforms for Petro Nigeria, which, despite its official sounding name, was one of the smaller Nigerian oil companies. For the previous ten years, Octagon Petroleum and the other international oil companies had been selling their marginal wells to local Nigerian producers like Petro Nigeria, who could extract the oil with fewer costs. It meant that a new local industry had arisen, one that Ifeanyi hoped would provide them with the cover they needed.

Olabisi drove the truck slowly, warily eyeing the reckless okadas. The last thing that Ifeanyi and Olabisi needed was an accident that would draw unnecessary attention to them. Up ahead was their second police checkpoint. They slowed the truck, and Ifeanyi took a deep breath. Just like at the previous checkpoint though, the officers merely waved them through.

The port of Onne had dramatically expanded over the past twenty years. Port Harcourt itself had a small port area that had long since proved insufficient for the large amount of boat traffic that came in and out of the Niger Delta. Given the relatively poor state of Nigerian roads and railways, the port and local waterways were essential for getting goods around the region. This newly paved road and modern signs were all evidence of the expansion. A large roundabout welcomed traffic to the port facility. Ifeanyi scanned the area for anything that looked suspicious.

A row of security booths marked the official entrance to the port area. Each booth had a gate that had to be raised in order to pass through. At the end of the day, only two booths were open. Ifeanyi pointed to one, and Olabisi drove the truck to the waiting security agent. They slowed to a stop, and Olabisi manually rolled down her window.

"What is your business?" the security man asked. He glanced at the truck, which was midsize, had no identifying markings, and was painted an indistinct white. Olabisi wore a baseball cap with **Petro Nigeria** on it. In the fading light, the security man couldn't tell whether she was a man or a woman, which was just as well.

"We're here to pick up parts from our warehouse," Ifeanyi said, as routinely as he could, while leaning across Olabisi to make eye contact with the guard.

"Let me see your papers," the guard demanded.

Ifeanyi handed over the forged documents to Olabisi, who handed them to the guard. The paperwork had lists of standard equipment for oil repair work. The Petro Nigeria logo ran across the top of each page.

"Alright." The guard handed the papers back to Olabisi, who passed them to Ifeanyi. They both sat back as the truck drove on.

At the first intersection, they took a left turn along the road that ran behind the warehouses. It was late enough in the day that most of the port workers had gone home. Some security guards patrolled the fenced-in areas around each warehouse, and Ifeanyi could see a few trucks here and there, presumably picking up parts. Inside the fences lay piles and piles of pipes. A single well often required ten thousand feet of piping. New wells being drilled weekly, both onshore and offshore, meant a lot of spare supplies stockpiled in Onne.

Ifeanyi quietly directed Olabisi to a warehouse at the far end of the port area. The sign on the outside read **Petro Nigeria**. A fifteen-foot-high fence surrounded the corrugated tin warehouse, and stacks of the ubiquitous drilling pipes were piled up outside. At the warehouse gate, a young-looking security guard came up to them. Even though he carried a semi-automatic weapon, it seemed old, and Ifeanyi guessed it had no bullets. The guard looked curiously at the truck.

"What you here for?" he asked, his voice a little squeaky.

In the light of the streetlamp, Ifeanyi estimated the guard was no more than seventeen years old.

"We're here with orders to pick up parts for Mr. Suleiman Yaro."

Suleiman Yaro was the owner of Petro Nigeria and would never be involved in ordering individual parts, but Ifeanyi assumed the security man did not know that. The guard seemed dutifully impressed.

"Do you have any papers?" the guard asked. He took another look up and down the truck, confused that there was no Petro Nigeria logo on it.

"Of course we have papers, boy."

Ifeanyi handed over his order manifest to the guard, who looked it over. The daytime guard would have been used to seeing similar orders and might have been able to spot the fake. Ifeanyi was certain this guard had no idea what he was reading.

"Okay, looks good." He handed the papers back to Ifeanyi and went over to the fence, which he slid back to allow the truck to enter. They drove over to the entrance of the warehouse. The large metal sliding door was open. Olabisi maneuvered the truck into position and carefully backed up. Once inside, Ifeanyi and Olabisi jumped down from the cab. Olabisi went to close the outer door while Ifeanyi took out his phone and texted a number. On the other side of the warehouse, he could hear a beep that indicated his text message was received.

A man walked slowly toward them out of the semidarkness. Only a few of the large fluorescent overhead lights were kept on through the night. As the man got closer, Ifeanyi could see he had a black cap pulled low on his face.

"Drake?" he called out.

"Yes. Who else would it be?" the voice, calm but firm, answered. The man Ifeanyi referred to as "Drake" was actually Wilson Chen, an arms dealer who worked all over sub-Saharan Africa. He had once supplied arms to MEND through Henry Okah, the assumed leader of MEND before the organization began to fall apart following the amnesty. Ifeanyi had been able to connect to him through Okah's brother. "Did you have any problems getting in?" Drake asked.

279

"No, none at all. Are there any Petro Nigeria workers here?"

"Yes," Drake nodded toward the rear of the warehouse. Ifeanyi noticed a light coming from what must be the office for the warehouse. "He knows not to disturb us." Their eyes locked.

Drake was taller than most Chinese that Ifeanyi had met before, and he had a hard time placing his age. Drake had an athletic build, and Ifeanyi guessed he was a former army officer, possibly with links to the Chinese intelligence service. The Chinese were all over West Africa, expanding their informal empire.

"Mr. Okah said there were some goods here for us to pick up," Ifeanyi said.

"Yes, we have them on several pallets in the back. I have two of my men to help you load. We'll also pack some spare parts for oil in case the truck gets opened. The weapons are not traceable back to us. Let me warn you: do not cross me." Ifeanyi tried not to think of what Drake might do to him. If Ifeanyi was caught by Godwin Ogbe or other Nigerians, the newspapers would cover it, and he might have a chance of living. With Drake and his associates, it would be a different story.

"Don't worry about that. I'm the only person who knows the details of our transactions, and if things don't go well next week, I'll be dead anyway." A slight smirk appeared on Ifeanyi's face. Fatalism was useful for confidence. Drake had no reaction.

"Let's get this over with," Drake said before whistling loudly. A few moments later, Ifeanyi could hear a motor running. It was a lift carrying the first pallet of weapons to the truck.

Ifeanyi turned to Olabisi, who was waiting near the truck. "Open the back," he ordered. Olabisi pressed a button near the back of the truck to lower the ramp. She then unlatched and lifted the door of the truck. The first pallet arrived, and she started working with the two Chinese men to get the weapons packed away.

"You have women working with you?" Drake asked, suspiciously eyeing Olabisi.

"I have people I can trust working with me. This is a delicate matter. What's in the shipment?" Ifeanyi asked. He had requested arms and explosives weeks before but had heard nothing back. Only after the kidnapping did Okah contact him with the time and place that Drake would meet him. He did not ask questions then and merely took down his instructions. The funds were sitting in an escrow account in South Africa until the shipment was finalized. The funds were theoretically for real estate investments, at least as far as the Nigerian government and Interpol were concerned.

"Ten cases of semi-automatic rifles, each with twenty weapons. One hundred sixty thousand rounds of seven-point-six-two-millimeter ammunition. Twenty-two grenade launchers with twenty-five grenades each. We have also included sufficient C-four explosive and detonating devices. Satisfied?"

Ifeanyi, trying not to show his excitement, merely nodded and said, "Yes."

They both continued to watch as the weapons and then the oil parts were carefully loaded. As the Chinese assistants jumped down from the truck, Drake said, "You will have no other reason to contact me. We don't expect to hear from you again."

Drake seemed as though he was going to say something else, but then turned and motioned to his two assistants. Together they disappeared into the rear of the warehouse.

Ifeanyi looked back at the truck. Olabisi had finished closing and locking it up.

"Well, Bisi, time to head off. We have some deliveries to make." The two of them climbed back into the cab and slowly pulled out of the warehouse. They waited at the fence for the security guard to open it. Ifeanyi didn't even bother to acknowledge him. They made their way out to the exit of the port area. A guard waved for them to stop.

"Papers," he said, matter-of-factly. Ifeanyi handed over the manifest. He glanced over it and then looked back at the two of them. "It's late in the day for a pickup."

Ifeanyi shrugged. "I just do what I am told now, boss. There is some work that needs to be done on a well, see. Big wahala. We need to drive there tonight." Ifeanyi smiled dumbly.

"Hold on," the guard said as he went inside his guardhouse. Ifeanyi could see him picking up the phone and calling someone. No one seemed to be answering his call. He came out a few moments later. "You better be on your way. Don't fall asleep."

"Thank you, thank you," Ifeanyi said in return. He nodded to Olabisi, and they drove away.

Aba, Nigeria

Two hours later, Ifeanyi sat down on a plush couch in a large house outside Aba, northeast of Port Harcourt. The house belonged to a family member of Emeka Nwosu's, and he had brought his family there for vacation, or so he told his secretary at work. Only a couple people knew of his whereabouts, and they were told to alert him if anyone started asking questions about him.

As Ifeanyi relaxed, Nwosu's housemaid brought him a Guinness Extra Stout, and he took a slow drag on the bottle. "Almost there," he said quietly to himself.

Olabisi was resting on the couch opposite him. Against his better judgment, or so he claimed, Emeka had allowed Ifeanyi and Olabisi to visit him to work out the next steps of financing and the final plan for distribution of arms. The home was gated and had its own security guard.

Even if the local police suspected something, they would need hard evidence before they entered private property. Emeka and his friends were very well connected with the governor. All the same, Ifeanyi was discreet. He had used the back service entrance and parked the truck out of sight from the street.

"The trip went well?" Emeka asked as he came down the stairs. He was tired from the day, and the anxiety about the upcoming attacks kept him sleepless too many nights.

"Very."

"Where to next?"

"We're heading out to my camp before dawn. We have to make a stop to drop off some arms on the way."

"How close are you to launching your attacks?" Emeka found a seat on the chair opposite Ifeanyi. His housemaid brought him a gin and tonic, his normal drink, and he took a long pull.

Ifeanyi thought for a moment. "Most of our teams are prepared. We'll be ready in a week. Not sure about Mama Sandra. If all goes according to plan, we should have an attack on twenty different major installations simultaneously, plus what the women can do."

The two of them carried on talking in low voices for another thirty minutes. Emeka was responsible for the distribution of money to the various MEND commanders, and Ifeanyi wanted the full report.

"Make sure you get some rest," Emeka said finally. "You don't look well."

"It's been a long several weeks."

"What's going to happen after the attacks? Where will you go?"

"I've been giving that a lot of thought. I'll head back north to my village and lay low for a time. From there I will write and try to encourage the movement for separation."

Emeka was glad he would stay away. Ifeanyi had already exposed them enough.

"I've always admired your passion, Ifeanyi. You never stop fighting." Emeka took another sip of his gin and tonic. "You have no interest in a family, my friend?"

Ifeanyi, at first, didn't answer. Then, in a low voice, he said, "I guess that is not for people like me." He swirled the remainder of his beer in the bottle. "I committed myself to something else long ago."

It was the first time Emeka could ever remember seeing a tinge of regret in Ifeanyi. "You'll be remembered long after your time. If only all of us had your courage." Emeka hoped his words reassured his old friend. Maybe Ifeanyi was human after all.

Chapter 34

Ichewa

Every time Captain Mustafa Musa ventured into the creeks of the Niger Delta, he knew he was in enemy territory. As the convoy made its way toward Ichewa, Musa took his Glock 17 handgun out of its holster. He removed the ammunition clip and examined the barrel. Satisfied that all was normal, he re-inserted the clip and loaded a round in the chamber before putting on the safety catch. It made him feel better to know he was prepared for anything that might come up. Looking down the road, which was choked with palm trees and green undergrowth on all sides, his mind drifted back to his conversation with Godwin Ogbe.

"Musa, I have a special mission for you," Godwin had said when Musa entered his office. "You have always been a loyal JTF commander, and I have not forgotten that. Now I need you to root out insurgents."

The prospect had excited Musa. Special missions meant extra pay and other side benefits if things went well.

"Thank you, sir. What do you want me to do?" Musa appreciated Ogbe's calculating mind. He was highly ambitious and never a friend to anyone but himself. His predictable motives made him an easy person to work with.

"Some men in the village of Ichewa were involved in a high-level kidnapping last week," Godwin had said, as if passing down a sentence. "We need to make an example of them before the violence returns. I know Ifeanyi Okoye has been planning something. I want to find out who his co-conspirators are. The people of the delta must know that supporting him will only bring trouble."

"Of course, sir. What would you like us to do?"

Godwin had sat back in his chair while Musa stood in his uniform on the other side of the gray metal desk. "Finding the insurgents in Ichewa would be too difficult. It is far too big a place to arrest everyone suspicious. Standard questioning in the village will lead nowhere. I want you to arrest the elders of Ichewa and bring them to Port Harcourt. I will speak with them one at a time and convince them how bad violence would be. We must turn the people in the creeks against Ifeanyi and his group. And I would bet some of them were involved. We might get lucky and find out all we need to know."

"What means are at my disposal, sir?"

"Any means you deem necessary." Ogbe had leaned forward and brought his clenched fist down onto his desk with a thud. "Those people must know that their actions have consequences."

Those words rolled over again and again in his head as Musa traveled at the head of the convoy. Their goal was obvious. Make other village leaders afraid of supporting Ifeanyi while encouraging those who wanted to support the government.

Musa had some ideas. He had five vehicles in his convoy and thirty soldiers at his disposal. Two of his trucks had mounted .50-caliber machine guns. His force had been increased for this mission, apparently with Octagon Petroleum funds. They even had an Octa-on Petroleum helicopter above them that could observe movements in and out of the village along the main roads. If anyone tried to flee, they would be sure to notice.

The first building Musa saw as they drove up the road toward

Ichewa was the new school, the same building that provided all the photos for the oil companies and the local Big Men. Would a school cure these people of their ills? No. Nigeria needs the right kind of education. The people here had no respect for the Prophet Muhammad or the great faith of Islam. Instead, they worshipped their various ju-jus cloaked in Christian language. As a Northerner from the Hausa tribe, Musa did not like delta people. They were superstitious and had little respect for authority. They did not know how to govern themselves. Their oil had given them an overinflated sense of their own importance. He was happy to teach them a lesson.

"Stop in front of the school," Musa ordered. His American-made Humvee pulled up to the building and stopped. There were a few people lingering outside the small houses across the street. Musa could see the concerned looks on their faces. He got out of the Humvee and walked around. The clearing here would be perfect for the public arrest and humiliation of the elders.

He turned to the nearest adult villager and motioned for her to come closer. She was no more than twenty years old and looked terrified. Reluctantly, she walked toward the uniformed captain.

"I want you to bring your elders here," Musa told the villager. She looked at Musa with a blank expression. He repeated his order more slowly and with greater emphasis, but this time he pulled out his gun. "I want you to bring your village elders here."

The woman nodded, then turned and ran off toward the center of town, her purple dress trailing behind her.

He shook his head. "These people."

Musa walked over to his Humvee, where a sergeant, his second-in-command, waited. "Unload the men. I want to speak to them here." The sergeant nodded and then started barking orders while walking back to the vehicles behind them.

There was a rustling of uniforms as thirty soldiers lined up in a semicircle around their commander. Each stood at attention. Musa was happy that the new soldiers seemed to fit right in.

"I want you to bring the villagers here to the clearing in front of the school," Musa began. "Go through the town and round up everyone. I want this done quickly and orderly. We are the law here."

The noncommissioned officers took over from Musa and began splitting the soldiers into groups to search the town. Within minutes, armed men in green fatigues were heading toward frightened villagers. One sergeant stayed behind with the machine gunners.

Musa leaned against his Humvee and looked at his watch. It was midmorning, and the sun was warming the pavement in the clearing. He could hear the sound of the helicopter overhead. Some villagers, accompanied by soldiers, were slowly walking toward him. When one of the returning soldiers was within earshot, Musa asked loudly, "Where is the village? Why are people not here? What is the delay?"

"Sir, we're having to go house to house. Some of the houses are empty."

This response infuriated Musa. How dare these people waste his time!

Musa went to his Humvee and grabbed his radio. He adjusted the frequency and began to talk. "This is Captain Mustafa Musa. Can you see any activity in or around Ichewa?"

There was a slight pause before the helicopter pilot above the town responded, "I see lots of hurrying, but no cars are leaving the village."

"Good," Musa replied. "I'll have my radio on me. Let me know if that changes."

"Roger that."

Musa put the radio on his waistband and looked at the small gathering of about twenty-five villagers in front of him. More were coming down the road. He glanced at the new school next to him. The more he looked at that building, the more he hated it. What did these people do to deserve a new school with its fresh paint and nice colors? The delta tribe swine were inside learning their lessons. Time to get the attention of these villagers.

He turned to the second vehicle in the convoy, which was pulled up alongside his Humvee and had a machine gun mounted on the back. Musa motioned to the schoolhouse. "Put some bullets into that nice, new school building."

The soldier responded, "Yes, Captain!" before climbing up onto the back of the truck. He cocked the weapon and turned it to face the school. A burst of a dozen rounds sprang from the machine gun. The sound from the large .50-caliber bullets echoed around the clearing.

The inexperienced gunner seemed almost surprised by the noise and let his aim slip. Bullets broke glass on the second story, and he could hear screams from inside the building. The children in the school were well protected behind the concrete walls, Musa reasoned. There was nothing like the screams of children to instill fear.

"No!" someone yelled from the small crowd of villagers in front of school. "Don't shoot the children!"

"Again," Musa ordered. The machine gun fired away. Concrete and paint shot off in multiple directions. More screams could be heard from inside the building. Several of the villagers moved toward the truck with the machine gun as though they were considering whether they could rush the Humvee.

"Enough!" Musa shouted to the gunner, and the firing ceased. He turned to the crowd and could see panic on their faces.

"How could you do that?" a man asked. "There are children in that building."

"I ordered the village to gather here. Where is everyone?" Musa looked around. "I don't see them." Glancing down the road, Musa was pleased to see that his ploy had worked. More than a dozen parents, mostly mothers, were running toward the schoolhouse with others behind. The banner over the main door of the schoolhouse was now in tatters. The places where the concrete had chipped off formed a stark contrast to the fresh yellow paint. When the first woman reached the school, she sprinted inside, yelling the name of her son, which Musa could not make out. Others followed her into the building.

A few minutes later, there was a sizable crowd of villagers gathered in the clearing in front of the military vehicles. Some people were speaking to one another, and a few called out questions at Musa, who simply ignored them. Not all of the villagers would be there, which was fine. He knew his message would be relayed to those too afraid to show up. As the soldiers trickled back, herding more villagers to the clearing, they walked back near the trucks until the two groups, soldiers and villagers, faced each other.

When he was satisfied that enough of the village was present, Musa walked to the center of the road. The crowd became silent, but the tension from the shooting of the school was palpable. Musa looked around and then bellowed, "Where are the elders of this village?" No one moved. "Don't make me lose my temper. Where are the elders of this village?"

Several people moved in the crowd, and soon there were four older men standing before Musa. "Where are the rest of your elders?" he asked.

One of the men spoke up, "These are all of them."

Musa took out his handgun. "That, I know, is a lie. It doesn't help that your pictures were splashed over all the newspapers." Musa reached into his breast pocket with his left hand and pulled out a folded newspaper. He shook it open and looked at the picture. "I count seven people from the village in this picture. Are you telling me that the other three merely stood there? I hope you can tell I mean business."

"What I meant to say, sir," the elder responded, his voice slightly quivering, "is that we are all the elders in the village now."

Musa thought about this for a moment. "You are lying to me, but we will deal with that later. It has come to our attention that this village has been supporting insurgents."

"That's not true," one of the elders interjected.

"Your denials will not help the cause of this village. It has been decided that the elders must report to Port Harcourt for questioning. The residents of this village must know that violence has consequences. I'm placing you four under arrest."

"You cannot do that to us. You have no evidence of any wrongdoing."

"Last week, after the dedication of your new school, several people were kidnapped and taken for ransom after leaving this village. There is no way the insurgents could have known they were not going back to Port Harcourt unless one of you, or perhaps several of you, informed them. That is evidence enough."

"I demand to have a hearing with the governor!" one of the elders shouted.

"Oh, you will have your hearing." Musa turned to his soldiers. "Arrest them."

Soldiers stepped forward and seized the four elders. People in the crowd started to yell: "Go!" "Leave us!" One of the elders, the youngest of the four, resisted and pushed the soldier away. The soldier reached out again and the elder slapped his arm defiantly while staring at Musa. Then a second soldier came up behind the elder and grabbed the back of his neck. Instinctively, the elder elbowed the second soldier in the face, cracking his nose. When the villagers saw what was happening, they cheered. Musa was losing control of the situation.

"Wait!" Musa shouted, infuriated by this act of defiance. He pulled out his handgun and walked over to the resisting elder. He raised his gun to the man's head and fired off a round without hesitating.

The shot momentarily stunned the crowd, and they went silent. The elder's body slumped to the ground with blood and brains leaking from his head.

Shock quickly gave way to outrage, and the people in the crowd shouted: "Killer!" "Get him!"

Without warning, the crowd surged toward the soldiers who had attempted to arrest the now dead elder. Musa fired his gun in the air, but it seemed to have no effect. The crowd was on top of the two soldiers and was wresting their guns from them. Musa then turned his gun on the crowd and fired at the nearest person standing over the soldiers. The man fell to the ground. The frenzied crowd continued to surge toward the soldiers.

"Fire!" Musa yelled. Five of the soldiers near the trucks started to unload the magazines of their AK-47s into the crowd. There were more screams. Bodies began to fall.

"Stop! Stop!" Musa bellowed. The crowd was silent. The smell of cordite was heavy in the air. There were nearly two dozen bodies on the ground in front of the villagers. A woman let out a loud wail. Then another wail went up. Musa fired off his gun into the air, and the women quieted down.

"This is what happens when you defy the authority of the government," Musa declared. He could feel his heart pounding as he surveyed the carnage before him. "I expect this village to cooperate. We will be back tomorrow to question your elders. We want law and order here. Know that you brought this violence on yourselves. All we want is peace."

Musa worried that the crowd of villagers might surge forward again, and he knew he had to diffuse the situation. He didn't have enough men to settle things without more violence. He turned to his men and motioned them back to the vehicles. He realized he was waving around his handgun, and he carefully put it back into its holster. He could feel the warmth of the tip of the barrel.

As soon as he was in his Humvee, Musa ordered his driver to go. The worried man nodded and turned on the engine. The rest of the soldiers were still loading into their vehicles, but Musa did not wait for them. His Humvee did a rapid three-point turn, and Musa caught the eyes of villagers. He knew that look well. It was the look of pure hatred.

Chapter 35

Port Harcourt

Julia O'Keefe parked her truck on the sidewalk in front of the Em-maus Ministries offices. As she rushed out of her truck, she didn't even notice that her front right tire was over the curb. She hoped that Chris was inside working. Without hesitating, she burst through the front door. Silas was sitting in his normal place.

"Hello, Ms. Julia."

"Is Chris in?" Julia asked, spitting out the words.

"Yes, he's upstairs, probably in the library."

Without waiting for a response, Julia ran down the hallway and up the stairs. Reaching the library, she stopped. Chris, his elbows on the table, had a book laid out in front of him. Julia took a moment to stare at him, lost in his book. When he realized someone was at the door, he looked up.

"Julia!" Chris had a big smile on his face. The night before, they'd had a long conversation at Julia's place. They talked through the trauma of their kidnapping and how they had been feeling the past few days. David Sloan earned some choice words from both of them. They even talked more about religion. Despite the shock and exhaustion of their ordeal, they found themselves laughing by the end. Maybe things would work out for them. The night ended with a passionate kissing session, which Chris still couldn't get out of his mind. He'd felt almost giddy in the office most of the morning. His mind kept drifting to Julia. But when he saw her in the doorway, he knew something was wrong.

"What is it?" Chris asked.

Even with all of her rushing to get there, Julia was now oddly frozen. "It's Ichewa," she said finally.

"What about Ichewa?"

"JTF soldiers showed up there earlier today and massacred the citizens."

"What?"

"I don't know how many are dead. Maybe as many as twenty or thirty."

"But why?"

"I don't know, but I'm afraid it had something to do with the school dedication and the kidnapping. I'm heading out there now. I have to know what happened."

Chris pressed a button on his cell phone, which showed that it was already after 3:00 pm. "Are you sure that's safe, Julia?" He saw how determined she seemed. "Okay, but we won't get back from there until late. We could run into more trouble."

"Chris, I have to see it. The New Africa Initiative has done work in that village. I'm going, either with or without you."

"Yes, yes, you're right." Chris stood and looked around. So much was racing through his mind that he had a hard time thinking clearly. He wanted to make sure he had everything, but he didn't know what he could possibly need.

"Come on!" Julia pleaded. "I want to beat the traffic out of the city.

Chris nodded and followed her out of the library and downstairs.

"Nice parking job," he said when they got outside.

Julia didn't respond. She was already opening the driver's-side door.

•••

Tim McAuliffe had finally finished his work for the day. In less than a week, he would be on his way home. His first several months in Nigeria had been frustrating but a good learning experience. He now knew firsthand the struggles of working with Octagon's joint partner, the Nigerian National Petroleum Company.

After the kidnapping, however, Nigeria had turned into a nightmare for him. His nerves were fried, and he'd barely slept since he was freed. He couldn't get the experience out of his head. His boss had agreed to let him return to Houston early and take some much-needed vacation. Tim had just logged off from his computer when his cell phone rang.

"Hello."

"Tim, this is Eli. There's something we need to discuss." Eli Schrimpf, the head of Octagon Petroleum in Nigeria's regional cleanup team, had never called his cell phone before.

"Now? I was just about to head out."

"Yes, now. Can I come down to your office? I'm glad you're still there."

"Sure." Tim hung up his phone. "Great," he mumbled to himself, "just when I was ready to take off." He started gathering his things anyway. That would give Eli the not-so-subtle sign that he should be quick about whatever was on his mind. His back was turned when he heard a knock on his door.

"Come in," Tim said.

Eli Schrimpf closed the door behind him. "I just spoke with one of our helicopter pilots."

"Are you planning on taking a trip?" Tim asked, trying to feign lightheartedness. Eli's expression showed it was something serious.

296

"No, this was one of the pilots you authorized to help the government."

"Oh, right. Was he complaining about something?" Tim asked.

"He was, as a matter of fact."

Tim let out an audible sigh. He just wanted to go back to his apartment and rest. "Well, what is it?"

"There was an attack on innocent civilians today in Ichewa."

"Ichewa? The place where we dedicated the school last week?" Tim couldn't believe what he was hearing.

"Yes. I have reports that over two dozen were killed."

"By whom?"

"The Joint Task Force, including soldiers Octagon financed on your orders. The helicopter pilot you lent to the government confirmed everything with me in person. He was over the village when it happened."

"Oh my God," Tim replied, collapsing down into his chair.

"What should we do now?" Eli asked.

"Let me make some calls. This is unbelievable."

Eli sat in the chair opposite Tim's desk. He glanced around at the walls with their posters of happy Nigerian citizens and the Octagon Petroleum logo displayed on the bottom with the tagline, Helping Develop.

Tim picked up the phone on his desk and started dialing. It was just before lunch in Houston. The phone rang several times before being picked up.

"Walter Cunningham's office." Tim recognized his boss' secretary's voice.

"I need to speak to Walter. This is Tim McAuliffe."

"Hold on one second, Mr. McAuliffe. I'll see if he is available." Tim waited, tapping his foot on the ground. A moment later the voice returned, "I'm sorry. He is in a meeting. Would you like to leave a message?"

"Tell him it's urgent!"

There was a slight pause on the phone. "Okay, hold on one minute."

"Come on, Walter. Pick up," Tim muttered. More time passed.

"Tim?"

"Walter! I'm glad I got you. We have a problem. There has been a massacre in Ichewa."

"What are you talking about? What's Ichewa?" asked the voice in a slow, East Texas drawl.

"It's the Nigerian town where we dedicated a school before my kidnapping. The army here killed two dozen people in that town earlier today."

There was a pause before Walter responded, "That's tragic, Tim. I am sorry to hear it. We should have our PR people in Lagos issue a statement of concern. We can have it on our Nigerian website tomorrow." Walter's voice was calm and unperturbed. "Now, I don't want to sound callous, but why call me in Houston?"

"Walter, they used some of our soldiers. Our money went into this."

There was another, longer pause this time.

"How did that happen, Tim?"

"Well, after the kidnapping, government officials here said they were afraid of a new insurgency. They said they needed more resources for protection of our oil facilities."

"And you promised them Octagon funds for that protection?"

"It was to safeguard our resources, Walter! How was I supposed to know they would go shoot people? My God, what is this place?"

"Tim, calm down. Let's take this step-by-step. Who knows that our resources went toward this?"

"I don't know, maybe ten or so people here. I really haven't checked."

"Well, check. I want a list of names by the end of the day."

"End of the day? It is the end of the day here." Tim could feel his exhaustion deepen.

"Get the names by the end of today, and I want you to talk to them all tomorrow. This was a tragedy, one that Octagon Petroleum had no part in. Do you hear me? We had no part in this. I want that to be made clear to everyone there. And tell them tomorrow that the home office has their names."

"Yes, Walter. I'll be sure to do that." Tim put the phone back on the receiver. He looked up at Eli, "Did you hear that?" Eli nodded. "I suppose that's that, then. Our money helped shoot people, and yet it didn't. Wonderful corporate logic."

How did I end up in this position? Tim wondered. He looked through the papers that were left on his desk. Where was that number? His secretary had already gone home. When he found it, he picked up the phone again. "I want to hear this from the horse's mouth," he said.

"Hello," a female voice answered when he dialed.

"Hello, I'd like to speak to Godwin Ogbe."

"I am afraid Mr. Ogbe has gone home for the day."

"Let me have his home phone number. This is Timothy McAuliffe from Octagon Petroleum."

Tim waited for a response. "Hold on, Mr. McAuliffe. I might be able to find him."

Tim covered the mouth of the receiver. "Typical," he said to Eli, who was lost in his own thoughts.

"Mr. McAuliffe."

The booming voice made Tim wince as he pulled the phone from his ear.

"Hello, Godwin, I'm glad to reach you. I heard there was a massacre in Ichewa." Tim could tell his nervousness was making him speak more quickly than usual.

"Rumors. Rumors, Mr. McAuliffe. Don't believe everything you've heard."

"I got it from an eyewitness! Are you telling me that he is lying?" Tim was sick and tired of dealing with Nigerians. "Now, what happened?"

Godwin sighed before replying. "I sent an officer out to the village to talk to the elders about the insurgency. The people there attacked one of my soldiers, who defended themselves."

"Defended themselves? I heard that two dozen villagers were killed. How many soldiers were killed?" Tim nervously ran his hand through his hair.

"I do not know about the numbers. This is a dangerous time in Nigeria. These insurgents must be dealt with. Sometimes bad things happen. Surely a man in your position can understand that, Mr. McAuliffe. It is about making Nigeria a safer place, especially for companies like Octagon Petroleum."

"But people were killed!"

"Mr. McAuliffe, this is not Texas. The police cannot easily enforce the laws here. Sometimes violence is necessary."

"What the hell does Texas have to do with this? Listen, I don't want Octagon Petroleum resources being used to kill innocent civilians."

"You are assuming those citizens were innocent," Godwin said in a calm voice. "They were not."

"Just no more using Octagon Petroleum resources to kill. Got it?"

"And what should I tell my men if the insurgents attack an Octagon Petroleum facility?"

"Just don't kill innocent people."

"Of course not. And don't worry about the newspapers, Mr. McAuliffe. We will take care of the newspapers. Octagon Petroleum's name will not appear."

"Good. Good. I have to go now." Tim hung up the phone. He couldn't deal with Godwin Ogbe anymore.

"God, please don't let this get out," Tim prayed quietly. "What have I gotten myself into?"

Ichewa

The first things Chris and Julia saw when they drove into Ichewa were the bullet holes in the new school building.

"Look," Chris said pointing up to the second story. "The windows have been shot out. I wonder if any of the kids were harmed."

"I hope not." Julia's voice was shaking.

They pulled up next to the school. The main road in the village was deserted. There was a stillness in the air.

"Where is everyone?" Chris asked, looking around the clearing in front of the school.

"I would bet they are caring for the wounded in the small clinic or preparing the dead for burial," Julia said. "It's eerie here." She nudged Chris and pointed to the ground. Bloodstains covered the road despite the afternoon rain that had come through earlier.

They wandered down the main road and waved down the first person they saw. The woman stared back, then turned and walked away from them. It was as though the whole village was in shock.

Julia led Chris to the small clinic in the village. It had been built, like the school, with Octagon Petroleum money. It had had a full staff for less than half of its ten years of operation. Fortunately, after the dedication of the school, the clinic had its full complement of two doctors and three nurses, which served Ichewa and the surrounding villages. The doctors rotated in from Port Harcourt. Given the violence, they would both be here, reasoned Julia.

Approaching the one-story clinic, they could see that it was full of activity. They entered through the main door, but no one was at the reception desk. A few people walked by but didn't seem to notice them. Finally, Julia reached out to someone. "Can you tell me where I can find Dr. Obe?" The person pointed down the hallway.

Julia and Chris walked down and peered into the first room. There was a small boy in the bed with an IV in his arm, his parents at his bedside. They looked up at Julia and Chris, then, realizing they were not doctors or a nurses, went back to focusing on their wounded child.

"I guess that answers your question about the school," Julia said. The door to the next room was locked so they kept moving. At the end of the hallway was a large room with several beds in it, separated by cloth screens. Julia spotted who she was looking for.

"Dr. Obe, how are you?" Julia went up to him and made a motion to hug him, then thought better of it.

"Julia O'Keefe, it's good to see you." Julia could see the strain on Obe's face. "Things are bad here, as you can see."

"What's the situation? I only heard a brief report."

"We have twenty-two dead and another twelve wounded. Four of the dead and five of the wounded are children. Thankfully, the clinic has just enough beds for the wounded. We're tending to them."

"Do you need more supplies? I am sure that the New Africa Initiative can help out with that."

"We do," Obe admitted. "Thank you for the help. I can have the nurse give you a list." Obe managed a smile through his exhaustion.

"Do you mind if we look around?"

"You are welcome." Dr. Obe waved his hand around. "Just be sure you wash up and take the usual precautions. We don't need any infection complications."

"Of course. Thank you, doctor."

Julia and Chris looked around the facility, careful not to touch anything. Chris leaned around one of the curtains in the main room and saw a man in his twenties with bandages around his right leg. When he saw the man's wife, Chris nodded and then felt embarrassed for his curiosity. Of course they wanted their privacy. There were far fewer machines and beeps than you would find in an American facility, but everything was clean, and the people seemed well cared for.

"It's just so sad," Julia blurted out before they even left the large room.

"What is?"

"All of this violence. I can't believe it." She put her hands up to her face. "It's as though all of the efforts with the school were for nothing. This clinic was never meant to be used for this, for children and victims of brutal violence!"

Chris put his arms around Julia's shoulders, which rose and fell with each of her deep breaths. A disturbing thought crossed Chris's mind. "Maybe I shouldn't have gone to see that man, Godwin Ogbe," he said, almost to himself.

"What was that?" Julia asked, looking up at him.

"After our talk about the rule of law, the next day I went to see someone named Godwin Ogbe. He's the government official in charge of hunting down insurgents. I told him about our kidnapping and that it had to have been someone in Ichewa."

Chris could see from the look on Julia's face that he had done something wrong. "What is it?" he asked.

"Don't you see?" she said, pushing away from him.

"See what, Julia?"

"This is all your fault."

Chris's face turned pale as he thought of the little wounded child in

303

the next room. "I...I only wanted to help. I wanted to make sure the bad people were punished. You said yourself the MEND people were bad, that we needed the 'rule of law.'"

"That's why the JTF came here," Julia said, averting her eyes from Chris as though he was too disturbing to look at. "You told them to come here."

"Hold on a second, Julia. You can't say that. I was trying to uphold the rule of law. I was doing the right thing."

"No, you thought you were doing the right thing. What you did had horrible consequences."

Chris was getting agitated. "I need to talk to Paul about this."

"Yes, run to Paul."

"Julia—"

"Let's get some air," Julia said. Her voice had become cold.

Julia walked ahead of Chris, not bothering to see if he was following. When she reached the main street, she slowed her pace, again struck by the surreal feel of the place under the specter of death.

Chris was at her side now. "Listen," he said, "you know I could never intend harm like this."

Julia took a moment to respond. "I know." Chris could see the redness in Julia's eyes, and he wanted to reach out and touch her. "Let me think about this some more," she said. "I have too many emotions going through me now, and I'm afraid I will say something I'll regret. But how could you be so naïve?" There was anger in her voice as she muttered the last phrase.

"Naïve? You were the one who said people were good and we needed the laws enforced. You were the one who said that material action, not moral transformation, was needed."

"Damn it, Chris. Of course society needs moral people to function."

"And how is that supposed to happen if not from enforcing the law?"

"Just shut up about you and your Christianity. Shut up, okay?"

"Alright," Chris said meekly.

Julia walked back to the truck. They returned to Port Harcourt in silence.

Chapter 36

Somewhere in Bayelsa State

Mercy Dublin-Green had lost her husband to a Joint Task Force bullet six years earlier. The first year after her husband's death, she had struggled to raise her three young children and spent many nights praying to God to alleviate her misfortune. The answer to her prayers came in the form of Mama Sandra.

Mama Sandra was not from Mercy's village. She was even of a different tribe. But Mama Sandra had made it her mission to support women in the Niger Delta, especially women whose husbands abandoned them or died. The local women's group helped Mercy with food, clothing for her children, and, most importantly, gave her friends and a community outside her family. Mercy's village and family had been helpful, but village custom did not often favor single women. For Mama Sandra and the women of her group, the only thing that mattered was supporting their fellow women, even if it sometimes clashed with tradition.

Mama Sandra was also deeply committed to the struggle of the whole Niger Delta. She remembered the Biafran War she'd experienced as a child and how the delta had been a pawn to larger tribes and forces. It imprinted on her forever that, even though the tribes of the delta differed, they had to band together if they wanted to resist the encroachments of the large Nigerian tribal groups—the Igbos, the Hausas and the Yorubas.

The widowed Mercy Dublin-Green went to all the local women's meetings, and she heard stories about the resistance efforts of Mama and the other women. Oftentimes, Mercy was surprised to learn that a woman not much different from her had helped smuggle arms to MEND or led a protest that shut down an oil facility. Now Mama Sandra was asking the women of the region to do something different. She was asking them to attack oil installations. The plan had been laid out in a matter-of-fact manner one meeting. The foreign-dominated oil industry had poisoned their water and stolen their resources. The only way to assert the independence of the Niger Delta was to push the oil companies out. The only way to do that was to make it so costly to do business in Nigeria that they either shut down production or sold their facilities to Nigerians.

The key, according to their meetings, was to attack oil installations across the delta region at one time. Mama Sandra had groups in Rivers State, Bayelsa State and Delta State. Each of those states contained extensive onshore oil operations. The women had gone out into the woods and scouted the various wells, pipelines and flow stations to assess security and the likelihood of disabling the facilities. From there, a list of targets was created with specific goals and outcomes. One of the biggest issues that they debated in their meetings was how to minimize oil spills, but they all admitted that a certain amount of spillage was inevitable.

In several villages, women were appointed to make homemade explosives. The bombs were rudimentary—ammonium nitrate mixed with diesel fuel and a detonator—but they did not need large or complex explosives for their purposes. Transporting the bombs was surprisingly easy. The JTF and other local enforcement authorities never suspected that the women were transporting anything other than local household goods. Every team of women had taken at least two trips out to their planned site to survey the task ahead. Everything was all set. All the women needed was the signal to go. That signal came the day after the

Ichewa massacre.

Mercy Dublin-Green was excited about her mission. She was doing it for her children so they could grow up in a Nigeria with more justice and opportunity. She met her best friend, Angel, at dusk, and they got on Mercy's okada motorcycle for the trip out. Strapped to the back of their bike, wrapped in one of Mercy's bags, was their explosive device.

They stuck to the main road for most of the trip. Every vehicle they passed made their hearts race. If they were discovered at that point, they would go to jail for a long time. But no one thought twice of two village women riding an okada. When they reached the turnoff for the local oil well, they pulled their okada into the bushes, making sure no one saw them. The okada was well hidden, especially in the fading light. Earlier, they had marked a path through the trees for the final mile to the well. Although Mercy had a flashlight with her, she did not have to use it. The path was familiar, and the light from the dying sun provided just enough illumination.

Mercy and Angel had been chatting to ease their nervousness while they rode along. Now, as they walked through the dark woods, they were silent. Approaching the facility, they eyed the fence with its barbed wire running along the top. There were so many wells throughout the region that they were rarely guarded, unlike the flow stations where the oil from the wells was collected and separated. Nevertheless, the women stayed hidden until they were satisfied that no guard or technician was around. They crept forward across the cleared ground that surrounded the well, nervously glancing both ways. If they were caught now, it would be difficult to come up with a viable excuse.

Mercy reached into her bag and withdrew a pair of wire cutters. Finding an inconspicuous location in the fence, she began to clip. The evening sounds of the surrounding woods drowned out any noise from the snapping metal. Mercy made the hole just big enough for the two of them to make a rapid escape, if necessary. They carefully withdrew the cut portion of the fence and made their way up to the well. The wellhead itself stood atop a low concrete platform. It was painted green and had valves coming out of several sides. About halfway up was a pipe that took the flow of oil from the well to a station a mile away. They carefully brought their device out of the bag and set it next to the base of the well. There was a simple timer on the outside of the device. When they were certain the bomb was in place, Mercy pressed the button that started the small, digital timer.

"Let's go," she said to her friend. She was relieved that this part was finished.

They hurried to the woods and made their way back to the road. The timer had been set for twenty minutes. They needed to be back on their okada and headed toward their village before the bomb went off. The scale of the damage would be minor, they had been told, and the well would non-operational for only a few weeks, possibly longer. If that well was knocked out of commission, Mercy knew that Mama Sandra would be happy. It would be something she would tell her children about. The night the women struck back all across the delta.

As Mercy and Angel approached the road, the traffic was light, thankfully. It was dark so they could see any headlights coming down the road in advance. The two of them waited for a break in the cars and then wheeled their okada out onto the road. Mercy and Angel climbed on the okada and kicked the starter. The engine sputtered and then stopped. Mercy tried again. Again, the engine sputtered and stopped. The bomb would go off soon. She began to panic. She tried a third time, and the engine began to catch. Mercy revved the engine with her right hand, but then it died. She hurriedly kicked the starter again and again, but nothing.

"The engine is flooded," Angel whispered to her from behind.

"What?"

"The engine is full of gasoline. It won't start."

They were on the side of the asphalt road, but it had no shoulder. They had both chosen dark-colored flower-print dresses that provided natural camouflage but also made it difficult for oncoming traffic to spot them. Mercy looked over her shoulder. She could see headlights approaching. The light was coming fast, too fast. She tried the engine again, but nothing happened. The lights were quickly gaining on them. Should she pull the bike off the road? Did the car see them?

At the last second, she and Angel jumped off their okada to the side of the road. The oncoming car swerved out of the way. It had caught sight of them at the last moment. The car's tires screeched, and Mercy could smell burning rubber as she lay on the side of the road. The okada looked undamaged.

The car was stopped ahead. Mercy made the fateful decision to stand up. She was sure the driver of the car could now see her in its rearview mirror.

"Sit down," Angel whispered loudly. "They can see us."

"I know. I want them to."

"What if they are with the government?" Mercy did not respond to Angel. The car began to reverse and made its way back to the two women. Angel stood up as well. Mercy walked over to the car.

The car window rolled down. There were two men in the front seat. Fortunately, neither of them was in uniform. "What are you doing out here?" the driver asked accusingly.

"We were coming back to our village from a women's meeting," Mercy said. "Our okada broke down."

"A women's meeting, eh?" The driver looked to his passenger, and they both snickered.

"Yes, the two villages are working on a quilt that will show our unity. Men fight and women unite." Mercy stood there staring at them.

"We can give you a ride. It's already dark. You women should learn how to drive an okada."

"Maybe our husbands will teach us. And we can teach them to make quilts," Mercy added. Angel carefully hid her smile at Mercy's comment. The men got out of their car and walked over to the okada. The driver shook his head and the two of them wheeled the bike over to the car.

BOOM! The bomb went off a mile away. The woods muffled the sound, but it was unmistakably an explosion. There was a visible flash in the woods that indicated the oil had caught fire.

Mercy screamed, "What was that?"

"Oh no!" the driver said. "It means trouble. Hurry up and get in the car."

"You're not involved, are you?" Mercy asked the driver haltingly.

The man shook his head. "No, no. Get in. Get in before soldiers arrive and arrest us all." The bike fit uncomfortably in the trunk of the car. The trunk could not be closed, but none of them cared. As soon as the women were in the car, they began driving. Angel reached across the back seat and squeezed Mercy's hand. They had done their part.

Chapter 37

Greenwich, Connecticut

The phone's ringtone penetrated deep into David Sloan's sleeping brain. He had a habit of always keeping his phone on. It was a relic of his days as a young trader when his boss would call him at all hours of the night to talk about the upcoming day's trades. Sadly, that former boss had committed suicide two years earlier. His manic depression and self-medication with cocaine and pills had finally caught up with him.

David heard the ring again. His body ached. The anti-malaria pills were working, but his body demanded far more sleep than he was willing to give it. He forced himself awake. Too much depended on him now to worry about his own health. When he grabbed his phone, he noticed it was a call from Eli Schrimpf.

"Hello," David said, still mostly asleep.

"It has begun."

David shook his head and tried to think clearly. "It has begun?" he repeated dumbly.

"The attacks have begun."

The words struck his mind with the same effect as his head being dunked in ice water. "What's the damage like?" he asked, his voice focused.

"I have reports that nearly eighty wells, mostly the larger ones, and half a dozen major pipelines were attacked throughout the delta."

"That is a big dent."

"Yeah, it has taken out nearly a third of Octagon's onshore production. The other majors were hit hard too. It's fucking chaos here."

David glanced over at his alarm clock. It read 2:30 am. Shit, he thought to himself. That means it is 7:30 am. in London.

"Thanks for the call, Mr. Schrimpf. This will be worth your while."

"I sure fucking hope so. I'm still waiting for the first payment you promised. I could always leak something to the papers if I'm not paid."

David hated people who made threats. He suppressed the instinct to make a threat in return. He knew Eli Schrimpf wouldn't rat on him. He'd have just as much to lose as David. "Don't worry. Just be sure to keep me updated on anything that changes."

"Sure. Will do."

David put the phone down next to him on the bed. He'd been too exhausted to have any of his several girlfriends over for the night, which was a good thing. He swung his legs over the side of the bed and slapped his face a couple times.

"Come on, David. Here we go. Don't fail me now." He let out a deep breath, then reached over for his phone and dialed a number. It rang several times.

"Hello?" He could hear a groggy voice on the other end of the line.

"James, it's David."

James Li had to think for a moment before he realized that David meant David Sloan, his boss. "Oh, David. What is it?"

"The violence has begun in Nigeria."

"It has?"

"Yes. So far, close to a third of onshore production is shut down. The London markets open in about an hour. We have to be there for this one."

"Of course. I'll get changed and be in the office as soon as I can."

"This will be big, James."

"I hope we bought enough."

"Just get to the office. And call whoever you have to. I'm going to call Catherine."

Port Harcourt

Chris Reed had barely slept the whole night. He kept staring up at the bug net above his head as scenes from Ichewa raced through his mind. He had blood on his hands, the blood of little children. Every time he thought of it, he cringed. But he hadn't intended to do anything wrong. He was trying to support the rule of law. Would Julia ever forgive him? Could he ever face her again?

All night long, the same thoughts were on repeat in his head. He almost wished there had been a mosquito buzzing around to take his mind off all the guilt he felt.

When he heard Paul and Rotimi downstairs, Chris decided it was time to get up. He put on a t-shirt from a pile on the floor and pulled on the same cargo shorts he had worn the day before. He didn't even bother looking in the mirror before walking out of his room.

"Morning, Chris. How's it hanging?" Paul asked once Chris walked into the kitchen. "Oh," Paul added after taking one look at him, "you look like you wiped out, got dragged under a wave and rolled around like a rag doll, man."

"I feel about that way too. Hey, Rotimi." Chris made his way to the kitchen table and dropped into a chair.

"Hello, Chris," Rotimi said. Chris was used to Rotimi and Paul sleeping in the bedroom next to him. It was good to see the two of them happy.

"Anything you want to talk about? Just finished making some grub.

Should perk you up a bit." Paul came over to the table and slid Chris a plate of eggs, toast and pineapple.

"Thanks, Paul."

Paul sat down across from Chris. Rotimi decided to give them some space and was eating standing up near the stove.

"Julia is blaming me for the attack on Ichewa."

"Did you join the JTF without telling me?" Paul asked, raising his left eyebrow.

"No. I went to a guy name Godwin Ogbe the other day and reported my kidnapping. I told him it had to be someone in Ichewa who tipped off the kidnappers. I can't think of how else the militants would have known we were on that route to the flow station."

"I see," Paul replied. His expression changed from one of care to concern. "And now you blame yourself for the massacre that happened there."

Chris nodded. He looked at his food but was not hungry.

"Well, man," Paul continued, "Julia's got a point. What you did was stupid. Definitely stupid. You should've talked to me first." Paul started tapping the table. Something was on his mind. He looked back at Rotimi but kept silent.

"I didn't mean anything to happen," Chris said. "Julia made this big point about the need for the rule of law in Nigeria. I wanted to show her I was listening. I was only trying to help."

"Yup. I know." Paul reached over to put his hand on Chris's. "Listen, you messed up."

"Should I experience this much guilt about it? I haven't been able to get it out of my mind."

"Chris, we're sinners not just because we intentionally do what's wrong. Living in the world, we are caught up in unjust systems. No one, not even the most virtuous person, can avoid sinning in that way. The person who grabs a cup of coffee at the local coffee shop participates in a system that often does injustice to farmers. The person who buys the coffee doesn't mean to exploit poor coffee growers, but it happens anyway, and his money contributes to it. It happens all the time in the US. Think of how many of our clothes are made in sweatshops. Anyone who fills up at the gas pump is contributing to brutal dictatorships. Nearly everything we do supports an unjust system."

"What does this have to do with me?"

"You didn't intend to cause harm by going to the authorities. You were trying to do what you thought was right, but you got caught up in an unjust system."

"So what am I supposed to do? Pretend like I had no role in Ichewa?"

"I didn't say that. Most people ignore their complicity in bad things altogether. They claim it's unavoidable and not their fault. Then there are the crusaders, those who try to change the system. For you, I would say take the Christian path. Admit your faults. Name where you did wrong and the people you harmed. Be brutally honest. Seek forgiveness from God and from those whom you injured, intentionally or not. Also, pray for the grace to be part of the solution and not the problem. We often cause more harm than good when we try to fix things, which is why you have to go about that humbly and seeking God while you do it."

"What do I do about Julia? I like her, Paul." Chris poked his pineapple with his fork.

"That's tricky. All depends what kind of person she is. Most folks have a difficult time reconciling their role and the role of others in the bad things that happen. They struggle to admit their own faults and have a hard time recognizing true contrition and then offering forgiveness to themselves and others. Secular society has the mantras: 'Never apologize!' 'Don't feel guilty!' 'Guilt only harms.' When someone can't see their own need for forgiveness, it's hard to forgive others. But we're all sinners. We're all separated from God and do wrong. We all need forgiveness."

"Julia might understand. She knows I didn't mean to cause any harm."

"Chris, you didn't pull the trigger. She knows that. This will be a test of your relationship. But beyond Julia, try to make amends with some of the people you actually harmed. That's the response to God's grace that's needed."

Chris finally took a bite of his food.

Before he could say anything more, Paul's phone rang. He picked it up, "Hello?"

Chris couldn't make out the words that the other person was saying to Paul.

"Really? Then it's started. Meet me at the Emmaus Center in an hour, and let's see who else we can get to show up. We gotta stop this before it gets out of hand."

Rotimi laid down his plate, came over behind Paul and put his hands on Paul's shoulders.

"Yup...Okay...Bye." Paul hung up. "Looks like there was a series of attacks against oil targets across the delta last night. A lot of them. This could mean trouble."

"May God have mercy on us all," Rotimi whispered.

Paul reached over his shoulder and squeezed Rotimi's hand.

"Alright, Chris, do some thinking and then try to find Julia. That's important for you to do. Rotimi and I have work of our own. Lots of prayers, guys. We're going to need God's power now. Things are about to get real."

•••

Tim McAuliffe stared at the report on his desk. How could this be happening to him? Forty-six Octagon Petroleum wells throughout the Niger Delta were damaged. Three of their largest pipelines were gushing oil. Other companies were hit, as well. All of it in one night.

He walked over to his office early that morning, as soon as he heard that something was up, but he never thought it would be this bad. He picked up his phone.

"Amaka," Tim said to his secretary, "get me Eli Schrimpf, the head of our cleanup efforts." His voice was curt and emotionless. A few moments later, his phone rang.

"Sir, he is out in the field. Would you like his mobile phone number?" Amaka's voice betrayed her concern. There was tension throughout the compound that morning.

"I have it already, thank you." Tim pulled out his Nigerian cell phone and found Eli's number before pressing send.

"Tim? Glad you called."

"What's the story? By the way, where are you? I am having a hard time hearing you."

"I'm in a chopper now. Just visited some of the worst sites. Tim, this is a shit show."

"Is it that bad?"

"I just don't have the crews to deal with this. It'll take weeks to stop up the wells, maybe longer. Most of them are still on fire. It's like Mordor out there."

Tim paused, trying to think of options. "How many crews can you get going?"

"I have my one crew, Tim. One. We never planned for this. We haven't had even close to this many leaks and broken wells at the same time."

"Can't we fly people in or something?"

"That's what it will take. You should get on the phone to Houston as soon as you can. We need crews from wherever we can get them."

"We can do that. How bad is the damage?" Tim asked. "I'll need an accurate an assessment when I call up Houston."

"The shit of it is that none of the damage is that bad on its own. All it is are some wellheads and pipe fixes, from what I can tell. Whoever did this did not even try to plug up the holes with anything to make our jobs difficult. The problem is the number, the scale of the damage. Honestly, if we can get enough crews and supplies in here, we might be able to have the production back to normal in four to six months."

"So whoever did this wanted maximum shock effect."

"Exactly. Someone wanted to rattle us and, probably, the international markets too."

"Well, it worked. Thanks for the update, Eli. I'll get back to you later today with what Houston says."

Eli hung up the phone.

Just when Tim was about to head home to Houston, this had to happen. He had always considered himself to be a levelheaded guy. He was the techie in high school who had all the answers. Been a nice guy. Done the right thing. Tim had never felt this out of control. Anger and frustration boiled up inside him. He picked his desk phone back up again and dialed.

When a woman's voice came on the phone, Tim said, "I'm looking for Godwin Ogbe. Tell him this is Tim McAuliffe from Octagon Petroleum."

"Yes, Mr. McAuliffe. Hold on." Tim seethed while he waited. The timing of these attacks could not have been an accident. Two days after the Ichewa incident. But why do they blame us for the attack? Tim thought. Why hurt Octagon Petroleum? We gave them a school, for God's sake!

"Hello?" Godwin's bass voice was calmer than it had been the day before.

"Godwin. This is Tim McAuliffe."

"Yes."

"What the hell happened?"

"There was an attack."

"I know there was an attack. Damn it! There were lots of attacks!" Tim caught himself screaming into the phone. "I thought you were supposed to take care of it. I thought you had everything under control."

"I miscalculated their preparations," Ogbe responded coldly.

"No shit." Tim couldn't believe he'd just sworn. He never did that. "But why this destruction? Don't these people know that hitting oil wells only hurts them? Nigeria needs this money."

"These people in the villages are naïve. I know these villages. They think they can intimidate you."

"Intimidate me?"

"Octagon Petroleum, Mr. McAuliffe."

Tim was sick and tired of dealing with Godwin Ogbe. "So tell me this," Tim continued. "How did your security not stop these attacks? Who did you catch?"

"It's not that simple. The insurgents chose their sites well. Their attacks were too spread out, too well coordinated. No one could have stopped this."

"You failed, Godwin. You failed. Your job was to prevent an insurgency and you failed. I hope the governor will enjoy reading my official complaint."

Images of prison flashed through Godwin's head. He should have killed Ifeanyi when he had the chance. "Don't worry, Mr. McAuliffe. We will find the insurgents and bring them to justice."

"You do that. And whatever it takes, make it happen. There's no point in us fixing these wells if they are only going to be destroyed again."

"We will do what we can."

"You better." Tim was unaccustomed to threatening people. Maybe in Nigeria it would actually get him somewhere.

"Is there anything else you wanted to say, Mr. McAuliffe?" Godwin asked. Tim realized he had been yelling again. The stress of Nigeria had really gotten to him.

"Just make this place safe. Make our oil production safe."

"We will. Trust me. We will."

Tim hung up the phone. It had felt good to yell and get the pent-up anger out of his system. He suddenly had a pang of guilt. Anger. Yelling. Swearing. Prioritizing oil production over people. Threats. What was he doing? He never had been this way before Nigeria. Tim looked at the clock. It read 10:00 am. Houston was six hours behind, which meant he had to wait another five hours before he could call Walter Cunningham.

When the line went dead, Godwin Ogbe put the phone slowly down on its receiver. He could feel the rage build up inside him. How dare that oil bureaucrat yell at him! He slammed his fist down on his desk. He stood up, went to the nearest wall and ripped the framed prints off. They smashed on the ground and spread glass across the floor of his office. He turned to his desk, walked behind it and then turned it over, his computer crashing to the ground. He barely noticed. There was a lamp behind him, and he threw it across the room, putting a hole in the drywall. His chest heaved. That bastard. All those fucking bastards. He looked down and saw his phone on the floor, a dial tone sound coming from it. He kicked it aside, which yanked the plug out, silencing it.

Godwin pulled his cell phone out of his pocket. Those villagers would pay for this. If he was going to end up with no job and possibly in prison, he would make sure they paid dearly for this.

Chapter 38

Ewu, a Village in Rivers State

Chris had spent the last day trying to track down Julia. He had run through in his head what he would say and how he would ask for forgiveness for his role in the Ichewa massacre. But would she listen? He texted her in the morning and said he wanted to talk. It took her an hour to text back. She was spending her day running medical supplies to local villages. Not sure what else to do, Chris offered to join her on a trip. The car ride would give them plenty of time to talk.

When Julia pulled up to the Emmaus Ministries office, she didn't get out of her truck, but merely texted that she was there. Chris took a deep breath and strolled out, still rehearsing his lines in his head. He saw the stacks of boxes in the bed of the white pickup. Julia wasn't holding back on the supplies she was willing to give away. Chris opened the door with a big swoop of his arm.

"Hello, Julia!" he said with his most upbeat tone.

"Come on, Chris. We're already late." Julia barely looked at Chris when he got in.

"How have you been?"

"Busy. I've been gathering supplies all morning. I want to visit several villages today."

Chris could see Julia didn't want to talk and waited until they were outside of Port Harcourt before trying again to start a conversation.

Nigerian traffic was not conducive to intense discussions. But once they were on the open road, Julia seemed to be in no mood to relax her focus on driving.

"Julia, no need to speed. We'll get there in due time." Chris noticed that the speedometer read nearly a hundred forty kilometers per hour as they raced down the road heading out of Port Harcourt to the west.

"We might be able to visit three places today, if we hurry," Julia said. Chris kept his mouth shut in response. He reached out to touch her arm, but she drew back without a word.

"You know, Julia, I do want to talk."

"About what?" she said without emotion.

"About Ichewa. About me having gone to the authorities. I'm sorry, Julia. I know now that I messed up. I was hoping you might be able to forgive me."

Minutes passed without a word. Finally, Julia said, "I'm trying, Chris. I'm trying to forgive you. I know you didn't mean to do anything wrong. I just hate seeing people suffer."

"That's one thing I love about you."

Reluctantly, Julia relaxed her grip on the steering wheel and eased back on her speed. "I guess I'm also mad, mad at you for being so naïve, mad at the corruption in Nigeria, mad that this damn world doesn't operate the way it should."

"You have every reason to be mad."

"Christianity wouldn't fix this world," Julia asserted.

"We have to start somewhere."

"I am starting somewhere! Why do you think I have all these medical supplies with me?" Julia took a deep breath. "I'm sorry for yelling, Chris."

"You're fine. These supplies are a good idea. I agree it's a place to start." Chris tried to force a smile but held back. He knew sometimes it's better not to try to lighten the mood.

After that, neither of them spoke for a while. Chris was happy that the tension had eased somewhat. The silence gave him a chance to take in the Nigerian countryside. A real hamlet in God's kingdom, despite its troubles.

Their first destination was the village of Ewu, which lay on a small inlet off the Niger River. Julia guessed it had fewer than two thousand residents, with clusters of small houses set back slightly from the water. From their truck they had a good view of the whole village, and they arrived in time to watch the local fishermen bringing in their boats with the daily catch.

Chris shook his head. "I would never eat that fish. It must have so many pollutants in it."

"I would hate to see the long-term cancer rates for a village like this," Julia replied.

Chris was happy the conversation seemed more normal. Julia parked the New Africa Initiative pickup truck in the main clearing at the village entrance and turned off the engine.

"Why are we in this village?" Chris asked.

"This is one of our malaria sites. I wanted to check with the locals we work with to be sure they have enough meds and to see what else we can provide."

"Do they know we are coming?"

"No. I just want to be sure they have what they need." Julia squeezed the steering wheel, her knuckles whitening. Then she pressed her forehead against the wheel. Seeing the village brought it all back. "I'm sorry, Chris. I feel powerless. Things are unwinding so fast in the delta. I don't know what to do. I thought this might be something."

"These supplies are important," Chris assured her. "I'm sure they will be happy to see you." Julia sat back and took a deep breath.

"How do I look?" she asked.

"You look beautiful."

"You would say that anyway."

"Only because it's the truth." Chris smiled. "Onward!" he said, trying to feign excitement.

Julia got out of the car and surveyed the village. It looked like one of the hundreds of small villages strewn throughout the delta region. The houses were small, no more than oversized huts. Women sat outside one of the nearer huts, chatting and pounding yams to break up the starch and turn it into a chewy accompaniment to fish stew. One of the younger kids waved at Julia, and she waved back. She remembered her contact in Ewu was a man named Hart, though she had a hard time recalling his first name. She knew she would recognize him, even though it had been more than six months since she had last been here. Usually, Hart came to a larger village to collect his medicines and make his report with other malaria workers, but Julia liked to visit all the communities they worked with at least once per year.

Chris trailed slightly behind her. "It's a beautiful day." He looked up at the blue sky and wispy clouds. There was a gentle breeze coming off the water. Chris guessed the temperature was in the mid-eighties.

Nigeria could be a wonderful place. Friendly people. Nice weather. Julia O'Keefe.

Somewhere the Niger Delta

This time, Mustafa Musa's orders were unambiguous. Godwin Ogbe ordered him to identify villages near damaged wells where militants were likely to be. Then Musa was to arrest every male between the ages of fifteen and thirty-five. If some villagers died while resisting, then so be it. As far as Godwin was concerned, they had been too soft on Ichewa. They were going to round up suspected militants and interrogate them until they found out who was behind the bombings. Godwin might lose his position because of the attacks on the oil wells, but he was not going see his family left destitute without proving he could get the job done.

Musa also felt slighted. The villagers in Ichewa had attacked his men, who had acted out of self-defense. Suddenly, the newspapers were labeling him and his men butchers. His own men accused of inciting violence, when it was the villagers of Ichewa who had plotted and kidnapped the Americans. The bombings that had followed only proved to Musa that he had been right. But he had not been firm enough. Their retreat from Ichewa showed weakness on the part of the government, weakness that the militants decided to exploit. That leniency would now end.

Musa planned to attack two villages today and then follow up with more attacks later in the week. Godwin, he was told, would commandeer several buildings on the outskirts of Port Harcourt for detention and interrogation. The interrogations would be brutal and efficient. He was sure they would get to the bottom of the violence.

Riding along the river, Musa was calmed by the beauty of the day. The warm sun bathed his face, and a soft breeze massaged his black skin. The rhythmic hum of the patrol boat's engines added to the soothing feeling.

He looked up and down the boat at the crew, who seemed to be doing even less than his soldiers. It frustrated Musa that his men had to rely on the Nigerian navy for transportation to the villages. The navy was well-known as the most corrupt and ineffectual force in the entire delta. No matter. Certain things were necessary to achieve larger goals. He glanced down at the map. The village of Ewu was first on his list. Two wells nearby had been damaged. It was time for redress. As they neared the final turn to the village, Musa said to the sergeant next to him, "Make sure the men are ready. We will land at the village dock and disembark. It must be quick. I don't want to give the villagers time to prepare."

The sergeant nodded and turned to the men gathered in the rear of the boat to convey his instructions. Another large patrol boat followed them. It would be filled with prisoners before the day was out.

When Ewu came into view, Musa reflected on how picturesque it was. Light glimmered off the zinc roofs of the huts, which were scattered away from the water in case of a big storm surge. Pulled up along the shore were the characteristic Nigerian fishing boats, long and narrow with makeshift sails, a patchwork of faded colors, wrapped around their masts. Along the shore, fishermen were mending their nets from the night before. How could such a peaceful place be home to militants? That was the deceit of it all.

The lead boat slowed as it approached the dock. When the fishermen along the shore saw the boats turn toward the village, they quickly stored the nets in their skiffs and ran back to the huts. Were they going to get arms? Musa reached down and took out his own handgun and checked it one final time, switching the safety latch to the off position.

Musa noticed that a few of his men were nervous. That was a good thing. Nervousness meant focus. He could feel himself getting excited. On the foredeck, a navy man prepared the bowline while two more men cocked and readied the .50-caliber machine gun mounted right behind him. In the event of trouble, Musa would not hesitate to use the machine gun to pacify the villagers

The boat eased into the dock, and Musa moved to the gunwales. He wanted to be the first one out of the boat.

Before disembarking, Musa turned back to his men. "You know your orders. I want every man in this village between the ages of 15 and 35 in front of the dock within the hour. They might resist you. Do not hesitate to respond with force. These people have been planting bombs. They seek to undermine Nigeria with their violence. We must send a clear message. There will be appropriate rewards for all those who act with vigor."

With that, Musa stepped out onto the dock and pulled his weapon from his holster.

The villagers on the beach had all fled before the soldiers reached the end of the dock. While his men went about their business, Musa motioned to the gunmen on the boat. "Decorate these boats for the villagers of Ewu. A good reminder not to harbor insurgents." The gunman nodded and began firing along the shore. The sound of the large-caliber machine gun echoed across the water. Each time a bullet hit a fishing boat, it made an audible thud as it pierced the wood. The gunman swept across the skiffs three times to ensure they'd be useless on the water. Repairing them would be no easy task.

Musa was pleased with himself. Now it was time to wait in front of the dock for his prisoners to arrive.

Chris Reed grabbed Julia's arm when he heard the sound of engines. "What's that?" he asked.

She looked toward the water and listened. "Sounds like a motorboat. A large motorboat." They both turned in time to see the first of the navy vessels rounding the river bend. The boats were headed toward them.

"What are they doing here?" Chris wondered.

Eyeing the machine gun on the bow, Julia said, "It can't be good. Come on." She pulled Chris with her as they ran to the nearest cluster of huts. Chris could see fear on the faces of the people around them. Damn the government.

Julia stopped a middle-aged woman. "Where can I find Mr. Hart?"

"Hart?" The woman looked back at her, sorting through Julia's accent. "Ah, yes, Hart. Over there." She pointed to a hut a hundred feet away, closer to the water. Julia started moving toward it.

"Shouldn't we get in our truck?" Chris asked, as he ran behind her.

"I want to find out what is going on. They need American witnesses for this, whatever it is."

"But this isn't safe, Julia."

"They would never hurt an American," she called back over her shoulder, not slowing her pace. When she reached the entrance of Hart's hut, Julia looked over at the dock. Soldiers were moving toward the village with guns drawn. The machine gun suddenly opened fire, and Julia involuntarily jumped back and screamed.

"They are shooting up the boats," Chris said. "Damn them. That's those fishermen's livelihood. Inside. Inside." Chris pushed Julia into the hut. The main room had a kitchen with a kerosene stove in one corner and a table with chairs not far away. Another corner had several handmade chairs in a semicircle. No one was in the main room.

"Hello?" Julia yelled. No one answered. "Hello? Where could they be?" Without waiting for a response, Julia went to the door of the hut and looked out. One soldier had a villager by the arm and was dragging him toward the water. He struggled to get free, but the soldier was bigger and stronger. The villager, who looked no more than twenty years old, stared over at Julia. Desperation was in his eyes. She heard more gunfire and yelling coming from somewhere nearby.

"What are they doing?" Chris asked, anger rising in his voice.

Julia looked at Chris and said, "I don't know, but it's not right." She ran after the soldier.

"Wait!" Chris yelled, trying to grab Julia to prevent her from going out. He just got hold of her t-shirt and forcefully pulled her back to the hut.

"What are you doing?" she screamed, looking back at Chris. Anger filled her eyes. "Let me go! Can't you see what they're doing?" They heard more scattered gunshots.

"Julia, this is not our fight. Anything can happen here. We must leave! Now!"

"I'm not going to abandon these people!" While Julia and Chris argued in the doorway, a villager was knocked to the ground not ten feet from them. They both turned in time to see a soldier kick the villager in the ribs with his boots. Tears welled up in Julia's eyes.

Chris had to make a decision. Without thinking any more about it, he gripped Julia firmly by her upper arms. "Come," he said.

Chris began to walk to where their truck was parked, taking Julia along with him. She resisted, but only slightly. She knew Chris would not let her interfere with the soldiers. Chris attempted to use the huts as cover, trying to stay away from the chaos by the water. Maybe the soldiers wouldn't see them, or at least ignore them. Another shot rang out, and Chris saw a villager drop to the ground from the corner of his eye.

"I hope the truck is undamaged," Chris said.

Julia stopped resisting Chris and let herself be led away. "I guess we're going to leave these people to their fate."

"Julia, I know you want to help, but we need to make it out of here alive. We need to report what we've seen." Peering around one of the huts, Chris could see the NAI truck parked safely about forty yards away. He could not see any soldiers around it. Chris turned to look at Julia. "We're going to walk briskly, but without looking at the soldiers until we get to the truck. You have the keys?"

"Of course I do," Julia replied. Her voice had an edge to it.

"Julia." Chris could see the pain in her eyes. "Are you ready to do this? We have to go now. Don't you see we can't do anything but get ourselves harmed?" Screaming and yelling, punctuated by sporadic gunfire, filled the air.

"Let's go," Julia said.

"One. Two. Three." With his left arm around Julia, putting himself between the woods and the soldiers, Chris walked toward the waiting truck. He didn't look toward the water.

"Hey, you!" Chris heard one of the soldiers yelling. He ignored the voice and kept the same pace. "You! White man! Where do you think you're going?" Chris's heart raced, but they maintained their pace. Almost there. Crack! He heard a gunshot ring out. "I said, 'White man!' You, tough guy. You better turn around."

Chris stopped, let go of Julia, and turned to face the soldier.

"What are you doing here?" he asked Chris and Julia.

"We are aid workers delivering supplies. It was an accident that we were here," Chris said, as calmly as he could.

"Accident, eh?"

Chris nodded. They were only ten feet from the truck.

"You wait here," the soldier said, pointing his gun to the ground at Chris's feet to indicate where he should stay.

"Okay," Chris said. "We'll wait here."

The soldier turned and began walking toward the shore. He was looking around, obviously trying to find his superior officer.

"Go!" Chris said, pushing Julia toward the driver's-side door of the truck. Chris sprinted to the passenger's side, jerked open the door and hopped in. He noticed the soldier turn back around. Without waiting, Julia turned on the ignition and threw the truck into reverse, turning the wheel quickly to the right.

Crack. Another gunshot hurtled in their direction. Julia put the truck into drive and floored the accelerator. More shots rang out. She and Chris ducked. Several bullets hit the boxes of supplies on the truck's bed. Moments later, they were down the road headed back to Port Harcourt.

Chris had never had so much adrenaline in his veins. He was glad Julia was driving. She was a lot better behind the wheel. After a few minutes, she slowed the car down to a safer speed. "You alright?" he said to Julia.

"Did you see the woman being dragged to the hut?" Julia asked.

"What?"

"The local village woman. She looked young. Two soldiers were dragging her to a hut."

"Julia, we're safe."

Julia turned to Chris. "Yes, but that young woman is not. They are raping her as we speak." Chris didn't say anything. "And we abandoned them," Julia added.

Chris didn't say anything in response but bowed his head in prayer. "Dear God, help these people in Ewu."

Chapter 39

Chris looked down at his vibrating phone and hit the talk button. "Hello." His voice was weak.

He glanced over at Julia sipping a cup of tea at her small kitchen table. On the drive back to Port Harcourt, Julia had been busy calling contacts at the New Africa Initiative so they could share what was happening with the press. She hoped there was some way they could confirm her account to get the news out. After several frantic calls, there wasn't much to do, and they rode in silence. Both of them were in shock. Once they were inside Julia's apartment, Chris went over to Julia and hugged her. Now they sat opposite each other, not sure what to do.

"Chris, my man. Where are you?" It was Paul on the phone.

"I'm at Julia's now. Leaving soon."

"Head on over to the office. I need your help. It's going to be a big one this afternoon."

"Big one?" Chris asked.

"Yeah. You didn't think I was going to do nothing about what happened in Ichewa, did you? Come on down."

"It's more than Ichewa," Chris said. There was a silence on the other end of the phone.

"Did something happen?" Paul asked after a moment.

"Yes," Chris replied.

"Is there anything I can do?"

"Not unless you can change the past."

"Meet me at the office, man. Sounds like we need to talk."

"I don't know. I'll have to ask Julia."

"Okay, Chris. Just let me know. We're on the edge of a major moment in the delta, a kairos moment, one of those times when God's presence brings true healing to a community. This is it. Things will change."

"Yeah. Things will change." Chris hung up the phone. He looked back at Julia.

"Go see Paul," she said finally.

"Are you sure? I want to stay here, to be with you."

"I want you to go see Paul."

"Is there anything you need?" Chris asked.

"Go, do your church thing. I need some time alone."

Chris got up and went to Julia. He leaned over and kissed her head. She didn't react and merely took another sip of her tea.

Chris drove the New Africa Initiative truck over to the Emmaus Ministries office. He had no interest in huddling in a Nigerian taxi bus. In truth, he wanted to be alone or with Julia, but he knew it was best to go speak to Paul. Paul was his only other friend in Nigeria. He might understand.

When Chris pulled up to the office, he was surprised at the crowd gathered outside. Dozens of Nigerians, mostly young, were talking excitedly. He made his way through the crowd and into the building. The din of nervous voices filled the main classroom and reception area. Posters were scattered on the floor amidst the crowd. He could read some of the messages: **Justice for the Delta, Love Not Violence, God Wants Peace**.

Chris didn't spend much time on the posters. He was looking for Paul. Where was he and why were all these people here? As he climbed the stairs to Paul's office, Chris weaved his way through the throng, avoiding eye contact with those he knew. Paul's door was closed. Chris knocked loudly.

"Paul?"

"Chris, come in!" he heard from the other side. Chris nodded to the man next to him, who obviously wanted to speak with Paul, and slid through the door, shutting it behind him. Rotimi and Paul were looking at a map of the city spread out on Paul's desk.

When Chris entered, Paul glanced over at him. Chris's face was drained of color, and his eyes had a vacant expression. His frame slouched as if someone was holding up his limp body. Paul walked over and hugged Chris.

"You look like you've returned from hell. Are you okay?"

Chris shook his head. "Julia and I went out to one of the villages that New Africa Initiative works with. It's…it's…out on the creeks, and we had brought some medicine. Not long after we arrived, the JTF showed up with the Nigerian Navy."

"What happened?" Paul's tone showed his concern.

"They rounded up all of the men in the village. I'm not sure what they were going to do with them. Some people were shot."

"What?" Paul asked. Rotimi walked the few steps from the desk to stand next to Paul. They both were stunned by the news.

Chris nodded. "I've never seen anything like it."

"I'm glad you got out safely," Paul said, lightly squeezing Chris's arm.

"Do you remember the name of the village?" Rotimi asked.

"A place called Ewu. It's very small. The soldiers might have gone to other villages nearby, as well."

"We have to let the newspapers know," Rotimi said to Paul.

"Chris, we'll need you to write up everything you saw while it is still fresh in your mind. You think you could do that, man?" Paul asked.

"I can do that. Julia's already called her people. I guess it's important to write it down," Chris responded vacantly.

The three of them walked the few steps to Paul's desk. Paul pulled the chair out and sat Chris down at his computer. Chris opened up a new document and titled it "Ewu."

"That's good, Chris," Paul said, tapping him on the shoulder. "Just type whatever comes to your mind. Try to remember as many details as you can."

Without really collecting his thoughts, Chris began to type. He let the whole incident pour out of him, not bothering to read what he was writing. Paul and Rotimi watched Chris for a while before turning their attention back to the map of Port Harcourt, keeping their voices low.

"Where's Julia?" Paul asked after a few minutes.

"Julia? She's at her place." Chris stopped typing as the scene flashed through his mind. "She wanted to stay and fight the soldiers or something. The whole thing was awful."

"I can't imagine there is anything you could've done."

"I know. We couldn't do anything but watch."

"You did the right thing to get out of there, Chris." Paul kept his eyes on Chris, who turned back to the laptop, his hands hovering over the keys, not moving. A tear hit the keys, and Chris wiped his eyes.

"I think it's time we pray," Paul said.

"Yes." Chris nodded. "I'd like that."

Chris stood up. Paul, Rotimi and Chris held one another's hands and bowed their heads.

"God," Paul began, "you put us in a world that is so often filled with evil, and yet we know that you desire good for all your children. God, we pray that you would bless all the people of Ewu, especially those who are injured in mind or body. Comfort those who mourn with your Holy Spirit."

Chris heard Rotimi mutter "Yes" under his breath.

Paul's voice began to rise in volume. "Heal the twisted souls of those who would commit wanton violence. Break down the barriers to Jesus's love. Help us see that you are at work now and deliver us from this present hatred."

Again Rotimi murmured, "Yes."

"And continue to work in your servant Chris. Make him and us your instruments in a fallen world. We pray this in Jesus's name. Amen." Rotimi and Chris each joined with an "Amen" of their own.

Paul held on to Chris's hand for a little while longer and gave it a squeeze. Then he pulled Chris toward him and hugged him. "This world is shit, man," Paul whispered to Chris. "No other word to describe it. We have to rely on love to transform hate. Only love can cast out this darkness."

"Thanks, Paul. Thank you." Chris wiped the dampness from his eyes and took a deep breath. He looked down at the computer, but he didn't have the energy to keep writing. "So what's going on downstairs?" he asked, his voice weak.

"I have gathered some of the churches together so we can march in the streets of Port Harcourt," Paul said. "We are going to hold a peaceful demonstration in front of the governor's house to protest the use of force. Time for God's voice to be heard. We want a new delta, but not with bombs and guns."

"Paul has been working hard on this, Chris. God is working through him." Rotimi beamed.

Chris looked at the two of them. "I'm glad you're doing this. They have to see this whole situation is wrong. Is there anything for me to do?"

"For sure, my man, if you're feeling up to it," Paul said. "We are now finishing the route. We have people gathering at several of the churches downtown. We will start marching soon, and other churches will meet us along the way. The protest will end outside the governor's residence. It should be massive. God's love is awesome." The more Paul spoke about the rally, the more animated he became.

"Do the police know you're doing this?" Chris asked.

"If they don't know, they will soon. Alright." Paul clapped his hands together. "I'm gonna make a few phone calls. Chris, why don't you go downstairs and see how the signs are coming along? You can finish your Ewu report later. Also, think of some good hymns we can sing while we march. I wish we could print out song sheets. There is nothing like the power of God in song."

This time Chris wrapped his arm around Paul's shoulders and then looked him in the eye. "Thanks again, Paul. For everything."

"No worries, man." Paul patted Chris's chest. "See you downstairs in a few." Paul's eyes radiated the depth of his empathy.

Somehow Chris felt a little better. He knew he had to focus on something other than the horror of Ewu. This march was what the Christians of Port Harcourt should be doing.

He headed downstairs and eased through the crowd, looking over the signs. They were crudely drawn, mostly with black sharpies on white oaktag, but they would work. He leaned over one of men finishing up another sign and offered a few suggestions about how to make the letters more readable.

He wished he had been around earlier to help make better signs. They had about twenty signs for seventy-five people.

He shook his head. He couldn't believe he would be leading a protest march in Nigeria. It was all so overwhelming. He took a couple deep breaths to tune out the din of voices. When he opened his eyes, he felt more at peace. He started to think. What should they be chanting?

A few minutes later, Paul and Rotimi came downstairs, followed by a half dozen others who had been waiting in the hallway. A couple people were chatting with Paul as he made his way into the main room.

"Okay, everyone," Paul said, his blue eyes beaming. "Are you ready for a peaceful protest?" His voice was rising as he spoke. All eyes were on Paul, but no one responded. "We can do better than that. Let's try again. Are we ready for a protest?"

"Yes!" a few people responded.

"Everyone, we have to be loud in our chants. Let's try it one more time. Join in. Are we ready to protest?" Paul asked, his voice rising in volume.

"YES!"

"That's better." Paul had a big smile on his face. "Grab those posters and let's head outside."

With people trailing behind, Paul led the way to the door. Out on the sidewalk, he addressed the full crowd. Chris had never heard Paul's preaching voice before. He was impressed with how loud the Californian could be. The sea of faces waited on every word.

"We are going to march through the city in good order and show the governor that we want peace in the Niger Delta. We want peace with justice. We are going to show the government in Abuja that the delta demands its due. Think of Christ marching into the city on Palm Sunday. The city of Jerusalem rallied to his cause, and we are rallying to the same cause, the cause of God's justice. Follow me!" A loud cheer arose in response.

Paul led the way down the edge of the street. There were well over a hundred people in the protest as they made their way toward the Anglican cathedral. People spilled off the sidewalks onto the main road, blocking half the street's traffic. Horns honked at them, but they were ignored as the protestors kept marching. The pace was deliberate, which allowed people to chat with those next to them. The collective energy fed the crowd's spirits. When those on the side of the street realized what was happening, more and more people joined in.

Chris was elated. It was turning into a mass movement. Everyone knew about the Ichewa massacre and knew it could lead to more violence. Too many people had felt the negative effects of the insurgency and its backlash. It was as though casual onlookers could sense that this was the moment, the time for change.

Paul started a chant, "WE WANT JUSTICE! WE WANT JUSTICE!" The crowd joined in, and their voices carried over the sounds of traffic. The marchers raised their fists in the air. Some people leaned out the windows of their cars to join the chant or to clap in solidarity. With this much support, the governor of Rivers State would not be able to ignore them. He would be forced to order a stop to retaliatory attacks like the one at Ewu that morning.

At the Corpus Christi Cathedral, another five hundred protesters, maybe more, joined them, swelling their numbers to well over a thousand. The crowd seemed remarkably diverse to Chris: women and men, some just off the street from selling wares, others in suits. A few women wore traditional Nigerian dresses, which added bright reds and greens and blues in a cluster near the front. The march continued through the streets, signs waving amidst the chants. A traffic jam spread in both directions. A few people parked their cars on the curb, leaving them to join the protest.

Paul elbowed Rotimi and began singing. Rotimi followed his lead.

"Amazing grace, how sweet the sound…"

Chris smiled and nodded. Yes, this was grace. Chris looked up at the sky and let his voice mingle with the ever-increasing volume. "I once was lost but now am found, was blind but now I see!"

The whole crowd was in a jubilant mood as they walked down Isaac

Boro Street toward the governor's house.

Noticing Paul looking around, Chris asked, "What is it?"

"There was supposed to be another large group here waiting for us. I don't see them. They were going to meet us just past the park."

"Maybe they're taking their time," Chris offered. "This is Nigeria, after all. Being late is part of the national psyche."

"No, I called the pastor who was leading those people just ten minutes ago." The crowd slowly marched on while Paul stopped to look for the other crowd up the cross streets. There were cars honking their horns at them, but no sign of any protesters. He called the number of the pastor who was leading them, but the phone went immediately to voice mail.

Paul hesitated and then shrugged. "Let's head on to the governor's house. It's not as big a crowd as I hoped it would be, but it will send a message."

Paul and Chris found themselves at the rear of the crowd. The protesters kept to one side of the street to allow some traffic to get through. But this prevented Chris and Paul from seeing down the road. Suddenly, they felt the crowd push back against them. A few cries rose up from the head of the line.

Paul grabbed the nearest person, who was moving past them in the opposite direction, away from governor's residence. "What's going on?" Paul asked.

"I don't know. It might be the police. I'm getting out of here."

Paul could see the look of terror on his face.

Paul weaved his way through the crowd, putting distance between him and Chris. There were more screams and yelling, and the crowd surged against him. Chris wondered where Rotimi was and if Paul was searching for him. Chris started to look around himself as the crowd became more aggressive, and he felt himself being pulled away from the governor's house. Soon he lost sight of Paul.

Then panic broke out. People started to rush past Chris, tossing their signs by the side of the road. When he turned, he found himself facing a line of police. They wore helmets and held riot shields in front of them. The governor must have ordered them to disperse the crowd.

The line of police marched toward him. Fear gripped Chris, and he raised his hands in surrender. He just wanted to get back to the Emmaus Ministries office and find Paul. While Chris tried to think of what to do, the police kept walking toward him. Before he knew it, the police line, a wall of plastic shields and truncheons, was almost on top of him. He turned and decided to run, but before he could get his legs moving, he felt a plastic shield hit him from behind. A blow landed on his shoulder. Then another one hit his side. Chris fell to the ground. He put his hands over his head as repeated blows rained down on him. Pain shook his whole body, and he struggled to protect himself from the assault, which became fiercer and fiercer. He could already feel his shoulders, arms and back bruising from the repeated blows. Chris did not know how much longer he could shield himself. What if they didn't stop?

Then the blows became lighter. The police were hitting someone else, another body on top of him. He opened his eyes and saw black arms enveloping him.

"Stop! Stop!" Chris heard the Nigerian yelling, and the police gradually melted away. Chris began to move, and his whole body ached. He looked over his shoulder and recognized Rotimi, who had blood streaming down his face.

"Rotimi."

"Are you okay, Chris?"

"Yes, I think so." He could see the police moving down the street, chasing the remainder of the protesters away. Chris rolled over on his back and sat up. His body had never hurt so much. "Where is Paul?" he managed to say.

"Paul is safe. He's hiding in one of the stores off the road," Rotimi answered.

Chris looked Rotimi in the eyes. "Thank you."

"It's nothing. Let's get you off the road before the police come back." Rotimi helped Chris to his feet. Chris could see that Rotimi was as badly wounded as he was.

The street was empty of protesters. A few groups of police were searching for stragglers. He could still hear a cacophony of horns and police voices shouting over megaphones. Traffic was surely backed up for miles. They limped over to the side of the road and made their way to a shop that sold radios and sound equipment. Once inside, Chris collapsed onto a plastic chair out of sight of the street. He saw Paul in the corner.

"Are you alright, Paul?"

Paul looked up, his face full of sadness. "I never thought they would do that," he said. "We weren't violent at all."

"Maybe violence is the only thing people respond to," Chris said. "I never knew what it meant to live in a fallen world until today."

"God's grace wins out, Chris. Don't ever forget that."

Chris could taste blood seeping into his mouth. "I'm still waiting to see it."

"Today might be a catalyst for something great. You never know. We have to keep the faith in God, especially in the face of sin. We can't hate back. That will get us nowhere. We have to forgive and believe in the power of love. If we give up on that, we've given up on everything. Remember the cross, Chris. The Christian way inevitably involves self-sacrifice. But that is not the end of the story. 'Blessed are you when people revile you and persecute you and utter all kinds of evil against you falsely on my account. Rejoice and be glad, for your reward is great in heaven, for in the same way they persecuted the prophets who were before you.'"

Chris wiped his face with his shirt. He realized one of the cuts on his head was bleeding badly. He applied pressure to it with his hand. As he felt the blood on his skin, one line kept coming back to him: "This is my blood, which is poured out for you and for many for the forgiveness of sins."

Chapter 40

Bonny Island, Nigeria

Ifeanyi Okoye crouched uncomfortably in the boat. There would be several more hours of waiting before they moved out, and his knees already ached. He wished he could get some rest, but he was too full of anticipation. This was the night he had been waiting for.

The boat was moored two miles away from Bonny Island, carefully hidden near the shore. With each gentle lap of the waves, the small metal boat rocked slightly and hit against the low branch they were tied to. In the boat with Ifeanyi were Olabisi and three men. Ifeanyi had hesitated to bring Olabisi along, but she had insisted. How would she respond when the fighting started? Had her torture depleted her ability to deal with stress? The other soldiers with them were young and inexperienced. Ifeanyi knew they did not have enough training for their mission. No matter, it will work, he assured himself. It had to work.

"It's unfortunate that Mama Sandra launched her attacks so soon," Olabisi whispered to Ifeanyi.

"I wish she had spoken with me, but it has turned out well for us. Godwin and the JTF reacted far more zealously than I expected. The whole delta is ready to explode. This will be the final blow. When the oil companies see the attacks tonight, they'll leave here, and we will be free." Every time he thought about the new future, it gave him new energy and focus. This was what he lived for.

"Tonight is the night," Olabisi echoed. She looked admiringly at Ifeanyi. He would be the hero of the new Nigeria, a Nigeria for the people.

Ifeanyi reached into his pocket and pulled out a folded piece of paper. He carefully opened it and then used his cell phone for light. The words were dim, but he could make them out. It was something his grandfather had given him many years before. He read the handwritten note once more:

A prayer of an African king before battle against the white colonists.

O Lord, despite a great many prayers to You, we are continually losing our wars. Tomorrow we shall again be fighting a battle that is truly great. With all our might we need Your help, and that is why I must tell You something: This battle tomorrow is going to be a serious affair. There will be no place for children. Therefore I must ask You not to send Your Son to help us. Come Yourself.

"Yes, indeed," Ifeanyi whispered. "Come Yourself." He folded the paper back up and looked around the boat.

"We will leave here at two," Ifeanyi announced to the men. "That will put us in place by three am. It will be quite a sight for people to wake up to." No one in the boat said anything in return. Ifeanyi knew they were too scared.

"How many others do you think will attack tonight?" Olabisi asked Ifeanyi quietly.

"I don't know. We've done what we can about the others, Bisi. All we can do is focus on our mission."

Off in the darkness beyond them lay the single largest storage facility for oil in Nigeria. Later that night, it would be in flames.

•••

Bight of Bonny

Fineface Pepple looked across at the boat thirty feet off his port side riding parallel to his own. Were they ready? he wondered. After his run-in with the Nigerian navy on the open seas, he'd had to find a replacement boat and recruit more men from the Lord Rules Brigade for their attack. The incident had been bad for morale, and Pepple feared the new men had not had enough training. He took a deep breath. It was too late for second-guessing.

The two boats were twenty miles offshore and cruising at close to fifteen miles per hour. The mufflers were off the engines, and Pepple tried to estimate the gas they were burning. He glanced at the reserve containers lying on the boat's floor. He hoped it was enough to get them to the oil rig and back. He had never taken his boats this far out to sea before.

Pepple moved to the console and looked over the shoulder of the driver. The compass reading was dead-on. Navigating was more difficult out in the open ocean because there were few obvious landmarks. At night all he could see was blackness, the water dimly lit by a sliver of moon. On his map, he had marked two oil rigs they should pass en route and written down the approximate distances and headings. With the rigs lit up at night, they should have no problem finding them, so long as they were on the right course and the ocean currents weren't drawing them unknowingly to a different location. If all went according to plan, they should be in sight of the target rig in a little over three hours.

"Everyone, eat something," Fineface said to his men. A couple of them nodded that they had heard him. Two others were trying to sleep.

He wanted them to preserve their energy for the mission. It would be a long night.

Bonny Island

Ifeanyi and his crew lay low in the boat, trying to keep their silhou-ette as small as possible. They were crossing the final stretch of open water, brightly illuminated by floodlights from the liquefied natural gas (LNG) plant and the enormous oil storage facility nearby, which was their destination.

Olabisi whispered to Ifeanyi, "It looks like their security is on high alert."

Ifeanyi nodded. Even at that hour, he could make out some soldiers moving back and forth near the facility, but he doubted there were enough soldiers to watch the whole area. He was much more concerned about being seen or heard as they approached. On the water there was nowhere to hide.

Olabisi had rigged up a muffler for their engine, as they used to do for MEND missions during the last insurgency. Even with that precaution, the engine still made noise. When they were about a half mile from the facility, Ifeanyi killed the engine. They pushed out the oars and tried to silently row their way in to shore. The men barely breathed. With each placement of the oars in the water, Ifeanyi looked toward the lurking sil-houettes of the oil storage tanks. Over five million barrels of oil were stored in those tanks. Somehow, they had to get to them. If they could set those tanks ablaze, they would shut down the main export terminal for Nigerian crude oil.

Ifeanyi could see the shoreline ahead. There was a small sandy beach that led to a strip of grass. A few feet beyond the grass lay the

349

facility's fence. He directed the boat to a section of the beach that had slightly eroded. He hoped it would give the boat some cover. The boat slid into the beach, and Ifeanyi could hear the bow grinding against the sand.

He gently slipped out into the shallow water, making a quiet splash. He paused, his heart pounding, and looked around to see if any guards were moving toward them. Everything seemed normal. Ifeanyi held the gunwales while the others stepped quietly into the water, which soaked them below the knees. Two men collected the explosives, safely packed in two black backpacks, while Ifeanyi and one other man lifted the bow of the boat and dragged it up onto the shore. Olabisi was already at the fence, looking for the right section to cut out. The floodlights were strong, but the shadows from the fence pole obscured them. No one had seen them, so far. Olabisi found a section of the fence next to one of the poles that seems to provide the most cover before returning to the boat.

Ifeanyi and Olabisi each took one of the backpacks of explosives. Without speaking, one of the soldiers took out a wire cutter and began working on the chain link fence. The nearby salt water made electrifying the fence impossible, which made things far easier for Ifeanyi and his crew.

Beyond the fence, a couple hundred feet away, Ifeanyi saw two soldiers lazily talking. One of them was smoking. He kept his eyes on them while his man cut a hole in the wire pattern. Each audible clip made Ifeanyi tense up, as if he was certain the soldiers could hear it. But as he peered across the alternating darkness and floodlit grass, they seemed deep in conversation and unaware.

When the man with the wire cutters was done, he eased the fence links out. With a final jerk, the roughly cut rectangle gave way. It stuck more than the man was expecting, and the sudden movement shook the fence. They all froze. Ifeanyi gave a sign for them to stay low. One of the guards, who must have noticed something, was coming toward the hole in the fence. With any luck, he might turn around and go back to his conversation. Ifeanyi eased the safety off on his weapon. The guard kept approaching.

Just then, a loud crack of gunfire went off near Ifeanyi's ear. He turned to see one of his men with a petrified expression on his face. Light smoke drifted out of the barrel of the man's rifle.

Ifeanyi quickly turned back to the guard. The bullet had missed. The soldier started to yell.

"Hey! Hey! There are people at the fence!"

The guard raised his gun in their direction. Ifeanyi fired off a short burst from his weapon, and the guard fell to the ground. He could see the other soldier at a distance moving toward his wounded comrade.

"Go! Go!" Ifeanyi said, pushing Olabisi through the fence.

The other three men followed her. The second guard left his fellow soldier lying on the ground and began running toward them. The guard fired several rounds in their direction, but since he was running, the bullets passed harmlessly above Ifeanyi and the others.

Olabisi fired back to give cover to the men sliding through the fence. The guard fell down suddenly.

"Did you hit him?" Ifeanyi asked when he was through the fence.

"In the leg," Olabisi responded. "Now what?"

Their intended target, the massive crude oil storage tanks, lay on the other side of the wounded guard and his fallen colleague. Ifeanyi was certain they had already radioed for help. Time was short. Ifeanyi couldn't make out what the wounded man was doing and assumed he was pointing his gun at them, waiting for them to move. The other guards and soldiers protecting the facility were stationed near the storage tanks behind him. How would they get to the tanks now?

Ifeanyi's mind raced through his options. They couldn't turn back.

They had to blow up those tanks, even if it cost them their lives. This was the moment, his moment.

"I have an idea." Ifeanyi pointed in the direction of the LNG plant with its egg-shaped tanks about a hundred fifty yards away from them. There were large, angled walls around each of the tanks and a maze of pipes that helped with the cooling needed to turn natural gas into a liquid. The LNG plant was on the opposite side of the facility from the crude oil storage tanks and away from the wounded guards. Looking over at the LNG plant, Olabisi wondered how they would double back to their target. She pushed the thought out of her mind. She had to trust Ifeanyi now. Crouching low, he started to move.

"Wait." Olabisi grabbed him. Ifeanyi looked back. One of their men had been hit in the stomach by the guard's gunfire.

"We should return to the boat," one of the men said. His friend was dying, and Ifeanyi saw the terror in his eyes.

"No!" Ifeanyi replied. "Not yet. You three stay here and defend our escape. Olabisi and I will go plant the bombs. We'll be back as soon as we can." Their boat beyond the fence was the only reliable way out.

"What if they come with a dozen men?"

Ifeanyi paused. "If it looks like you can't hold here, go through the fence and take the boat across. Olabisi and I will find a way to escape on foot to the town on the other side of the facility."

"Okay, sir. Okay." With a slight tremble in his hands, the young soldier pointed his gun in the direction of the wounded guard, a hundred yards away.

Ifeanyi tapped Olabisi on the shoulder, and they moved quickly across open ground toward the array of pipes that led to the LNG plant. He heard another burst of gunfire but kept running. The darkness provided some cover, but with the floodlights, Ifeanyi was certain the guard must have seen where they were headed. When they made it to the pipeline, they took a quick rest, both of them breathing heavily in the damp early morning air.

"Ifeanyi," Olabisi began, after she caught her breath, "how are we going to get to the crude oil storage tanks? They're on the other side of the guards." She pointed in the direction in which they had to go.

"I know," Ifeanyi replied.

"What will we do?"

Ifeanyi nodded to the egg-shaped LNG storage tanks towering behind them. "We will plant the bombs there."

Olabisi gave a start. She could not believe what Ifeanyi was saying. "Ifeanyi, we discussed this. If we do that, we will be consumed in the blast. When liquefied natural gas ignites, the explosion can be like a small atomic bomb. You said so yourself."

"Yes, and it will push the oil companies out for good. It's the only way we can destroy the oil storage tanks. The blast will take everything else with it too."

The implications of what Ifeanyi was saying frightened Olabisi. She looked into his eyes and saw a determination that bordered on madness. She reached out and touched Ifeanyi's arm. "But the blast would also destroy much of Bonny. Think of all the innocent people." A small inlet separated the oil and natural gas plants from the town of Bonny, where thousands of Nigerians lived.

"It would. They will be martyrs to the new Nigeria."

Scattered gunfire echoed through the night. The two of them looked back toward the fence. They could see their two comrades hunched on the ground with the third lying down. From another direction, they heard a commotion. A group of soldiers was moving toward the fence.

"We have no time to lose," Ifeanyi said. "Let's go."

"No, Ifeanyi. We cannot do this," she pleaded. "We are fighting for those people in Bonny! To kill them would go against everything we stand for. Think of the children and—"

Ifeanyi turned away from Olabisi and moved along the pipes toward the LNG tanks, trying to stay hidden.

Tears welled up in Olabisi's eyes. A loud air raid siren rang out, filling the night air. T

he entire town of Bonny would be awake soon.

Olabisi began to follow her hero, but her legs failed her. "There must be another way," she said to herself.

Ifeanyi kept moving down the pipes. He didn't look back for her.

Suddenly, she felt a pinch in her side and instinctively moved her hand to the pain. When she looked down, her hand had blood on it. Turning around, she saw three men with semi-automatic weapons running toward her. They kept firing.

Olabisi didn't know what to do. She unslung her rifle from her shoulder and threw it to the ground, then raised her hands into the air. More gunfire followed. The bullet that hit her skull knocked her backwards, and her lifeless body struck the ground.

Bight of Bonny

Fineface Pepple cursed under his breath. The seas had been rougher than he had expected, and their pace much slower than it needed to be. He could already see light on the horizon, and they were not yet at the rig. Two hours earlier, he had made the decision to send the other boat back to shore. Two of his men in his boat went back with the others and, in exchange, they loaded more gasoline and explosives with Fineface. That left four of them in a twenty-five-foot open-decked boat: himself, the driver, and two others. Fineface had assigned the two other men the job of bailing out the boat to keep it as light as possible. He knew they all were well beyond exhaustion and working on adrenaline. They had been on the water for the past eight hours. His watch read 4:57 am.

Fineface took out his binoculars again and scanned the horizon. As he was finishing his sweep, he caught sight of it. "There! There!" he yelled to the driver. The driver nodded and turned the boat in the direction of the structure on the horizon.

The rig rose several hundred feet out of the water and sat on a single spar that looked like a giant tree trunk. Fineface hoped they could make it there before it became too light. He had no idea what their defense weapons were like or if they had any. Ifeanyi had told him that this rig cost Octagon Petroleum several billion dollars to build and was one of the newest deep-water platforms in Nigeria. The destruction of that rig, especially so far out to sea, would send fear into the bellies of every oil executive, or so Ifeanyi had assured him. This would change everything.

Fineface looked back at the two large duffle bags. The explosives inside had been carefully wrapped in plastic. He hoped it would be enough to do the job. They had never before attempted anything so ambitious.

Bonny Island

Ifeanyi had turned around in time to see Olabisi fall to the ground. She had bravely sacrificed herself for him and the cause. He must avenge her. Without waiting, he sprinted down the final stretch of pipeline that led to the four large LNG storage tanks.

Ifeanyi reached the base of the wall that separated him from the first of the egg-shaped tanks that held the liquefied gas. His only way over was to climb the series of pipes that led in and out of the tanks beyond. Even though they were insulated, the cold pipes were covered in condensation, making them slippery. The extreme cold nearly burned his hands as he climbed up them. He heard gunfire ricocheting off metal not far from him.

What would happen if the pipes burst? Ifeanyi paid no heed to his fear and kept climbing.

There was a fence at the top of the pipes and a catwalk that ran toward the storage tanks. Reaching the bottom of the chain link fence, Ifeanyi grabbed hold of the links above him and heaved himself up, resting his elbows on the catwalk. Losing his footing on the slippery pipes, he reached his right hand as high up the fence as he could. Pulling with all his might, he could feel the wire dig into his fingers under the weight of his whole body and the explosives in his pack, cutting off their circulation. He ignored the pain and kept climbing the fence with his arms until his toes touched the catwalk. The floodlights made his position obvious to anyone who glanced in that direction. He felt totally exposed. His only chance was that the natural gas tanks and pipes might discourage soldiers from firing in his direction.

Ifeanyi could hear shouting behind him, but he focused on quickly getting over the fence. Once at the top, he let his body fall onto the metal catwalk below him. The sporadic gunfire had become such a regular part of the background that Ifeanyi didn't notice it. He assumed the men by the water were already dead or captured. If he could only make it to the LNG tank, he will have done it.

He got to his knees and took his sidearm out of its holster. Aiming his gun through the chain link fence, he fired three random shots into the darkness. With the bright lights around him, he couldn't see where he was shooting.

He just needed to buy a little time.

He got to his feet and began to run down the catwalk, which led to the nearest storage tank. As more bullets ricocheted near him, Ifeanyi ignored the gunfire and stared at the goal in front of him.

He reached the ladder that led to the tank, turned around, and climbed down as quickly as possible. The tank was just forty feet in front of him now.

Not glancing behind him, he sprinted. Ifeanyi felt a sudden pain in his lower back and then another in his right leg. He fell to the ground, but kept his eyes on the tank, now only ten feet away. He managed to get to his feet to walk a few steps before falling forward again. Slinging his backpack off his shoulder, he reached inside and took out a block of the C-4 that Drake had given him in Onne. He flipped the switch that armed the detonator while crawling to the tank on his forearms. He heard yelling not far behind him. With the last energy remaining in him, Ifeanyi lunged and placed the explosive next to the cold metal.

Ifeanyi smiled. He rolled onto his back and looked up at the stars, which were fading in the dawn light.

A great place to die, he thought. As his eyes closed, he knew he had done it.

"Get the device," he heard above him. "Who is this one?"

"That is Ifeanyi Okoye."

"What a way to die. Disarm that device. This insurgent should have been smart enough to detonate the bomb on the spot. Then we would all be dead."

With that, Ifeanyi Okoye slipped out of consciousness.

Bight of Bonny

The whole superstructure of the great oil platform was ablaze with lights. Atop the platform, a flare burned around the clock to dispose of the methane gas brought to the surface with the crude oil. From a distance, it looked like a floating refinery, with masses of pipes and holding tanks.

Fineface Pepple had to marvel at its sheer size. The entire structure sat on a giant pillar that disappeared into the water some five hundred feet down. Below that, flexible pipelines stretched the full mile down from the surface to the seabed. In its own way, caught in the dawn light, the platform was beautiful.

Approaching the platform in their boat, Fineface and his men were entirely exposed. There was no place to hide on the open ocean, and with light dawning, they lost the crucial cover of darkness that Fineface had counted on for the element of surprise. No need for any engine muffler. It all depended on what kind of defenses the rig had.

No cigarettes and no booze: the two things Jack English didn't like about working on oil rigs. At least working on the rig forced him to be a bit healthier than he would be otherwise. He had started his shift that morning at 4:00 am, and now he was on his first break. He went outside and leaned over the railing of the Eureka spar platform, admiring the scene.

Stranded on an oil production rig like this, you are away from everything. You could look out over the ocean and see nothing but the sea in every direction. Jack breathed the ocean air in deeply and watched the shimmering effect of the sunrise on the water. The whole world emerged from the darkness of the night. These were the best moments on a rig. He wished he was facing the rising sun, but this view was good too. Savoring the scene dawning before him, Jack noticed something moving on the water. He squinted.

"Holy shit!" Jack called out in his thick Louisiana drawl. A small boat was approaching. It did not take long for him to realize that this was not good. He ran inside and picked up the nearest emergency phone. It rang once and then a voice answered.

"Hey, this is Jack English. I'm on my break on the west side of the rig. There's a boat approaching."

"A boat? We don't have any scheduled dockings today."

"Not an oil boat, you idiot. It's a small motorboat. Militants on board it! You hear me?!"

"Are you sure?"

"Yeah, I'm sure! I know what a fuckin' motorboat looks like."

"Okay, we'll send someone down."

Jack hung up the phone and went outside to see the boat again. It was approaching quickly.

"Son o' a bitch," Jack said to himself, moving about nervously. A moment later, he heard someone coming toward him. "Look at that!" Jack said, pointing to the boat.

"Fuck, man," the shift supervisor said.

"What do we have for weapons on board?" Jack asked.

"There aren't any weapons on board. Why would we need them? It is just an additional security risk to have weapons here."

"Damn it!" Jack yelled. "There has to be something we can use to defend ourselves."

"The only thing we have is our fire-suppression equipment."

"Then we better learn how to aim 'em down at the water."

"We haven't done any training on that." The shift supervisor was new and several years younger than Jack. "We'll figure something out."

"What should I do?" Jack asked.

"Keep an eye on that boat and stay near the phone."

The rig supervisor took one final look toward the motorboat and went inside. A few moments later, the emergency siren started wailing across the rig. Jack pitied the bastards who just got off their shift an hour and a half ago. No sleep for them.

•••

The siren carried over the water at a deafening volume. The driver turned to Fineface with a worried expression on his face.

"Keep driving!" Fineface yelled to him over the sound of the water and the engine. The boat plowed forward through the small waves. The other two men had stopped bailing and had their guns out. Just a few hundred more yards, Fineface thought.

As the boat approached the rig, Fineface could see men scrambling on the deck. He thanked the gods that he didn't hear any gunfire. It meant they did not have any guns on the rig. Otherwise, his boat would have been an easy target.

Suddenly, Fineface saw a torrent of water rain down not two hundred feet ahead of them. It was coming from the water guns the rig used to put out potential fires. The force of the water hitting the ocean made a thundering sound. More pillars of water appeared as the rest of the fire-suppression equipment came alive.

"Turn!" Fineface yelled. "Avoid the water guns." He pointed above so the driver could see where the water was coming from. The boat sped left and then maneuvered back toward the central spar, lurking beneath the superstructure a couple hundred feet ahead. But wherever they turned, the water gun followed. Fineface realized the only way to the spar was to brave the blast of the water gun.

"You're going to have to go through it." Fineface turned to his other men. "Hold on to something!" The men nodded that they had heard him.

The boat drove around the rig and, when it was out of range of one water gun and before it hit the next, the driver turned the boat toward the spar and put the engine on full throttle. All of a sudden, a waterspout appeared ahead of them. The four men held on to the boat as they went under it. The water pelted the boat and pushed it down.

Fineface feared the boat might sink...but then they were through into the clear dark water in the shadow of the vast superstructure. The boat was half-full of water and moving much more slowly, but they had passed under the rig. Since the water guns were designed to bathe the superstructure with water in case of fire, they could not hit anything near the supporting spar.

They were safe, for now.

The two men in the front frantically bailed water out of the boat while Fineface picked up the bag with the explosives. He unzipped the bag and unwrapped two large pieces of gray C-4. He also took out two rolls of duct tape.

The boat neared the spar and then slowed. The driver let the boat float up next to the rig. With the waves rising and falling, Fineface and one other man struggled to strap the explosives to the side of the rig with the duct tape. The boat pulled away right when they were attaching one block of explosives, and it fell. Fineface reached down and caught it just before it hit the water. The other man helped support him, and they brought the large gray block into the boat.

"Stop bailing and help hold the boat steady," Fineface ordered his other two men. After attaching the second block, he removed two more packs of explosives from the other duffle bag.

Finishing the job, he took out the detonator and timing device and set the timer to five minutes.

"We bail the boat out first, before setting the bomb. We will never make it past the water cannons with this much water in the boat." Fineface wished they had another pail for bailing water. All they had were two empty plastic fuel cans with their tops sawed off. They dumped and dumped and, ten minutes later, Fineface thought they had enough of the water out.

He looked up when he heard a sound. The men from the rig were looking down on them through one of the hatches above. Could they possibly disarm the device? Did they have handguns? He ignored the thought and hit the button to arm the bomb. The clock on it began to tick down.

"Let's go," he said. The three men pushed off the spar while the driver pointed the bow to sea. He jammed the engine on full throttle. The bow lifted high out of the water and then began to plane as they reached the edge of the shadow from the superstructure above. Fineface hoped they could make it out of the range of the water cannons in time.

Approaching the edge of the platform, they could see water from two cannons spraying the ocean in front of them. At full speed, they shot out from under the rig. One of the water cannons caught them, but their speed prevented it from dousing the boat for more than a moment before they were out of its range.

Fineface looked back up at the mighty rig. Its mass towered over him. In just a few minutes, it would be at the bottom of the ocean.

The boat was a quarter mile away when Fineface heard the explosion. He brought his binoculars up to his eyes. The force of the initial blast rocked the platform, and then another, larger explosion hit as the fuel stored in the base of the platform ignited. The whole structure lurched away from them, then righted itself. Fineface could see the platform begin to sink as the central spar filled with seawater. When the superstructure hit the water, the sinking slowed and the mass of metal settled on the waves.

Fineface put his binoculars down. He felt suddenly drained of energy. He had not slept in twenty-four hours. Somehow, they still had to avoid the Nigerian navy on the way back to the creeks.

"How do you think Ifeanyi did? Will this be the start of the new Nigeria?"

Fineface looked over at the man who was speaking. Brave and hopeful, he was no more than twenty years old.

"I don't know," Fineface replied. "But I pray your children will know a different Nigeria than this one."

Chapter 41

Greenwich, Connecticut

David Sloan was positively giddy. All morning, he had been pacing around the small trading area at Sulla Partners, delivering whoops of joy with every increase in the price of crude oil. He had long since given up on his nicotine gum and had been smoking one cigarette after another.

The price of crude futures on the New York Mercantile Exchange and ICE in London had jumped nearly ten dollars in intraday trading and showed no signs of slowing down. The markets had been artificially down with Josh Cohn's trades and those who'd followed him. Now, the reality of the tight supply and the violence in Nigeria had caused a panic. By leveraging all the available capital they had, Sulla Partners had over five billion dollars invested on a billion dollars of capital. By noon, they had already made nearly a billion dollars in profit.

David pulled out yet one more cigarette and stood over James Li's shoulder, his eyes scanning the three large screens above his desk. Every number was good. Futures of all types were rapidly changing hands. The era of computerized trades had made the action even brisker. Various algorithms at hedge funds around the globe were executing trades at lightning speeds.

"This is it!" David blurted out, slapping James Li's shoulder. James winced from the blow but did his best to ignore his boss and the foul odor of smoke. Both of them were pale from the stress and lack of sleep, which the overhead florescent lights only made more obvious.

"When do you want to begin selling?" James asked his boss without looking up.

David ran his hand through his hair and tried to think clearly. The key was to sell at the right moment. Over ninety-two million barrels of oil were produced daily around the world. Nigeria produced a little over two million barrels of that. Production in Nigeria had been cut by at least a million barrels, but the dip in production would only be temporary.

"What are you thinking?" David asked James.

"I say we begin selling now. We've already made a killing. Let's lock in these profits."

David paused while he thought some more. This was not the time to let his emotions take over. "Let's start selling," he replied. "Slowly."

"Got it. It's going to take some time to offload our position anyway."

James turned to the other two traders at the desks around him and relayed his instructions. It was time to take some profits. The situation reminded David of the final sprint in a rowing race. Push all out to the end. Don't give up. Be persistent. He could hear the voice of his old coxswain blaring over the speakers in the racing shell.

"Mr. Sloan?" David recognized the voice of his secretary, Martha Childs, behind him. He swirled around to face her.

"Yes?"

"You have a pile of messages waiting for you. Most of them urgent."

"Right, right. I'll take them in my office." David strode across the pale gray carpeting to his office door. Once inside, he kept the door ajar so he could hear the commotion from the traders. He loved that noise. It pumped him up. Sitting down in his Steelcase leather chair, he looked up at his secretary standing on the other side of his desk.

"Here is a list of the trading firms that put calls in to you in the last hour." Martha handed him a yellow pad with a list of names and phone numbers. He glanced at the names and smiled. They all wanted a piece of the action, and they knew he, David Sloan, was holding the best hand.

"Thanks, Martha. I'll get on it."

Martha hesitated before leaving. "One more thing, Mr. Sloan."

"Yes?" David was getting impatient. He wished she would just spit it out.

"You have another message from Eli Schrimpf at Octagon Petroleum. This is the third one in two days. Do you want to handle it or should I?"

"Eli," David muttered as he rubbed the stubble on his face. "Let's hold off on that one for now. We've got more important things to deal with. Eli can wait."

Martha nodded. "Whatever you say."

David watched her leave the room and took one more look at the names on the yellow pad. It was time to do a little gloating. He couldn't wait to send out the note to his investors the next day.

Aba

Emeka Nwosu sat on his cousin's plush couch and watched the rain fall outside the window. Spread out before him on the coffee table were the day's newspapers. He took a break from reading them to sip his coffee and collect his thoughts. He hadn't bothered to get dressed that morning and was still in his bathrobe as the afternoon light began to fade.

He wished that he felt something other than sadness. The attacks across the Niger Delta had been a success. The reports in the papers gave various estimates as to the extent of the damage, but Emeka could not get Ifeanyi out of his mind. The reporting said that he and Olabisi, along with the others in their team, had all died in Bonny the night before. How many others had died remained unclear.

For the first time since Ifeanyi had been released from prison, Emeka had feelings of regret. Was it all worth it? He still didn't know if he would ever be able to return to his life in Port Harcourt. Deep down, he knew things would never be the same for him. Surely, someone would make the link between his bank and the insurgents. It was only a matter of time.

With Ifeanyi's death, the cause would shift. There was now no obvious leader to advocate for change. Would anything be different for the people of the Niger Delta? Had he been naïve to think that the international oil companies would leave or that their departure would even make a difference? The oil was still there. The players involved might shift, but then what?

Emeka sighed. He loved his country so much and especially the people, but there was no way to change history. The legacy of British colonialism had left them in this mess. Now they had to find a way forward, somehow.

"How are you doing?" The voice came from behind Emeka, and he turned his head to see his cousin's wife coming over to him.

"Pensive."

"I'm sorry about Ifeanyi," she said, sitting down next to Emeka.

"I'll miss that passion the most," he replied. "He had such energy. Part of me wonders what would have been different if he could have directed it elsewhere."

"He had his destiny to fulfill."

"Something like that. I only wish he hadn't been so fixated on his one solution, on the violence. He would have made a great politician or preacher. If only he had put his faith in something else."

"Do you want any food, Emeka? You've barely eaten all day."

"I'm not hungry." Emeka had a glazed-over look in his eyes and kept staring at the rain.

"We'll get through this." His cousin's wife squeezed his hand and then got up. "Let me know if you need anything."

"Thank you, dear. I will."

After she left the room, Emeka looked back down at the newspaper headlines on the coffee table. Most of them broadcasted the extent of the violence or included photos of Ifeanyi Okoye. At the bottom of the page on one of the papers, he noticed a story about Godwin Ogbe. It seemed he would be leaving his position in the government. Good riddance, Emeka thought to himself. Another article quoted the head of Octagon Petroleum in Nigeria, Olufemi Adebayo. Octagon would be speeding up their sale of their onshore oil wells to local Nigerian firms. Emeka reflected that he could have gotten in on some of that action, but it was too late for second-guessing. His friends in Lagos had taken their path, and Emeka had taken his own. At least he had a clear conscience. There was more to life than money.

Chapter 42

Littleton, Massachusetts

The campus of St. Luke's Episcopal School was designed by the famous landscape architect Frederick Law Olmsted. The central feature of the design was a grass oval around which stood the main campus buildings. At one end of the oval was the chapel, a beautiful neo-Gothic stone building with a world-class Aeolian-Skinner organ.

Sitting in that chapel for his daughter's baccalaureate service, David Sloan reflected on the starkness of the interior, with its undecorated stone walls and vertical lines that lifted your gaze heavenward. It fit with the Spartan ethic of the school's early days. St. Luke's had been a place that taught "Christian manliness." Hot water for showers only appeared sometime in the 1950s. Boys were required to play football to be toughened up. Arts and artistic pursuits were discouraged because they led to effete gentleman not prepared for the rigors of life in the world. Success meant leadership, sacrifice and service to God and country. And it was the chapel that nurtured the moral and spiritual lives of the boys.

Those days were long gone. Now the chapel represented the old WASP establishment of the Episcopalian elite. Parents sent their sons and daughters to St. Luke's to share a part of that establishment ethos, carefully stripped and scrubbed of outdated notions of "Christian manliness" or really any Christianity at all. What a pity, David thought. At least the old St. Luke's stood for something.

David looked back up at the pulpit. The chaplain was offering a few banal words about the journey of the past year. David was tempted to excuse himself to check his e-mail on his phone, but he knew his wife, Sally, would kill him for it. So he sat there along with all the other parents of the graduating class. The service ended with a hymn from the 1982 hymnal that David didn't recognize or care to sing. The chapel had bad acoustics for congregational singing anyway. Looking around, David could see that he was not the only one who didn't even bother to crack the old hymn book.

After the service, everyone marched out to the grass oval, where a large white tent had been set up for the graduation ceremony itself. The graduates led the way with their straw boaters and school ties. It was a beautiful sunny day, which matched the mood of everyone there, or nearly everyone.

"Aren't you proud of Mary?" Sally asked David as they strolled to the tent.

"I would be prouder if she had gotten into Harvard."

"Oh, David, you can be so nasty."

"Honest, Sally. I can be so honest," David corrected her.

"Mary was never an academic."

"I'm well aware of that. She'll be happy in college. Four years of insulated living, happily spending my money and learning about things like social justice from the confines of her college quadrangle. Then afterwards she'll realize that social justice won't get her an apartment in Brooklyn with her friends, and she will become another boring yet fashionable liberal."

"It's fine if you're in this kind of mood, just don't let Mary or Elizabeth see it."

"As I said, Sally, insulated living. It's what St. Luke's specializes in." David turned to Sally and smiled. "I wouldn't want to ruin the facade."

They made their way over to the white folding chairs that had been set up under the tent. As parents of a graduate, they had a special area where they could sit.

"Mom!" Elizabeth, David and Sally's younger daughter, came running up to them.

"Hey, sweetheart." David Sloan went to give his daughter a hug, but she ignored him and hugged her mother instead.

"Wonderful to see you, honey," Sally said when Elizabeth pulled away from her. She had just finished her freshman year at St. Luke's. "Say hi to your father."

"Hey, Dad," Elizabeth said, giving her father a perfunctory hug. Their relationship had never been the same after Elizabeth had met one of her father's girlfriends while staying with him in Greenwich. "Did you really get kidnapped?" she asked. "It sounded scary."

"Not as serious as it sounds, sweetheart," David assured his daughter. "Daddy wasn't in any trouble."

Sally looked over at David and didn't say anything.

"So, where are we supposed to sit, Liz?" Sally asked.

"Over here." Their daughter led her parents to the three seats she had reserved for them. Sally said hello to a few other parents while David followed Elizabeth to their seats. Sitting down, he noticed Josh Cohn up on the dais. He had been appointed a trustee of St. Luke's the year before. David made eye contact with him and nodded. Cohn pretended like he didn't see him. David looked through the program for the event. The usual variety of speeches and then the diploma ceremony. He glanced at his watch, wondering how long it would take.

The chairman of the board of trustees opened the ceremony with standard sentences about education and its merits, combined with a few words about the greatness of this year's graduating class. Undoubtedly, the words were intended to make the parents feel better about the two hundred and fifty thousand dollars they had dropped on four years of private education. Then the chairman introduced the St. Luke's headmaster to make some remarks.

"As we gather on the oval," the headmaster began, "to honor and celebrate another class of graduates from St. Luke's, we cannot help but think of those in other parts of this country and the world who are suffering today. Let us pause for a moment as we think about the conflict in Israel and Palestine and, more recently, the violence in Nigeria." The headmaster became silent for a moment, then said, "We treasure a place like St. Luke's in the hope that such violence and turmoil will be a thing of the past. This new generation, with its optimism and idealism, will have its opportunity to lead us all to a peaceful world." The audience clapped. David Sloan didn't bother. Where did people think the money for all of this came from anyway?

"St. Luke's is a school founded on the principle of service to others, and that is my theme for this afternoon. It is up to you, our graduates, to dedicate yourselves to helping others and our world. Over the past four years, you have heard a number of our distinguished alumni return here to inspire us with what they have done in service to others. The baton is now passed to you, our graduates. Earning money is all well and good, but it is not what will not make you happy. Service to others is where you will find the most fulfillment. Remember that you can do well while also doing good..."

David stopped paying attention to the speech. He had heard similar platitudes ever since he was a boy. One of the best books he had read at St. Luke's in his day was Reinhold Niebuhr's Moral Man and Immoral Society. He was sure they didn't read that anymore. The one lesson he took from that book was that all of this do-gooder stuff would never bring justice because people were not willing to sacrifice their own self-interest. Collective selfishness would always get in the way unless people had loyalty to some power higher than themselves. It was something he hadn't forgotten. Since he never believed in Christianity, or any other religion, he'd ditched the 'service to others' bullshit long ago and devoted himself to his own self-interest. And things had worked out pretty well for him.

David reached into his pocket to pull out his cell phone only to have his hand subtly batted down by his wife. Oh well, the boredom continued. What were the games they used to play during chapel? He began scanning the crowd for someone who was more bored than he was.

At the close of the ceremony, all the graduates tossed their straw boaters into the air. Many pictures were taken. Time for the kids to decorate social media. The thought of all that narcissism disgusted even David.

"I need a drink after that," David said to Sally. "Where's the refreshment tent?"

"Don't you want to say congratulations to Mary?"

"Doesn't she have lots of pictures to take with her friends so Instagram can have them? I hear Instagram loves private school graduations." He smiled.

Sally didn't answer David but grabbed his hand and led him to the front of the tent. "Oh, honey, congratulations!" Sally said to her eldest daughter.

"Hold on, Mom." Mary was in the middle of a selfie with her two roommates. David spotted Josh Cohn a few feet away and made his way through the crowd toward him.

"Josh, you're looking very official today," David said, relishing the afterglow of his victory. Josh Cohn looked around to see if he could ignore David.

"Thank you, David. Good to see you actually made it to your daughter's graduation."

"I wouldn't miss it for anything."

"Come to gloat about your Nigeria coup, I assume."

"You say that with such venom, Josh. How much did you lose again? I think I lost track."

"We all have our ups and downs. By the way, I heard you were in Nigeria shortly before the violence began. How exactly did that happen?"

"God works in mysterious ways, Josh."

"Right. You've always been such a devout man."

"Well, I'm sure you have a lot of hands to shake. Don't let me get in your way."

"Pride goeth before the fall, David. Remember that."

"Is that a line you said at the benefit in New York four weeks ago? I'm trying to recall. Somehow I missed that part of your speech."

Josh Cohn glowered at David and then walked away.

"David!" David turned to find his wife motioning him over. "Come over and take a picture with the new graduate."

When David made his way over to Sally, he said, "Are you sure you want this one for the Christmas card?"

"Holiday card, David. When are you ever going to learn? Now stand next to Mary and smile."

After several pictures, David said, "Can we find some refreshments? Mary, where's the reception?"

"It's over in the dining hall, Dad."

"Lead the way." Mary and Elizabeth walked ahead to the dining hall with David and Sally trailing behind.

"You have to admit that you're proud of your daughter," Sally said.

"She's great. I just wonder why schools like this have to insist on teaching a lame secular humanism. They ditched any real sense of Christianity years ago. They might as well be honest about the world and teach nihilist realism."

"What would you propose? Stock-trading classes for freshmen?"

"That would be a start. And a rewritten values statement."

"Maybe you can suggest something to the headmaster over your third drink."

"Don't tempt me, Sally."

"So, have you thought of a gift for Mary?"

"That is one advantage of my ethics, Sally. I can buy her whatever she wants."

As they approached the large brick building that served as the dining hall, David noticed two black SUVs pull up with government license plates. Three men in dark suits got out of the lead SUV and walked toward them.

David stopped. He could feel his heart rate rising.

Sally turned toward him. "What is it, David? You look like you've seen a ghost or something." Turning back around, she noticed the three men in suits coming closer to them.

"David Sloan?" the man in front asked.

"Yes." David could feel the sweat on his palms.

"Mr. Sloan, you're under arrest." The two other men stood on either side of David, and Sally slowly backed away. By now, others around them realized what was happening.

"Under arrest? What for?" David asked.

"Insider trading, insurance fraud and bribery." The lead FBI agent had taken off his sunglasses and stared David down. "We've had some nice conversations with your friend Eli Schrimpf."

"I want to speak to my lawyer."

"You'll get that chance. In the meantime, let me read you your Miranda rights."

"I'd prefer we do that elsewhere," David said.

"No," the agent replied, looking around at the crowd of graduates and their parents. "I think here will do fine."

Chapter 43

Port Harcourt

As soon as Julia texted, Chris Reed was on his way to her apart-ment. He kept rehearsing in his mind what he was going to say. He knew he wasn't going to convince her to stay in Nigeria, but he wanted things to end on a good note. So much was going through his mind when she opened the door and invited him in. Now, sitting on her couch, where they shared their first kiss, he was at a loss for words.

"What are you going to do with all your stuff?" Chris asked as he watched her take down the prints and objects from her walls. It was the first time he had seen her since Ewu.

"I don't know. I was thinking of giving it away, but I'll ship some of the art. I just have to decide what to keep. Why? Is there something you want?"

"It would be nice to have something to remember you by." Chris looked around the familiar apartment, with its sea-blue walls and Nigerian art, half of which was now on the floor. The place was so Julia. The pain of nostalgia lodged in his stomach.

"Chris, we'll stay in touch. I hope you know I'm not mad at you."

"But why leave now? What about the New Africa Initiative?" Chris asked.

"Everything has changed, Chris. NAI has designated the Niger Delta as unsafe. They're suspending their programs and evacuating all foreign workers."

"What's going to happen to your work? The people who still need malaria treatment and the other help NAI offers?"

"I don't know. I guess the people in the villages will have to go a lot farther to get medication."

"Will you ever come back?"

Julia stopped her packing. She came over to sit next to Chris on the couch.

"Honestly, Chris, I don't think so. The past week haunts me."

Chris turned and looked at Julia's familiar eyes through the rims of her glasses. She was there but still seemed distant.

"I'll miss you," he said quietly before reaching out to grab her hand.

"It's like everything I've worked for has been for nothing. I came here determined to save the world, to save the people of the Niger Delta. It seems so foolish now."

"You did great work, Julia. You made a difference in a lot of people's lives."

"It doesn't seem like anything's changed. Things have only become worse. The problems are bigger, more complex than I had imagined. Implementing top-down development goals devised by someone at the UN won't fix them." Julia sighed. "When I came here, I was so idealistic. I thought we could solve malaria, at least. Now, I don't know."

"I hope you never lose your idealism. The world needs that."

Julia took Chris's hand in both of hers and gave them an affectionate squeeze. "You're a good egg, Chris Reed. How about you? Are you staying?"

"For now. Professor Mendes was right. Nigeria is what I needed. And I've learned so much from Paul."

"How do you do it, Chris?"

"Do what?"

"How do you maintain any optimism after what we've been through?"

"I know it sounds cheesy to you, Julia, but it's God. When I came here, I never thought much about faith. But working with Paul and trying to process everything that's happened has changed me. I believe now more than ever that God is real. God is here. In spite of everything, and maybe because of it, I can see that now. I can't really describe it. I just feel it. The Israelites had their time in slavery, their time in the wilderness, in exile. But through it all, God was still there. That's what Paul was reminding me of yesterday. The Bible is God's narrative, the narrative of redemption. We have to see ourselves in that narrative and to tell that story. It's really shifted how I see things and how I make sense of it all."

"Paul's quite a guy, I have to admit. I'm glad he's been here for you." Julia stood up. "Alright, I've got to get back to packing."

Chris stood up, as well. "I hope we stay in touch," he said.

"We will." Julia leaned in and gave Chris a kiss. They both held it. Chris felt the pit in his stomach return. He already missed her.

After they kissed, Chris gave Julia a hug.

"Be well, Julia. E-mail me when you get home."

"Will do. And you know what?"

"What's that?"

"I think I might actually wander into a church when I get back."

Chris looked surprised. "Really?"

"I didn't say I'm going to become a Christian, but, for some reason, I want to sit in a pew again and just think. Trust me. It won't be during a service."

Chris smiled. "I hope you find what you're looking for, Julia. I really do."

•••

When Chris returned to the Emmaus Ministries office, Paul tapped him on the shoulder and said they were going for a ride. Seated in the familiar Honda, Paul kept silent while he drove through the Port Harcourt traffic. Even the radio was turned off. After about ten minutes, Paul pulled off to the side of the road near a bridge over one of the small rivers that flowed into the delta. Without saying a word, Paul got out and Chris did the same.

"Where are we going?" Chris finally asked Paul.

"Just follow me, man. I want to show you one of my favorite spots in PH."

Paul Wisner, flip-flops clicking, walked ahead of Chris down a dirt path from the car. The path winded down the steep bank to the water. The ground was a little unstable from erosion, and Chris nearly lost his footing on the sandy path. When they reached the bottom, they were standing on a small beach at the edge of the river.

"This is one of your favorite spots?" Chris asked. "I don't get it." The houses by this part of the river were mostly shacks. There were empty plastic bottles strewn along the shore. Cars rattled over the old bridge nearby. Chris could smell the burning flesh from the local open-air slaughterhouse on the other side of the bridge.

"You're not looking, Chris. For a moment, try to get beyond the fact you're in Port Harcourt. This is a part of God's creation."

Chris looked around again. He watched the gentle flow of the water. The shacks across the river were painted in bright pinks and greens with scattered palm trees swaying above them. A group of four children, no more than eight years old, played by the water's edge, using the plastic bottles to make a fort in the grainy brown sand. One of the children was laughing at something another one had said.

"Isn't this a beautiful town?"

"Parts of it, Paul. For sure. But I'm not sure I could ever love it as much as you do."

"You might someday. By the way, I wrote to Professor Mendes." Paul was rocking back and forth on his feet with his hands buried in the pockets of his board shorts. "I let him know that I'll be moving back to the States."

"Really? I assumed you would be here forever."

"I'm sure I'll be back at some point, but having you around has reminded me how much I miss home. It's time to hand over Emmaus Ministries to a Nigerian. And the violence has made me concerned about Rotimi. Our relationship. Is it safe? You know." Paul broke off, deep in thought, and let his pale blue eyes settle on the water.

"You guys will be happy, Paul. I know it."

"Thanks, Chris. That means a lot. So tell me, what have you learned from your time here?"

"I keep thinking back to something Professor Mendes said to me. He said that so often we can only really find God through suffering. We're like those who watch for the morning in Psalm 130. Out of the depths of suffering, out of the darkness we wait for the light and see the world in a whole new way when it dawns."

"There is a lot of truth to that."

"That's what's so revelatory. I don't feel lost anymore. Before coming here, I still had my childhood view of a God who controls everything. God was up there in heaven directing all of life. When Abby died, I was so mad at God for letting it happen. But now, I see God differently. It's hard to explain. It's as though God is a presence, the source of love and compassion in the world. God is constantly loving a world that so often doesn't love him back. But God is still there, inviting us into a relationship with him, supporting us through the people who love us. I really feel that God weeps when we weep and feels pain when we feel pain. We only have to hear God's call and be reminded of it again and again, especially when life is hard."

"Sounds like you've become a theologian, Chris."

"That's the funny thing, Paul. This change hasn't come about through reading books. It seems as though I've lived several years in these past few months. For me, now God simply is."

"Believe it or not, theologians have written about that, Chris. We have ways of knowing and understanding the world that go beyond rational arguments. It's like how I know that God supports Rotimi and me. Life teaches us about God, if we're only open to listening. That's why it helps to read other people's experiences of God, not just ivory-tower arguments. You're not the first person or first Christian who has lost someone dear to you and wrestled with it. There is something about suffering that clarifies our thoughts on God and makes them so much more profound."

"The world seems like it would be so lonely without God, so dark, so meaningless. I can't imagine going through all of this without faith," Chris replied.

"Chris," Paul said looking at him, "everyone has faith in something. What we have faith in is what we value most, where our center of meaning is in life. Humans are hardwired to need meaning and purpose. For some, they have faith in money and make money or ambition their god. I've known hedge fund managers who make their pile of money a god. It drives them and means more to them than anything else, even their families. For others it can be an institution or a non-profit like the New Africa Initiative. They are willing to sacrifice everything else for the institution because it's the institution that gives their life meaning. That's what happened with the Catholic Church and its abuse scandal. Those bishops put the church above the gospel. Others have faith in a cause or a political party. We see that in the US now, and that was true for Ifeanyi Okoye. He became so obsessed with his cause of Nigerian freedom that he was willing to sacrifice everything else for it. Without it, he had no meaning.

"True Christians put their faith in God, in love and compassion and peace and healing, and also in that presence you feel, as though God is the very ground of your being. You're not always aware of it, but God is there."

"I never thought of faith that way, but it makes sense."

"When we put our faith in something of this world, it can always collapse. Faith in God endures because God, that ground of our being, never goes away. Having faith in God allows us to stand and live courageously even when the worst things happen."

Chris thought for a moment. "You know, my thoughts on Jesus have changed too."

Paul chuckled. "As long as we're talking about theology, why not lay it all out? Maybe we should call those kids over for a sermon."

"I'm serious, Paul. I used to put Jesus on such a pedestal that I lost sight of the person, of who he was and what he did. When I was a kid, I got caught up in seeing Jesus as God and trying to prove that and believe in it so I could be saved."

"What? You don't believe Jesus was the son of God now?" Paul smiled.

"No, not that. I just see him differently. Nigeria highlighted things about Jesus that I never realized were so important. Here was someone who stood against those in power because power so often corrupts. Here was someone who stood by the powerless and the marginalized. He healed and taught the importance of love and forgiveness, even when it seemed impossible, which it certainly has seemed here at times. He showed how material possessions are not what matters most. Even our lives are not what matters most, because anything can happen. We have to be willing to struggle for God's love and justice even if it leads to the cross. We have to believe in the resurrection even in the darkest times, otherwise evil will overwhelm us. And we have to believe that through Jesus, we all are truly forgiven and accepted as who we are in our core. We have to embody the grace that God gives us and share that grace with others, even when they don't seem to deserve it."

"Well said, padawan," Paul replied, trying to mimic Alec Guinness's voice from Star Wars.

"I don't think there can be any other way for us to live. Without love and forgiveness and grace, everything else only leads to more harm and evil. It amazes me how often I forget that. It's so easy to hate and chase after things that don't matter."

"That's why we need to pray and worship God, the living presence we feel and believe in," Paul said. "It's too easy to lose sight of God amidst the cares of the world."

"You know, Julia said she might visit a church back in New York."

"See?" Paul's face brightened. "Miracles do happen, man."

Chris and Paul stood next to each other for a while before Paul turned and walked back up toward the road. "So what's next for you, Paul?" Chris asked.

"Lunch."

"You know what I mean. When you and Rotimi get back to the States, what's next?"

"Proclaiming the love and mystery of God in some way. Lifting up the importance of centering ourselves in God and forgiving others. Trying to live into the kingdom of God. What form that takes doesn't really matter to me. The future is wide open. I'm sure something will come up. God will show me. And for you?"

"I don't know. Back to school, I suppose. I think I do still want to be a professor."

"You'll make a great one. It's been a pleasure knowing you, Chris. I'm glad you came here. I know it's been tough at times, but it has meant a lot to me."

"It's meant a lot to me, too."

When they climbed back up to the road, Paul looked back down at the children by the river. "I have always enjoyed theology because it can help me see the world differently. I feel as though I should be sad now that I'll be leaving, but I'm not. I keep thinking about the notion that God is beyond time, that God sees all time simultaneously." Paul grew quiet then added, "Our time on Earth, whether one year or a hundred, is infinite before God. I guess I see our time together in the same way. It came and it went, but somewhere it plays back eternally."

"I like that image. Each moment of life is being held with God."

"Including this one."

Acknowledgments

I'd like to thank all the many people who have been involved in this project. Many close friends took the time to read the manuscript and offer helpful comments, including Nate Gray, Christina Rosenberger, Kaji Dousa, Jeremy Faro, Peter Overland, Josh Owens, Peace Conant, and Rob Newell, to name a few. I cannot thank all of you enough for your guidance. Special thanks are due to Shelby Condray, who had to deal with an inordinate number of requests, and to my mother, Nancy Blackburn. Obeleye Krubrubo and Emeka Dike and his family provided incredible hospitality while I was in Nigeria. I'm grateful to Chase Bice and Carlton Cook for their encouragement when the book lay dormant. I'd also like to thank Joe Flood and Lynsey Griswold and N2 Communications for their help. Matt Roeser did an excellent job working with me on the book cover. Finally, I am grateful for the patience and support of Jess Burgess and Oliver Russ. They both heard far more about this book than they ever wanted. Every book has its share of limitations, and those all fall on me. I hope the book both entertains and leads people to think about the value of religion in a complex world.

About the Author

Jonathan Page is the Senior Minister of the Wellesley Hills Congregational Church in Wellesley, Massachusetts. A graduate of Harvard College and Yale Divinity School, he previously worked as the undergraduate chaplain at Harvard's Memorial Church and served congregations in Ames, Iowa, and Houston, Texas. He is the author of *Ringing the Gotchnag: Two American Missionary Families in Turkey, 1855-1922*, which examines the evolution of American Protestant foreign missionary policy. To learn more about Rev. Page, visit his website: www.jonathancpage.com.